Done with You

WHITLEY COX

Cover Design: EmCat Designs

Editing: Proofreading by the Page

For Janna.
You, lady are a fucking warrior and I love you.

Contents

Chapter One

"You know, one of these days you should probably say something," Greg said with a slight chuckle in his voice as he rested a hand on Aiden's shoulder. "You can't just come to an anger management class and not participate."

Aiden glared at the man and jerked his shoulder, so Greg's hand slipped away. "Start seeing a therapist tomorrow. There's no need to talk here. Just gotta show my face, so you can sign the papers."

Greg's brown eyes turned sad. "No, Aiden, it doesn't work that way. You need both. You need to participate in *both*. Therapy *and* anger management together. The therapist is going to help you in a different way. Discuss your trauma and triggers more in depth, get to the root of it all, and give you long-term coping tools. But anger management will help, too. It's comforting to be around others who experience similar intense emotions. To hear how they cope. To hear how they have slip-ups and how they handle day-to-day triggers. How they can come back from difficult episodes, and make amends with those they've hurt. We have tools here, too. But *both* this class and therapy are required for you to get back to work."

Aiden ground his teeth together and bunched his fists as he slowly turned around to face the gray-haired man old enough to be his father.

Greg's dark brown eyes shone like a glass of Coke being held up to the light, with sincerity, then slowly drifted down Aiden's body until he focused on his fists. His mouth twisted beneath his thick mustache, which had twice the amount of salt as it did pepper. "You want to punch me, don't you?"

"Did you drink and then drive here?" Aiden asked through clenched molars.

Greg's brows pinched together in confusion. "No."

"Then it's not you I want to punch."

"See, now we're getting somewhere. Why can't you discuss this in class?"

"Don't need everyone else knowing my business. I'm a cop, and I've probably pulled over at least a few of these people. And I *know* I went to a domestic dispute regarding that tall motherfucker over there and his wife."

Greg pivoted for a moment to see Damien, who was closing in on six-foot-seven, standing next to the refreshment table with a paper coffee cup in his hand. He was smiling and talking with Terry, a long-time participant and a veteran.

Understanding flashed in Greg's eyes when he faced Aiden again. "That's fair. Perhaps this might not be the *right* class for you. Maybe you need to go to one out of town, or geared specifically for police officers, where you don't run the risk of being in a class with civilians you've witnessed at their worst."

Aiden snorted and rolled his eyes. "I just want to get the fuck back to work. So just let me come here, sit, listen and stay quiet. These people don't need to know why I'm here. We're all here for the same reasons, anyway. We're angry and we can't control it."

Greg shook his head. "No, that's not it. At least, not all of it."

Huffing out a breath in frustration, Aiden shoved his fingers through his short brown hair. "Look, I'm doing the best I can. I've been waitlisted for this therapist for months, and I finally got in to see her. She's apparently *the best* for PTSD and anger. So that's gotta count for something, right?"

"It definitely does. But you need to actually go to your appointments with her for the healing to begin. And you need to actively participate in anger management, as well." Greg pulled his phone from his pocket. "Let me call around and see if I can pull some strings to get you into a class elsewhere, where you're less likely to run into people you know. People you've encountered while on the job."

Aiden grunted. He appreciated Greg's effort and understanding, but the whole situation just pissed him off. Yes, he'd overreacted when he punched that drunk driver he pulled over. But the guy had his fucking nine-year-old daughter in the car with him. They'd been at a friend's barbecue, and the dad tied on one too many, thought he was fine to drive home, and was swerving all over the fucking road.

Aiden pulled him over and was furious enough to see the man had been drinking and was driving, but when he noticed the kid in the back, Aiden lost it. He lost his temper, his cool. He lost all sense of composure, reached into the car, hauled the man out, and decked him hard across the jaw.

That's when he saw the camera-phone vigilante who'd pulled over behind them and was filming the entire thing.

It went semi-viral, and Aiden was cast as the villain in the story.

Not the negligent father who could have killed his daughter.

Aiden was suspended from work—normally he'd have been fired, but some-one somewhere was apparently looking out for him—however, in order to return to work, he had to attend mandatory therapy and anger management classes.

But everything was full and wait-listed because the world was an angry fuck-ing place.

He'd been out of work for four and a half months and was going stir-fucking crazy doing nothing every day as he waited for the call that he was next on the list to see the therapist.

He was even willing to see other therapists. And travel to do so. He didn't *have* to see this Dr. Young. But apparently, she was the best and the one who was recommended for him. So he had to at least try to see her first. And besides, all the other therapists were booked, too.

"If you want to come by and just chat one-on-one, I'm happy to listen," Greg said. "I understand what you're going through."

"Do you?" Aiden bit back, his voice loud enough that it echoed around the room. All other conversations halted like cars screeching to a stop so a mother duck and her ducklings could cross the road, and every set of eyes in the room pivoted to him.

Greg swallowed, and his eyes darted sideways.

With his face on fire, Aiden squeezed his fists even tighter, shifted his eyes around the room for a hot minute, then spun on his heels and stalked out of the rec center basement into the frigid early December evening in Montreal, Quebec.

He hit the fob for his truck and the auto-start button so the engine roared to life before he was even at the door.

Normally, an event like this would make a person turn to booze. Hit up a bar and grab a drink—or several—to numb their feelings. But Aiden didn't drink.

He didn't use any kind of substance, illegal or legal.

His only *vice* was coffee. The stronger and darker, the better. He drank at least four cups a day. But he was also strict about that consumption and never took a drop after three o'clock, since it would just keep him up. And as a cop who worked two day-shifts, then two night-shifts, then had four days off, his sleep cycle was already fucked up enough.

He climbed into his truck, which was already getting toasty warm, since he made sure to leave the heaters on full-blast before he left, and the seat-warmers were at max, too.

He might not drink alcohol, but that didn't mean he couldn't just go sit at a bar, watch the hockey game on the screen, indulge in some nachos and just exist among the carefree.

Besides, it never hurts to have a cop in the bar in case things get rowdy. More than once, he'd had to jump in and help a bartender throw out some degenerates who were getting obnoxious after one-too-many beers, and their team lost the game.

He did a quick Google search for a nearby bar with televisions and nachos and lo and behold, there was a hotel only two and a half kilometers away with just what he was looking for.

With his face still full of flames from that outburst in the rec center, he put the truck into gear and pulled out of the parking lot, careful to keep his eyes peeled for black ice. They hadn't had a big dump of snow yet, but it was coming, and soon. He could smell snow in the air, and the clouds above were a dense, dark and gray blanket. The thermostat on his dash said it was minus eleven Celsius.

Fuck, he hated the cold.

He drove to the hotel, parked his truck further away than right in front of the front door, so that hopefully nobody would park right beside him and scrape his shiny black Dodge Ram, then hoofed it across the slick parking lot to the entrance.

The hotel wasn't huge, but the parking lot was absolutely packed.

As he opened the front door to the lobby, a roar of a crowd, followed by applause, made him pause.

The bar was to the left, but the cheering was coming from the right.

"What's going on in there?" he asked the red-vested hotel staff behind the front desk.

"Monthly pole and burlesque show," the guy with the name tag that read Rakesh, replied, his smile big and showing perfectly straight white teeth. "Always pulls in a huge crowd."

"A what?"

"Pole and burlesque. You know, pole dancers."

"Like strippers?"

"Well … it's more than that. In fact, I don't think they take their clothes off at all." He scrunched his nose. "I mean, they're not wearing a lot to begin with, but it's not a strip show. We're not licensed for that." He tipped his chin toward the door to the show, just as another cheer made the pictures on the walls tremble. "You should go check it out. These women are crazy strong and fit. It's an art form. I couldn't do it."

Aiden grunted and was about to scoff at the idea when he was interrupted by a loud announcement from inside. "And please welcome the beautiful, the talented, the brilliant … *Luna Love.*"

The crowd went bananas.

"They do know it's Monday, right?"

Rakesh shrugged. "Doesn't seem to matter what night of the week it is; the house is always packed when these ladies perform."

Another cheer shook the walls.

"How much?" Aiden asked.

"Fifteen, or twenty, and that gets you two drink tickets. Otherwise, drinks are five bucks each."

"Don't drink," he said, reaching into his wallet and pulling out a ten and a five. He took a step toward the room filled with music and more cheering, but then paused. "Can I order food from the bar and have it sent in there?"

"Afraid not, sir, but the show in there will be over in a little over an hour, then you can move to the bar."

Aiden grunted again, nodded, said a quick *thanks*, then headed toward the music and cheers.

The place was dark and filled with round tables that sat four people. All the tables were full, and people stood around the edges, drinks in their hands, eyes glued to the stage, as a caramel-haired beauty with a super-sexy silver bathing suit thing that was up her ass crack like floss, and giant cut-outs on her abdomen, hung from a metal pole by nothing more than one bent leg.

Her body was at a ninety-degree bend outward and she was spinning around the pole—or the pole was spinning her around—backward, her arms out.

"Fucking hell," he murmured under his breath.

"Drink, sir?" a chipper-voiced male server asked.

He glanced down at the kid, who was probably no more than twenty and weighed less than a Great Dane. "Club soda with lime," he said.

The kid nodded. "Be right back."

Aiden meandered through the crowd, his eyes glued to the woman on stage. So, this was *Luna,* as the announcer had called her. She was in ridiculously high, clear, plastic, chunky heels and had just hoisted herself into the air by holding onto the pole with her arms. She spun around a few times, continuing to stay off the ground, then, while still in the air, she flipped herself upside down, hooked one leg around the pole, maneuvered her body so her head was hanging below her legs, and bent the other leg so that she could grab the heel of it with both hands. All while still spinning. All while holding onto the pole with just that one leg at the knee. Squeezing it with her calf and hamstring.

Then, still just using her arms, she lifted her bent leg back up and held herself on her back in the air, in the splits with the pole between her legs, before finally dropping to the ground to her knees in a sexy way, then standing up by pushing her ass up first and flipping her high ponytail.

The crowd went apeshit.

Aiden hadn't fucking blinked, and when he finally did, his eyes stung and he realized he had a dry mouth from standing there with his mouth open.

"Club soda, sir," the server said, approaching him with his drink on a tray.

Aiden grunted. "Thanks." He handed the kid a five, knowing that the drink was probably no more than three bucks since there was no booze in it.

"Change?" the kid asked.

Aiden shook his head, pulled out the straw, and put it back on the tray before taking a sip from the glass.

"Thank you very much," the server said, his grin getting bigger before he disappeared into the masses.

Luna continued to do tricks and spins on the pole, defying gravity and all other laws of physics, while simultaneously blowing Aiden's mind.

He'd been looking for nachos and a hockey game to ease his temper, but this was somehow doing the trick, too.

Eventually, Luna's time on stage was over, but as she bowed and left, the crowd stood up from their seats and gave her a standing ovation.

She bowed deeper, then hopped back up onto the pole for an encore. This time, the move she did certainly had to have wires or something because nobody had that kind of upper body strength. Especially someone who didn't have enormous biceps. She went upside down, parallel to the pole, hooked one foot around it just at the ankle, then held on with one hand and spun around, giving him a clear view of the tattoo she had on her left shoulder blade, as well as her right tricep. Her other hand and leg just hung out away from her body.

How?

Just. Fucking. How?

Then she did a move where she held onto the pole with one hand, made her body go parallel with the floor, split her legs like chopsticks, and grabbed one foot. Only to then slide to the floor, almost licking the ground with her body, stick her ass in the air again, and finish in the fucking splits.

The crowd continued to go insane and the applause followed Luna off the stage for another thirty seconds after she was gone.

The performers that followed Luna were good, but they were no Luna.

The woman had a presence about her. An almost aloofness that Aiden felt in his very marrow.

She made eye contact with the crowd, but in such a way that he was sure every person in there thought she was looking at them. That she was performing only for them. Like Mona Lisa's eyes, they followed you no matter where you were in the room. And even though he was sure she was doing it all for show, that it was just part of the performance, the way she looked at him, the way her light brown eyes bore into him, had him believing that this was all for him. That he was the only person in the crowd, and this was a private show.

He stuck around, hoping that the lovely Luna Love would return to the stage. He'd paid his ticket, and the front desk guy said there was only a little over an hour to go, so he may as well see the hour through.

After his second club soda with lime and the third performer after Luna, there was a ten-minute intermission where the lights came on, and people quickly grabbed more drinks or used the washroom.

Aiden took this as an opportunity to find a better vantage point.

He didn't want to steal a seat from anyone, but he made his way closer to the front along the side wall, picking a spot that would give him a clear view of the stage.

A man wearing all black wandered onto the stage and removed the pole, then other props were dragged onto the stage. All gold, black, and red, as well as five black folding chairs.

Everyone returned to their seats, and the lights dimmed. The stage went completely dark and the crowd went silent. Five dark, shadowy figures stepped across the stage and took their places in the chairs.

Then there was a thump from the speakers, followed by another, and the lights on stage came on, revealing five beauties—with Luna in the center—all decked out in lingerie and feathers.

This was the burlesque part of the show.

Aiden's heartbeat mimicked the thumping of the bass.

The music picked up tempo and the women started to move, giving the chair a lap dance.

Four of the five removed a few articles of clothing as the song and dance progressed, until all that covered their chests were black flower pasties, but Luna remained dressed. She kept all her clothes on. But the clothes she kept on were sexy as fuck. Black fishnets, mile-high black heels, a black and red corset with lace and bows, and a black thong that went up her ass crack to show off her taut, round cheeks. Her hair was pinned up in a glam kind of way with red and black feathers in it. She was stunning.

Her makeup was dramatic, and the jewelry on her neck and ears was sparkly as hell and probably added a couple of pounds to her fit frame, but she was breathtaking. For the second time that night, Aiden's mouth was dry and his eyes burned from not blinking.

The way she moved on the chair—doing a handstand, then the upside-down splits, sticking her ass in the air, caressing her body in a seductive way. He was mesmerized. Transfixed.

Before he knew it, the show was over. The five women on stage held hands and bowed, while the entire crowd stood up and rattled the rafters with their applause and cheers. The crowd was made up mostly of women between the ages of twenty and sixty, but there were quite a few men in the mix, too.

"Give it up for Margo, Juanita, Cherise, Daphne, and *Luna!*" The way the announcer said Luna made it clear that she was the center of this show. The star performer and the reason everyone came to watch. Even if he hadn't emphasized her name that way, Aiden wasn't an idiot and could easily tell that Luna carried that group. But maybe she was the leader and their teacher? Everyone has to start somewhere.

He set his empty drink down on a ledge and clapped, then put two fingers in his mouth and whistled. His whistle was loud enough to pull Luna's attention, and her heated gaze pivoted toward him.

She batted long, fake lashes at him and smiled demurely. Almost shyly.

The women bowed once more, then stood up, waved, and filed off stage.

Aiden elbowed his way through the crowd to the door, then booked it across the lobby to the bar. He needed to grab a seat before all those people at the show followed their rumbling bellies next door, and he was once again without a place to put his ass.

He grabbed a stool at the bar, which gave him a perfect view of the television overhead. The Montreal Canadiens (Les Habitants or Habs for short) were playing the Rangers and it was the second period. Habs were up by two.

"What can I get you?" the bartender asked.

"Nachos. Loaded, with extra guac and a club soda with lime," Aiden said, settling in for a bit.

"You got it."

He tried to focus on the hockey game overhead, and his nachos when they came, but his mind kept drifting back to Luna.

The way she moved, and the way her eyes filled with fire. But he already knew there was incomparable intelligence behind those eyes. He was exceptional at reading people, and he could see that there was a hell of a lot more to the lovely Luna Love than just plastic high heels and a lot of makeup.

With a chip hanging midair, loaded with far too much guacamole for any sane person to put on one chip, he was lost in thoughts of Luna and staring blankly ahead when the bartender's voice broke through his fog.

"Usual?" he asked.

"Please, Pedro," said a soft female voice.

Aiden's chip broke and the guacamole plopped back onto his plate. He turned his head to find Luna Love, of all people, beside him at the bar. There was one empty stool between them. She had removed her makeup, put her caramel-colored hair up in a ponytail midway down the back of her head, and was dressed down in dark jeans, a gray sweater that fell off one shoulder, revealing the strap of a red bra, and black ballet flats.

She was beautiful on stage all dressed up, but holy fucking shit. Now, she was ... he was speechless.

Swallowing, he cleared his throat. "Saw the show."

She glanced at him, and her dark brows lifted. "Yeah?"

"Impressive. Not sure that I have the upper body strength to do that and I work out every damn day."

Her smile was small, but also tired, like she'd heard that line more than once and wasn't exactly impressed with it.

The bartender placed a drink in front of her, and Aiden knew immediately that it was a Shirley Temple. Non-alcoholic and fruity.

"Not drinking?" he asked.

"I don't drink very often. And not when I'm out. Only at home or with friends, and maybe one or two glasses of wine. Besides, the adrenaline is more than enough for me."

He could believe that.

"You ordering food tonight?" Pedro, the bartender, asked Luna.

She nodded. "Yam fries, chicken strips, and chili prawns, please."

Pedro cracked a smile, then tossed her a wink. "Luna Love appie platter, coming right up."

"You're welcome to share my nachos," Aiden said, sliding the platter normally meant for four people, closer to her. "I *could* finish it myself, but I probably shouldn't."

She eyed him suspiciously for a moment, then her gaze fell to his drink. "What's in the glass?"

"Club soda and lime. I don't drink—ever."

Her brown eyes, flecked with different shades of gold, flared and she held his gaze for a moment, then reached forward, grabbed a chip, and dipped the corner of it into the sour cream. "Thanks ..."

"Caden," he said. He liked this woman, but he already knew there was no future for them. He was a broken human being, and she deserved so much better than him. No sense getting attached to real names and torrid pasts. He stuck out his hand.

She took it. "Luna."

Chapter Two

Caden was good-looking.

Like really good looking.

He hadn't stood up yet, but she already knew he was tall. His torso was long, and so were his legs. And he had a breadth to his shoulders that she liked. Not to mention those thick arms that were threatening to pop the seams of his long-sleeve white waffle-knit shirt.

Oona spotted him in the crowd during the show almost as soon as he walked in. Which wasn't easy, since she was basically blinded on stage. But he was off to the side, and, depending on the angle, she could see people standing on the fringe when the overhead lights weren't trying to burn holes in her retinas. But he had a presence about him that screamed military or paramilitary in some way. His posture, shoulders back, head up, eyes taking in his surroundings—looked like he was scanning for threats. This man probably didn't know how to slouch.

She couldn't make out his eye color from where she was on stage, but the man had an intense stare about him that just ratcheted up her heart rate until she was slightly out of breath and the blood in her ears made a *whooshing* sound.

What she could see from the stage, though, were those dimples.

He didn't smile much or for very long, but she caught him smiling a few times, and holy nail gun to the face were those babies deep and disarming.

Then he went and whistled at the end of the show, which had her lower belly fluttering and her cheeks flooding with heat as the corners of her mouth pulled up even higher like they had marionette strings attached, and some sadist above her was tugging on them extra hard.

She couldn't pinpoint why, but she had always been attracted to a man who could whistle like that. Loud and commanding.

Well, actually, she could pinpoint the reason. It was her eighth-grade soccer coach. She'd had a terrible crush on Jaxon and he could whistle like that. He was twenty-four at the time and had a girlfriend, but she'd still say to this day that Jaxon Hannigan had been her first love.

And the fact that Caden didn't drink was refreshing.

Not that she had anything against alcohol in general, but her ex had been an alcoholic, and ... well, now she was really careful about who she spent time with and how much alcohol they consumed.

She would never tell a man to give up alcohol for her, but she also knew that she would never go back to a situation where the person's disease made her fear for her life.

Her appetizers came and she shared them with Caden while he shared his nachos. She drank her Shirley Temple and he ordered more club sodas and they watched the rest of the hockey game. The Habs won in overtime, which made the entire bar erupt into cheers. People were patting each other on the back and high-fiving like they were the ones on the ice sweating their butts off and scoring goals.

She never could wrap her head around intense sports team fandom and athlete idolization. She understood the admiration and enjoyment of playing sports and watching them, but not the shaping of one's identity around their favored sports team or athlete. It was another red flag for her, actually. Russell, her ex, had been a passionate Toronto Blue Jays fan and dragged her to too many games to count. And God help everyone within shouting distance if they booed "Russell's team" or the team lost.

When they lost to the Seattle Mariners one time, Oona ended up with a cracked rib.

That had been the start of her escape plan.

She was gun-shy when it came to relationships now, though. Hadn't had one since Russell, which was back when she was doing her masters. And since then, she had barely dated. She had the occasional fling with someone she connected with on a sexual but superficial level, but nothing ever became serious. Nothing stuck.

Then there was Ben. He was a research scientist at McGill. He flitted in and out of her life like a zephyr, and that was something that worked well for both of them. Not only that, he wasn't in town for more than a week before he went off on another grand adventure to investigate turtles in the Galápagos or stingrays on the Great Barrier Reef. They had fun when he was in town, but she knew he was having fun with other women wherever he was, and he didn't expect her to be celibate while he was away. Though she usually was.

But she hadn't heard from Ben in nearly six months, which was a rather long time, all things considered.

"Are your legs littered with bruises?" Caden asked, breaking her introspective train of thought as they sat side-by-side at the bar eating nachos, yam fries and watching the highlights after the hockey game.

"They used to be," she said, dipping a yam fry in the chipotle mayo. "But I've been doing it so long now, my body has adjusted and I don't get too many anymore. When I first started, though, you should have seen my legs. More blue and purple than my skin-tone. And of course, I started in the summer, so I couldn't even wear dresses or skirts for fear of someone thinking I was being viciously beaten."

Besides, Russell never left bruises that were visible. He always made sure to allocate them to her torso or upper arms.

"I've got some pretty gnarly callouses, though," she said, holding out her palms to show off her leathery pads of pride.

Caden reached out with his right index finger and gently rubbed her callouses. "Jesus. You sure do. Those are like ... I dunno." He scratched the dark scruff on his chin until it made a raspy sound. "It's like you work in the coal mines with a shovel or in the woods with an axe, with hands like that."

She grinned, grabbed a tortilla chip, and dipped it into the salsa. "Nope. Just spin my body around a metal pole."

"You sure do." Out came the dimples and she had to inconspicuously keep herself from falling over from their intensity. She also made sure to keep her swoony sigh on the inside. "So what do you do for work anyway?"

Her gaze slid sideways as she chewed. She was already using a fake name with him. Her stage name. *Luna Love.* And she rarely told a stranger what she did for work. As soon as anyone found out she was a psychologist, they immediately assumed she was analyzing them—which she was—and either went into protective mode, or spewed their guts and life problems at her as if she'd fix them in an hour for free. But she also hated lying, so she kept things vague. "I'm in healthcare."

His green eyes widened. "Oh, okay. A doctor?"

"Sure."

That wasn't a lie. She *did* have her PhD. She was Dr. Oona Young. And she was in *mental* healthcare. So she wasn't really, truly lying.

His head cocked to the side like a curious puppy for a moment, but then he smiled and nodded, catching her drift that she didn't want to get too serious and personal. "I'm a first responder," he said, also deliberately keeping it vague. Yep. Just as she suspected. Probably cop or a firefighter.

"Thank you for your service."

"Thank you for yours, *doctor.*"

His smile was coy and sexy and she slid one similar right back at him.

The sexual tension that rippled off him was making her lightheaded, and she hadn't had a drop of alcohol. He glanced up at the television over the bar and took a sip of his club soda, allowing her a moment to study his profile.

He was even more handsome in close proximity. His bottom lashes had an exaggerated curve and were as black as coal. They were long—like the length that a lot of women paid a great deal of money to achieve—and delicate, kissing the skin below his eyes. A faint smattering of freckles, faint but there, dotted his upper cheekbones and ran across his long, prominent nose. Some might say his nose was a touch *too* long, but she thought it suited him perfectly. It was a good-looking nose. A nose with character.

"You from around here?" he asked.

"Beaconsfield area," she said. "You?"

"Charlemagne," he replied.

"Opposite sides of the city. And yet, here we are in the middle."

He lifted his club soda and held it out halfway, waiting for her to touch it with her Shirley Temple. "And yet, here we are in the middle."

She tapped his drink, then took a sip. "What brings you this way?"

His brow lifted. "Do you really care?"

No. She didn't. "As long as it wasn't to murder someone and bury the body, I suppose not."

Caden snorted and sipped his drink. He'd removed the straw every time the bartender set a new drink down, preferring to drink it straight from the glass. "Not hiding any bodies. Just here for an appointment."

"Married or in a relationship?" she asked, sliding her gaze down to his left hand to see if he was being a dick and had just slipped off his wedding band. There was no tan line, though. And wedding rings mean very little in the way of attachment these days.

He shook his head. "You?"

"No."

17

The way his smile caused his cheeks to apple, pulled her attention to a small, puffy scar on the right side of his face. It was probably only an inch in length and fell in a vertical line from the outer right corner of his eye, maybe three and half inches below it. It didn't take away from his beauty, though. If anything, it added to it.

"Then ... I guess you don't have a room?" She bit her bottom lip for half a second, then averted her gaze up to one of the televisions over the bar and popped a chili prawn into her mouth, removing the tail and placing it on the side of her plate.

"Don't, but I could," he said without any inflection of excitement in his tone. He was playing this just as cool as she was.

"You don't have work in the morning?"

"No."

"Days off?"

He paused for just half a second, then said, "Yeah."

He didn't ask her if she worked tomorrow morning.

She did. She didn't have a client until eleven, but regardless, if she was at home, she'd still be up at six o'clock. Then she'd do twenty minutes on the rowing machine, twenty minutes on the elliptical, and twenty minutes of weight and strength training, followed by a shower.

Then she'd make her breakfast smoothie, which she'd take with her to work. It took her exactly twenty-two minutes to drive to work where she listened to a podcast and drank her smoothie. By the time she got there, she was ready for her Earl Grey tea, her morning poop, and her first client. Whether her client arrived at nine, ten, or eleven, she was in her office, with her butt in her chair by eight-fifty without fail. If her client was later in the morning, she filled the first few hours with emails, notes, and other menial tasks.

She couldn't afford an assistant, yet, so the administrative stuff still fell into her lap. Which she didn't exactly hate, given how much of a control freak she was about things, anyway.

But if she set the alarm on her phone for five o'clock, she could slip out of bed with this tall, handsome stranger with the big arms, deep dimples, and nice smile, and get home in time for her routine to be undisturbed. She probably wouldn't fall asleep with him, though. So she could have some fun, then leave, getting back to her own bed for a few hours with her thousand thread-count cotton, luxurious down comforter with the lilac duvet cover, and her lavender sachet under her pillows.

"Should I, uh ... go get us a room then?" Caden rasped.

She squeezed her legs together beneath the bar, took a sip of her Shirley Temple, and smiled over the straw before giving him one small head bob.

"Be right back."

He slid off his stool, leaving his coat, but taking his wallet, keys, and phone.

A tremor of excitement traveled through her.

She hadn't done anything like this in a long time.

And not with someone as handsome or ... mysterious as Caden.

This was completely out of character for her.

Well, for *Oona* anyway. When she was Luna, she allowed herself to do things a little differently. She embraced the freedom that a fake name gave her. She could do things she would never normally do. Like accompanying a total stranger up to a hotel room for sex.

But if she had to choose one thing, pole and burlesque had given her more than anything else—besides incredible upper body strength—it was empowerment. Russell had stripped her of so much, that, by the time she left him, she didn't even know who she was anymore. Didn't recognize herself in the mirror. And pole gave that back to her. She was able to cultivate a new identity, embrace her body and all the curves and jiggly bits, and feel more beautiful and graceful than she ever had before.

And even though uptight, rigid, overly-organized, and extremely type-A Oona would never dream of following a stranger to his hotel room for meaningless sex, Luna was excited and here for it.

19

The freedom that her alter-ego allowed her was something so liberating, and addictive, that she had to remind herself on more than one occasion that she was actually Dr. Oona Young, *not* Luna Love, and that being Luna Love was fun for a short time. But Oona Young was who she was and who paid the bills and kept Luna Love strutting in her six-inch plastic heels and brand-new corsets.

Opening her purse, she checked if she had condoms. Yes, she had an IUD, but that didn't prevent STIs. In one of the inside pouches, she found a strip of five condoms. *Phew.* She checked their expiration dates. They were still good. *Double phew!*

After the pole and burlesque show ended, she wiped off all her makeup and put on fresh deodorant. She had baby wipes in her purse, as well, so a quick duck off to the bathroom to freshen up wasn't a terrible idea.

"Pedro?" she asked, grabbing the bartender's attention.

"Another Shirley?" he asked with a big smile that showed off the slight chip on his left front tooth.

"No, I'm good. I'm just going to duck to the ladies' room, so don't clear my stuff."

"You got it."

She finished her drink, then grabbed her purse and rounded the bar to the far side, where the washrooms were located.

She was in and out in a matter of minutes, having used some mouthwash, slathered on some lip gloss in the bathroom mirror, and freshened up with a wet wipe.

Caden was back at the bar, and when he saw her, his face lit up. An explosion of grass-green eyes, white teeth, and devastating dimples. "Thought you might have ditched me for a second." The way his lips lifted higher on one side had her panties getting damp. "But then Pedro set me straight."

Pedro shot her a wink.

"At the very least, I would have paid my tab first. I don't stick people with my bill."

"Mighty kind of you," he said as she reclaimed her seat at the bar. He discreetly slid a key card over to her elbow. "We have a room."

She glanced down at it, and her lip twitched. "I guess we do."

You'd think they were drunk based on how they burst into the hotel room with gropey hands and sloppy kisses. But they were both stone-cold sober. They were just really horny.

He'd unhooked her bra in the elevator, and she had to keep herself from unzipping his jeans in there, too, when what lurked beneath that denim prodded her in the hip as he ground against her and his lips found her neck.

Thankfully, their room was only two doors down from the elevator, and the key card worked.

Then they were in the room, and clothes were flying everywhere as hands roamed and lips found new patches of bare skin to explore.

Her calves hit the end of the bed and he pulled his lips away from her shoulder, then with a grin, pushed her backward, so she fell to the bed with a bounce. She smiled at him when he reached for the ankles of her jeans and tugged them off.

He was shirtless, and the realistic and intense expression of a big horned owl tattoo on his left shoulder and part of his bicep made her insides hum. The eyes of the owl were vivid and sort of glaring at her. But she wasn't scared by the intimidating expression that regarded her as prey, she was intrigued and excited by it. She wanted him to devour her.

He'd relieved her of her shirt and bra just moments after the hotel room door closed. She wasn't ashamed or embarrassed of her body, so to tumble back to the bed topless while still in her jeans didn't faze her at all.

But now she was just down to her panties.

His eyes lasered in on the V of her legs, where she was positive he could see the damp patch she'd created on her cornflower blue cotton underwear. If she knew she'd be having sexy-time with a man, she would have put on something a little less practical, with maybe some lace or satin. But whatever. He'd already seen her all glammed up in a corset and six-inch plastic heels. Now he could see her for how she was the other ninety-percent of her life. Practical and in a breathable fabric.

"I like your tattoo," he said, which came out more like the purr of some wild jungle cat. He stepped between her spread legs, which dangled over the edge of the bed, and traced the fine-line tattoo of a lily on the bottom of her left ribs. "You also have one on your shoulder blade and," he said, pointing to her right tricep, where the compass done in pointillism was. "Anything else?"

She scraped her teeth over her bottom lip and nodded.

His brows lifted, but then his gaze slid across her body, leaving a warm, glowing heat on her skin wherever his eyes touched, until he focused on her belly button and the waistband of her underwear. "I have to finish unwrapping if I want to see them all?"

She swallowed and lifted her hips as he hooked his fingers into the elastic sides of her underwear and slowly slid them over her thighs, revealing her last tattoo.

It was the smallest of all her tattoos and the simplest. But it was also the most meaningful.

Because she wasn't the only one who had it.

It was five intersecting hearts in a row, each one slightly smaller than the one that preceded it. All but one heart were colored in. And in this case, for her, it was the fourth one—her place in the birth order of her and her four sisters. She chose hot pink just to be different.

"What do the hearts mean?" he asked, tossing her underwear to the floor and running his big thumb over the tattoo.

"For me and my sisters."

"Five girls?" He blew out a breath. "Are they all as hot as you?"

She rolled her eyes. "You'll never know. I could be the ugly duckling of the bunch."

"Jesus, I highly doubt it, but if that is the case, then fucking hell. Damn good genes in your family if *you're* the ugliest." He licked his lips, and his eyes turned serious as he dropped to his knees at the foot of the bed. "Gonna suck your clit now."

All she could respond with was a gasp as he leaned forward and did just as he promised. He pulled her throbbing, needy clit in between his lips and gave it mouth-to-mouth—or, in this case, mouth-to-clit—like it was circling the drain and about to die.

Only he didn't breathe life into it. He sucked the life into it.

Okay, so maybe that analogy was terrible. But she was getting incredible head from a gorgeous stranger, her brain wasn't running on all cylinders.

As he sucked, he ran his hands up the backs of her thighs, tickling behind her knees, until he reached the callouses on the inside bend of her knees. He paused and lifted his head from her center.

She glanced down her body at him. "Yeah, that's a pole callous."

He grinned up at her and gently stroked the rough spots on either side of her legs with his thumbs. "It's hot knowing how you got these." He turned his head and pressed a kiss to each one before dropping his mouth back to her clit and giving it another suck.

Her head tilted up so her chin was pointed at the ceiling as her back bowed and her toes curled where they now rested on his shoulders.

He released her clit with a wet *pop* then began to lick.

And, oh God, could the man lick.

His tongue was ... magical.

It was like a soft, slippery wand that he wielded and kept putting her deeper and deeper under his spell, until her hips churned and bucked of their own volition. She pinched her nipples and pressed her pussy harder against his face

23

just as he slipped two fingers into her wet channel and curled them upward, hitting her right where she needed him to the most.

"Oh God ..."

Around and around and around he swirled his tongue on her clit, then down to where his fingers pumped and entered her, only to backtrack his journey and start from the beginning, all the while alternating his licks with sucks and scrapes of his whiskers against the most sensitive, swollen parts of her.

She wasn't going to last much longer if he kept this up. She was going to blow, and given the way Caden seemed to have set up camp, he was in it for the long haul and wanted her to come. He wasn't just trying to get her close so he could drop trou and climb on her. He was a real gentleman that wanted to get her off first, before he even got his dick wet.

That seemed to be a rare breed of man these days.

So she was going to take advantage of having a gentleman with his face between her legs and get off.

"Can feel that you're close, Luna. Let go, baby. We have the place for the night."

He went back to the clit sucking, pulling that tender little bundle of nerves so deep into his mouth that she thought he might suck it clean off. Then he pressed up even more on her G-spot and she let go. Like an invisible zipper had just been pulled up from her tailbone to the nape of her neck, she shuddered and her muscles went tight. A weightlessness overcame her body as warmth infused its way through her limbs in a tingling surge that started between her legs and followed her nervous system into her toes and up to her chest. Out to each fingertip and to each earlobe.

Her lower belly fluttered like it was filled with butterflies, and sunbursts clouded her vision as the rolling waves of euphoria pitched her higher and higher up into the ether. All tension left her body, and she was nothing but a puddle of blissful, warm goo.

By the time her orgasm receded enough for her to open her eyes and see more than spots, and for her legs to unlock and her toes to wiggle, it was impossible for the giddy smile on her face to fall away.

She hadn't had a non-self-induced orgasm like that in a very long time.

She wasn't even sure she could give herself one like that.

A toy could, but her own hand couldn't.

Exhaling through her mouth as her chest continued to rise and fall rapidly, she glanced down her body at Caden who was now lazily licking her pussy like it was a lollipop, not an ice cream cone he needed to finish before it melted in the hot sun.

"Can I return the favor?" she asked, her voice deep and husky and catching her off guard by how sexy it sounded.

"Sure fucking can, beautiful," he said with a big smile, giving her one final sweep of his tongue between her folds, before standing up and dropping his boxers to reveal his cock.

He wasn't huge, but he wasn't small, either.

The crown was a deep, dark purple and the shaft was veiny with a small, trimmed patch of hair at the base.

He took himself in his big palm and gave his length a couple of strokes. That's when she realized just how big his hands were. Like really massive.

Not freakishly big, like he wasn't a gorilla or anything, but they were big. However, they didn't dwarf his cock, so maybe he was bigger than she initially thought. Or he was still growing. But the sight of his large hand stroking his cock like that, sent blood rushing to her ears so loudly that it was like waves crashing inside of her head.

It was hot, and the sudden desperate need to have that cock in her mouth while his big hand wrapped around her ponytail was alarming, but in a really exciting way.

Sitting up on the edge of the bed, she gently swatted away his palm and wrapped her fingers around him, then she leaned forward, swiping her tongue across the head to gather that bead of precum that leaked from the slit. Humming, because that's what guys liked, she swirled her tongue around her lips before parting them and taking him into her mouth.

"Fuck," he breathed when she took him to the back of her throat almost immediately. She alternated between deep-throating and swirling her tongue around the crown while stroking him. He bucked forward slightly and growled like a bear when she took him deep. But he also seemed to like it when she held him by the base and just licked his shaft from root to tip. He made more noises when she did that, and at one point, he gripped her by the ponytail—which she didn't really mind—and pulled her from a deep-throat to do the licking thing again.

His balls were hairless, so she cupped those with her free hand, then at one point, while stroking his cock, she dropped her head lower and licked his sac before taking one, then the other, into her mouth and gently sucking.

"Fucking hell," he grunted right before he yanked on her hair—*yes*— then tossed her to the bed, covered her, and kissed her like he was out of air and she was the only remaining source of oxygen.

His cock fell right between her legs and he rocked against her, the head knocking her clit and reawakening it from its cat nap. She lifted her hips and ground against him, but before they could get too carried away, she put a hand on his shoulder and pushed so he would stop kissing her. "Condom," she whispered. "In my purse." She pointed to where her purse was on the table.

"Right." He nodded and climbed off her so she could get up and grab a strip of them from her bag. He had one on in seconds, then was back on top of her, kissing her again, bringing the flavor of her own release on his lips and beard, as his cock once again knocked her pussy.

"Fuck, you're beautiful," he murmured, breaking their kiss and dropping his mouth to her neck, clavicle, shoulder, and finally her nipple. "Fucking gorgeous." He scissored his teeth across her tight bud and she arched her back, gasping and then moaning from the pain that was quick to be extinguished and replaced by pleasure. "And holy fuck, can you suck a cock."

Pride swelled stupidly in her chest at his praise.

She knew she had a praise kink.

Always had.

It came from being raised in a family and by parents who only ever pointed out your faults and failures, never your successes. Who sought to shame and humble you until you couldn't even feel good about getting ten out of ten on your spelling quiz.

She hadn't discussed it with her sisters before, but she wouldn't be surprised if all five of them had a praise kink of some sort.

He moved over to the other breast and offered it the same attention from his mouth. All the while he continued to rock against her, his cock sliding between her slick pussy lips, the head knocking her clit and getting it all excited.

"Your pussy tastes so fucking good, too," he rumbled, raking his scruff over her nipple before kissing up the other shoulder, side of her neck, and then back to her mouth. "Goddamn delicious." Then he lifted up on his arms, tipped his hips forward so his cock was notched at her center, and as he locked eyes with her and held her gaze, he slowly slid home, sheathing himself inside of her. "Perfect fucking fit," he said, once he was all the way inside. "Goddamn it, Luna. You're the whole damn package, aren't you? Brilliant, sexy, and great at head. A triple threat."

"You need to start moving," she said, a slight shake to her voice. "Like now."

His smile was bright and brilliant, beckoning his dimples so completely that it winded her a little. There was a raspy chuckle that followed as he nodded and started to move, sliding in and out of her at the perfect speed. Hitting her in the perfect spot and making the perfect orgasm build inside of her faster than she was prepared for.

The way his lower belly scraped her clit had her legs shaking. She clawed at his back, and her head thrashed side to side on the bed, the harder she tried to keep the orgasm from bursting free so she could ride out the journey a little longer.

"Don't hold on, baby. Just let it go," he said. "It won't be your last tonight. I can promise you that. Many more in store."

He'd dropped his mouth back to her breast, but then he lifted his head again, grabbed her right leg, and bent it so her knee pressed into her belly, allowing him to go deeper, to change the angle, and hit her in new and glorious places.

Their eyes met, and a knowing, cocky smile slid slowly up on his mouth, one side slightly higher than the other, which only made him sexier. "I can feel your control fading. Just let go. I'll catch you."

She bit her bottom lip as her heart hammered against her rib cage.

"Luna, I mean it. Come."

Then, to drive home the point that he meant what he said, he wedged a hand between them—somehow—and pinched her clit.

She exploded.

"Good girl," he purred, but his praise barely resonated inside her brain because it was made mostly up of warm happy goo as the orgasm rippled out of her center and back into every limb. Into every cell and forgotten erogenous zone of her body, until her skin hummed and prickled like it was being kissed by the first rays of spring sunshine after a particularly long and cold winter.

Her toes curled, and her pussy squeezed and trembled around his cock.

He was still pumping. Still thrusting forward, but then as she was still floating high in her own euphoria, he stopped moving, his back muscles went tight, he grunted and released a long, slow breath accompanied by a groan. His cock twitched and pumped inside of her as he came, his corded arms bunching and twitching slightly beside her, his muscles straining from holding up his own weight above her.

She wanted to tilt her head and lick one of those veins.

So she did.

His eyes flared as he dropped his head back down to look at her. Green flames danced beneath his thick brows and hooded lids.

His chest heaved against hers, and after a few more moments, he exhaled, and his soul reentered his body. "Did you just lick my arm?"

She pulled her bottom lip between her teeth. "Maybe."

"That was hot."

She grinned.

He grinned.

Then he rolled off her and went to the bathroom to dispose of the condom. "Give me like thirty minutes, then we can go again, okay?"

Her mouth dropped open. Thirty minutes? That was it?

Russell was a once-a-day ejaculation guy. Not that they did it once a day—thank God. But he could never go more than once.

Before they got together, and when they first got together, she'd had a particularly high sex drive. But as he grew abusive, she looked for every excuse in the book not to have sex. Which was what she figured pushed him to cheat.

She still didn't have the sex drive she once had, but she was getting it back slowly.

But a man like Caden, who only needed a thirty-minute refractory period ... he seemed like just the right solution to her lull.

He returned from the bathroom with two glasses of water and a big smile on his face. "Well, if that's not the most beautiful sight. You, naked, flushed, and fresh off two orgasms." He handed her a glass, and she sat up, but before she could take a sip, he kissed her. "Would it be cliché for me to ask you to treat me like your pole and climb me?"

She snorted and rolled her eyes. But the smile that graced her mouth was unavoidable as she took a sip of her water. "A little cliché, yeah, but ... if you can hold me up, I can think of a few creative positions we could do."

There were the dimples again. "Luna Love, I am your pole for the night, use me, abuse me, and climb all over me."

She set her water glass down on the night stand and he did the same, then she pushed him back to the bed and straddled him. "Sure, but first, let's see how well you can hold your breath."

Then she climbed over him and sat on his face just as he cupped her ass cheeks and murmured, "Good girl."

Chapter Three

She might have been delirious from all the orgasms, but she wasn't drunk, and she had the forethought to set the alarm on her phone for five o'clock during one of their sex-lulls.

Because even though she hadn't planned on staying the night with Caden, she ended up falling asleep with his arm around her from behind, her bare ass nestled in the crook of his body, against his finally flaccid cock as he breathed lightly and evenly behind her.

And it was nice.

Really nice.

She hadn't cuddled with anyone in a really long time, and she forgot how *nice* it was.

Yes, the sex and orgasms were amazing, but you still got that surge of oxytocin from cuddling, too.

Her alarm went off at five, but Caden didn't stir more than to roll over and hug his pillow.

She quickly got dressed, double-checked she had everything, then dug into her wallet for money, scrawled a note that said *My share of the hotel room* before setting them both next to his wallet and keys and leaving quieter than a church mouse.

The smile on her face as she took the elevator down to the lobby was hurting her cheeks by the time she reached the main floor. She was also walking a little funny.

Caden No-Last-Name was hands down the best sex she'd ever had.

And he was a total stranger.

How peculiar.

She'd had sex with strangers before. Hooked up with people, had one-night stands—who hadn't?—but more often than not she came away slightly disappointed. She usually had to intervene with her own hand to get off, and no man had ever been that enthusiastic and thorough going down on her. Caden seemed to genuinely love it. While he was waiting for his balls to reload (his words, not hers), he'd slide down onto his belly and push his face between her legs just because "I like it here," he said more than once.

Where did Caden come from? Heaven? Because it sure as heck seemed that way.

They did have some actual conversations, too. Chatted about their hobbies—both were into fitness; he liked to run and lift weights—favorite restaurants in the city; places they'd traveled, places they wanted to travel, and of course, how she got into pole and burlesque.

She remained vague about that bit, merely telling him that she'd been in an abusive relationship and that doing pole and burlesque helped with her trauma and regaining her power and sense of self. She'd been asked this question more than once, so she had a canned, but honest response. Most people dropped it after that, since her tone usually left little room for continued questioning.

Caden, like everyone else, said how sorry he was that she experienced that and that he was glad she found something that helped her. Only, unlike other people, there was a tendril of anger woven through his words. Not at her, she knew that. But at the fact that she'd had to experience anything like her abuse at all. A protective anger she appreciated, even if it was a little odd coming from a complete stranger.

He was an easy person to talk to. Didn't seem to be overly critical or narcissistic. He asked her questions about herself and seemed genuinely interested in what she had to say. He was a little more evasive when she asked him about his life, but no red flags started to wave with his answers.

She just hoped he wasn't in a relationship, or out on parole for spousal abuse or something. That would really suck.

It was well below freezing when she reached her car in the parking lot at five-fifteen. The pavement was slippery and the sky was still dark. Her breath cast a thick fog in front of her face as she fumbled with her key fob to open her black Toyota Corolla, and she shivered when she finally got it open and slid in behind the wheel.

It took another twenty minutes for the car to heat up enough that she could drive it. She also had to scrape the windows and defrost them from the inside.

Ugh. Winter was the worst.

By the time she got home, it was twenty after six, since she took it slow, navigating icy patches all over the city.

Quickly changing into her workout gear, she cut her rowing and elliptical exercises a little short and only did twelve minutes of strength and weight training rather than twenty. Her shower afterward was glorious and she smiled when she saw the whisker burn on her inner thighs and breasts.

Her smoothie was extra-delicious, not that she added anything extra to it, and the sun seemed to be shining brighter than ever when she headed back out to her car from her third-floor condo, to head to work.

Was this because of all the great orgasms? Her smoothie was tastier, her shower was better, and the sun was brighter? What next? The best, most understanding, and easy to work with client of her life?

Maybe.

She got into work at the same time she always did, finishing her smoothie as she unlocked the door to her office.

Then she brewed herself her double-bergamot Earl Grey Stash tea, visited the bathroom that all the offices on the second floor shared, and returned to her office to start her day.

And she already knew, it was going to be a great day, she could just feel it.

He took the stairs up two at a time to the office of his new therapist.

She was located on the second floor of a professional building dedicated to multiple different businesses. By the looks of the nameplates in the lobby, the second floor was almost entirely allocated to therapists and psychologists of some nature, while the bottom floor was a chiropractor, massage, and physio office, and the third floor (also the top floor) was a dermatologist's office.

Aiden heaved on the door to enter the second floor hallway, and was greeted by an endless corridor of closed doors.

Slowly, with his gut spinning and the dread that had formed invasive roots in his feet and ominous twisting branches that spread into his arms and shoulders, weighing them down and making them ache, he walked the hallway reading each nameplate on the doors until he reached the one he was meant to stop at.

Dr. Oona Young.

She came highly recommended and had a waitlist that was months long.

Didn't stop him from getting itchy and twitchy at the thought of having to share his innermost thoughts, anger, and details of his life with a total stranger.

You just ate the pussy of a total stranger for hours last night; seems like you're okay getting personal.

That was entirely different. And by the end of the night, Luna didn't feel like a stranger at all.

Probably because he knew every inch of her body intimately, but also because she was one of the easiest people he'd ever talked to, or ever been around. She was sweet and funny. Smart, sexy and hell, the woman knew how to suck cock like nobody he'd ever been with before.

He was a little heartbroken to wake up earlier that morning and find her gone.

Then, she had the audacity to leave him money for half the hotel.

What the fuck?

But he didn't even let that irritation overthrow the joy he felt from spending the night with such a wild and wonderful beauty. She was uninhibited, generous, and brazen. But he could also tell she had a deeply rooted praise kink and loved it when he called her a good girl. The way her cheeks streaked with pink and her eyes flared brightly when he praised her just made his pulse race.

So despite the inevitable difficult appointment ahead of him, his spirits were high when he checked out of the hotel and headed home for fresh clothes. Not much could deflate his mood after a night like that, after spending time with a woman like Luna.

Too bad he'd probably never see her again.

He knew that Dr. Young had a file on him. That she read up on most of what he'd already been through, why he was there in the first place, and his prior warnings and recommendations for anger management.

But she'd want to go deeper. She'd want to study his childhood like a bug under a microscope. Dissect it until all the fragile pieces were spread around him in total, unrecognizable disarray, and then after an hour, send him home to try to reassemble them the best he could.

He finally reached her door and stopped. His hand fell to the metal latch, and with a deep breath, he turned it and entered.

He loved his job as a police officer, it was what he was born to do, so if speaking with a shrink and going to anger management was how he got back in the field, then so be it.

He'd chased down bad guys, been punched by wives whose husbands had just given them a black-eye because suddenly the husband wasn't such a bad guy and Aiden was a dick for arresting him.

He could do this. He could spend an hour with a therapist if it meant he got back to protecting the good people of Montreal from drunk drivers and abusers like the guy who'd hurt Luna.

Maybe when he got back in the field, he could do some digging and see if he could find the guy who hurt her.

Luna probably wasn't her real name, but he could bring up victim photos and see what matched her. If the scumbag ever got reported, that is.

He stepped into a small waiting area with two chairs, a side table filled with various magazines, and a burbling fountain with a skinny Buddha on it was next to a big fern-like plant in the other corner of the room.

His phone said it was ten-fifty-five.

His appointment was at eleven.

There was another door and he assumed that was the therapist's office. Should he knock? Or would she come out and get him?

He sat down on one of the seats and rested his hands on his jean-clad knees.

The left knee started to bounce. It often bounced when he was nervous.

Glancing at his phone every twenty seconds did nothing for his nerves, but he couldn't stop himself.

Then, when the time switched over to ten-fifty-eight, he stood up from the chair and was about to knock on the door when the latch turned and the door opened.

"Aiden?" came a confident, slightly robotic voice.

"Dr. Youn—" His mouth hung open.

Her brown eyes, the ones flecked with different shades of gold, were the size of twin Frisbees.

"C-Caden?" she stammered.

"*Luna*. Or should I say *Oona*."

Her slender throat moved on a swallow as she continued to stare at him. "Are you Officer Aiden L?"

As a second line of privacy, the police department had taken to issuing the officers names to mental health professionals with just their last initial. There'd been a recent breach in confidentiality concerning a therapist and police officer in Ottawa, so now all departments were upping their privacy regarding their officers and submitting paperwork with only their first name and last initial.

He nodded.

"Are you Dr. Oona Young?"

She nodded. "I—" Exhaling, she released the door latch on her side and stepped into her office, leaving the door open for him to follow. She circled around her obnoxiously tidy desk, but didn't sit down in the chair. Everything on her desk was at a right angle and arranged either according to color or size. She had very little in the way of decorations besides a purple orchid on her filing cabinet behind her. No pictures, no paintings, or art. Her diplomas from Brown University and McGill University were the only things on the wall. "I can't see you," she finally said.

He wasn't quite at the two comfy chairs she had facing her desk, but was close enough that he was able to take another step and rest his hand on the plush back of one. "What do you mean?"

"I can't treat you. I'm sorry."

"But ... but you have to. I've been on the waitlist to see you for months. If I don't see you, if I don't complete anger management, I can't go back to work."

"I know that. And I'm happy to refer you to someone else, but—"

"But then I'll just be stuck on their waitlist for another four months-or longer! You're holding my job hostage because we slept together *once*?"

Anger bubbled up hot and heavy in his chest, like a pot of thick gravy on the stove that somebody had left on to boil.

"It's unethical."

He rolled his eyes. "Didn't stop you last night."

"I thought you were *Caden* last night. I had no idea you were *Aiden*, my new patient."

"So, you're not doing anything wrong, then. I wasn't your patient last night. It's not unethical. What would be unethical was if I bent you over that desk right now and called you a good girl."

A high tide of blood rose up her neck and into her cheeks, turning them blotchy and red. "It's still unethical to treat someone I know personally. I could lose my license. I could lose my job."

He snorted and shook his head. "What about *my* job?"

"I don't want you to lose your job, either. But if I treated you and someone found out that we ... were *together*, they could invalidate your treatment. Accuse me of manufacturing the data, of declaring you fit to return to work when you're not. I'm looking out for *both of our careers.*"

His palms curled into fists on the top of the chair, and her eyes lasered in on them. She took a half-step back. "Being suspended and forced to attend anger management classes should be enough penance for what happened," he ground out.

"You punched a person after you pulled him over. And apparently after prior warnings for over-the-top behavior regarding drunk drivers. I'd say all things considered, you're lucky they're not firing you after the investigation from the Civilian Review and Complaints Commission came back. The fact that they're giving you a second chance and simply asking you to *learn* from your mistakes before you return to active duty is HUGE, and not something I've ever seen before. Take this as a win. But if I treat you, it will compromise this second chance significantly."

"He was a drunk driver and he had his daughter in the back! As far as I'm concerned, *he* got off pretty lucky just getting punched. No charges were ever filed. So he's free to do it again."

"I understand that, and as horrible as that is, you are an officer of the law and are supposed to conduct yourself in a more professional manner. You are supposed to be able to restrain yourself. The judge made the ruling that in order for you to return to active duty, you need to complete twenty hours of therapy and six months of anger management."

He gnashed his molars together. He was well aware of the facts, and it grated on him that she was, too.

Not that Dr. Young was aware, but that *Luna* was aware. That Luna, or Oona or whatever the fuck her name was, the woman he'd spent the night with last night, the first woman he'd really connected with in ages, and liked, knew his history.

All of it.

All the dirty, humiliating, shameful details. He saw his file sitting on her desk, and it wasn't a thin file. This was his first suspension, but he had prior warnings for over-the-top behavior regarding drunk drivers. He had anger issues, and when he saw that poor child sitting in the backseat after her father had been swerving all over the road, Aiden let his rage spill over, and he wound up suspended.

It didn't matter that he was suspended with pay. He wanted to be working for that money, not sitting at home with his finger up his ass, waiting while more drunk drivers swerved in the streets and killed people.

Her gaze softened and she pressed her lips together before she spoke. "I will write the court and simply state that there is a conflict of interest and I am unable to treat you. I am sorry. I will make a recommendation for a colleague and see what I can do to expedite your time on the waitlist."

But even with that softened gaze, her sympathy felt forced. She was cold and ... robotic in the way she spoke to him. This wasn't the Luna he'd met last night. The Luna who had confidently, salaciously swung around a pole on stage while wearing six-inch plastic heels. The woman who'd worn a corset and thong and gave a lap dance to an empty chair at the same time she gave everyone in the crowd come-fuck-me-eyes. The woman who'd climbed over him, straddled his face and asked him how long he could hold his breath. That woman was pure heat. Pure fire.

This woman, this *Dr. Oona Young*, wore a boring beige pantsuit with a light purple blouse underneath. Her caramel-colored hair was pulled back and twisted up into one of those French twist things. She had on minimal makeup, nude lipstick, and pearl studs in her ears. She looked a lot older, too. Lines he hadn't seen before—and he'd studied every inch of her, including her face—were fine, but noticeable around her eyes and between her brows. If it wasn't for the brown and gold eyes and that tiny little freckle or beauty mark below her right eye, he would have thought she had a stuck-up twin or something.

But her frigid approach to their situation only made the waves of anger lash harder against his insides until his throat burned with a frothy bile and his pulse hammered wildly in his ears. "Forget it," he gritted out.

"I really am sorry, Ca-Aiden."

"Yeah, you really *sound* sorry."

"I *am* sorry. But I can't jeopardize my career, or yours."

"I can pretend I've only just met you," he said, in a last-ditch effort to get her to change her mind. "I mean, in theory, I have. Last night I met *Luna Love*."

Something weird passed behind her eyes, but it was there and then it was gone. He couldn't place the emotion she just felt, couldn't even put a label on it, but the closest he could come to describing it was *envy*. Like she envied her alter ego. But why? Couldn't she just *be* Luna Love if she wanted to? Act like Luna even when she wasn't on stage? He didn't get it.

Did this chick have split personalities? Would he meet a Russian mobster named Uri in a few minutes?

She shook her head. "We can't." Nibbling on her bottom lip like she had last night, she cast her gaze toward his file. "But I um ..." That ice-cold wall she'd built around herself showed signs of a fissure. Her shoulders dropped away from her ears a little, and the color in her cheeks faded to a pretty pink. He suddenly saw glimpses of Luna from last night. "I like you, Aiden. And even though I can't be your therapist because of the conflict of interest, perhaps … maybe we could go out again?"

A fresh, warm rush of frustration sprinted up his spine like someone behind him had just scraped the pointed, hot edge of a knife along his vertebrae. "What the actual fuck? Are you kidding me right now?"

He practically heard the walls around her get thicker and the bricks stack higher. That fissure sealed up fast, and the woman in front of him hardened to granite.

"So because I've seen all your tattoos and know what your pussy tastes like, you can't keep me on as a client, but you're asking me out? Isn't *that* a conflict of interest and unethical?"

"I haven't treated you, so no," she enunciated through clenched teeth. He could see the regret in her eyes and ignored the flickers of guilt in his belly. He was too angry to care.

Huffing a laugh, he shook his head. "You're a real piece of work, Dr. Young. Real piece of fucking work."

He knew he was stretching. He knew he was just adding fuel to the fire, goading her. Pushing her buttons and pushing her away. It was what he did best. Make them angry, so they get angry back. Call him an asshole, because he is one. He had no doubts about that.

"But I'm going to have to pass. Thanks. You've read my file, so you know my shit. I'm not interested in dating someone who knows all my secrets, when apparently, she has a buttload of her own. Not exactly *fair*, you know."

Her back straightened, and her gaze flew up to his. With each even breath, her nostrils flared, but it took several agonizing heartbeats for her to speak. "I will do my best to find you another therapist," she bit out the words once more.

"Whatever." He turned to go, the blaze of rage burning everything inside of him to the point where he thought he might start to breathe fire. His hand rested on the door handle. He could feel his career, everything he'd worked so hard for, slipping away and it hurt like a gunshot to the gut. He wanted her to

41

feel a bit of his pain. To know what she was doing to him. "You weren't good in bed anyway." Then he left, making sure to slam the door behind him, so she couldn't see the shame that he knew was all over his face, because how could it not be when it filled his entire soul.

Chapter Four

The full weight of Oona's humiliation pressed down on her shoulders like two large birds of prey, waiting for her tattered heart to leave her chest so they could feed on it.

Her temples throbbed with an angry supply of blood as she stood behind her desk, staring at the closed door of her office. She had no idea how long she stood there, but it was a while.

By the time her breathing finally reached a point where she wasn't going to see spots if she moved too quickly, Oona gathered her wits—or what remained of them—and slowly, methodically left her office.

She walked down the hall two doors, and didn't bother knocking when she turned the handle. The space was identical to her own setup. A small waiting room with two chairs and a side table with magazines, as well as a door leading into the main office.

While her office had a big fern and a Buddha fountain, this office had a palm tree and small Easter Island Moai statue.

Voices on the other side of the door had her sitting down in one of the two empty chairs, and just as her butt hit the seat, the door opened. "All right, we'll see you next week. Take care, Viola."

"Thank you, Dr. McRobb," the woman said, offering a small, embarrassed smile at Oona before quickly vacating the waiting room.

Dr. McRobb's dark brown eyes lasered in on Oona and their brows shot up under the aquamarine shock of hair that tumbled over their forehead. "I didn't think I had another appointment until one."

"I messed up," Oona said.

Dr. McRobb smiled, rolled their eyes, then tilted their head to indicate that Oona should step into their office. Dr. McRobb was nonbinary, which meant—at least in their case—that although they were assigned female at birth, they did not feel overly female or overly male. As they often said, "I just feel like a person." So their preferred pronouns were they/them.

"What's going on, Oons?" Dr. McRobb—or Teal—to their friends, asked. Because Oona and Teal were friends. Actually, Teal was Oona's supervisor. Even though Oona had her PhD and could practice psychology, she still had a supervisor for a little longer, which she didn't mind. She and Teal were friends more than anything. She went to Teal with her work issues, life issues, and now, in this case *boy* issues.

Teal turned on the electric kettle at their tea station, which was set up on top of a filing cabinet, and then sat down in the chair beside Oona, rather than the one behind their desk. "Spill."

Oona tipped her head back against the chair and let out a sigh. "I slept with a client."

"You what?!" Normally, Teal was the most even-toned person around. Not much ruffled their turquoise feathers, except this.

"It's not like that," she quickly said, taking in Teal's petrified expression. "He wasn't a client when I slept with him last night. We gave each other fake names. It turns out he was my new client."

"The super broken cop with PTSD and anger issues?"

"Is that your professional diagnosis, Dr. McRobb?"

Teal smirked. "Obviously, you told him you couldn't treat him."

"Of course. He didn't even sit down. I opened the door, and once I got over the shock of seeing him again, I told him I ethically couldn't see him as a patient. But—"

"He showed you why he's in anger management?"

She exhaled. "Yep." She buried her face in her hands. "But only after I made the colossally stupid mistake of asking him out again."

"You didn't."

She peeked at Teal between her fingers. "I did."

The kettle let them know it was at a full boil. Teal got up and didn't even bother to ask what Oona wanted. Her answer would always be the same. Earl Grey, no sweetener, a splash of oat milk, and leave in the teabag.

Teal handed Oona the mug of Earl Grey, then blowing on their own mug, which would undoubtedly have raspberry rooibos in it, sat down in their chair again. "And he shot you down?"

"Yep, then said I was bad in bed, just to drive that stake a few inches deeper into my chest."

"Ouch."

Oona merely raised her brows to agree.

"You did the right thing, though. Know that. Because regardless of our friendship, if I found out you were sleeping with, or had slept with a client whom you continued to treat, I'd be ethically obligated to report you."

"I know."

Teal offered a grim, understanding smile. "Doesn't mean it hurts any less."

"Nope."

They both blew on their tea before taking cautious sips and letting Oona's issues percolate through their analytical minds in companionable silence.

Teal had been born into a very religious and traditional Korean family in New York, their birth name, or, in this case, now, *dead name* was Ju-Won, which ironically means *beautiful woman*.

They laughed about it now. How their parents just set themselves up with naming their child that, even though they tried with all their might to shape Teal into the person they wanted them to be. Forcing them to wear the girliest dresses imaginable, go to church, and worship a God that considered Teal's existence a sin.

Teal was set up on dates by their mother with Korean boys whose families went to their church and drank the same bigot-flavored Kool-Aid. Teal often said that their upbringing was a lot like Lane's from Gilmore Girls, only instead of harboring a love for punk music, they harbored a love for girls, ska music, and pantsuits.

They came out as gay to their family at eighteen and were instantly shunned. Teal had not spoken to their parents in almost twenty years. Not even their siblings. And even though they pretended it didn't bother them, Oona knew that it did. Oona knew that the pain was still deep and the scars would probably never fully heal.

Teal revealed that they were nonbinary around the age of twenty-three, and married their long-time girlfriend, Penelope, when they were both twenty-six. Penelope was cis-gender, identifying as female and using the pronouns she/her. And, oh wow, was she ever a girly girl. A kindergarten teacher and maker of homemade soap, Penelope wore dresses almost every day. Often ones with flowers and or lace. She had long blonde hair down her back and even her laugh was like a little bird tittering. But she and Teal made a beautiful couple. And Penelope's family was extremely accepting and open-minded. They welcomed Teal into the McRobb fold with open arms. Called Teal their *Dr. In-law*. Which was why Teal took Penelope's last name when they got married. Teal wanted nothing to do with their former life or family.

And now, Teal was a very successful psychologist, specializing in therapy geared toward those in the LGBTQAI2+ community, those going through transition, and their family members who required a bit more support to understand.

They also kept their hair color a cool shade of blue, usually teal or aquamarine, but sometimes, they'd mix it up and went with cobalt or navy.

After a full five minutes of silence where the two of them were just sitting there blowing on their tea and taking gingerly sips, Oona finally let one of those birds of prey fly off her shoulders. "I liked him."

"I know you did. You wouldn't have put yourself out there like that if you didn't. You also wouldn't be sitting here with that scrunched up look on your face if there wasn't more to this story."

"But his reaction just confirmed why I never put myself out there anymore. The rejection just hurts too much. And to be called bad in bed ..."

Teal pressed their lips together and hummed. "Well, it sucks for sure. But you have to look at this as an opportunity for learning and growth. We all have clients that we have to eventually decline for one reason or another. Yours just happened to be because you slept with him. And I highly doubt you're bad in bed. Maybe a little rigid ... but," they shrugged, "maybe not. I've never had sex with you, so I wouldn't know. But I have been to your shows, and based on how flexible you are and how high you can lift your legs, I highly doubt you're bad in bed."

Oona groaned.

"The sex was good, wasn't it?"

She closed her eyes and reluctantly nodded. "So good."

"That sucks."

"Seriously sucks."

"Want to come over for dinner tonight? Pen is making her *famous* paella. We can drink wine and you can let the Luna side of Oona come out, tell us how you really feel." Teal snorted, then smiled. Teal and Penelope's house was one of Oona's few safe places where she could drink more than a single glass of wine. She had nothing to worry about when she was there, and allowed herself to overindulge on more than one occasion. To the point where Penelope made up the guest bed for her so she could sleep off the wine spins. But they were her people. Her sanctum sanctorum. She hadn't told a lot of people about what Russell did to her, and although Teal and Penelope weren't in her life when all the shit with him took place, they knew enough to give her the breadth and safe space she needed.

Oona nodded. "I'd like that."

"In the meantime, we need to figure out who else we can refer him to, since the man clearly needs some help."

Oona nodded again. "I was thinking of Astrid Kramer."

Teal nodded and tapped their chin. "Yeah, I think she might have the space in her schedule, plus she owes me a favor. Let me call her." Teal brought out their phone and tapped the screen half a dozen times before putting the phone to their ear.

While Teal handled that, Oona's gaze drifted around the room, her mind fading back to the heated conversation she'd just had with Aiden. His physiological responses had been more akin to pain than rage. Yes, his nostrils flared, he bared his teeth, and his words were sharp and meant to hurt, but his grimaces also lingered, which indicated pain. Not necessarily a physical one, but an emotional one. His swallows were hard, and his head shakes slow and disbelieving.

Did he feel the connection between them that she felt, too? And was he hurt by her unwillingness to help him? His shoulders had cinched up so close to his ears, which was a sign of panic. She understood it, because the tension she felt in her shoulders every day around Russell was debilitating. But there was no need for Aiden to be afraid of her. So it had to be a panicked response to losing her as his therapist. To having to go back onto a waitlist.

Either way, the array of emotions that creased the man's handsome face in the span of their three-minute conversation were astounding. His anger was paramount, but there were a lot of secondary emotions there, too.

Her heart went out to him.

Sure, he didn't react well to the drunk driver, but his intentions were in the right place.

She believed that, despite his poor choices, that Aiden was deep down a good person.

Or at least, he was, until he made those cutting remarks about seeing her tattoos, tasting her pussy, and that she was terrible in bed.

Now, she wasn't so sure.

"All right, thanks, Astrid. I appreciate it," Teal said into the phone. "Have a great day." They hung up and turned their attention back to Oona. "Astrid's assistant is going to reach out to you later today to get the cop's information, then they'll contact him and set up an appointment. She said she can't squeeze him in until the new year, though. She's swamped with patients, then taking two weeks off to go to Mexico with her family."

"It's better than nothing," Oona said glumly.

Teal sipped their tea and tilted their head to the side, gauging Oona. "You'll get over this. It just stings right now because you put yourself out there and he behaved like an ape."

"Your professional assessment?" Oona asked dryly.

"I'll put it in writing if you like."

They smirked at each other and sipped their tea, both of their gazes drifting out to Teal's big office window that had the drapes pulled open, to reveal a gentle fluttering of snow falling from the sky.

"When do you leave for your sister's wedding?" Teal asked.

"A week from today."

"And you're gone for two weeks?"

"Ten days."

"I think this is exactly what you need. Time with family, partying, celebration, and getting away from this bitter cold and the idiot men of Montreal."

Oona knew Teal wasn't just referring to Aiden. They were also referring to Russell.

It was a constant fear of all of theirs that Russell would one day just show up somewhere where Oona was. It was one of the reasons she always carried pepper spray and a small switchblade in her purse. She'd also gone and taken self-defense classes after leaving Russell. She never wanted to be put in a position where she was the victim again. Where she couldn't fight back.

Oona finished her tea and smiled over her mug at her friend. "Thanks. I needed this."

"I know you did." Teal smiled. "See you tonight?"

"I'll bring the wine and dessert."

"Malbec and mille-feuille, please," Teal said.

Oona sucked in a deep breath through her nose and stood up from her chair. "Then I guess I better go to Dominque's Bakery now; otherwise, they'll be all out of mille-feuille by the time I get there after work."

Teal sipped their tea. "Chop, chop."

Oona left Teal's office feeling better about what happened with Aiden. But she still didn't feel great.

For the first time in a very long time, she put herself out there, and it backfired exponentially. She thought that what she and Aiden shared last night could turn into something more, and went for it. And he shot her down, laughed in her face, and said she was bad in bed.

If that wasn't enough to turn a person off from putting themselves out there, Oona didn't know what was.

Tightening the collar of her coat around her neck as she walked down the road to Dominique's, she passed a plant shop and stopped to gaze through the window.

Maybe she was just meant to be a plant-mom.

No relationship. No children.

Just friends, pole dancing, and plants.

It was better than becoming the crazy cat-lady, right? Besides, she was allergic to cats, so the only kind she'd be able to get would be a hairless one, and those freaked her right out. Their foreheads looked like a wrinkled scrotum.

Gripping the handle of the door for the plant shop, she heaved it open and took in a deep breath of the warm, balmy air.

"Bonjour," the shop girl greeted.

"Hello. Bonjour," Oona replied. She'd learned quickly after moving to Montreal that if she spoke French, the people around her assumed she knew French—which she did not. And then she got confused and embarrassed when she told them they'd have to repeat themselves in English. She was trying to learn the language, though. And knew some phrases since moving to the city. But languages—particularly the romantic ones with the masculine and feminine, were not her forte. So she made sure to always throw some English into her greetings so they knew she preferred English.

"Can I help you with anything today?" the woman asked, her French accent as thick and beautiful as her eyelashes.

"That big plant in the window with the cutouts on the leaves. What is that?"

"Ah, the Monstera. She is beautiful, no?"

"She is," Oona agreed. "I'll take her."

The woman beamed. "Wonderful."

Plants, poles, and pals. Not such a bad life. Now all she needed to do was find a vibrator that sucked her clit the way Aiden had last night, and then she'd be all set for spinster life.

Sigh.

Chapter Five

One week later...

This was a bad idea.

What the fuck was he thinking?

Aiden hadn't seen his brother in years. They were estranged after what went down with their father. Not because they disagreed with what happened or how they handled it, just that the devastation Dallas's death caused, followed by the alienation of their parents and the town, was just too much. Aiden and his brother both thought they should have done more. They blamed themselves, and rather than have that bring them closer, it drove them apart.

And yet, there he was, boarding a plane to head to Victoria, on the west coast of Canada, to attend Jordan's wedding.

But he had to try.

He needed to try to fix the wedge between him and Jordan. After all, he was the only family he had left. Jordan was his little brother, and he was getting married. Aiden needed to be there.

He was still attending anger management classes, and by grace and fucking God, the assistant for another therapist called last week to set up an appointment for him for the second week of January.

A little late for his liking, but he'd take it over months of having to wait.

In the meantime, though, he needed to try to repair some of the damage in his life *before* the therapist wielded her magic wand and fixed the rest.

Because that's all therapists were, right? Wizards with PhDs.

He was supposed to fly out yesterday, but because of snow, ice, and probably fucking reindeer on the runway, his flight was canceled and he was tossed onto a new one today. No select seating this time, and he would only land in Vancouver, then be forced to catch a tin can with wings over to the island.

Whatever. He'd get there eventually.

He had his audiobook downloaded, his earbuds fully charged, and his brand-new travel pillow. He could just crash against the window—thank fuck he had a window seat—and wake up when the plane landed.

The airport was choked with winter vacation enthusiasts. Everyone wanted to escape the frigid weather and piles of snow for warmer temperatures. There were loads of direct flights down to the Caribbean, Florida, and the Gulf of Mexico. But like some idiot, he wasn't heading south, he was heading west.

The temperatures out west weren't as bad as they were here, but he knew he would still need his winter coat, boots, and gloves.

No Tommy Bahama shirts or linen shorts for him.

His gate was reduced to standing room only, which meant a full flight. Lots of kids, crying babies, and people with runny noses and persistent coughs.

Lovely. He'd probably have some kind of bug percolating in his system and baby vomit on him by the time he reached Vancouver.

He just needed a window seat. That was it. He could make do with the rest.

He could handle a crying baby beside him or a guy with a chronic cough who wanted to hog the arm rest. He just needed the window seat so he could lean against the wall, tune out the world, close his eyes, and pretend he wasn't jammed into a tiny space with a shitload of mouth breathers thirty-thousand feet in the air.

Keeping the volume low enough that he could hear announcements, he put in his earbuds and started up his audiobook. It was a memoir from a man who'd sailed around the world in a small sailboat. He'd been alone and barely spoke to a soul for nearly three years. His tales were astounding, but the reviews also said that the guy also sounded a little nuts. Like all that time as a nautical hermit and out in the sun had wrecked his brain just a smidgen.

Either way, Aiden was excited to dive into it.

He closed his eyes and leaned back against the small bit of empty wall space he had near his gate, letting the narrator's deep timbre calm his nerves.

He'd done some traveling over the years, but flying never got easier or more relaxing.

Once he was in the sky, it was better, but the lead up to the take-off and being with so many people always made him jittery.

He wasn't one for tight spaces in general, or crowds, but he'd learned how to cope over the years.

Tune out the world, close your eyes and just pretend you're alone.

The announcement to board came sooner than he thought, and before he was even on chapter three, he was lining up with everyone else, then taking the jet bridge to the plane.

It was a Boeing 747, but an older version. He'd checked his main bag, but had a backpack as his carry on. Slowly, like a sheep being led to slaughter, he followed the bleating person in front of him down the aisle until he reached his designated seat—24A.

He stowed his backpack beneath the seat in front of him, then quickly buckled up, draped his coat over his body, pulled the hood of his hoodie over his head so nobody could see his face, adjusted his travel pillow, and leaned against the wall, closing his eyes.

Even turning up the volume didn't completely drown out the cacophony of passengers boarding, but he was determined not to open his eyes.

Someone sat next to him. He didn't even lift a lid halfway.

He didn't care.

The *clunk* of the overhead compartments being closed registered in his head, but he still didn't open his eyes.

He'd pulled up his hood to obstruct his face and turned away from the masses as much as he could.

The person beside him shuffled a little, said something, and then their knee started to bounce furiously.

Aiden peeled one eye open and glanced over and down just enough to see the knee.

It was slim and bony and covered in brown pants that seemed a few sizes too big.

The hand that gripped the knee had knobby fingers, nails nibbled down to the quick, and the way the person—obviously a man based on the musky scent of aftershave—was bunching his fingers and knuckles said he was nervous.

Stress sweat filled the air and Aiden peeled another eye open and turned his head a little more to take in the Panicky Pete beside him.

The guy was thin, short, probably in his mid-fifties, with a shiny bald head, thin gray hair at his temples, and round glasses. He was blinking a lot and kept swallowing. His nostrils flared and his movements were jerky.

He was making Aiden nervous.

Aiden's knee started to bounce, too, but he put his hand down on it firmly, and it stopped.

"I don't like flying," the man said, catching Aiden watching him. "And in this weather." He shook his head. "Nuh-uh."

Aiden nodded. "It'll be fine, man. Not a huge fan of flying myself, but you've gotta have faith that they wouldn't take off if the conditions weren't suitable."

The guy's head bobbed a little.

That's when the person in the aisle seat spun around from where they'd been speaking to the flight attendant, and Aiden's jaw dropped while his stomach nearly hit his feet.

Her brown eyes with the different shades of gold went wide, and her mouth opened. "What are you doing here?"

"What are *you* doing here?" he spat back.

"You two know each other?" the balding man asked, his level of panic rising.

"Sort of," Oona said with a sarcastic bite.

"A-and you get along?" the middle-seat man asked, clearly reading the tension rolling off Oona and the way she was glaring at Aiden like he was dog shit on the bottom of her shoe.

Aiden lifted a brow and snorted. "I wouldn't say that."

A rush of heat flooded Oona's cheeks turning them pink. "We did. Now we don't, apparently."

The middle-seat guy's eyes were as dark as an ink spill and nearly doubled in size, and his hand shot up in the air. Then he started pressing the "call" button above profusely before waving his hand to get the flight attendant's attention.

A flight attendant came down the aisle. "Yes?"

"I-I need to switch seats. These two are enemies."

Aiden snorted at the word *enemy.*

That seemed a bit extreme of a term. Like he and Oona were two knights on opposite sides of a battlefield, fighting for different monarchs, swords drawn, chain mail rattling, and horses stomping hooves as the fog settled over the moor.

"I can't be between them," the man continued to say. "It's bad luck and I'm already terrified of flying. I need to either get off this plane or switch seats. I can't. I just can't. Please. Please." He tried to stand up, but forgot that he was buckled in. He unbuckled his belt, then stood up, pushing past Oona and heaving on the seat in front of him.

The passenger in front of him had her hair up and resting against the back of her seat, his fingers got tangled in her ponytail, making the woman yell out, "Ouch."

"Sir, you need to sit down. We're about to take off," the flight attendant—a woman in her forties with dark red hair and lipstick to match—said.

"I can't sit between them. It's bad luck. I can't." He shook his head and was now in the aisle, trying to open the overhead compartment. "I need to get off the plane. I can't. They are baaaadddd energy. Bad. The way he's looking at her." He directed his focus back on Aiden. "I don't like it."

"How am I looking at her?" Aiden asked, lifting his arms so his palms faced up.

"Like you want to *kill* her," the bald guy said.

"I don't want to kill her. I mean, I don't *like* her. But I don't want to *kill* her. I'm a cop, dude. One of the good guys."

"And yet you two don't get along. Something is *off* here. I can feel it."

Yeah, Aiden could feel that something was *off*, too, and it was this melodramatic man in the baggy brown pants and freshly waxed skull.

"Even cops can have people they don't get along with. Doesn't mean they want to kill them," Aiden protested. "We *are* human."

This man was off his freaking rocker. He was going to get the whole plane grounded, maybe even get Aiden thrown off the flight.

"Sir," Oona said, her voice cold but calm. "I'm a trauma therapist, and can assure you there is nothing to worry about. The other passenger and I may not see eye-to-eye, but there is no bad energy that will cause the plane to crash."

The bald guy's eyes went even bigger. "CRASH!"

People around them groaned.

"I'll switch seats with the little guy if it'll shut him up and get us in the air," came a deep voice from the back.

The balding man's expression lit up and he started to nod vigorously.

"But no middle seat. I want the aisle," the guy said. "Too big for the middle seat." And he wasn't lying. When he stood up from his aisle seat closer to the bathroom, he revealed that he not only had height, but also breadth. No way could he cram his telephone pole legs and linebacker shoulders into a middle seat, and they were in the emergency exit row, too, since Aiden needed space for his legs, as well.

"Thank you," the flight attendant said to the man who lumbered forward, then patted the balding guy on the head as he waited for Oona—who was glaring at Aiden like she *did* want to kill him—to move over to the middle seat.

Once the behemoth white knight from 32F took his seat and buckled up, all the passengers settled down. The guy had no hair—but it wasn't like the previous man. This guy was completely bald and it looked like he preferred it that way. The back of his skull had those weird folds, too. He was probably in his mid-forties and had a dark scruff covering his angular jaw and chin. He turned to face Aiden and Oona. "Let's have a smooth flight, hmm?"

Oona nodded. "Wouldn't dream of anything else."

Aiden merely jerked his chin at the dude, then turned to Oona, bringing his voice down to a whisper. "Why the fuck are you going to Vancouver?"

"To visit my sister," she said, matching his hushed volume, her brown eyes hard and angry. "Not that it's any of your business."

He could see the curiosity burning in her gaze to know why he was going west, as well. But too fucking bad, he wasn't going to satisfy this little split-personality kitten's nosiness. All he did was go, "Huh." Then he turned up the volume on his audiobook again, pulled his hood back over his head, and faced away from her.

She was just another passenger on this plane. He could ignore her like he would ignore the rest of them.

Only, he hadn't had his tongue between any other passengers' legs for the better part of a night, didn't know the noises any of the other passengers made when they came, and sure as hell hadn't had any of the other passengers' lips wrapped around his cock.

So ignoring her wasn't as easy as he thought it was going to be.

Particularly since whatever the fuck shampoo she used was driving his senses wild. Something floral, but with a nutty undertone. Almond, maybe?

Then there was the fucking arm rest.

Yes, he knew that the rule for air travel was that the middle person got both middle arm rests, but she seemed content giving the other one to the big dude on the aisle, and because of the man's size, Oona was forced to lean a little toward Aiden—for the entire flight. Their arms and hands brushed more than once, which only made his entire body erupt into fresh flames.

Then, when the flight attendants came through with their drink carts and she ordered a ginger ale—what he was also going to order—he felt compelled to order something else and stupidly said, "Tomato juice," before he could come up with something better. And honestly, anything would have been better than that metallic-tasting, thick, cold soup that resembled blood. *Blech.*

He also normally never pissed when he flew. He kept his liquid consumption to a minimum and just blocked out the world for the entire flight.

But fuck him and his bladder, because about two hours into the flight, he was going to fucking burst if he didn't do something about it.

Pausing the audiobook, he pushed his hood off his head and put up his tray table, then glanced over only to find Oona gone and the bald monster in the aisle seat snoring.

Fuck, fuck, fuck.

Swallowing, he reached over and gently tapped the man's shoulder.

It was made of goddamn titanium.

The bear didn't move.

He tapped a little harder.

All the bear did was grumble.

Aiden cleared his throat, then shoved the man's shoulder a little.

He stirred, grunted, and groggily opened his eyes. "Eh?"

"I need to piss, dude. Sorry."

The bald gorilla rolled his eyes, then took his sweet-ass time unfolding himself from his seat. "Should have thought of that before I fell asleep," he rumbled as Aiden carefully maneuvered past Oona's purse on the floor and the bald man in the aisle.

If you choose the aisle seat, then you need to be prepared to get up for people. That's just the way it goes. And how the fuck was Aiden supposed to know when Frankenstein's monster decided it was nap time? Did he pass around his sleepy-time schedule and forgot to give it to Aiden?

Fuck him.

Aiden murmured a thanks, then made his way down the aisle.

It was nighttime outside now. The flight left at three o'clock, and since it was almost the winter solstice, it was dark earlier than ever.

His brother's wedding was on Christmas Eve—terrible time for a wedding—but apparently, he and his bride-to-be met on Christmas, so they wanted to come full circle. But Jordan asked Aiden if he could come out a week early to help with wedding stuff, attend the stag, and spend some time together to reconnect. Jordan even offered to let Aiden crash on their couch. Not ideal, but he'd slept in worse places.

He got to the bathroom, and holy shit, there wasn't a line. Both stalls were occupied, though, so he resisted the urge to cross his legs and waited as patiently as he could.

The *click* of the lavatory lock disengaging made helium fill his chest and his bladder squeeze. Then, of course, because fate was a miserable bitch, who should be in the bathroom and ready to exit, but Luna Love herself.

Her brown eyes went wide in surprise when she saw him, and she sucked in a breath, inflating her chest and pushing out her tits. Like they were made of fucking magnets, his gaze was drawn to her chest, where he knew she had raspberry nipples that were probably beading that very second. But just as fast as she grew surprised, she replaced the look of shock with one of irritation. And that just pushed his need to piss to the back of his mind and ignited something feral deep down inside of him.

Before he could stop himself, he stepped forward, crowding her and pushing her back into the lavatory.

"Wh-what are you doing?" Her hands landed on his chest.

She glared at him, but the way her pupils dilated, her chest rose and fell rapidly, and her nostrils flared, he could tell that it wasn't panic or fury causing those physiological reactions—it was arousal. Her tongue darted out and slid along the seam of her lips. "Aiden!"

If he offered her a fuck right now, he was ninety-nine percent sure that even though she hated him, she'd have her pants around her ankles in record time. The noises she made and the way she came when they were together told him so much about her.

She was a little closet sexpot.

An uptight bitch on the outside, a wanton little slut on the inside.

Leaning forward, he sucked in a deep breath, pulling her floral, nutty scent deep into his lungs. But that only made his cock twitch and his balls ache.

"What. Are. You. Doing?" she bit out, dropping her hands from his chest, which only propelled him even closer to her. Close enough to count each gold fleck in her irises—if he wanted to. Close enough to kiss that beauty mark beneath her right eye—if he wanted to.

He lifted a brow at her, and the same side of his mouth hitched up, as well. He had no idea what he was doing, but he knew he was getting a kick out of pissing her off. Out of seeing her so flustered. Out of knowing he aroused her so easily. "If I told you to turn around, bend over, and stick your ass in the air, you would, wouldn't you?" he said, leaning forward, so they were close enough that his nose bumped the side of her cheek.

"N-no."

The stammer proved she was lying.

He was trained to detect when people were lying, and right now, everything about Oona Young said she wanted him to spin her around, pull down her pants, and take her from behind.

He inched forward until his mouth was near her ear. "Still dreaming about my tongue on your clit, Dr. Young?"

She pulled in a sharp breath, shivered, and closed her eyes. He smiled in satisfaction, but that only lasted a second before she placed her hands on his chest again and shoved him hard backward. "Get out!"

Smiling at her sufficiently ruffled feathers, he rolled his eyes. "Pretty sure it was *my* turn in here."

"You pushed me *back* in," she protested. "I was coming out. Then you went all weird, feral, alpha asshole."

He snorted. Yep, he had, and he couldn't figure out why he'd done it.

Growling, she awkwardly shuffled past him, but because the space was so small, they wound up crotch to crotch, and her tits grazed his chest. He stifled a groan, kept his asshole smile on his face, and waited for her to exit. "You are such a prick," she grumbled.

She finally got the door open and stepped out of the tiny space.

"It's not what it looks like," he heard her murmur to someone as she left.

Resisting the urge to laugh out loud, Aiden locked the bathroom door and finally relieved himself.

He studied his face in the bathroom mirror for a hot second as he washed his hands. Yes, he was an asshole. He knew that. But what he didn't know, what he couldn't explain or understand, was why he'd done what he'd just done with Oona in the bathroom.

He didn't like the woman.

She was a cold bitch. A split-personality shrink who was probably just itching to use all the ammo she had against him—after reading his file—to humiliate and belittle him. She couldn't put their brief encounter aside and help him. But rather, she had to hold his career hostage to further her own.

And yet, deep down inside of her somewhere was Luna. Warm, soft, sweet, and sensuous Luna.

He exited the bathroom and made his way back down the aisle. The bald gorilla was snoring again, while Oona sat in the middle seat reading on an e-reader. She didn't look up at him.

Sighing, he tapped the bald walrus on the shoulder again. "Sorry man."

The walrus lifted one eyelid and glared at Aiden before grumbling and unfolding himself from his seat. He was probably double pissed off because both Oona and Aiden had asked him to move on what were now four separate occasions.

Oh well, buddy. Them's the breaks when you fly coach and insist on the aisle seat.

"Thanks," Aiden grumbled, having to shuffle past Oona who hadn't moved, but rather just pulled her feet up onto her seat.

She glared up at him, and her mouth curled into a sneer.

The gorilla sat back down and resumed his snoring.

Aiden's elbow landed on the armrest just as Oona's did. She gave his elbow a hard shove and tossed him some serious *I will murder you in your sleep*, side-eye.

He let her have the armrest, put his earbuds back in, and tried to ignore her as best he could.

But he kept his awareness of that armrest and its occupancy at the forefront of his mind, and as soon as she dropped her elbow away from it, he pounced.

For the next hour, they fought over those few inches of communal space, to the point where, at one point, she elbowed him in the ribs, she jerked her arm so hard.

He was getting a kick out of pissing her off more than he was getting annoyed. A pissed off Oona was better than a cold, robotic one. The pissed-off version reminded him more of the fiery Luna, and he liked her.

The drink cart rattled down the aisle, and he licked his lips. To fuck with copying her, he needed to get the taste of tomato juice out of his mouth.

It was a different flight attendant than before, and this time she asked Aiden what he wanted first. "Ginger ale, no ice, no cup, please," he replied, the burn of Oona's gaze warming his cheek.

The flight attendant handed him the can, then focused on Oona. "Ginger ale, as well, please," Oona said sweetly.

The flight attendant nodded, then ducked down, disappearing behind the cart, only to reappear a moment later with a frown. "I'm afraid we're out."

Aiden snickered, but not quiet enough to avoid a kick from Oona.

"Apple juice then, please," Oona said, accepting the can of Minute Maid from the attendant a moment later.

The bald yeti in the aisle seat woke up enough to ask for a Coke, then promptly conked back out, not even bothering to take a sip.

Aiden cracked open his ginger ale and took a sip. "Ah," he said loudly, licking his lips.

Oona glared at him, her eyes thin slivers.

He grinned at her and sighed. "This is delicious."

"I need this plane to land so I can be done with you once and for all," she gritted out, tapping the screen on her e-reader and focusing back on it.

"The feeling is mutual, babe. Trust me." Then he put his elbow on the armrest, only for her to knock it off again, this time making him spill a little of his ginger ale.

It was worth it.

Chapter Six

Longest. Flight. Of. Her Life.

Oona would rather spend eighteen hours on a flight between two hairy hippies who considered deodorant and bathing optional, and brought their own sauerkraut onto the plane, than even another minute next to Aiden.

The man was insufferable.

And what the hell was that in the bathroom?

Was it a power play?

Was he trying to seduce her? Did he want to make her crack?

It certainly seemed that way when he insinuated they should engage in a dangerous public display of indecency. Because she was pretty sure that's what having sex in an airplane bathroom was. And that was illegal.

And he was supposed to be a man of the law.

Then he rubbed it in like lemon juice in a paper cut when he got the last ginger ale.

She didn't hate apple juice. It was fine.

But as someone who rarely drank soda to begin with, she liked to treat herself to ginger ale when she flew.

Ugh!

He was such a jerk.

And bringing up his mouth on her clit? Really? Could he be any more crass? *Didn't stop you from getting hot and wet, though.*

Yeah, the physiological reaction her body had to Aiden was in complete contrast to the one her brain experienced. Her brain hated him. Her body wanted him naked and on top of her more than she wanted all the ginger ale in the world.

Add in the fact that she was reading a spicy romance on her e-reader, and she was a lost cause with a puddle in her panties by the time the plane landed in Vancouver.

It was too quick of a layover between when she landed and when her flight to Victoria left. Fortunately, she didn't have to claim her bag and recheck it; she just had to find her new gate and hustle. There were only thirty minutes between when she landed and when the next plane departed.

She was running through the airport, but that only made her need to pee, so she ducked into a bathroom and sure enough, her panties were frustratingly damp.

Well, at least she wouldn't have to see Aiden again.

But what in the world were the odds of him being on her flight to Vancouver? What was he doing here? And the fact that she was seated next to him? Fate had a messed-up sense of humor.

She resumed her hustle through the expansive YVR, reaching her gate as people were boarding. Then she handed over her boarding pass, smiled at the flight attendant, and slowed her roll behind an elderly couple on the jet bridge. She made it. No need to build up any more sweat under her pits. She'd be on the island in half an hour, then hugging her baby sister ten minutes after that.

It was still hard to believe that Rayma was getting married.

Rayma, the wild child of the Young sisters. The free spirit that their parents couldn't handle.

But she'd come a long way since her teenage days, where she was hanging out with the outlaw biker gang The True Destroyers, showing up at home in the wee hours of the morning and passing out drunk on the front lawn.

Now, she was twenty-five, a social worker, and about to marry the man of her dreams.

If she was being completely honest, Oona was a little envious of Rayma. Here Oona was, thirty years old, with a PhD and a rewarding career, and yet, she had nobody to share her life with—well, besides her new plant, which she'd named Harmonia, after the Greek goddess of harmony. Daughter of Ares and Aphrodite.

So far, Harmonia hadn't brought too much harmony to Oona's life, but she was still getting adjusted to her new home. Oona needed to give the plant some time—or a friend. Maybe she'd buy Harmonia a companion when she got home. So her big-leafed friend wasn't lonely.

But even with a rewarding career, and a gigantic tropical plant, Oona was petrified of commitment after Russell. She silently convinced herself that this was what she wanted. That her solitary life with its militant routine was enough.

And since she'd yet to find a vibrator that did the trick like Aiden's tongue, and Harmonia didn't say much, she was growing less and less convinced that this *was* enough. Even if she was terrified of the alternative.

Rayma was only twenty-five; had the job, the man, and support around her. Their sister, Pasha, also lived in Victoria. She was married to a man with a big family, and that family had welcomed Rayma in like one of their own. Heath's mom, Joy, had even taken Rayma in when she was seventeen, and set her straight when nobody else could.

Oona only had Teal and Penelope, and even though she loved them, they had their own family and more often than not, Oona felt like an interloper when she tagged along to McRobb family events.

She sighed and smiled as she stepped onto the plane, saying hello to the flight attendant—a young woman probably in her early twenties with tawny-colored hair and dark gray eyes. The plane was significantly smaller than the previous one, and the seats were in pairs on either side of the aisle. She was near the front in 11A and quickly took her spot, stashing her purse below the seat and her carryon bag overhead.

She'd reached a really saucy part in her e-book and even though her underwear might need a little wringing out by the end of the flight, she was itching to get back to Pascal and Helena. It was a modern-day twist on Romeo and Juliet that was supposed to deliver a much happier ending than the original. Two well-to-do New York upper westside families, where the fathers were business rivals. Then the young adults of the family fall in love, and against their families wishes, wed in secret. The steamy scenes were hot. Pascal was a very thorough and generous lover.

Oona squeezed her thighs together. She knew another thorough and generous lover ...

Damn Aiden. Why did he have to be such an asshole?

And why was she always attracted to assholes? First, Russell, and now Aiden.

Aiden was mean. He might not be physically abusive like Russell, but he had a way with his words that could draw blood.

That didn't seem to bother her libido or imagination, though, because as much as she knew she should stop thinking about the damaged cop with a chip on his shoulder, he was all she pictured when she thought of Pascal, and she pictured herself when she thought of Helena.

The fact that Helena was blonde with blue eyes meant nothing to her pleasure center, though. They were color-blind.

The flight attendant stood at the front and went through the safety protocol.

The aisle seat beside Oona remained empty. She glanced behind her. It wasn't an overly full flight.

The plane ascended, and so did Oona's heart rate.

Pascal was using his tongue on Helena, and Helena was loving it.

Just like Oona loved it when Aiden used his tongue.

Fucking Aiden.

And yeah, if he'd spun her around and yanked down her pants in that airplane bathroom, she probably would have given into temptation and let the jerk fuck her. Because he was just that good, and she was just that desperate. Just that turned on.

Fucking Aiden.

By the time the plane landed, Oona was a hot bundle of horny nerves.

Not the best state to be in to meet your sister's fiancé for the first time, but whatever.

It wasn't like she was going to have to take her pants off and show them all her wet underwear. She was probably just a little flushed, and that would disappear in no time. Particularly because the Victoria airport was small and there was no jet bridge. They climbed down the stairs and walked across the tarmac, getting whipped in the face by the chilly, salt-scented wind. But there wasn't any snow or ice in that wind, so she had to take the little victories when they came.

Rayma said it snowed earlier in the week and hadn't really disappeared, but the roads were clear and there wasn't any snow in the forecast for the next several days.

The warm rush of air that greeted her when she stepped back into the airport was like a long-lost friend hugging her while they both wore one of those super comfy oversized hoodies.

She exhaled in relief, and kept her chin up and eyes alert for signs of her sister.

The *arrivals* sign overhead called to her and Oona picked up her pace, eager to wrap her arms around Rayma and finally meet this *Lassie* that Rayma was madly in love with.

She was behind a few passengers, but not many. Her quick pace had her ahead of the pack. She still had to wait for her suitcase, but her eagerness to see Rayma propelled her forward.

She spotted her sister almost immediately. And not because Rayma was smiling and jumping up and down, but because she was holding a sign that said, "Welcome home from prison, Sis!" She also had an enormous, pleased-with-herself grin on her pretty face.

"Aaahhh!" Rayma squealed, handing the tall, handsome guy with the blocky shoulders and green eyes her sign, then throwing herself at Oona. "You're here! You're finally here!"

Oona dropped her carryon to the ground and wrapped her arms around Rayma. "I'm here, you nut."

They held onto each other for well over a minute, each of them squeezing just a little harder until Rayma made a, "Gak" sound like Oona squeezed too hard. It was all in jest. All part of their game that had spanned decades. "Uncle. Uncle," Rayma finally said with a laugh.

Even though they were five years apart, Oona was closest in age to Rayma. They'd both been oopsie babies, since Oona came four years after Mieka. And even though Oona and Rayma didn't always have a lot in common, they bonded over the fact that they were the youngest and the last two stuck at home. Their "love you more" game started when Oona was seven and Rayma was two. Whoever cried "uncle" first, when they hugged and squeezed each other, loved the other one less.

"I win," Oona said, letting go of Rayma and pulling away, smiling. "I love you more."

Rayma merely beamed, as beautiful and radiant as ever. Probably more so because her life was on track and she was in love.

"You finally get to meet Lassie," Rayma said. "Since he couldn't make it out to Triss's wedding." She elbowed him. "Something about being a team player and a man of the law, blah, blah, blah."

The man she called Lassie rolled his green eyes before sticking out his hand. "Nice to finally meet you, Oona."

They shook hands and smiled, but Lassie's attention was pulled to something over Oona's shoulder.

His mouth split into an even bigger smile. He dropped her hand and stepped to the side. "Aiden."

Aiden?

"Little brother," the smoky voice behind her said just as she turned around and watched Aiden—yes, *that* Aiden—embrace Lassie.

Oona blinked like she had dust in her eyes. Her heartbeat was everywhere—in her lips, her throat, her fingertips, and most definitely in her chest. Couldn't they all hear it? It was a heavy thud of warning throughout her entire body.

This was not happening. What were the odds? Did he know all along?

"Were you guys on the same flight?" Rayma asked, entirely oblivious to the way Oona was close to having an apoplexy.

Aiden flicked his gaze to Oona, adopting a look like he'd never seen her before in his life. "Guess so." He stuck out his hand. "Aiden Lassiter, Jordan's older brother."

Jordan's. Older. Brother.

Oona's baby sister was marrying Aiden's baby brother?

Oh, fate, you fucking bitch.

She took his hand, and the zap of electricity that ran up from their clasped palms right to her clit was like a bolt of lightning. She yanked her hand back and shook it out.

"You okay?" Rayma asked, tucking her long caramel-colored hair with the blonde balayage behind her ears. She rubbed Oona's back affectionately. "Hungry?"

Now that she thought about it, yeah, she was a little hungry. But that wasn't what was making her lightheaded.

The look burning in Aiden's eyes—the identical shade of green to Jordan's—was equal parts amused as it was intense. Like he was daring her to tell them the truth, but also daring her to grab him by the scruff of his shirt and kiss him.

"Let's order a pizza and pick it up on the way home," Rayma said, turning to Jordan. "I stopped and grabbed wine after work."

"I don't drink," Aiden said quickly.

Rayma's brows shot up, but only for a second, then she shrugged. "More for me." Her nose wrinkled. "What *do* you drink? I'm happy to stop if it's something specific."

"Water is good," he said casually.

"Sounds like the baggage carousel has started to move," Jordan announced, falling in line with his brother as the two of them turned to head to the baggage pickup area. He'd rolled up the sign Rayma made and was carrying it like a tube in his big left hand.

"How were your flights?" Rayma asked as she bent down and picked up Oona's carryon and slung it over her shoulder. "Did you have to sit next to anyone insufferable?"

Oona nearly choked on her own spit. She was burning two symmetrical holes in the back of Aiden's head with her eyes right now. She hoped he felt the heat. Hoped he itched and was uncomfortable from her death stare. "Yeah, unfortunately, I did," she finally said. "But I survived."

"You're a tough cookie." Rayma's smile was so innocent and carefree. Oona needed her sister to stay that way. This trip, this wedding — all of it was about Rayma. She deserved nothing but goodness and joy, and Oona was going to do her very best to give her sister that.

"Do we have to stop off at a hotel to drop off Jordan's brother?" she asked, stopping just shy of knocking her shins on the edge of the baggage belt.

"No, he's staying with us." Rayma's gaze flicked to where Jordan and Aiden were standing off to the side. Her eyes turned curious, then she brought her voice down to a hush. "They've been estranged for years. Devastating family drama. This was Jordan's attempt to mend things between them. Aiden is the only side of Jordan's family invited, since there is no-contact with the rest. He asked Aiden to come out early so they could reconnect, and he invited him to stay with us, but only after I offered you our guest room. So Aiden will be on the pullout couch in the living room."

They were staying in the same house!

Oh, God.

As much as she wanted to give her sister the drama-free wedding of her dreams, Oona wasn't sure she could if she had to stay under the same roof as Aiden for a week.

"Oh, wow, no. I don't want to interfere with their bonding. He can have the guest room and I'll go stay at Pasha's," Oona said.

"Can't. Mieka and Triss are staying there with their men. And Pasha has the two kids, and Heath is the size of two normal people, their house is packed. We have the space. You just have to suck it up and be okay sharing a bathroom with a stranger."

Well, he wasn't *exactly* a stranger.

"We have an ensuite off our room. But the other bathroom is a full bathroom with a shower and tub. I'm sure it's not going to be that awkward." Rayma's gaze slid down to the baggage belt. "Which one is yours?"

"That one," Oona said with a defeated sigh as she watched her bag travel past her. She hadn't been paying attention.

"Lassie!" Rayma called out, grabbing her fiancé's attention. "Grab that purple suitcase." She pointed to Oona's luggage.

But before Jordan could step through the crowd, Aiden was on it, reaching his long arm between two people, and wrapping his big hand with its skilled fingers around the handle, and heaving it off the belt.

"Yay, Big Lassie," Rayma cheered, beaming again as she gripped Oona by the arm and hauled her over to where the guys were. "Thanks, Big Lassie."

Aiden's eyes met Oona's and he silently extended the handle of her rolling hard-cased suitcase with four wheels and pushed it toward her.

"Does that mean I'm now Little Lassie?" Jordan asked. "Because I don't know if I'm okay with that."

Aiden snorted. "I'm okay with it."

Jordan gave him a glare, but it was all for show.

"Why Lassie?" Oona asked, only just registering the fact that Aiden didn't have his luggage yet.

"Because our last name is Lassiter and Rayma is cheeky," Jordan said, looking at his fiancée with nothing but pure love.

She wrapped an arm around his waist, and he did the same to her. "You love it when I'm cheeky." Her brows bounced on her smooth forehead. "When I misbehave."

Aiden cleared his throat. "I see my bag." He left their awkward trust circle of four and stepped toward the carousel, grabbing an army-green duffle bag off the belt and heaving it over his shoulder. "Ready to go."

Jordan was glancing down at his phone, his thumb sliding over the screen, and his brows knitted in concentration. "All right, I just ordered a couple of pizzas for pickup. They'll be ready in twenty."

"Which is exactly how long it takes for us to get home," Rayma said with a smile and bouncing on her toes. "Oooh, I'm so excited. Now that the guests are starting to arrive, it really feels like this is happening."

"Are Mieks and Triss already here?" Oona asked, her gaze fixated on the wide space between Aiden's shoulder blades as he glided behind Jordan with unimaginable confidence through the crowd, toward the automatic sliding doors that would take them all outside. Maybe it was the sweater he was wearing, but he seemed larger than life. Larger than she remembered, and she remembered that he was tall. But right now, he was skyscraper-tall and had impossibly broad shoulders.

And for some weird reason, she didn't even want to attempt to understand, the gulf between his shoulder blades on his back was really turning her on.

"They arrived earlier today. I went with Pasha to pick them up. We're all getting together tomorrow afternoon for you four and Peyton to try on your bridesmaid dresses," Rayma said, pulling Oona's attention away from Aiden's sexy back and back to reality.

Oona smiled at Rayma. "Sounds fun." Peyton was Rayma's best friend in Victoria and a social worker, as well. Oona had never met her, but she'd heard all about her and saw tons of pictures of Peyton and Rayma on social media.

Rayma wrapped an arm around Oona's shoulders and pulled her close. "I'm just so glad you're here, Oons. I've missed you."

Oona tipped her head into Rayma's. "I've missed you, too, kiddo."

"And who knows? Mieka and Triss hooked up and are now with brothers, maybe you and I will do the same." She dropped her voice to a whisper. "Aiden's single, and you both live in Montreal, maybe it's meant to be." Her brown eyes glittered beneath the recessed lighting of the airport arrivals overhang as they stepped out into the chilly evening.

Heat raced into Oona's cheeks despite the outside temperature. All she could do was laugh, but it came out slightly frantic. "Don't hold your breath, kiddo."

Rayma shrugged. "You never know. He is *very* nice to look at. You can't argue with that."

No, Oona couldn't. And she'd seen every inch of Aiden up close and personal.

The problem was that, for as dangerously gorgeous as the man was, he was just as insufferable and rude.

This was no doubt going to be the longest week of her life. The ultimate test of her patience.

He craned his head around and shot her a smug smirk that she wanted to punch off his face ... or wipe off with her own mouth.

Yes.

This week would not only test her patience, but also her willpower, because as much as she hated Aiden Lassiter, she also wanted him, and that was a huge problem.

Chapter Seven

Jordan and his fiancée lived on the bottom floor of a condo building. But rather than having to go into the building to get to their place, the front door was a walk-up style. They had a little patio with the smallest patch of grass Aiden had ever seen, but it was more than a lot of people had—more than Aiden had—so good for them.

Only, according to the very chatty Rayma, it had snowed earlier that week, so their grass patch was currently white and sporting a snowman the size of a Pomeranian.

Twin turquoise Adirondack chairs sat on the other side of the patio, where there were paving stones, and small outdoor Christmas lights framed the overhang above their door.

There was also a tasteful cedar bough and holly wreath—which looked to be real—hung over the etched glass of the door.

The twenty-minute ride from the airport to his brother's place, crammed into the backseat of Jordan's truck with Oona was awkward as fuck.

And not just because Aiden sat behind Jordan and Jordan was tall so he needed to push the seat back, which forced Aiden to damn near fold in half, but because the woman sitting beside him was constantly shooting daggers into the side of his face from her eyeballs.

They stopped and grabbed pizza, the smell of it in the cab of the truck making his belly growl and flip, then drove another five minutes to the condo.

"It's actually not a terrible pull-out couch," Rayma insisted as they all trudged into the foyer of their place, kicking off boots into the boot tray and setting down bags. "We got it brand new when we moved here last month. And I bought one of those really nice memory foam toppers, so we put that on the mattress and it's nearly as comfortable as our bed."

"I'll be fine," Aiden insisted, offering his sister-in-law to-be a smile.

Jordan set down the pizza boxes on the kitchen island, then went about grabbing plates, napkins, and drinks.

Rayma led Oona through the house to the guest room.

There was a small, probably five-foot-tall, fake Christmas tree in one corner of the living room, draped in gold and red baubles, with a gold star on top. A few other Christmas decorations freckled the living room and kitchen, but nothing gaudy or over-the-top.

Until he spied the kitchen counter, that is. There were six, yes, six, pineapples lined up on the counter.

Did anybody need that many pineapples?

Scratching his chin, he shook his head to dismiss the idea of asking why they needed that many pineapples and just said, "Bathroom here on the right?" instead, directing his question to Jordan.

"Yep," Jordan said with a nod.

Aiden didn't really need to piss, but he did need a moment to himself.

Between finding out Oona was Rayma's sister, that they were going to be staying under the same roof, and seeing his brother after so long, Aiden was a little overwhelmed.

Why couldn't anger management have sponsors like AA?

Because now would be the perfect time to call a sponsor.

Not that he was angry, but he was just ... struggling to cope with everything that had been thrown at him. Maybe he didn't need a sponsor, but just some better coping tools.

The thought of having a lack of coping tools sent a flash of red-hot anger coursing through him. If he had a therapist, he'd fucking *have* tools. But the woman with the beauty mark under her eye and great legs turned him away. She refused to treat him because he'd seen all of her tattoos ... *once*.

He pissed, washed his hands, and then splashed some cold water on his face. He could do this.

This week was not about him. It was about Jordan and Rayma. Jordan had extended an olive branch to Aiden with the hopes of rebuilding their relationship. This week was about that. About family and two people who loved each other coming together.

He needed to get over his own shit, get over Oona and be there for Jordan.

He opened the bathroom door, only to literally bump into Oona as he stepped out.

"Oh, sorry," she said, the shock in her voice dousing the anger he'd felt toward her a moment ago. She had linens and pillows piled in her arms and couldn't see where she was going.

He cleared his throat.

"Just toss the stuff on the couch, Oons. I'll make up Aiden's bed later," Rayma said, emerging from her and Jordan's bedroom.

Jordan settled them in the living room, which was painted in soft beige and brown. The sectional was a dark brown leather, and a black La-Z-Boy sat invitingly in the corner.

Plates, napkins, pizza, sparkling water, and wine were out for everyone, as well as some cut up veggies and dip.

"My baby knows how to put out a spread," Rayma said with a hint of sarcasm as she took a seat at one end of the longest part of the sectional. Jordan took the La-Z-Boy, which left Aiden and Oona to sit closest to each other on the other side of the couch. "So, Oons, how was your show last week? You said you were going to send me pictures, but you never did."

Aiden could tell Oona really wanted to look his way, but she was resisting the urge so forcefully, that a cord in her neck popped out. She reached for a slice of pizza and a plate, which forced her to lean closer to him, her elbow brushing his knee, before sitting back against the couch, and turning her focus away from Aiden completely. "Yeah, sorry. I have some, our photographer took some great ones. I just haven't gone onto my Google Drive and downloaded them yet."

"Oona does pole dancing and burlesque," Rayma said to Aiden. "It's so freaking hot, right, Oons?"

"It's uh … it's fun," Oona replied, taking a bite of her pizza.

"Sounds fun," Aiden said. "You have to have a lot of upper body strength for that, I hear."

"I'm just taking beginner pole classes, and so is Pasha," Rayma added. "But we only go like once a week, so we're nowhere near as strong as Oona." Her eyes glittered with pride as she smiled at her big sister. "And the burlesque is just hot. I mean, the pole dancing is hot, too. But that chafes your thighs and is really hard work. The burlesque is just sexy."

"I feel like that would really work your inner thighs from all the squats," Jordan added. "At least from the short clips of the videos Rayma shoves into my face and makes me watch." He took a sip from his beer and winked at Rayma when she stuck her tongue out at him.

"It's a lot of squatting and stuff, yeah," Oona said. All Aiden could see of her at the moment was her profile, but that was enough. A sexy pink flush crept up from her neck into her cheeks and even her ears, the more they talked about pole and burlesque. Clearly, she hated the attention on her, which sat so weird with him, considering she performed on stage with barely any clothes on in front of dozens of people.

Then again, that was *Luna Love* on stage, not Dr. Oona Young.

Maybe she really did have a split personality.

Was that safe for a therapist?

What if the patient suddenly found themselves being treated by Luna and not Oona? Was Luna also licensed to practice therapy? How did that all work?

He'd taken a few training courses in mental health and how to deal with people and situations concerning mental breakdowns and stuff. But it'd been more about risk management and deescalating a dangerous situation, not diagnosing someone's disorder, or how to deal with specific disorders.

"So I want to hear about the wedding," Oona said, reaching for the glass of wine that Jordan had set down for her. She put the glass to her lips, but her throat didn't move. She didn't actually take a sip.

Did her family not know she didn't drink?

What the fuck?

Rayma started to talk with a loud voice and wild hand gestures, bouncing on the couch cushion and regaling them with wedding details that Aiden didn't give a fuck about.

He grabbed himself a slice of pizza and cracked open a can of mango flavored sparkling water that Jordan had set down for him. It was weird being with Jordan after so long, and when he flicked his gaze up to his brother, he could feel the worry and tension rolling off Jordan from the way he was looking back at Aiden.

Jordan tipped his head sideways toward the door, and Aiden nodded.

Taking his pizza, he pried himself up from the couch and followed Jordan to the door. They slipped into their shoes and coats and ducked outside.

"It's weird," Jordan said, his breath making a big puff in front of his face as he shoved his hands into his pockets and let his shoulders round forward. "Us, you and me, being together after so long."

"Yeah." Aiden finished his pizza, then pushed his hands into his coat pockets, too, and fell in line with Jordan as they made their way up to the sidewalk.

"Never meant for it to go this long, you know?"

"I know. Me either."

Jordan glanced at him. "I just ... I didn't know what to say."

"Me either."

"I still see him, you know?"

"Dad?" Aiden slid a sideways glance toward his brother. Jordan was half an inch shorter than Aiden, but his shoulders were slightly broader.

Jordan shook his head. "No. Dallas."

Aiden swallowed and bobbed his head in understanding. "Me, too."

"I replay that day over and over and over again in my head. On a loop like fucking Groundhog Day. And no matter what I do differently—"

Aiden exhaled. "Same fucking outcome, I know."

"I see him across the street. Then, when I blink or take a second look, he's gone. Sometimes I hear his 'Hey Jordan!' and think I'm losing my mind."

Aiden just continued to nod. He knew exactly what Jordan was referring to, because even after all this time, Aiden was still haunted by Dallas's ghost, too. Still saw the kid, still heard him, and I still dreamed about him.

Jordan cleared his throat. "When we started planning the wedding, Rayma had me make a list of everybody from my side that I wanted to invite." He snorted. "Shortest fucking list in the world."

"Yeah?"

"Only one name was on it."

Aiden smiled but kept his head down.

"I know we haven't seen each other in years and we're not close, but ... you're my brother, and I was hoping that you'd also be my best man?"

They stopped in their tracks, under the orange glow of a streetlamp. A large church parking lot was behind them, with piles of snow from the plow crammed into the corners.

"I mean, I get it if you don't want to. Totally, I'm just glad you're here," Jordan said quickly, his eyes darting around the road as he uncomfortably shifted from side to side on his feet. Then he was walking again, they both were. It was easier to talk about serious shit when they weren't looking at each other.

"I can ask someone else. I should have asked you sooner, honestly. But I wanted to see you, to ask you in person—I can ask my buddy Jace, I'm sure he'd—"

"Dude, I'd be happy to," Aiden said, stopping them again, reaching out, and resting his hand on Jordan's shoulder. Hard muscle bunched beneath his fingers. "Just 'cause we're not close now, doesn't mean we weren't at one point, and it doesn't mean we can't be again. Just tell me what you need from me, and I'll do it."

Jordan grinned at him, and for a brief moment, all Aiden saw was their mother. He hadn't realized how much Jordan looked like their mom when he smiled. He dropped his hand from his brother's shoulder and fought the urge to step away, instead, he cleared his throat and cracked his neck from side to side.

"Do I need to plan a bachelor party or something?"

"That's being planned already. Didn't expect you to pull that together on such short notice. But just stand there with me on the big day, that's what I need most of all. Hold the torch for my entire side."

Emotion clawed hard and thick in Aiden's throat until all he could do was nod. He couldn't even swallow, let alone say anything.

"Should we head back? I'm fucking freezing."

Aiden's head bobbed again. "I thought the West Coast was warmer than back home. This is fucking gross."

"It's a different cold, bro. A wet cold, from being right on the ocean. Blasts right past the layers and sets up camp in your fucking marrow until spring."

"Ugh."

Jordan huffed a laugh. "Yeah, but at least we don't get the dumps of snow like you guys do. Don't miss that."

Aiden made fists with his fingers inside his pocket to keep them from freezing. He knew it would take a bit of time before he and Jordan were completely comfortable with each other again. It'd been over ten years since they last saw each other, and a lot had changed. A lot of time had passed, and they both harbored guilt and anger over what happened to Dallas.

Over what happened to their family.

But Jordan asking Aiden to be his best man was not something Aiden ever expected, but was overjoyed to be asked. He'd never been *best* anything, let alone a best man.

"So Rayma is intent on playing matchmaker with you and her sister," Jordan said, changing the subject.

Aiden stopped on the sidewalk. "With Oona?"

Jordan peered at him curiously. "Yeah, why?"

"I just ... what the fuck? Why?"

"Because you're both single, in your thirties, and coincidentally live in Montreal. It doesn't help that Mieka and Triss—two of their other sisters—have found love with brothers. Triss married Asher a couple of years ago and they're expecting a baby, and Mieka is now with Asher's brother, Nate. They all own a big ranch in Colorado together. They built Triss a clinic for her speech pathology, and are building Mieka a dance studio to teach dance. All on the property. The guys aren't coming out until the day before the wedding, though. Need to stay and work on the ranch."

"Fucking hell."

"So, Rayma thinks it would be cool if she and Oona also ended up with brothers. I told her to cool her matchmaking jets, but she's determined." He glanced over at Aiden. "Figured you deserved a heads-up, in case you're not single, or just not interested."

What the hell was Aiden supposed to say to that?

Did he tell his brother that he'd already banged the sister and now they were enemies? Or did he keep it hush-hush to avoid any kind of drama before the wedding?

"I mean, she's pretty cute," Jordan said. "And a doctor. Like a psychologist type doctor. And she does pole dancing and burlesque. I've seen some of the videos, and like I said, she's talented."

Oh, Aiden knew she was talented. Oona had used him like a pole and climbed him, swung around his body while naked, then given him a lap dance like she had that chair during her burlesque performance.

"Yeah, she's cute," Aiden murmured. "But the focus is on you guys this week. The wedding. Not my love life."

"Try telling that to my fiancée. It doesn't help that we were set up. So she is a firm believer in matchmaking, not that she's ever done it before."

Aiden sorted. "As long as she doesn't go hanging mistletoe around the house expecting me to kiss Oona, I think I can handle her." They reached the front door again.

"Don't give her any ideas," Jordan replied, his chuckle lighthearted as he turned the handle and opened the door, a warm, pizza-scented waft of air flying toward them.

Rayma and Oona were on the couch, both of them in a fit of giggles with tears streaming down their cheeks. Rayma took one look at Aiden, then glanced over at Oona again, only to topple sideways and start laughing all over again.

What the fuck?

Did Oona just tell Rayma about them?

And if she did, what exactly did she say?

Chapter Eight

Even after her shower and getting into her pajamas for the night, Oona still smiled to herself at the memory of seeing the look of terror on Aiden's face when he and Jordan walked back into the house and found her and Rayma laughing.

He thought she'd told Rayma about them. She could tell by the way his skin went lily-white and his mouth dropped open. Then his eyes darted back and forth between both women like he was watching a tennis match.

It helped immensely that Rayma had looked at the guys right before she toppled over into another laughing fit. And Aiden—being the self-absorbed idiot that he was—assumed that she was looking at him and laughing, when in reality she was looking at her fiancé.

She'd just told Oona a story about Jordan and how Rayma had—in her filter-free way—embarrassed him. They'd gone to a hot yin yoga class together, since Rayma figured it would help Jordan learn to relax after a stressful day "fighting crime" and "chasing The Joker and Penguin around Gotham." Only, they went to the class in the evening, after dinner. And that night for dinner, she made turkey chili. Well, poor Jordan got gassy, and when he lifted his legs into the air for *happy baby*, he let out a pretty loud and smelly fart.

Rayma hadn't even gotten to the best part, and already she and Oona had tributaries of tears running down their cheeks, and Oona's face hurt from smiling.

"I mean, farts are a natural bodily function. A buildup of methane gas. It's gotta go somewhere, right?" Rayma said between giggles. "Otherwise, we're uncomfortable. And they're so cute coming out of babies. Like when Raze and Eve farted, we all thought it was adorable." Raze and Eve were Pasha's kids, Oona and Rayma's nephew and niece. "But suddenly, we hit a certain age and farts become gross."

"I mean, to men, I don't think they're ever gross. I think men always find them funny," Oona countered.

"In certain circumstances, yes. But I think we need to just erase the stigma. Everyone farts. Even the Crown Prince of Monaco. And I'm sure he farts a lot given his rich diet."

Oona snorted. "Probably."

"So, I simply patted Jordan on the arm and said, loud enough for everyone to hear, but not so loud that I disturbed their meditation, 'It's okay, Lassie, that just means you're really relaxed. Then in solidarity, I farted, too."

Oona gasped and started to laugh again.

"He didn't like that. Got really red in the face and pissed off at me. Then our whole corner of the room smelled like turkey chili and people started coughing. In hindsight, maybe I shouldn't have farted in solidarity. But I did it out of love."

It was at this point that Jordan and Aiden walked back into the house. Oona and Rayma were in stitches. Rayma looked up at her fiancé and just doubled over again with laughter.

But Aiden thought they were laughing about him, and Oona was under no obligation or interest to correct his assumption.

She hopped into the shower first, ahead of the tall jerk with the chiseled jaw and sexy back, then yanked on her comfy plaid pajama pants, a black tank top, and a gray McGill hoodie. She was just putting her hair in a braid when there was a knock on the bathroom door. "Other people need to shower, too," came his rough and smoky grumble.

"Yeah?" she replied, deciding that today she would brush her teeth for an extra couple of minutes.

"Yeah."

"Be out soon," she sung.

She would not be out soon.

She finished braiding her wet hair, then she did her nighttime moisturizing routine—something she easily could have done in the mirror in the guestroom—then she brushed and flossed, and finally, at long last, she emerged from the steamy bathroom.

"Leave me any fucking hot water?" he growled, passing her in the doorway with a towel slung over his shoulder. He was so big beside her that his hand brushed her arm, and heat raced through her from that connection point.

"I'm sure your hot head will warm it up if I didn't," she replied sweetly.

Jordan and Rayma had retired to bed, closing their door. It was just Oona and Aiden now, along with their big secret and the tightly wound tension twanging and buzzing between them.

"We agree not to tell them, right?" she asked, turning to face him once she was out of the bathroom and before he shut the door. "That this week is about them, not about our ..."

His brows lifted.

"Drama," she finished.

His single nod was curt and to the point before he shut the door in her face.

She narrowed her gaze at the closed door, huffed out a frustrated breath, then spun on her heel and stalked to the guestroom, closing the door behind her.

She didn't toss and turn much before she finally fell asleep, but the tossing and turning that did happen was because of the thoughts that rattled around in her brain like marbles in a tin can.

Aiden, naked in the shower, and only a thin layer of drywall between them.

She'd seen him naked. Had run her tongue across the smooth ridges of his abs, kissed the silky skin of his chest and clavicle, but that only made it worse.

She had firsthand knowledge about what she would see beyond the bathroom door and it was driving her insane.

She should not be this bothered, this flustered by a man who clearly hated her and wanted to do nothing more than ruffle her feathers and piss her off.

Aiden was an angry person who needed help. But she was not the person to help him.

However, they needed to put their drama aside for the time being and focus on Rayma and Jordan.

She could do that.

For Rayma, she *would* do that.

The bathroom door finally opened and she could just picture him sauntering out with his sexy owl tattoo all covered in water droplets, while the towel hung dangerously low on his hips and his skin was a tantalizing rosy pink from the warm water.

She licked her lips, groaned, and flipped over onto her belly, squeezing her eyes shut so tight it made the skin at her temples tingle.

"Go. To. Sleep," she growled at herself.

Eventually, she did fall asleep. Only to be bombarded with sexy dreams of Aiden seducing her.

They weren't on a plane this time, but the seats were arranged like airplane seats. Numbered and narrow. But they were inside the bar, where they first met back at the hotel. Pedro was shaking drinks behind the it, but when she tried to order a Shirley Temple from him, he passed her a can of ginger ale instead.

"I didn't order this," she said.

Pedro ignored her.

"Here, you can have mine," came a husky voice, followed by a big hand sliding a can of tomato juice toward her.

"I don't drink tomato juice."

"Neither do I. I'd much rather drink you down." Then he—a fuzzy image that looked a lot like Aiden—dropped to his knees, hooked her legs over his shoulder and she suddenly found herself sitting in an airplane seat, with the big bald man from their first flight beside her snoring, while Aiden ate her out.

Her groan of pleasure woke her up with a start. Her chest heaved, her body was warm and she didn't even have to check her underwear to know that she was aroused. Every inch of her skin tingled, and there was a thin layer of sweat forming along her hairline.

"What the fuck?" she breathed out into the dark, quiet room.

Grabbing her phone off the nightstand, she checked the time.

It was eight-thirty in the morning. Wednesday. Right. She was at her sister's place in Victoria. Not her apartment in Montreal. It was a work day, but she didn't have to work.

"What the fuck?" she said again. She'd never in her life slept that late. She was an early riser, and given the time difference, she thought for sure she'd be waking up earlier than ever since she was conditioned to wake up at six every day. So that would be three in the morning Pacific time.

How had she slept so long?

Swinging her legs over the side of the bed, she didn't bother with her hoodie, since her body was still hot and bothered, and she padded barefoot to the door, slowly opening it.

The apartment was quiet.

With her phone in her hand, she stood on the bedroom side of the door and checked her messages. There was one from Rayma.

Hey sleepy head. Figured you would want to sleep in. I had to head into the office for a couple of hours but I'll be back in time for the dress fittings. Jordan is working a day shift, so he'll be home around dinner. I want you to look at this as a vacation, so take a load off. Veg and unwind. Aiden is still at the house, so maybe, I dunno ... have some fun. See you in a bit. Love you, Oons!

Oona gaped at her sister's message.

What the hell?

She texted Rayma back. *A head's up last night would have been appreciated. I'd much rather go to the gym than hang out at your house all morning with a stranger.*

Rayma texted back almost immediately. *He's not a stranger. He's family. And if you jump his bones and grind them into dust with your crazy-strong stripper thighs, then he definitely won't be a stranger. Xoxo*

Oona growled. Rayma was such a meddler.

She had the best of intentions, and an enormous heart, but her filter was nonexistent, and her mouth was colossal. If there was ever a person on that planet who gave less fucks about what people thought of her than Rayma Young, Oona would love to meet them.

Scratch that, no, she probably didn't want to meet them, because they were probably just a never-ending runaway train terrorizing their way through life, wreaking havoc and causing bedlam wherever they went.

Jordan had certainly tamed Rayma in a lot of ways. She was still wildly inappropriate most of the time, but her intentions were slightly less misdirected.

But she'd missed the mark in a big way this time.

A worse match did not exist. And even though the sex had been great, and the conversations stimulating, Aiden and Oona were less compatible than a fox and a house full of hens.

Her bladder reminded her that it needed to be relieved, so she lobbed a weary sigh, resigned to her fate, and silently crept out of her bedroom and into the bathroom.

And yep, her panties were soaked. Which meant she'd probably actually orgasmed in her sleep. Not the first time, but she hadn't done it in a while.

It was essentially the female version of a wet dream.

Fucking Aiden.

Yeah, fucking Aiden, or at least dreaming about fucking Aiden was what had caused such a puddle.

Growling, because what else was there to do besides channel her inner honey badger, she used one of the wet wipes from the package on the back of the toilet to clean herself up properly, then she washed her face, brushed her teeth, and, holding her bunched and damp underwear in her fist, tiptoed back to her bedroom. She put on new underwear, but didn't bother getting dressed. Her pajamas were loose flannel pants and a black tank top. She was still too warm for the McGill hoodie, but she did throw on a thin cardigan just to cover up a bit more.

Rayma had already pointed out where the blender was and all the smoothie making ingredients, so at least Oona would be able to hold onto that part of her routine.

She continued to tiptoe through the house, not wanting to attract any attention to herself if she could help it.

A quick glance into the living room showed the pull-out couch all folded up blankets and pillows stacked neatly on one side.

Where was Aiden?

Unease and relief ran neck-and-neck inside of her. She was alone. Thank God.

Relaxing, she went about making herself a smoothie, forgoing any tiptoeing and just enjoying the peace, quiet, and aloneness.

Rayma had a Costco-sized bag of spinach in her fridge, so Oona grabbed a cup and a half of that, along with a frozen banana from the freezer, a cup of frozen blueberries, a scoop of vanilla protein powder, and oat milk. She considered cutting into one of the six pineapples on the counter, but then thought better of it.

Someone with six pineapples had to have a plan for them, so she didn't want to dip into their supply and ruin something.

And also, the pineapple fibers always seemed to get tangled in the blades of her blenders.

The whirr of the blender was noisy, but nothing she wasn't used to. It did, however, drown out the sound of the door opening, and since her back was turned, when the door closed—and not gently—she jumped and squealed.

Turning off the blender, then whipping around, she found Aiden, a smug smile curving up the corners of his mouth. He was dressed in a pair of running shorts over top of running pants that were skin tight. His long-sleeved black running shirt was pasted to his body like a second-skin, and his face was flushed. Black earbuds were in his ears, and he had on a black running ball cap. Everything he wore was black, but he also had reflective gear—straps around his wrists and ankles, a blinking light on the back of his hat, and white reflective stripes on his shirt.

Her tongue turned into the consistency of stale bread.

"'Morning, *Luna*," he said. "Nice of you to finally join the land of the living."

Glaring at him, she returned to her smoothie and turned on the blender again.

He ditched his shoes and came around the other side of the island to stand directly in front of her. She kept her head down, watching her purply-green concoction whirl around in the glass pitcher.

Once it was sufficiently mixed, she turned it off and poured the entire contents into a tumbler along with a silicone straw. It wasn't easy avoiding eye contact with Aiden, but she did it. She was proud of herself.

"Seems like there is enough there for two people," he said just as the icy drink hit her soft palate and icicles formed in her gray matter, making her wince.

Once the brain freeze was gone, she blinked up at him. "Yeah, there probably is."

His lips pursed for a moment, then curled up slightly, more so on the left. "Classic *Oona*. Only thinking about herself. *Her* career, *her* hunger. Nobody else matters but *Oona*."

A rush of fury buzzed through her at his words. Her nostrils flared, and she narrowed her gaze. A mean, sarcastic response sat impatiently and ready on her tongue, but the difference between her and Aiden was that she thought before she spoke. She had impulse control and knew when to keep something in her head and on her tongue, rather than release it into the world to cause more pain.

Because as much as she now disliked the man in front of her, she knew he was in pain, and the last thing she wanted to ever cause anyone, regardless of how she felt about them, was pain.

She might not have taken a Hippocratic oath to do no harm like an MD, but she went into her profession—psychology—and specialized in trauma and PTSD for a reason. Because she hated to see people hurting and wanted to do whatever she could to ease their suffering and help them live more peacefully.

She sipped her smoothie.

Huffing out a derisive laugh, he shook his head, and then, because he knew exactly what he was doing, he removed his hat, tossing it onto the island. Then, reached behind his back and yanked his shirt off over his head, taking the tank top beneath with it, to reveal all the rippling, defined ridges of his abdomen.

Did the owl tattoo on his shoulder and pec just wink at her?

Oona nearly choked on her smoothie.

She dropped her gaze to the floor, studying the white laminate that was meant to look like tile.

She could feel the owl's eyes on her, burning into the side of her face like a brand. But she refused to look up. Refused to give in to even the owl's temptation.

He ditched his phone and earbuds on to the island, too, then stalked toward the bathroom. Only then, when he finally wasn't facing her, did she hedge a glance upward, taking in the wide expanse of his back, his thick traps, and broad shoulders.

Her pussy quivered and her lower belly fluttered.

Fucking Aiden.

The bathroom door closed and she heaved a sigh of relief.

She needed to get away from this man. Get out from under the same roof as him. Somewhere. Anywhere.

She pulled out her phone and shot off texts to Pasha, Triss and Mieka, asking them for reprieve. For anything. But nobody responded.

Where the hell were they?

Aiden was correct. The smoothie was more than enough for two people. She made too much.

But she was normally used to her personal sized smoothie maker, not this gargantuan blender meant to feed an army.

Her belly was full before she was even halfway through, so she poured the rest into a mason jar, secured the lid, and stored it in the fridge. Then she cleaned up her mess in the kitchen.

She was just finishing the dishes when the bathroom door opened again.

Oh, please come out covered up, you dickhead.

But, of course, he didn't.

He knew precisely what he was doing. And it was working like a charm.

Why she hadn't rushed to her room when she heard the water shut off was beyond her. Probably because, deep down, she wanted to see him all glistening wet and half-naked again.

But she shouldn't.

He was an egotistical jackass with anger issues. She should stay as far away from him as possible.

And yet, she couldn't.

Because she knew he wasn't *just* an egotistical jackass with anger issues. She'd seen the other sides of him. Good sides. Soft sides.

Holding his running clothes in one hand, and the towel at his hips with the other, he shifted his weight with practiced ease through the apartment into the living room, to where his duffle bag sat on the floor tucked out of the way. Bending over, which just caused Oona's insides to get hotter than the surface of the sun, he rifled through to find clothes.

She was trapped in her own body, which had somehow become glued to the floor. Her muscles refused to listen to her brain and move. Her feet forgot how to walk, her legs pretended they weren't listening when she told them to engage and take her to the bedroom.

She just stood there like an imbecile, watching him, hoping, praying for the towel to drop. Because she knew exactly just how nice his ass was— she had experienced it with her teeth—but the memories were already a little fuzzy and she needed fresh fodder for her dreams.

What is wrong with you? Move! Move! Stop staring at his ass. It might be a great ass, but it's attached to a jerk. A jerk who said you were bad in bed, let's not forget.

That last reminder is what did it.

It jostled her from her petrified state of intense arousal. She blinked a bunch of times and shook her head. Lifting one foot, then the other, she exhaled in relief that her legs and feet were listening again.

Two steps toward her bedroom, and she was stopping again, only this time it wasn't of her own volition.

It was because of Aiden.

He'd crossed the room with alarming speed and, still in the towel, was crowding her until she had to back up against the small space of wall between the kitchen and bathroom.

"Wh-what are you doing?" she stammered, swallowing hard as her thighs begged to be squeezed together.

He hadn't touched her, but she could feel his heat. He'd boxed her in, his forearm resting on the wall next to her head, while his other hand was on the wall beside her arm. His breath was minty and cool on her cheek as he stared down at her, his green eyes hooded and gaze soft. He leaned in even closer, and this time she noticed the slight flare in his nostrils and his pupils widening, that was after they took in the curve of her breasts beneath her tank top. Slowly.

And since she wasn't wearing a bra, he could see her peaked nipples protruding through the soft, thin, black fabric.

He licked his lips a little.

May as well have flicked her clit with this tip of his tongue, for how it made her panties turn instantly damp.

"What did you tell Rayma?" he asked, his voice brushing over her name in a rough rasp.

Oona blinked. "What did I tell Rayma when?"

"Last night?"

"Huh?"

"Don't play dumb, Oona, it's not a good look. Did you tell her about us? About me?"

"No," she whispered, making sure her answer sounded confident.

"When Jordan and I came back from our walk, you two were cackling like a couple of old hens. Then she took one look at me and burst out laughing again. What. Did. You. Tell. Her?"

Swallowing again, Oona lifted a hand and placed it in the middle of Aiden's chest, pushing him away a little. He didn't budge.

"A little breathing room, please," she said, loathing the idea of having to remove her hand from his warm skin. There was a light dusting of dark brown hair between his pecs, but it just added to his over all sexiness.

He shook his head slowly. "Only after you tell me what you told her."

Oona sucked in a deep breath through her nose and rolled her eyes. "I didn't *tell* Rayma anything. It was *her* telling *me* a story about Jordan. Then you two came in and she looked at *him*, not you; he was just behind you, but your inflated ego made you think she was looking at you, then she burst out laughing again."

His brows pinched together on his forehead, and he narrowed his gaze.

"I swear to God," she said, impatiently. "You can ask Rayma. I didn't tell her anything about ... *us*."

"And you can't. Doctor patient confidentiality."

"Well, technically, you were never my patient, so ..."

Anger flashed in his eyes.

"But yeah. I would never breach confidence and tell her—or anyone—anything I knew about any of my patients or *non* patients. And I certainly never told her about ... *us*." Though Rayma was hell-bent on setting them up anyway. But Oona didn't say that part. The less Aiden knew about that, the better.

He was quiet for a moment, then hummed, which was like warm fingers dancing up her spine. "What did she tell you?"

"Nothing terrible."

"Then you'll have no problem telling me."

She rolled her eyes again. "She told me about how she took Jordan to a hot yin yoga class, he farted, it stunk, so to make him feel less embarrassed, she farted, too, in solidarity. But then they ended up stinking up their whole corner of the studio, to the point where they made a dude start coughing. It was a whole thing. Jordan was not happy."

Aiden's eyes widened again, and his lips twitched. "That was it?"

Oona nodded. "That was it. I swear. I get giggly when I'm with my sisters. We haven't always been close, but we're working on that. And since Rayma and I are the youngest, she and I have a lot of little inside jokes and stuff."

"Noticed you didn't drink the wine last night."

She shook her head. "If you weren't here, I would have had a glass. But ..."

"But what?" he rumbled, the timbre having the same affect on her like melted chocolate on a sun-kissed strawberry. He leaned in closer. So close, their noses practically touched.

"But, my wits and smarts can sometimes be affected when I've been drinking and I wanted to make sure I didn't say," or do, "anything that could ..."

"That could?" Her pussy vibrated from his purr, as if he'd spoken while his lips were rested directly against her heated, damp flesh.

She swallowed hard and breathed out through thinly parted lips. "Compromise or add drama to this week for Rayma and Jordan."

"You mean like the fact that you and I slept together, then you refused to help me."

Sucking fortifying oxygen into her lungs, she placed both palms into the center of his chest and shoved him away. "I *ethically* can't. I could lose my job."

He rolled his eyes and scoffed. The look and sound far sexier, far more arousing, than it should be. But he was right there in front of her in nothing but a towel, smelling delicious and radiating everything she knew was wrong, bad. and off-limits, but wanted nevertheless.

Her muscles went rigid in frustration and she pressed her fingers to her forehead before dropping them to her thighs with a *slap*. She was annoyed with herself for being turned on and attracted to him, but that needed to come out in another way, and being pissed off at Aiden and his unbelievably thick skull was the way to do it.

"Are you really *that* self-absorbed that you can't see past your own needs?" she asked, wrangling every last ounce of disdain she had for this man and holding onto it with both hands in tight fists. Because if she didn't, she was going to throw caution to the wind, whip off his towel, and bend over.

"*My* own needs?" he said with indignation. "You're just thinking about your career while holding mine hostage, because you can't put one night where we used aliases and were not even therapist and client, aside, and do what's right."

Ooh, this man was infuriatingly dense. Why did the dense ones have to be so hot?

"What's right? What's right?" Her voice went up a couple octaves until she was on the south side of shrill. "If I lose my license to practice, if I lose my job, the fifty *other* clients I have right now would suddenly be without a therapist, not to mention all the future clients that I can help, will be trapped on waitlists for even longer. Not getting the help they sorely need. The help that *I* can give them. Did you think about that? No, of course not, because Aiden Lassiter doesn't think about anybody but himself. My refusal to see you, based on *ethics,* based on a conflict of interest because *we slept together,* is bigger than just keeping you on the waitlist longer. In fact, that has nothing to do with it. I don't *want* you to be on a waitlist. I feel bad for everyone that is stuck on one.

"But I had to refuse *you* treatment so that I could continue to help a lot of other people." She plunked her hands on her hips. "And I happen to know that Astrid Kramer has agreed to start seeing you in the new year, so you're really only waiting like three more weeks. And yet you still can't get over it. It's like you've never been told *no* before. And now that you have, you're behaving like a toddler who was denied a second cookie for the first time in his life. I'm surprised you haven't stomped your feet or thrown your body to the ground."

Her chest rose and fell like she'd just done twenty minutes uphill on her elliptical. Her body was hot, and her temper was raging.

But it was nothing compared to the inferno that was staring back at her. Green flames danced in his eyes, and his defined chest expanded and deflated quickly, which caused his nostrils to flare like a bull preparing to charge. His chin jutted out, and the muscles and tendons strained from his neck. A quick glance down at his hands made her pulse spike. His fists were bunched and the veins and cords of his arms stood out like a map with three-dimensional topography. Valleys and ridges were broken up by planes dusted with soft, dark brown hair.

Despite the burning ire inside of her, she couldn't deny how much she appreciated his beauty.

How much she was attracted to him.

Usually, people become more attractive when their personality was attractive. The two really did go hand-in-hand. But the more she got to know Aiden, the less she liked him. And she hoped that she'd eventually find him less attractive, too. But that simply wasn't the case.

The man was a work of art.

A miserable, broken, hurt, and hurtful work of beautiful art.

"Just leave me alone and I'll leave you alone," she said, her shoulders dropping as the tension started to seep from her body. "I don't want to do anything to cause Rayma or Jordan any extra stress. And *this*," she pointed back and forth between them, "isn't healthy for anyone. This is stressful. My cortisol-level is probably through the roof."

She turned to head to her room, but found herself plastered back up against the wall, this time, he made sure he was touching her. One hand was on her hip, the other on the back of her head. "Think you're better than me?" he asked. His words, his breath, stirred the strands of hair that had escaped her braid throughout the night. They stirred feelings deep down inside her she'd never experienced before.

Not with anyone.

Not like this.

His eyes followed the roll of her throat as she tried to swallow ...

Heat erupted from her center and filled up every nook and cranny of her body. The flicker at her center grew stronger. More demanding. More distracting. But, she still had her wits. Some of them anyway, and she shook her head. "No. Do *you* think I'm better than you?"

Something strange flashed in his eyes, but it was gone a second later as he growled and crushed his mouth against hers.

She managed to worm her arms between them, and for the third time that morning, she placed her hands on his pecs and shoved him away.

Their chests heaved as they stared at each other. Her body was a maelstrom of conflicting sensations. Her brain was short-circuiting because it didn't know what to feel or how to respond. A fire roared deep in her belly, drowning out the thoughts that told her this was a bad idea.

She wanted this.

Wanted him, of course.

But she knew she shouldn't.

Knew it was a bad idea, and yet ... the choice seemed perfectly clear.

She was drawn to Aiden Lassiter like a moth to a flame, a mouse to a chunk of cheese in a trap. Aiden was dangerous. He was broken. But that didn't stop the searing desire that threatened to burn her from the inside out. The unbridled need that consumed her, or the powerful desire to feel his lips on hers again and go back to that night at the hotel where they were just Luna and Caden and nothing else mattered.

As if drawn by an invisible force, he rushed her, she rushed him and leaped up onto his hips just in time for him to slam her back into the wall, as his mouth continued its siege on hers and his towel finally gave up the fight and fell to the floor.

So much for them leaving each other alone.

Chapter Nine

Just like that night at the hotel, they were all hands, teeth and lips as they crashed around her sister's apartment, grappling at each other. Each of them trying to climb deeper inside the other, get more skin-to-skin, more lips to flesh. More everything.

It was a battle of wills.

A challenge.

A duel.

Who would come to their senses first and stop this?

Stop it before it went too far.

Before they reached the point of no return.

It wouldn't be her.

He was already naked, and his hot length prodded her thigh as he spun them around and into the kitchen, plunking her ass on the island—and not gently.

Everything about the way Aiden moved was rough, gruff, and possessive.

And she was here for it.

She'd never let another person manhandle her like this before, not after Russell, anyway, and yet with Aiden, she was okay with it. She relished it. She invited more of it. She wanted to see bruises tomorrow from how tightly he gripped her hips, wanted to see his bite marks on her neck and across her shoulders and collarbone.

It got her heart racing. Her juices flowing

The savage, desperate need in his eyes turned those sparks of heat inside her into licking flames.

He pulled away from her just enough to finish sliding the sleeves of her cardigan off her arms, then he reached for the hem of her tank top and ripped it off, tossing it somewhere behind him. His eyes took in her bare breasts. Her nipples were so puckered, she could have sworn she felt them throbbing, swelling under his scrutiny, and begging for his mouth.

Just his eyes on her, devouring her with such blatant desire, had her pussy pulsing, and another trickle of arousal filled the already apparent puddle in her underwear.

Heat bloomed from her core, and her body quivered with need.

Bending at the knees, he leaned forward and cupped both breasts roughly, squeezing and kneading as he brought his mouth to one nipple while the thumb and forefinger of his hand tugged and tweaked the other puckered bud. A sigh slipped from her, followed by an unrestrained groan.

He switched sides, ravaging the other nipple with his mouth, scraping his teeth across it and sucking it to almost the back of his tongue until she gasped from the pain, then moaned loudly from the warm blossom of pleasure that quickly followed.

Rising back up to his full height, his eyes hooded, he caught her gaze.

Her breath snagged harshly in her throat, and she tried to swallow.

He smirked in a smug way that normally would have made her temper flare, but at the moment, it just turned her on even more. The glint in his eyes turned wily. Nothing about the way he looked at her said, "I'm done with you." Not at all. And certainly not when his hands were working down the waistband of her pajama pants. Everything about him, the way he moved, looked at her, and touched her — said, "I'm nowhere near done with you."

Without really even thinking, she lifted her hips so he could drag her underwear and pants down to her ankles, then he yanked them off fully and tossed them to join her tank top. They were both naked now.

Only, she was sitting with her bare ass on her sister's granite counter.

And she didn't care.

His teeth raked across her clavicle and up her jaw, the sharpness of them almost breaking the skin, causing goose flesh to rise on her arms and legs in excitement, and her breath to rush from her lungs. He nipped her jaw, sending a wave of heat to race down her body. A jolt of awareness directly to her clit.

"I can smell you," he growled, trailing his fingers delicately up her inner thigh, gathering some of her arousal that coated her inner lips, and pressing the pad of his thumb against her clit. "Smell how bad you want me. How bad you want my cock in your tight little cunt."

Normally, a man smelling her arousal would be something that would embarrass her. Yet, with Aiden, she was turned on by it. She didn't care. Didn't give a damn that he knew how hot she was for him. How much she wanted him. He clearly wanted her, too, otherwise, he wouldn't have attacked her with his mouth and undressed her.

Her body was open and ready for him. Ready to welcome the enemy.

They could keep things drama free for Rayma and Jordan's sake, but right now, they had things they needed to clear up. Closure sex.

Yeah, that's what this was.

Angry, hateful, closure sex.

That was a thing, right?

Like a bookend to a bad story. They had sex as strangers. Albeit strangers who seemed to like each other and get along. Then things turned ugly. And now, they were at the end of the book, and although it wasn't a happy ending, they were attempting to wrap things up with a hate fuck of closure.

That made very little sense to her, but whatever. That was what it was.

Reaching between them, she wrapped her fingers around his cock and stroked him, pulling a bear-like growl from deep within his chest. "Why?" he breathed, dropping his mouth next to her ear.

She had no answers. She couldn't push a word from her tight throat if she tried.

"I hate you," he said, his mouth next to her temple.

Yeah, and she wasn't overly fond of him, either.

"But I ... I can't resist. No fucking self-control."

Whoa! Her pussy spasmed and she nearly came from that tortured confession.

With her free hand, she shoved her fingers into his hair and wrenched his head back, only to take his mouth with force, wedging her tongue between his lips. He bit her lip and growled again, taking control of their kiss, and forcing her to tilt her head the other way.

She ripped her mouth away, pulling in air like she'd just resurfaced from a record-breaking free dive. She needed to keep hold of at least some of her wits. To keep her desire for this man, whom she definitely shouldn't want, from completely drowning her. To remind him that he hated her, and this was a terrible idea.

But still, no words formed on her tongue. The ability to put vowels and consonants together to form words eluded her.

And it wasn't just because she didn't want to be the one to break, it was because even though she knew this was a terrible idea, a colossally disastrous idea, she couldn't stop.

She didn't want to.

Then, he pushed one finger, and another into her channel and pumped. Their cheeks were glued together, sweat forming between their pressed-together skin, as they both panted, his cock throbbing hotly in her palm while she stroked him. He curled his fingers inside of her and she ground down onto his palm, biting her lip and tipping her head back. But he wasn't having any of that, apparently, and pulled his fingers free of her almost fast enough to give her pussy whiplash.

Then she was off the counter and bent over the arm of the couch, ass in the air. She didn't remember leaving her purse in the living room last night, but there it was, right on the floor beside his big, bare feet. He bent down and rifled through it until he found a condom. The sound of the wrapper being ripped open was deafening, and the anticipation of what was to come, agonizing and glorious.

Her legs shook and her pussy pulsed, causing another trickle of arousal to run down her inner thigh.

Once he rolled on the condom and grabbed her hip with one of his big hands, she sighed in relief. Only to realize just how premature that sigh was.

The press of his cock, encased in latex, to her swollen lips, had her moaning and pushing back, opening for him. But he moved his cock head away just enough that he didn't enter.

Did he want her to beg?

Because that wouldn't be happening. She wouldn't give him the satisfaction.

She was a patient woman, and knew he wanted this just as much as she did, she'd wait. She'd torture him in her own way. By *not* giving him what he wanted, which was her crying out for his cock. For him.

Slowly, he dragged the head of his dick up from her soaked pussy, through her crease, and to her anus, then back where she was open and waiting for him.

Over and over again, he dragged the thick head back and forth through her folds, gathering all the natural lube, then pushing against her anus. He never breached her, but he came close.

Her muscles there puckered on instinct each time he pushed, and she had to bite her lip to keep herself from asking him to slide a finger there. To relieve the surmounting pressure and tension that had her close to snapping.

The hand on her hip snaked around her body and between her legs.

With one of his feet, he encouraged her to widen her feet, much the same way cops probably did to felons they had up against a wall or vehicle so they could search them.

She spread her feet wider, and the fingers between her legs opened her pussy lips and two fingers found her clit.

She whimpered when he pinched it, then groaned and rolled her hips when he started to work counterclockwise concentric circles. Behind her, he continued to slide his cock up and down her crease, pressing just a little harder against her anus each time he reached it. She couldn't tell if that was a promise or a threat, but either way, it made her pulse roar in her ears and her lower belly somersault.

She was close, and he hadn't even entered her.

They'd started out frantic and raging at each other like two furious animals in heat, why was he slowing down now? What was with the fucked-up foreplay?

Did hate fucks usually involve foreplay?

Shouldn't he be inside her right now, pounding into her with fury, as words of disdain flew from his lips and painted the room, competing with her whimpers of pleasure?

At least that was how the romance books she read did it. No drawn-out play or sensual touching. Not when the sex was angry.

Or was this psychological torture, too?

Was he going to get her so turned on she begged for it, then turn around and say, "Haha, baby, like I'd ever fuck you again."

A part of her thought she should stop it right then. Save herself embarrassment. Save herself from any prolonged torture.

But she didn't move.

She didn't say stop.

Her inner thighs were slick now, and the scent of her arousal filled the room, along with her whimpers and mewls, which she couldn't control, no matter how hard she bit her lip and tasted blood.

Aiden remained quiet behind her, but more than once, he leaned forward and raked his teeth over her shoulder and up her neck, biting her earlobe and breathing heavily into her ear.

She was close.

They both knew it.

He had brought her there with just his fingers on her clit. Just his cock sliding through her slick folds, hinting at more, but never giving it.

The orgasm hit her hard, and she broke with a harsh, strangled cry, pinching her eyes shut and bowing her back. Her legs widened just a little, but she wasn't sure if it was her own doing, or if Aiden did it with his knee. The waves of pleasure swept her away. The long-awaited release eviscerating the tension that had wound like an unforgiving cord around her muscles, squeezing tighter but never allowing any reprieve.

Her pussy throbbed, and her body trembled as the climax continued to ripple through her. She didn't know when, but Aiden had removed his hand from between her legs. She couldn't feel his cock behind her either. She knew he was still there, behind her, because the soft hair of his thighs tickled the backs of her legs. She could feel his heat, smell his delicious body wash.

Once the orgasm dissipated enough for her faculties to return, she craned her head around, catching his gaze. His top teeth sank into his bottom lip hard enough to make little white marks form on the otherwise red flesh. He had his cock in his hand and was stroking it slowly.

The words, "Fuck me," sat eagerly on her tongue. But she refused to let them fly.

She would not ask him for anything. Ever.

If he wanted her, he had to make the move. She'd already gotten off, in her head, she was the winner of this sick little game. Could she get off again? Yes. Did she want to? Of course. Did she want to get off with a cock inside her? One hundred-percent.

But she would get up, get dressed, and walk away from him with little regret if he made her beg. If he made her ask him. He knew she was consenting, that wasn't the issue here. Her ass was literally in the air, what more did he want?

Reaching forward with the hand that had been on her clit, he grabbed her braid, his other hand was still holding his cock.

Their eyes remained locked as he ran the crown up and down between her folds again, pausing at her anus and giving an even harder push. He still didn't breach, but the way his mouth curled up on one side into an off-kilter smirk, said he wanted to. Said he was testing her.

She'd had anal sex before, but only with someone she really trusted and after they'd been together for a while. Aiden was neither of those things.

She tipped her hips so he got the message, and he slid his cock further below her to her pussy.

When his crown reached her opening again, his eyelids slid down even further, until he looked almost sleepy. But she knew otherwise, then he tilted his pelvis forward and he was inside her.

Finally.

Filling her up.

The stretch that instantly followed had her moaning and pushing backward to take more of him. But the harsh and sudden yank on her hair made her yelp. She hadn't realized she'd glanced forward again.

"Eyes on me," he barked, pistoning in and out of her, the hand that had held his cock, now on her hip, the fingers digging in almost to the point of pain.

He tugged on her hair again.

She liked it.

Liked the burn of pain on her scalp. The rough, forcefulness of his demand. Of his need for her.

She was soaking his cock now, the wet, squelching sound of him entering her, then receding, echoed around the room. He used her braid as a tether, to pull himself deeper into her, to control her, and keep her head craned around and looking at him.

The feral, lustful look in his eyes made her squeeze her muscles around him, had her wishing for a hand to wedge between her legs. But the sheer force of his thrusts required her to have both elbows on the couch for support.

He wasn't messing around now.

His fucking was rough and angry and she wanted all of it.

The way he bared his teeth and glared at her. Confliction in his gaze. Hate and want blurring into one, penetrating, soul-shattering look that she felt all the way down to her toes.

If he was any other person, and this was any other circumstance, she'd consider asking him to spank her. Or, they would have discussed that bit of play ahead of time. She wasn't deep into BDSM, but she dabbled. She liked being tied up, like being spanked, a little choking now and then, orgasm deprivation could be fun when there was edging involved, and of course, she loved being called a good girl.

But just like with anal sex, that would not be happening with Aiden.

He was not that person. This was not that kind of sex.

She didn't trust him. They had no safe word, and more importantly, they couldn't stand each other.

This was one last bang to get the tension out of their system so they could be around each other without issues for their siblings' wedding.

One and done.

She could do that.

She did like the hair pulling. That he could do more of. That he could do all day long.

He probably thought he was being an even bigger asshole by pulling her hair. But what he failed to realize was that what was turning him on was also turning her on. She liked the pain. She liked submitting in the bedroom and being told what to do.

Her life was so controlled and organized all the time, it was a welcomed change and release to hand that control over to someone else for a while.

She moaned and pushed back, dropping her belly lower to the arm of the couch, which caused her ass to push up higher. His cock twitched and thickened inside her from the sudden change of angle, which allowed him to go even deeper.

She had to fight back her grin since he was still making her face him, still making her watch him fuck her. And she could tell that he was getting close.

He was unraveling and she was excited to watch.

"Touch yourself," he barked, his gaze dropping to her mouth.

She tried to move her hand between her legs, but he hadn't let up with the force of his thrusting, and she fell forward onto the arm of the couch with an "*Oof*."

Using her hair, he yanked her back up until she was fully standing. She had to go onto her tiptoes for his cock to remain inside of her.

He continued to use her hair like a leash and guided her around the couch, having slipped out of her in the process. She climbed up onto the longer part of the sectional and onto her knees. He followed, also on his knees, then pulled her down onto his lap so they were both still facing the same way. He slid back inside her with ease.

Grabbing several throw pillows, he stacked them in front of her, then pushed a hand between her shoulder blades so she hinged forward, her belly landing on the pillows.

He sat up on his knees, and still hanging onto her braid with one hand, he wrapped the other hand below her again to find her clit.

His thrusts grew harsh and punishing once again as he yanked on her hair and strummed her clit with his thumb, causing her lower belly to become a vortex of heat and need.

He tried to get her to look at him again by yanking on her hair, but the angle had changed and her cheek was pressed into the couch. She couldn't turn her head that much, but she was able to glance up at him, taking in his wild expression out of the corner of her eye.

Every drive forward of his hips, had her seeing more and more stars. Pushed her closer and closer to sweet release. Skin slapping skin co-mingled with their heavy breathing to create a filthy soundtrack to their hate-filled lust.

Finally, he let go of her hair and brought that hand on top of her ass, the thumb pressing against her anus. She puckered, but then—against her earlier convictions—pushed out. He slid his thumb inside, and she detonated.

Bigger than the first orgasm, this one atomized her entire body. Made her limbs go stiff and her body shake, as if she'd just stuck a fork in an outlet, as the bliss traveled out of her center. Like ripples on a pond after you throw in a stone. Giant white stars burst behind her closed eyes and her clit pulsed like it had a heartbeat of its own beneath Aiden's thumb.

She barely registered that he went still behind her, paused his efforts with his thumb, grunted and started to come.

She was still flying high around her own summit, as he breathed heavily behind her, his cock twitching against her pulsing walls.

She reached Earth roughly the same time he did, her chest heaving, limbs gelatinous and body thrumming.

Vaguely aware of the fact that this was her sister's couch and *not* a bed, she was careful not to get any bodily fluids on the cushions or pillows.

Aiden stood up behind her, and that's when she remembered he had a condom.

That would help, but she was still a leaky fucking faucet and would need to make sure she didn't make a mess of her sister's stuff.

He walked to the bathroom to dispose of the condom, and she extricated herself from the couch, checking the pillows for wet spots.

Phew. There weren't any.

Then, still naked, she went about finding an air freshener spray of some sort. She found some orange-scented antibacterial Febreze under the kitchen sink, and gave the couch and pillows a healthy douse. Then she wiped the counter with Lysol.

Neither she nor Aiden had said a word to each other. But when she turned around after throwing the paper towel with Lysol on it into trash, he was rummaging around in his duffle bag and gathering clothes.

She couldn't pinpoint why that bothered her so much, but it did.

Something to unpack with Teal when she got home, perhaps.

Standing there, still naked, she plunked her hands on her hips and stared at the wide expanse of his bare back right before he tugged a black T-shirt over it. He was already in boxers and slid effortlessly into a pair of dark-wash jeans that made his ass look delectable.

Only when he spun around and sat down on the square black leather ottoman that matched the recliner, and also served as a coffee table to put on his socks, did he notice her standing there.

He snorted and cocked a half-smile that had her seeing red. "You want to go again?"

"No."

One of his shoulder's lifted.

"That *can't* happen again," she said, the words tasting foul on her tongue.

"Believe me, it won't."

Why did that sting?

He finished pulling on his socks, then stood up, his gaze on her breasts and he wasn't hiding that that was where he was looking. "Can I help you?"

"You have absolutely nothing to say after ..." she pointed to the couch, "what just happened?"

He wrinkled his nose and glanced to where she pointed. "What the fuck *should* I say?"

"I don't know? Maybe ..."

But she was at a loss for words. What was she expecting him to say? What would make the anger burning in her heart cool off? What words could be the balm to soothe the sting?

He lifted his brows. "When you think of them, be sure to let me know. Then I'll be happy to say them." Sarcasm dripped from each syllable.

Then, before she could scream, he slouched into his coat, slid into his shoes and was back out the front door, leaving her standing there, naked, furious, and seriously contemplating murder.

Chapter Ten

Oh yeah, he was an asshole.

A big one.

And he had absolutely no idea where the fuck he was going, he just knew he couldn't be in that apartment for another second with Oona. Otherwise, he was going to say things he would surely regret and definitely fuck her again.

But it was the saying things part that really scared him.

She made him want to open up.

Which was probably why she was such a highly regarded therapist. She manipulated people into trusting her so they would tell her their deepest, darkest secrets.

He didn't want to be any more vulnerable around her than he already was. Because truth be told, he was at his most vulnerable, at his absolute weakest when he was with her.

She knew all his dirty secrets. Had read his file and knew why he needed therapy and anger management. And then she wasn't even treating him. So now *another* person was going to read his file and learn how he'd failed. Learn how he continued to fail. How he let his emotions get the better of him and his past haunt his present and damage his future.

But she was like a drug.

Bad for him in every way, but so fucking addictive, he craved her to the point of obsession. To the point, where, if he thought about her too hard, about their first night together in the hotel, he started to get the shakes.

Or at least that's how it felt.

And now he'd had her again.

Not a smart move.

There's a reason dealers give you the first hit for free. It's to get you hooked. But what they don't tell you is that the second hit is the one that makes you really feel alive.

And holy fucking shit, did Oona ever make him feel alive.

The way he fit inside her so perfectly—like her cunt was made for him. The noises she made, the way she moaned when he pulled her hair, pushed her ass in the air and welcomed his thumb ... He could tell she wasn't an anal sex virgin. And based on her personality and the way she gasped and crooned from any kind of pain, told him she probably liked to be spanked. Maybe even choked.

As he stalked down the sidewalk, his hands shoved deep into his coat pockets, he reflected on everything that had transpired between them in the house.

What she'd said to him. Calling him out the way she did.

She was right.

Completely and utterly right. And being called self-absorbed stung like a basketball to the face.

The reason he got in to see Astrid Kramer had to be because Oona had made a phone call. Pulled some strings or called in a favor. And yet, the idea of thanking her sat jagged and awkward in his craw. Like a popcorn kernel stuck between your teeth.

He had no idea what was in his file. How much the HR person at the station sent to his therapist ahead of time. Did Oona know about Dallas? Did she know about his and Jordan's dad and mom?

Did Rayma know?

When Jordan brought up Dallas last night, the hot pokers of dread began to burn in his gut. He thought about Dallas all the time, but hadn't spoken about him in years.

And the fact that Jordan still saw him, still heard him, too, it was both comforting to know that Aiden wasn't alone seeing a ghost, but it also made him feel like total shit that his brother was still dealing with the consequences of their actions over a decade later, too.

Aiden was the older brother, it was his job to protect Jordan. It was his job to keep Jordan safe.

And he'd failed.

He'd failed his brother, he'd failed his family and he failed Dallas.

The small shopping complex where they grabbed the pizza last night was only a short fifteen-minute walk and it boasted a bunch of different retailers. A drug store, a grocery store, an optometrist and even a Starbucks.

His brain hurt from lack of caffeine, so he headed into the Starbucks and ordered himself a venti black with two shots of espresso. He liked his coffee like he liked himself—tall and bitter.

Not that he liked himself bitter, he just was, so he accepted it.

A seat became available at the window bar and he took it, bringing up his phone and scrolling through the news while his brain righted itself on its axis now that the coffee beans were doing their job.

His belly grumbled after about twenty minutes, so he ordered a sandwich using the Starbucks app on his phone, so that he didn't lose his seat.

Jordan mentioned that he needed to work today, but Aiden hadn't really thought about what that would mean. What it meant, though, was that Aiden was trapped at Jordan's house with Oona.

A woman he wanted.

A woman who grated on every one of his last nerves and pushed him to push all her buttons.

Fuck, this was all so fucked up.

He closed his eyes, but that only made him picture her naked, bent over the arm of the couch, ass in the air, the hummingbird tattoo on her shoulder blade mocking him.

He opened his eyes, blinking them several times to dislodge the images of her from his brain. To scrape his mind clean of the vexing, irritating, split-personality Oona.

Fucking her this morning had been a huge mistake, but when she called him self-absorbed, when she taunted him with her head shakes and laughs, his brain became one-track. The way she looked at him like he was an idiot for only thinking of himself burned sharp, like a lance to the sternum.

But what hurt more than anything, was that she was right.

He was behaving and thinking selfishly. He thought only of himself and his own needs. His own career, his own problems.

The guilt weighed him down until he had a hard time putting weight on his feet to put his trash in the bin. He was a little wobbly, but tried not to let it show.

He'd been gone from the house for nearly two hours, and it still wasn't even lunchtime yet. What the hell was he going to do?

There was no text or voicemail from Jordan, so he caught the next bus that passed by and took it wherever it was headed.

He needed to stay out of the house, at least until he knew Oona was gone. Which he soon realized, he had no way of knowing.

A thick gray blanket of clouds hung over the city, but the wind was minimal and it wasn't raining or snowing. He found himself down in the inner harbor where the parliament building stood tall and colonial along the edge of a big bay full of boats moored at a dock, and seaplanes that were buzzing in and out.

No matter where he walked, he could hear the faint tinkle of a Christmas song. It wasn't necessarily the same Christmas song, but eventually they all sounded the same.

He was just going to give the happy couple cash for a wedding gift, but it was still Christmas, so he probably needed to get Jordan and Rayma some kind of gift, too.

Only problem was: he didn't really know either of them, or what they liked.

Besides fucking pineapples, apparently. And they had enough of those.

Great.

Making his way up Government Street, an area of town that reminded him of an old British town with its cobblestones, brick buildings and ornate street lamps, he glanced into various shops. They all had their window displays decorated for the holiday in one fashion or another. Some had painted glass, with Santa Claus and reindeer, or snowmen and trees, while others just used what they had in the shop, along with some red baubles and garland to make it look festive.

He stopped in front of a hemp store. The window display was eye-catching but not gaudy. It had a couple of mannequins decked out in winter gear. Nice looking toques, scarves and sweaters. There was lumpy fake snow on the floor of the display, and a red and black plaid blanket hung behind the mannequins as a background. You got that it was meant to be wintery and Christmas, but it wasn't obnoxious like a loaf of fruitcake to the face.

He heaved on the door, welcomed by the jingle bell overhead, and stepped inside.

The warmth of the space was inviting and he exhaled in relief. His shoulders also left his ears. He hadn't realized they'd been hanging out there until the tension fled from his upper back.

A young guy in a dark orange toque greeted him, but didn't hover.

Aiden liked that.

He figured a toque for Rayma and Jordan each would probably be a safe gift to get. Who didn't love a snazzy new toque that didn't itch? He had one on his head at that very moment, however, his wasn't organic hemp and as soft as a baby rabbit.

He grabbed matching his and hers toques for Rayma and Jordan in light gray, then a black one for himself. He was just heading up to the cash register when he passed a copper-colored scarf draped around another mannequin's neck. For some reason, the color reminded him of one of the shades of gold in Oona's eyes. He unraveled it from the mannequin and added it to the pile, not really thinking about why he was doing it. He'd probably just end up giving it to Rayma. She had similar eyes, though they did seem to have less gold in them than Oona's.

As he was handing over his credit card, he spied a basket of warm-looking hemp gloves. Again, there was a pair that matched the scarf.

Still, not totally thinking—or at least not reading into his actions too much—he tossed the pair onto the pile, then grabbed two more pairs for Rayma and Jordan.

He left the store with his paper bag and a weird sense of calm. Just as he was passing by a shop with a window full of different fudge flavors and contemplating getting a chunk of the orange creamsicle flavor, his phone buzzed in his pocket.

It was Jordan.

It was still weird seeing his brother's name pop up on his caller ID. The first time it happened a few months ago, when Jordan called to invite him to the wedding, Aiden had let it go to voicemail. He had no idea what to say to Jordan and was in a bad head-space when his brother called.

But Jordan left a brief voicemail, telling Aiden he was getting married and to call him back.

It took Aiden three days to work up the courage to do it.

"Hey," he answered, putting the phone to his ear.

"Hey, where are you?"

"Downtown. Took the bus, why?"

"Just checking in. I'll be off at six, thought we could ... I dunno, grab dinner together or something. Rayma is going to be off with her sisters doing who knows what, so I thought it'd be a nice opportunity for us to ..." he cleared his throat, "bond or whatever."

Abandoning the idea of fudge, Aiden continued to walk, that's when he spied a sandwich board and an arrow pointing around the corner. His mouth split into a big grin. "I know exactly what we can do tonight."

"Axe throwing?" Jordan asked as he parked his truck next to a meter later that night.

"I've never done it, have you?" Aiden asked.

Jordan shook his head.

They'd stopped off at Subway and grabbed a couple of foot-longs, then made their way downtown to the axe throwing place Aiden had noticed earlier that day. He'd followed the sandwich board after he ended his call with Jordan, then went inside, chatted with the guys behind the desk, and booked them each an hour of axe throwing and an hour of knife throwing.

He'd kept his plan secret from his brother and only when they pulled up to the curb, did he finally reveal his plan. He couldn't tell if Jordan was excited or not, though.

He really didn't know his brother at all.

"This feels like something Rayma would be really into," Jordan murmured, taking his sandwich off the bench seat and bringing it with him as he exited the driver's side.

Aiden grabbed his own sandwich and joined his brother on the sidewalk. "Really? Is your fiancée violent?"

Jordan snorted and cast his brother a side-eye. "Not *violent*, but mayhem does seem to follow her around like a lost puppy." He smiled as he thought about his bride. "I took her to the gun range when we first started dating, but she showed me. She'd been going for a while before that. Pasha and her husband were adamant that she learned self-defense and how to handle and shoot a gun. But she's always been ballsy and I feel like she'd be into this."

"Can always bring her another time for a date." Aiden held the door open for his brother and they stepped inside. The *clunk* of metal embedding into wood greeted them, along with the raucous laughter and cheers of participants.

The same guy from earlier that day was behind the desk and greeted Aiden with a familiar smile.

Then they got set up.

"How much time did you get off to come out here?" Jordan asked, putting his foot on the line and giving the axe a couple of practice swings as he lined up his target.

Aiden hadn't told Jordan that he was suspended. He hadn't told many people. Not that he had an overly big friend circle to begin with. It was mostly other cops that he hung out with, and although they hadn't left him to the wolves, he was learning who his true friends were based on who reached out since his suspension, and who stayed silent.

"Enough," Aiden said, sipping his water.

The desire to ask Jordan how his day was burned hot on the back of his tongue. He wanted to know. He wanted to put himself in his brother's shoes, in his uniform and feel what he felt. He missed it. He missed his job, his life as a cop. But he didn't ask. Because as badly as he wanted to know how Jordan's day was, he also didn't. He didn't want the sour taste of envy to taint their time together.

But Jordan was oblivious. "Got a fucked-up call today, man," Jordan breathed out before adjusting his stance a little, then he let the axe fly. It had a weird spin on it, the blunt part hit the wood, then it fell to the ground. "Shit."

Aiden stepped up to the line and decided to do a two-handed throw rather than Jordan's one-handed throw. He lifted it over his head, holding it like a golf club, with his thumbs aligned on the handle, then let it fly at eye level. It sailed through the air and struck the board, embedding in the upper right corner. It didn't even touch the bullseye.

"Better than me," Jordan said. "I didn't even get it to stick."

Aiden merely grunted and retrieved his axe.

Jordan got back up to the line, deciding to go with the two-handed throw, as well. "I hate being a cop this time of year. People go crazy."

Aiden grunted again. Yep, they sure did. As much as he missed working, he was kind of glad to be off over Christmas. People did go crazy. Lots of drinking, lots of families getting together who shouldn't, people desperate for money, and of course, people who shouldn't be driving on the road in either a vehicle not prepared for the weather, or alcohol in their system—or both.

His curiosity used his fear of envy as a punching bag and he muttered a, "What happened?" Just as Jordan threw the axe with both hands. This time it made contact with the board and stuck. And it was well within the bullseye, too.

Aiden's competitive side was waking up.

Now that Jordan had made it into the bullseye, Aiden had to, too. He got up from his seat and picked up an axe.

"Oh, it was just triggering. Kid got struck on the side of the road today."

Aiden dropped the axe onto his foot.

Motherfucker, that hurt more than he thought it would.

"Shit," Jordan said, his eyes going wide. "You okay?"

Aiden grunted, grit his teeth and nodded. "Yeah, it was the blunt end." He tapped his foot. "Still have all my toes."

Understanding dawned in Jordan's eyes. "I should have warned you. I'm sorry. I ... I've been talking with a therapist and it's helped me work through all that shit, you know? I'm still triggered, still see Dallas, but it doesn't affect me the way it used to." He made a dismissive noise in his throat. "Should have talked to someone about it a long time ago, but you know, that Lassiter ego is strong."

Aiden grunted and picked up his axe. "It is." He gripped the handle with both hands and heaved the thing toward the bullseye.

It stuck again, and it was closer to the center of the bullseye than Jordan's. "The kid okay?" he asked, walking forward to unstick his axe.

Jordan nodded. "Won't be having much fun this Christmas—two broken legs—but he's alive. His cat got out—an indoor cat—and he took off after it. Wasn't even looking at traffic, was just too concerned for his pet. Nine years old. Thank God it wasn't a busy road, and the person that hit him was only going fifty."

"Person sober?" Aiden asked. He had to ask.

Jordan nodded. "Yeah. It was at like ten this morning. A mom heading out to do some last-minute Christmas shopping. Her kids were with the sitter. She sneezed and that was all it took not to see the kid on the road."

"Fuck," Aiden groaned.

"She's devastated, of course. Was barely consolable. Ended up having to sedate her, she was losing her shit so bad."

That had probably also been pretty triggering for Jordan to witness, since they'd both been there when the news of Dallas's death was broke to his mom. She'd collapsed to her knees and sobbed, screamed and raged unlike any person Aiden had ever witnessed before. Mind you, he'd just been a teenager then, not a cop, so he hadn't seen much in the way of breakdowns yet. But that had been his first and it stuck with him.

"Family pressing charges?" he asked.

Jordan shook his head. "Don't think so. It was all an accident. Security footage from a neighbor's yard saw her sneeze and close her eyes, just as the kid stepped in front of the car. Total accident. No fault."

"Doesn't mean they're all not going to suffer."

Jordan threw his axe again. It landed even closer to the center than Aiden's had. "Nope. But at least the kid survived and the collateral damage seems minimal."

"Yeah, at least." Unlike the collateral damage that Dallas's death had caused. And Dallas's death could have been prevented. Jordan and Aiden had *tried* to prevent it from happening. But they clearly hadn't tried hard enough.

They took a break to eat their subs, then resumed throwing.

"You ever talk to anybody?" Jordan asked, having decided after their dinner break that he was only going to throw with one hand.

"What do you mean?" Aiden asked, scrunching up his wrapper and napkin and tossing them into the trash.

"About Dallas. About Dad and all that shit that went down. I was pretty messed up for a long time, took losing Rayma to finally get me to see that I needed to talk to a pro."

Aiden swallowed. "I uh ... I'm 'sposed to start seeing someone when I get back. Long waitlists and shit."

Jordan nodded and retrieved his axe from the board. "Yeah, I know. I'm lucky that Joy—who you'll meet—is a licensed therapist. Specializes in family and sexuality, mind you, but she knows her way around PTSD and grief counseling, too. Her first husband was a cop, so she gets it."

All Aiden could do was grunt. Talking about Dallas and their parents was the last thing he wanted to do right now. But he could tell that it was eating away at the stress Jordan carried for them to discuss it. To get out in the open the wedge that had destroyed their family and the talk about the grief and regret that he and Jordan shared and had ultimately driven them apart.

Did he tell his brother that he was suspended because of anger? That he'd punched a guy he pulled over because he'd been drunk and had his kid in the car? How would Jordan react? What would he think? Maybe he wouldn't want someone so volatile in his house around his fiancée. Maybe he wouldn't want someone with anger issues in his life at all.

Jordan seemed to be in a way better place than Aiden. He was talking through his issues with someone, he had his job, he had a family and was about to get married. He had picked himself up after losing their family and built himself something to be proud of.

What the fuck had Aiden done? Not much besides become a cop.

But he had no relationship, no *family* and at the moment, no job. All he had to keep him warm at night was his anger, and that wasn't the most comforting or understanding of bedmates.

Their hour was up before they knew it. Next came the knife throwing, but Aiden was tired and asked Jordan if he minded if they rescheduled. Jordan seemed disappointed, but he agreed and drove them home.

They were almost at the front door when Jordan rested a hand on Aiden's shoulder and had him stand still for a sec. "I can give Joy a call and see if she can squeeze you in," Jordan offered. "If you're itching to talk to someone?" His smile was lopsided and small. Hopeful, but also wary.

Aiden made a noise in his throat. "Thanks, but I think I can wait until I get back."

All Jordan did was nod. "Thanks for the subs and the axe throwing, that was fun."

"Yeah, no worries. Sorry about the axe throwing, I didn't sleep great."

"Is the couch uncomfortable?"

"No ..." But his hard cock the entire night because of the sexy pain in the ass in the other room was sure uncomfortable. Just because he got his rocks off this morning, didn't mean he wasn't going to endure the same bullshit tonight. He already knew he would. Oona infuriated him as much as she turned him on. And she really fucking turned him on. "Just new house, new bed, time change, all that shit. I'm sure I'll be better tonight."

They entered the apartment, once again to the roaring laughter of two women sitting on the couch. This time Oona had a stemless glass of red wine and was holding it on her knee as she sat cross-legged on the couch facing Rayma. He could tell by the flush to her cheeks and the fact that the glass was nearly empty, that she'd imbibed this time.

Her smile fell and her gaze narrowed to nearly slits when they walked in.

Rayma jumped up from the couch and rushed Jordan, throwing her arms around his neck and giving him a kiss. "Missed you, Little Lassie. How was your day?"

Jordan grumbled at her new nickname for him, but his annoyance seemed put on as he wrapped his arms around her and kissed her back. "Not great, not terrible. Nobody died, so I'll take it for the win it is."

"Do a lot of people die here?" Oona asked, getting up from the couch and joining them in the kitchen.

Jordan shook his head. "No, so I have more good days than bad."

Oona's smile was small as she nodded.

Rayma turned to Aiden. "And how was your day, Big Lassie?"

Aiden snorted from his new nickname and cast a teasing glance Jordan's way. "Hopped on the bus and explored downtown. Seems like a nice place to live. Lot of homeless people, though."

Rayma pouted and nodded. "Yeah, it's gotten really bad. I feel for them." Then her brows shot up nearly to her hairline. "Well, we had a great day at the dress fittings. Didn't we, Oons?" She released Jordan and turned to acknowledge her sister.

"Yeah, Rayma has graciously chosen dresses that make us all look good. Nothing froofy or hideous."

Rayma scoffed. "Like I'd ever *dream* of having something like that in my wedding photos. I want everyone to be hot." She snapped. "Which reminds me, Little Lassie," she turned to Aiden, "Big Lassie, you're scheduled to go for your fitting tomorrow night after Little Lassie gets off work. He's going to wear his blue serge uniform. Jace, too. And we weren't sure if you'd say yes to being a best man or not, so we ordered a set of blues for you, too."

"I really wish you'd just go back to *Lassie*," Jordan said. "The *Little* part is a bit emasculating."

"Don't mind my new nickname," Aiden said with a chuckle.

127

Movement to his right made him pivot his head. Oona fidgeted next to the island, twisting a couple of rings around her fingers and contorting her mouth so her lips puckered and moved side to side across her face.

"How was axe throwing?" Rayma asked, switching gears faster than a Formula One driver.

"Really fun," Jordan replied. "I think you'd like it."

"Well, we'll have to go sometime."

Aiden yawned, which set off a stream of yawns among all of them. The couch hadn't actually been uncomfortable at all, but his lack of sleep last night had him exhausted now. However, since he was sleeping in the living room, he had to wait until the rest of the house was ready to retire before he could.

"I'm gonna hit the hay," Jordan said. "Gotta be up early."

"I hear The Penguin and The Riddler are hatching a new scheme," Rayma said. "And only Sergeant Little Lassie can save the day."

Jordan rolled his eyes. "You coming to bed, Brat?"

She nodded. "Yeah, I think so." Her brown gaze swiveled to Oona. "Do you mind?"

Oona shook her head. "Not at all. I'm pretty beat, too."

The sisters hugged, then Rayma and Jordan retired to their room, shutting the door, leaving Oona and Aiden alone in the rest of the apartment. Without really realizing it, his gaze swung to the couch where they'd ... *been* that morning.

Her eyes tracked his and they both stood there, staring at the spot where he'd fucked her over a mound of pillows and stuck his thumb in her ass.

Heat filled his cheeks and his pulse picked up speed.

He wanted to swing his gaze to hers, but also knew it was probably a really bad idea.

He showered that morning after his run and planned to go for another run tomorrow, if the weather cooperated, so he didn't need to shower again. Continuing to avoid looking at the woman who he couldn't stop thinking about, he walked over to the couch and unfolded it. He knew Oona disappeared into her bedroom and was grateful for it.

When she wasn't around, he could breathe. He could think clearly and his cock wasn't nearly as confused.

He finished making the bed, then was in the middle of yanking off his pants—his shirt already off—when a bedroom door opened. He knew it was the guest room door, because it made a slight creak, whereas Jordan and Rayma's door didn't.

He could have just ignored her, could have just gone about his business, continuing to get ready for bed, but he didn't. He stepped to the side to see her, with her towel and pajamas, head into the bathroom. But before she closed the door, a cry from behind Rayma and Jordan's door made her pause and open the bathroom door again.

She knew what kind of a cry that was.

He knew what kind of a cry that was.

Another one. Followed by an, "Oh God, Lassie, harder."

Oona's mouth opened and her cheeks turned pink. Then her eyes flashed up to his.

He held her gaze for several long, agonizing heartbeats, then followed the roll of her throat as she swallowed, the dart of her tongue as she licked the seam of her lips.

His cock twitched and that's when he remembered he was no longer in his jeans, but his tight navy-blue boxer briefs. Her eyes fell to the front of his boxers and he could see her breathing heavily as her nostrils flared and pupils dilated.

A manly grunt from the bedroom fell heavily between them.

He thought about rushing her. About shoving her into the bathroom and taking her in the shower, but before he could act on that terrible idea, she squeezed her eyes shut, blinked them open, shook her head, then disappeared into the bathroom, closing *and locking* the door behind her.

Aiden exhaled a deep breath and dropped his chin to his chest.

At least one of them was making the right decision this time.

Too bad it was the one that left his cock hard and angry with him for the rest of the night.

Chapter Eleven

She was in and out of the shower and bathroom lickity split this time, making sure she sent the right message to Aiden. That she didn't want to see him, let alone stand awkwardly in the hallway, listening to their siblings having sex while he got an erection.

She disappeared into her room and stayed there. Of course, she heard him use the bathroom to brush his teeth and whatever, but he didn't have a shower, so she was safe—sort of—from picturing his soapy, naked body just beyond the drywall.

It was roughly three o'clock in the morning on Thursday—according to her phone—when she woke up needing to pee. Normally, she never woke up in the middle of the night, but she'd had one and half glasses of wine with Rayma and any time she had alcohol, she had to pee during the middle of the night.

Groggily, and still mostly asleep, she swung her legs over the side of the bed and carefully opened her bedroom door, grateful that it didn't creak this time. The last thing she needed was Aiden's wrath for waking him up because she didn't want to pee the bed.

The wood floor was cold beneath her bare feet and a chill swept up the length of her spine from her toes to the nape of her neck, making her shiver. She was in flannel pajama pants and a black tank top. And for half a second, she thought about ducking back into her room and grabbing a hoodie. But she ignored the chill and pressed on.

Curiosity competed with the need to pee and she considered checking on Aiden in the living room, but then she talked some sense into her half-asleep self, and just opened the bathroom door.

And what she found inside was Aiden standing over the toilet, yanking it. In the dark. His eyes closed, mouth open as his hand slid over his shaft from base to crown and back.

"What the—" She closed the door quickly.

"Would it kill you to knock?" he barked, not quietly.

She opened the door again and he was just pulling up his sweatpants. "Would it kill you to *lock the door*? What the hell?"

Rayma and Jordan's bedroom door opened and two very sleepy-looking people gazed back at them, their eyes thin slits, hair all wonky.

"Everything okay?" Jordan asked, rubbing his green eyes, pillow marks criss-crossing one side of his face like he'd been attacked by a dog.

Oona's chest rose and fell quickly and she cast a harsh glare toward Aiden.

"Your sister needs to learn how to knock," Aiden grumbled, directing his words to Rayma.

"It's the middle of the night, the light was off," Oona protested. "And if you're going to ..."

Aiden gave her a warning look.

"If you're going to *pee,* when you share a bathroom with a stranger, the smart thing to do is lock the door. I didn't want to knock because I didn't want to wake anyone up." She rested her hands on her hips and Aiden's gaze fell to the thin strip of skin exposed between her tank top and pajama pants. She hastily tugged down her shirt so it met her waistband.

"Dude," Jordan said, scratching the back of his neck. "Lock the door, okay?" He turned around and headed back into their bedroom

Aiden grunted, then washed his hands.

A gentle, barely noticeable tap to Oona's shoulder had her spinning to face her sister. Rayma had one brow up and her lips twisted. "He wasn't peeing, was he?"

Oona took a deep breath and pushed it out in a quick *whoosh*, then dropped her voice low. "I try not to overly familiarize myself with the idiosyncrasies of a man's time in the bathroom. He could have been painting you a picture as a wedding gift with his dick for all I know or care."

Rayma snorted. "There are a couple dudes who do paint with their cocks. Saw it live when I went to Taboo in Vancouver last year. It was wild. He probably has callouses on his dick if he was doing that."

Oona could without a doubt verify that Aiden did *not* have callouses on his dick, but she wasn't about to divulge that to her sister. She blinked and shook her head. "I just need to pee, then I want to go back to bed."

Aiden walked into the living room, but she could still feel the heat of his stare burning into her back like the summer sun at high noon from where she stood in the hallway with her sister.

Rayma gave her a small, cheeky smile, squeezed her arm, then retreated to her bedroom, closing the door behind her.

She knew better than to poke the bear, but call it delirium, disbelief, or inconvenient desire, because despite all the reasons she shouldn't, she walked into the living room, her hands still on her hips and cast a menacing, confused glare at the man getting himself comfortable on the pull-out. "Seriously?"

"What?"

"You ... you're ... look, I know masturbation is totally healthy and normal, but ... why couldn't you do it in the shower, or lock the freaking door at least?"

Unless ...

No, that was impossible. He didn't leave the door unlocked with the *hopes* of her walking in on him. He wasn't that deranged, was he?

Yes, what she'd walked in on was hot and had immediately caused a flush of heat to crawl up her neck and pool between her legs, but still.

The living room was dark, so it was tough to see his eyes. She liked their greenness and how, when he was angry or aroused, they turned a darker shade. Like the color of cedar boughs. Otherwise, they were more of a grass-green with veins of brown meandering outward from the pupil. But she couldn't see any of that right now. Just the scowl on his face and the narrowing of his thick brows. "It was an accident."

He was shirtless, and even though she'd seen him a lot more naked than that, her heart rate spiked and a lump lodged in her throat when she let her gaze roam across the valleys and contours of his torso, and arms as he sat there on the pullout bed, sheets tangled around his legs, staring at her.

"Can I help you with something else?" His tone was dry and bored-sounding. "Or were you going to help *me*, seeing as your interruption kept me from finishing." He smirked.

Her eyes went wide and she growled, stomped her foot, bunched her fists, and spun on her heel, stalking off to the bathroom. "You are a pig."

"Remember to knock next time, fuckyouverymuch," he called out after her just as she closed the bathroom door.

She wanted to scream. The man was ...

The man was impossible.

Impossibly handsome.

Impossibly sexy.

Impossibly good in bed.

Impossibly infuriating.

Impossibly arrogant.

Impossibly hurtful.

Impossibly hard to resist and get out of her head.

She splashed cold water on her face after she finally relieved herself, but that did very little to cool her off.

Sleep eluded her after that.

She tossed and turned for hours, tuning into the light sounds of the house, sure that Aiden was going to get up again and finish the job in the bathroom.

So what if he does?

A big part of her thought that if he did, she'd get up and help him out. But an even bigger part of her said that was a terrible idea and she would need a frontal lobotomy if she actually went through with it.

She never heard him get up. So she never got up.

All for the better.

Even though she didn't feel rested at all, she must have fallen back to sleep at some point, because she woke with a start around seven-thirty, where she found yet another puddle in her panties. But at least this time she couldn't remember her dirty dream, so if anybody asked—not that anybody would—she'd had a filthy, satisfying dream about Scott Eastwood *NOT* Aiden Lassiter.

Dead on her feet, she schlepped her way out of her room and into the living room. The only person there was Rayma. She was dressed in professional casual clothing; gray slacks and a cotton button-up shirt the color of a candy apple. Her hair was pulled back into a ponytail and curtain bangs framed her face. She looked so ... grown up.

"'Mornin', sunshine," Rayma said with a grin, pouring herself a cup of coffee from the French press. "You get any sleep last night? Or were you too riled up from the pop-up show you walked in on in the bathroom?"

Oona groaned and took a seat at the island on one of the bar stools. "Where is he?"

"Who? Aiden?"

Oona nodded.

"Out for a run. He left about ten minutes ago."

Even though Oona had no idea how long Aiden's run would last, she allowed her shoulders to leave her ears and she leaned forward and rested her head on the cool granite countertop.

"Okay, what the hell is going on?" Rayma asked, the sound of the electric kettle whirring behind her. She'd gone out and bought Oona's favorite stash brand, double bergamot Earl Grey tea, which was so thoughtful. And now, she was brewing her a cup. Rayma really was such a grown up now. So thoughtful. So put-together and organized.

All her sisters were.

Even though Oona had a PhD and was a successful therapist, hanging out with her sisters yesterday—who were all happy and in love—just reconfirmed that Oona was the one with her life in the most amount of disarray. She felt like an unlovable, broken mess compared to her sisters.

"Oons!" Rayma said louder, snapping Oona out of her self-deprecating fog. "What is going on?"

Oona lifted her head and blinked a few times. "What do you mean?"

"Between you and Aiden. *Did* something happen? Is he being an asshole?"

Yes. An enormous, gaping, shit-filled asshole, to be precise.

"Um ... no. It's just ... it's weird. Knowing that you're trying to set us up, and I just ... we're very different people. I don't think it's going to work out. He's a jerk."

"Okay ..." Rayma said with an upward inflection to her tone. "Then just be friendly. You don't *have* to cram your genitals together just because I want you to."

Oona groaned and rolled her eyes. "There are about a billion different ways for you to describe what you just said, that would be far less graphic or vulgar."

Rayma snorted. "Yeah, but none of them would make you make *that* face." The kettle beeped and Rayma went about making Oona her tea just the way she liked it. She also had fresh muffins on the counter, popped one in the microwave for fifteen seconds, then passed it to Oona with the butter dish. "Because I know you get an upset stomach if you drink black tea on an empty stomach."

"Still filter free, but all grown up," Oona said, taking a small wedge of butter off the main brick and smearing it onto half of her steaming orange cranberry muffin. "Did you make these?"

"Nana Joy did. I can cook, but baking has never been my forte. Too precise."

"And that conflicts with the rebel image you're trying to portray?" Oona asked with a teasing smile as she took a bite from the muffin.

"Damn straight. Measure this, sift that. *Pfsst*. Fuck that noise. If I want to add more vanilla, I'll damn well add more vanilla. See if I care." She sipped her coffee. "Vanilla extract is to baking, as garlic is to cooking."

Oona lifted a brow.

"In that the amount I add to my food is guided by reckless extravagance and utter disregard, verging on mild contempt for the recipe as written." Then she flashed a big smile.

Oona snorted and shook her head, marveling at her sister's wit and accuracy. Oona could cook and bake—though living alone and being very busy with work and pole dancing, she did very little of it—but she often disregarded the suggested amount of both vanilla and garlic and usually double or tripled it. Maybe it was a Young family thing? She'd have to ask her other sisters if they went rogue, too.

"Well, Nana Joy makes a mean muffin."

Rayma smiled and sipped her coffee. "She's helping Jordan, too. He sees her once a month for therapy to talk through some of the childhood shit he and Aiden went through."

Oona's interest piqued, but she had to be careful not to show it. All she did was nod. She'd read Aiden's file cover to cover—twice. Once before he came into her office, then again after he stormed out and said she was bad in bed. But there wasn't anything about his childhood in there. Just that he was triggered by drunk drivers due to a childhood trauma, and had, on more than one occasion, over-stepped as an officer of the law. This last time, he'd hauled off and punched a drunk driver in front of his kid and someone else with a cellphone caught it all on camera, posted it online and it went viral.

But for his trigger to continuously be drunk drivers meant there had to be a history there. Something specific happened in his life that made him react outside the scope of the law on so many occasions.

Her curiosity niggled at the nape of her neck like a persistent, thirsty mosquito. She scratched at the phantom bug and nibbled on her muffin. She needed to change the subject, otherwise, she was going to ask for more information, and that was not something she needed.

"You're at work today?"

Rayma nodded. "Yeah, sorry. I tried to take this time off, but shit's hitting the fan with a few families. It happens this time of year, so my caseload is bigger than ever. I'm going to try to cut out early, but we'll see. I talked to Pasha, though. She, Mieks and Triss are going to come and pick you up in a bit. Something about planning a bachelorette party for someone or something?" She smiled and shrugged, pretending to be completely oblivious. "Who could that be for?"

Oona played along. "Some brat, I'm sure."

Rayma's grin brightened even more. "She said they'll be here by nine."

"Cool. I'm excited. We have a group chat that we've been planning in for months, so most of it is taken care of."

"Just as long as there are strippers, we go to Vegas, I don't remember a thing, and Triss winds up with a face tattoo. That's all I ask." She sipped her coffee, the corners of her mouth trying desperately to touch her glittering eyes.

"Of course. Totally makes sense for a very pregnant woman to get a face tattoo. I bet for you, she'll even get shit-faced drunk at eight months pregnant," Oona said dryly.

"I think so. Imagine the stories she can tell her kid when he's older," Rayma threw right back.

Oona snorted. "Grab me another muffin, you nut. These are really good. Nana Joy follows the recipe like a champ."

Rayma obliged.

They sat in the kitchen a little longer, chatting about various things. There was rarely any awkward silences between Oona and Rayma. Either Rayma just always had questions and knew how to keep the conversation flowing, or she and Oona really just had that much to talk about.

When eight-fifteen rolled around and Oona had had two cups of tea and three muffins, Rayma pecked her on the side of the head and said goodbye. That she was "off to the office."

"Did you ever think you'd say those words?" Oona asked her baby sister as Rayma wrapped a scarf around her neck.

"Sure didn't." Her expression sobered. "Wasn't sure I'd live that long, to be honest."

Oona's smile was sad.

Rayma rallied fast, though, and blew her a kiss. "But, people change, and look at me now. Responsible and shit, and I'm even getting married. I still rebel in the kitchen, though. Can't completely lose myself. That's why our garlic and vanilla extract bill is almost as much as our rent." Then she was out the door.

Oona leaned her elbows on the counter, emotion pulling hard on the back of her throat. "Yep, kiddo, look at you now."

Her time in the house alone as she got dressed for the day allowed her some quiet, much-needed reflection. Even though Aiden wasn't anything like Russell, his behaviors were still triggering her.

She knew that.

She recognized the signs.

And she was working extra hard not to let herself revert back to old habits.

Instead of clamming up, apologizing, and making herself smaller like she did with Russell— because if she didn't, he'd lash our physically—she snapped back at Aiden. She retaliated with words. She put him in his place. It was unlike her. But it was also a sign that she wasn't the meek and cowering little lamb she'd been with Russell. She was stronger. More resilient. And she took shit from no man.

Russell had also been a silver-spoon fed, privileged shit-head who came from an upper middle-class, suburban nuclear family that loved him. She'd met his parents and they were lovely people. How they managed to create such a monster still eluded her to this day. As far as she'd been able to tell, Russell had no demons that haunted him. So, he had no excuse for his behavior. No childhood trauma that led to his drinking. No deep-seated resentment or monsters that made him lash out physically to those that upset him.

His life had been peachy from the day his father cut the cord.

Russell was just a bad seed. And that was her professional diagnosis.

He was just a crap human who took pleasure in hurting her and other people.

Teal had suggested on more than one occasion that Russell could be a sociopath, and possibly suffer from borderline personality disorder. But Oona still wasn't convinced her mentor was right. Sometimes people didn't have a mental health diagnosis, they were simply just shit humans.

The world was full of shit humans who woke up every day and chose to be shitty. Their brains were fine. Their pasts were fine. There was no chemical imbalance or repressed memories of abuse. They were just plain shit. And even though a part of her hoped that Russell *did* have a diagnosis to explain his behavior, her gut told her he was just one of those people that woke up every day and made the conscious choice to be terrible.

Aiden, on the other hand, was a wounded soul. But he had goodness inside of him. He wasn't a bad seed. He didn't wake up in the morning and *choose* to be awful. He was just an angry, confused, and emotionally stunted man who needed help. A lot of help.

She'd met him when he was Caden and *not* letting his anger rule his choices. And she'd witnessed glimmers of that same goodness when he was with his brother.

Something haunted him. Deeply.

And although it was no excuse for his behavior, it did help her understand him more. It helped her have empathy for him, and hold on to hope that he would see Astrid and get the help he needed.

Aiden wasn't back by the time Pasha picked her up, and thank God for that. It only briefly registered with Oona that it was pouring rain and windy as a hurricane and Aiden was out running in it, when she ran from Rayma's front door to Pasha's SUV. Whatever. He deserved all the rain in his face and she hoped it felt like tiny bullets against his skin.

"Doctor," Pasha greeted her with a cheeky smile and a slight bow of the head.

Oona bowed her head, as well, and returned the grin. "Doctor." This was always how they greeted each other. It was wildly pretentious and they knew it. They mostly just did it for the eye rolls that accompanied it from the peanut gallery. And in this case, the peanut gallery was Mieka and Triss in the backseat.

"Not a pretentious doctor," Triss said, bowing her head at Mieka.

"Not a pretentious doctor," Mieka echoed, bowing her head, as well.

"Your tea, madame." Pasha tilted her head to a Starbucks to-go cup in the cupholder for the front seat. "It's not Stash, but I got you two teabags and oat milk."

"I'm sure it'll be delicious," Oona said, grabbing it and taking a sip. "Thank you." She blew her sister a quick kiss.

"So, we need decorations and all things penis-shaped, right?" Mieka asked. Oona craned around in her seat just as Pasha drove away from the curb.

"Is that really what Rayma wants?" Triss asked, making a cringy face. "Because I was adamant that nothing would be phallic-shaped at my bachelorette party."

"We remember," Oona and Pasha both said, making exaggerated eye rolls and sarcastic tones.

Oona grabbed her phone and brought up the list of specifics that Rayma said she wanted for her bachelorette party. "Penis-shaped everything. Then she even said in the *notes* section that she wants this to be obnoxious and tacky."

They all snorted and shook their heads.

"All right then, obnoxious and tacky it is. To the party store for penis-shaped everything!" Pasha announced, pointing her index finger up and forward like she was a cowboy on the open range.

"Speaking of penises, heard you walked in on Jordan's brother tugging it last night," Mieka said from the backseat. She wasn't quite as filterless as Rayma, but she was close.

"Nothing is sacred, apparently," Oona murmured. "And I can't be for certain that was what he was doing."

Her sisters scoffed.

"We know you're not a virgin, Oons. We all know what a dude looks like when he's rubbing one out, and it doesn't look like he's peeing. The penis is very differently shaped for each of those activities," Pasha said, stopping at a red light. "He was jerking it, wasn't he?"

Oona shut her eyes and nodded. "Yeah."

"Awkward," Mieka sung.

Yeah, it'd been awkward all right.

Awkward, wrong, and hot.

And she hated that she found it hot.

She hated that she still found *him* hot.

But she did. There was no turning that attraction off. Despite how badly she wanted to.

Aiden was gorgeous with all his broodiness, and even when he scowled, and his brows dipped and pinched in the middle, her belly fluttered.

If only he wasn't so hurtful. If only he wasn't so hurt.

Because hurt people, hurt people.

And Aiden was one of the most wounded people she'd met in a long time. Only, it wasn't her job to fix him.

Chapter Twelve

As far as avoiding temptation was concerned, Aiden figured he was doing a pretty bang-up job.

He and Oona stayed out of each other's way, and he was grateful for it.

Sort of.

Yes, he'd been masturbating in the bathroom when she walked in on him, but hearing her moans of pleasure on the other side of the guest room door was driving him batshit crazy. She was obviously getting herself off in there, and not being quiet about it, which blew his mind, considering it was her sister's house—but we all had our quirks.

But he needed to fucking sleep, so yanking it was the best course of action.

He just never anticipated Oona getting up and walking in on him.

Should he have locked the door? Of course, but he had other things on his mind and at three o'clock in the morning, he wasn't really thinking that others would come barging in. Mostly, though, he just forgot. He was so pent-up, hearing her moans and whimpers that he just needed to knock one out, put his pillow over his head and finally get some fucking sleep.

It didn't help that before they went to bed, they'd both heard Rayma and Jordan going at it, that was like adding gasoline to a house fire.

He made sure he was up and gone for his run before sleeping beauty woke from her chamber, and he was really fucking glad she wasn't home when he got back. He had the apartment to himself and was able to finish what he started last night and jerk off in the shower—with the door locked.

But of course, even when he was sliding his soapy palm over his cock as the water beat down on him, his mind kept drifting back to Oona. To the roundness of her ass cheeks and the way they jiggled just the right amount as he pounded into her from behind.

The perfect noises she made and the way her leg twitched when he scraped his thumbnail over her clit. And those tits. The woman had glorious fucking tits. A little more than a handful which was how he liked them. Her nipples were like two perfectly ripe raspberries and the way they puckered and hardened when she was aroused made his dick thicken and his balls tighten.

She was a hot piece of ass, he couldn't deny that. But she was also a thorn in his side who was as rigid as an icicle and equally as cold.

He definitely wouldn't deny that.

Once he finished what needed to be done in the shower, he dried himself with the towel, and wrapped it around his waist, then headed back to the living room where his phone was warbling on the kitchen island.

He didn't recognize the number, but the area code was local to the island, so it had to be someone regarding the wedding.

"Hello?" He put it on speaker then went about getting dressed.

"Hey, is this Aiden?" said the deep rumble.

"Yep."

"Cool. This is Jace, I'm a friend of Jordan's and I'm planning his bachelor party."

"Cool."

"Anyway, Jordan gave me your number and I wanted to run a few things by you, if you don't mind."

"Don't mind."

145

"Cool."

Aiden tugged his long-sleeve, dark gray waffle-knit shirt over his head. "When is it again?"

"Saturday. Tomorrow night."

"Right." That crept up fast.

"Anyway ... so Joy's husband, Grant, drives the courtesy bus or whatever for an old folk's home and he managed to get it for us and is going to be our driver."

Aiden resisted the urge to snort. They were going to drive around in an old geezer bus for a bachelor party? Okay ...

"Not the coolest, I know," Jace went on, as if reading Aiden's mind. "But it's free and thankfully, it's not ugly in comparison to some of the old people buses out there. It's black and has gold lettering. Just the initials of the care home. Nothing too ..."

"Embarrassing?" Aiden added with a snort.

"Yeah. And Grant has big black magnets that he can put over the writing so it just looks like a nondescript black bus-thing. It'll be fine."

Aiden sat down on the leather coffee table and yanked on his socks. "I'm sure it will be. What do you need from me?"

"Well, the party is going to start around three."

"In the afternoon?"

"Yeah."

"Okay ..."

"We're going rock climbing at the climbing gym, Jordan has really gotten into climbing lately, then to the brewpub—I know you don't drink—I hope the brewpub is okay?"

"It's fine," Aiden said blandly.

"Okay, cool. Then after the brewpub, we're heading to the billiards hall, I enrolled us in their pool tournament."

"Seriously?"

"Why?" Jace sounded worried. "You don't think that's a good idea?"

"Does Jordan like pool?"

"I mean, we've played it once or twice when we've gone out for drinks. Why? Do you have a better idea?"

"Gun range? Axe and knife throwing? Jord and I went and did it earlier this week and he enjoyed it."

"Okay ... um, I can look into that. Then, after that, we were going to head out for dinner to the steakhouse. You're not like a vegetarian or vegan are you?

"No."

"Cool." He was quiet for a moment. "There aren't really any strippers or anything in town worth seeing ..."

"Does Jordan *want* to see strippers?"

"No."

"Then don't give it a second thought."

"Right. Right." Jace seemed like a nice guy, but there was a nervousness to his voice that grew increasingly frustrating. Like he was just pulling this entire bachelor party out of his ass at the last minute. It also didn't seem like he knew Jordan that well.

To be fair, Aiden didn't know his brother that well, either, but he already knew he could do a better job planning his bachelor party than this guy.

"Do you need help?" Aiden finally asked. "I'm literally sitting here twiddling my thumbs while everyone is at work. If you need me to call around and make reservations or do something, I can."

Jace exhaled loudly into the phone. "Oh, fuck man, that would be great. I'm training for E.R.T try outs right now and am fucking exhausted. I can barely lift my arms or see straight. I wanted to start planning this ages ago, then lost track of time."

E.R.T or Emergency Response Team was the Canadian version of S.W.A.T. The training was rigorous and intense. Aiden knew of a couple of guys who tried out and made it, but he knew even more guys who tried out and didn't make the cut.

Jace's behavior was beginning to make more sense now. The guy had stretched himself too thin and was running on fumes.

"Text me what you have so far and I'll see what I can do," Aiden said, his respect for Jace growing, now that he knew how beat and sore the guy probably was. It wasn't his fault he was shitty at planning Jordan's bachelor party, he was just terrible at time management and organizing.

"Thanks, man. I really appreciate it. When I'm not working, I'm training. And even days I work, I still fucking train for a minimum of three hours a day. My girlfriend broke up with me because she said I was never around, that training and work were consuming my life."

"Jeez. Sorry about that."

"Thanks." Jace stifled a yawn over the phone. "Okay, I just sent you everything."

Aiden's phone vibrated several times to indicate new text messages. "Got 'em."

"So, the invite list is: you, me, Brock, Chase, Rex, Heath—those are the Harty Boys if you didn't know—and like three other guys from the precinct. All cops. All good guys. And besides you and me, the rest are married or engaged. I don't anticipate this getting too wild."

"Got it."

"I've sent you all their contact info, too."

"Okay."

Jace yawned again. "Okay, I took a fifteen-minute break, now it's time for the kettlebell. Text me if you have any questions."

"Will do."

The call disconnected and Aiden brought up his text messages. Turned out Jace was more organized that Aiden gave him credit for, the guy was just exhausted and over-scheduled. He sent Aiden all the phone numbers, the plan and the websites for the restaurant, climbing gym and billiards hall.

Then Aiden got to work.

148

It was great having a task and not feeling like an imposing guest just sitting around with his finger up his ass waiting for everyone to get home.

By ten-thirty, he had the entire party planned, everything booked and everyone but Jordan notified of the changes.

It wasn't even noon, though, and as much as he enjoyed wandering around downtown yesterday, he wasn't keen on doing it again.

He had a couple of the cranberry orange muffins on the counter and two cups of coffee. That only brought him to ten forty-five.

What the fuck was he going to do with the rest of the day?

He could beat off again, but that just seemed excessive. He also had no idea where Oona was or when she would be back, so he didn't want to risk it.

He checked the fridge, and found it on the south end of empty. There was still food in it, but nothing substantial to make a decent dinner.

That's when the lightbulb in his head finally turned on.

He was going to make dinner for Rayma and Jordan. And Oona, he supposed

...

Finding a few cloth grocery bags, he set out back to the same shopping complex that had the Starbucks he visited yesterday. There was a grocery store, a drug store, and a health food store in the shopping center, so he figured for sure he could find everything he would need.

Hope and purpose added buoyancy to his steps as he made his way up the hill, the wind chilly but not icy enough to make him shove his hands in his pockets. The rain was abstaining for now—because it all pelted his face that morning when he was out for his run—so he needed to make haste.

Yes, he was going to make a delicious dinner of Caesar salad, a creamy leek and potato soup, fried oyster mushrooms, and bacon wrapped scallops. Since being suspended from work, Aiden had diverted his attention to the kitchen, taking online knife-skill classes, spending way too much money on decent knives, and even more money on primo ingredients for some pretty epic dishes. He found joy in cooking that he'd never had before. It was as rewarding as it was therapeutic, and when he perfected his first savory soufflé, he actually teared up a little.

Yes, this would be how he would show his appreciation to Rayma and Jordan for hosting him. He would cook them dinner ... and Oona, too.

Where was Oona, anyway?

What was she doing?

And was she allergic to anything?

"Holy fucking shit balls, that smells amazing," Rayma said with a groan as she opened the door to her apartment and let Oona step inside first. "What is that?'

Oona's eyes nearly popped out of her skull in surprise when she entered the kitchen and found Aiden wearing a baby blue apron covered in cherries. He was standing over the sink holding an immersion blender and there was a big pot on the stove steaming, and torn lettuce in a big bamboo bowl.

"Are you cooking?" Rayma asked, hanging up her coat and ditching her cute gray ankle boots in the boot tray.

Aiden nodded then held up one finger. "Just a sec." Then he flicked on the immersion blender.

Oona and Rayma exchanged bewildered expressions as the roar of the hand-held kitchen appliance echoed around the apartment.

Oona spent the day with her sisters while Rayma and Jordan worked. They gathered everything they would need for the bachelorette party tomorrow, then had lunch, then Oona accompanied them back to Pasha's house, where she got to spend time with her niece and nephew. She certainly didn't want to head back to the apartment where she might run into Aiden, so she just hung out with people she actually liked, and Rayma picked her up on her way home.

It was just past six o'clock, so Jordan would be home shortly.

Her belly rumbled as the decadent smells wafted up her nostrils. She'd had a wonderful lunch out with her sisters, and snacks over at Pasha's, but whatever Aiden was making smelled incredible, and she was hungry all over again.

The blender switched off and Aiden lifted the tall tumbler from the sink to reveal homemade salad dressing.

"What prompted this?" Rayma asked, dipping her finger into the salad dressing and popping it into her mouth. "Yum."

Aiden shrugged. "Just wanted to do something nice. Since you're putting me up, figured it's the least I could do to show my appreciation." His gaze flicked to Oona and silently asked the question, "And what do you intend to do to show *your* appreciation?"

She glared at his handsome profile.

"Well, this is great. We usually do our grocery shopping on Saturdays, so by Friday we're tapped out of energy and food. Takeout is our friend on Fridays." Rayma wandered through the kitchen, checking out everything else he was making. "What soup is that?"

"Potato leek."

"Yum."

She opened the oven. "And what's in there?"

"Bacon wrapped scallops."

"Fuck yeah." Then she lifted a piece of foil. "And these?" She grabbed what looked like a breaded chicken finger off a plate and took a bite. "Fuck, that's hot." Her tongue juggled the piece around and she breathed out dramatically until it cooled off a bit.

"Breaded and fried oyster mushrooms."

Rayma's brown eyes were wide. "Amazing. Who taught you to cook?"

Aiden's eyes flicked back to Oona's when he answered, "I taught myself."

"Well, props to the teacher," Rayma said, opening the fridge and pulling out a bottle of white wine.

She waggled it in the air to ask if Oona wanted any, but Oona shook her head.

Rayma pouted. "Seriously?"

Oona rolled her eyes. "Are you honestly trying to pressure me into drinking?"

"You're home. We're not going out anywhere, and it's Friday. Plus, you're on vacation. You're supposed to have a perpetual buzz on your vacation. I'm sure there's a rule about that written somewhere. *Must be slightly or more than slightly inebriated for entire duration of vacation, otherwise punishable by death. Or fine of twenty-five dollars.*"

"Death or twenty-five bucks?" Oona asked with a laugh.

Rayma shrugged. "Depends on the judge doing the sentencing. I don't make the rules." She brought down two wine glasses with stems, then cast Oona another pleading look. Aiden's gaze burned into the side of her face. She didn't need to look at him to feel him watching her with intense curiosity, and ready-to-pounce judgment.

She had a drink last night.

And it wasn't like he was the alcohol police. He wasn't police of any kind right now.

She turned to face him, gave him a challenging, smug smile, then nodded at her sister. "Sure, pour me a glass. Throw in some ice, though. I like my white wine really cold."

"I can do you one better. I have frozen grapes," Rayma said with enthusiasm, opening up the freezer and pulling out a Zip-loc bag of frozen green grapes. "They won't dilute the wine like ice cubes will."

Aiden cleared his throat, and Oona pivoted to face him. She could tell he had something snarky sitting on the tip of his tongue. He had a look on his face like he'd just bit into a lemon.

She knew he didn't drink, and that was fine. She also knew he had zero tolerance for drunk drivers, but did that intolerance also stem to people who drank in general? Because neither Oona nor Rayma had plans to get behind the wheel at all tonight.

Surely, he wasn't that much of a hard ass?

Rayma finished pouring Oona's glass over a handful of green grapes, then handed it to Oona, bringing her glass, as well, and clinking it playfully against Oona's. "To men in the kitchen and women enjoying a toddy after work. I like it!"

Oona smiled at her sister and took a sip of her wine, casting a cursory glance at Aiden, who was busy slathering what looked to be clarified butter on sliced ciabatta buns.

"Now, if only we could train him to bring us our slippers and a cigar, then we'd be sitting pretty." Rayma wandered into the living room with her drink and Oona followed. "Do you do a lot of cooking, Aiden?" Rayma called to her brother in-law to be.

Aiden nodded. "Yeah."

"On your days off?"

"Yeah."

Oona startled and glanced quickly between Rayma and Aiden. Aiden's gaze turned hotter than ever—but not in the way that said he wanted to burn off all her clothes with his secret laser vision—more in a way that said, "Say anything and I'll burn a hole in the center of your forehead."

Did Rayma and Jordan not know that Aiden was suspended? Had he not told them?

The harsh warning glare from the man in the cherry-covered apron said his brother and his betrothed were in the dark.

Shit.

Another secret that Oona now had to keep from her sisters.

She hated having secrets.

She kept so many of them when it came to her patients, that she tried to live her non-professional life transparent and open. Granted, her sisters had no idea about Russell, but other than that, Oona was an open book. Not having anything to hide made life easier. It helped her sleep, and helped her keep her work and personal lives separate. Because if she were forced to keep a million secrets in her own life, in addition to all the confidential stuff she was told by patients, her brain would explode.

"Mmmm, this is a good Riesling," Rayma hummed. "Jordan chose it. What do you think?"

Oona took a sip and nodded. "Yeah, very nice."

"I'm more of a red wine drinker, usually. But sometimes we like to *spice* it up with a fancy white we find on sale at the liquor store." Her smile was cheeky. "So, what kind of fuckery are we up to tomorrow night? Sublime fuckery I hope." Rayma bobbed her thick brows. "I want to be hungover on Sunday, please and thank you."

Aiden glanced up at Oona and his gaze hardened and narrowed.

Oona glared back at him and mouthed the words, "Fuck off," which caused his eyes to widen and his mouth to open with indignation and shock.

If he muttered so much as a fucking word to Rayma about drinking or wanting to enjoy her bachelorette with a little lubrication, Oona would be on him like a mama bear on a group of hikers who tried to pet her cubs. She would gut him with her claws.

They were all very protective of Rayma. Even though she'd been a wild teenager, what their parents did to her—giving up on her and shipping her off to Pasha—was beyond reproach and unforgivable. The girls had never been particularly close with their parents, and all of them left home as soon as they could, but abandoning Rayma just drove the wedge even deeper. However, it also helped the sisters grow closer. They banded together as a united front against their parents and their judgmental ways, and protected Rayma from their comments. Because even though Rayma had turned her life around and was a successful social worker now, they still threw out way too many barbs of disapproval that had the ability to send Oona's baby sister into a spiral.

Rayma had seriously debated even inviting their parents to the wedding, which was something they all supported. But in the end, she relented and sent them the invitation. But as the wedding drew closer, Oona—in fact, all of them—could tell that Rayma was having second thoughts about inviting their parents, and was probably secretly praying for a freak snowstorm in Baltimore that prevented them from flying out.

A key slid into the front door and it opened a moment later to reveal Jordan, his hair damp from the rain that had started again around three that afternoon, his green eyes bright, and cheeks rosy. "Wow, that smells amazing," he said, ditching his shoes and coming into the living room to kiss Rayma hello.

"I know, I could get used to this," she said. "Little Lassie, let's make more money so we can afford a private chef. Or ditch the badge, and let's knock over a bank."

Jordan snorted and rolled his eyes. "We'll call that Plan B." He lifted his chin to Oona. "How are you?"

"Pretty good. Spent the day buying obnoxious and tacky things for this one's party tomorrow. So much stuff comes in the shape of a penis these days."

Jordan laughed. "Yeah?"

"Dinner's ready," Aiden said from the kitchen, his tone terse.

"Just let me get changed and wash my hands," Jordan said, heading to the bedroom.

Rayma and Oona pried themselves off the couch and brought their wine over to the tall four-top bistro style table that served as Rayma and Jordan's kitchen table. Aiden had set it already and there was garlic bread in a basket, the Caesar salad tossed with croutons, bacon, and fresh grated parmesan, as well as a plate of the bacon wrapped scallops and the fried oyster mushrooms. He'd already placed steaming bowls at two of the place settings and they were expertly garnished with what looked like pine nuts, brown butter drizzle, and fresh scallions.

Oona never would have pegged Aiden as a cooking enthusiast like this. Then again, she really didn't know the man, as hard as she tried to analyze him, she could only assume so much. And he also probably had a lot of time on his hands, so maybe he took up cooking to keep himself from going stir-crazy.

Of course, she was the last person he dished up, and he set the bowl in front of her with a harsh *plunk* that made the soup slosh slightly in the bowl and over the side onto her plate. She glared at his back when he returned to the kitchen to ditch his oven mitts. He was still sporting that apron, though.

And as much as she didn't want to admit it, he pulled it off rather well.

Jordan joined them, then finally Aiden. Unfortunately, due to where Jordan and Rayma sat, Aiden was forced to sit next to Oona, and his intrusive knee brushed hers under the table when he pulled in his chair. Their eyes met, and both of them narrowed their gaze.

"Well, this is absolutely amazing," Jordan said, having grabbed a beer from the fridge on his way to sit down. "Bro, I had no idea you were like Gordon Ramsay or something."

Oona nearly choked on her wine.

What an accurate celebrity chef to choose. Gordon Ramsay was known for his temper and tirades, and Aiden was currently in anger management for his temper and tirades.

He must have picked up on her wave-length, and a sharp but inconspicuous pinch on her calf under the table made her squeak. It wasn't a painful pinch, though. More of a cheeky warning.

She knew the difference between being playful and deliberately inflicting pain.

And Aiden wasn't deliberately trying to inflict pain on her.

"You okay?" Rayma asked her, patting her on the back. "Go down the wrong pipe?"

"Something like that," Oona said, still coughing a little. She glanced at him out of the corner of her eye and dished back a heel dig to the top of Aiden's foot, but all that got her was a murmured grunt that nobody seemed to notice.

When they were Luna and Caden, she'd mentioned her ex and that he'd been physical. Aiden, for all his flaws, probably remembered that even though they were enemies, he was staying within her boundary of acceptable behavior.

Because even though he'd been rough with her, he'd never made her fear for her life. Never made her worry that he was going to punch her in the stomach, break her ribs, or give her a black eye.

Break her heart? Maybe. But never her collarbone.

"Anyway," Jordan went on, none-the-wiser, "this looks great, Aiden. Thank you."

"Yes, thank you," Rayma said, lifting her wine glass into the middle of the table. "To family. It just keeps growing and I couldn't be happier."

Aiden had a glass of sparkling water, which he lifted to join Rayma's wine. Jordan lifted his beer bottle, and Oona lifted her wine. She and Aiden made a point of *not* clinking their glasses with each other, and she thought it went unnoticed and she was in the clear, but ol' eagle eyes Rayma picked up on it.

"You didn't clink," she said, looking at them both like they'd each sprouted a second head. "You need to clink and you need to make eye contact; otherwise, it's bad luck and bad sex for seven years."

"I thought that was if you broke a mirror?" Aiden asked. Which echoed the confusion Oona also felt.

"That's just bad luck for seven years. But not making eye contact when you clink your glass in cheers, is bad luck *and* bad sex for seven years. I mean, do any of us want to risk that?"

Oona slowly, reluctantly, and with anger bubbling up inside of her, lifted her wine glass and her gaze toward Aiden. She focused on the brown tributaries that ran through his green irises and waited for his glass to touch hers.

His focus on her was unwavering.

Unsettling and unnerving.

She squirmed where she sat and squeezed her thighs together.

He knew what he was doing, and the corner of his mouth lifted up on one side a barely noticeable amount. But she noticed.

She noticed the way his nostrils flared.

The way his pupils dilated and the color of his eyes went from grass-green to forest-green. A muscle in his jaw pulsed and jiggled, and the slow roll of his throat as he swallowed made her breath catch in her chest.

"All right, I think that's enough eye contact," Rayma said slowly. "Like, enough for fourteen years of good sex."

Oona blinked and shook her head, dislodging the spell or whatever it was Aiden had cast on her and turned to face her sister. "Just following the bride's orders."

Rayma grinned.

They dove into dinner, and although sitting beside Aiden and feeling his heat radiating off him in rolling, intoxicating waves had Oona feeling light-headed, despite not even consuming an entire glass of wine, she was in a good mood.

They chatted together, but she made sure to direct her conversation to Jordan and Rayma, ignoring Aiden as best she could, and he ignored her in turn. But that didn't stop his knee from constantly bumping hers under the table, or their knuckles from brushing when they both reached for a bacon wrapped scallop.

And of course, with each of those little, innocuous grazes of skin against skin, she felt an electric zap that landed right between her legs.

Did the man know what he was doing? Was he wearing some kind of weird electric conductor? Because those things existed. Rayma sent her pictures of one she saw at Taboo last year. It turned the person into a conduit for an electric current, so when they touched another person, there was an electric charge.

Not entirely her cup of tea, but she wasn't against something like that, either. With the right person, of course.

And Aiden Lassiter was absolutely NOT the right person.

"Well, Big Lassie," Rayma said, sitting back in her bar stool and patting her flat belly, "that was extraordinary. You've set the bar mighty high."

Aiden's smile was small. "There's dessert."

"Shut the fuck up," Rayma said, slamming her hands on the table, her mouth opening. She turned to Jordan. "I might be marrying the wrong Lassie. I mean, yeah, you can cook, I particularly like your puttanesca, but you don't cook like this."

Jordan cast his fiancée an irritated side-eye, but it was all for show.

"What's for dessert, Big Lassie?" Rayma asked.

"Tiramisu," he said, getting up from his seat and taking Rayma and Jordan's empty plates and bowls.

"Shut the fuck up," Rayma said again. "That's one of my favorites."

"Is it?" Aiden asked slyly as he loaded the dishwasher.

There was no reason for his tone of voice or anything else that he was doing right now to annoy Oona, but it all did. His food was delicious and she would have probably used her finger to lick the bowl clean if it'd been anybody but Aiden who'd cooked it, but that just annoyed her more.

He was sending some kind of hidden message and expecting her to decode it.

Well, she had.

His message was: You're a freeloader and I'm not. *Na-na-na-boo-boo.*

Or something like that.

Well, two could play this game. She slid off her stool and gathered more dishes from the table, as well as her and Aiden's plates and bowls. "I can do this. You've already done *so* much." She hip checked him out of the way so she could load the dishwasher, barely catching the exchange of glances between Jordan and Rayma.

"It's really quite all right," Aiden said. "I just want my hosts to know how much I appreciate them putting me up."

Oooh, his tone was like a glove slap to the face. He was challenging her to a duel.

Well, little did he know, but she brought her travel sword.

"And I also want my hosts to know how much *I* appreciate them putting me up." She snagged her purse from the coat hook by the front door, pulled out her wallet, and grabbed a fist full of cash, slapping it down on the counter.

"For groceries, gas, and the hot water I've used and will use for my showers and laundry."

Rayma and Jordan's eyes were wide, and their expressions very confused.

"Oona, take back your money. We're not hard up. And you're definitely not paying our utilities. "What the fuck is going on?" Rayma asked, slowly. "You two have been acting weird a lot. Why?"

"It's nothing," Oona dismissed, sashaying back into the kitchen to tidy up. She didn't take her money back. "Just pulling my weight." Aiden had brought out the tiramisu from the freezer. "Oh, let me." She reached for the dish.

"I made it. I'll dish it up." His tone was cold and stern, along with his glare.

"It's really no problem. You've already done so much. Been on your feet in the kitchen all day." She tugged on the dish, but he tugged back.

"Sit. Down. Now, Oona," he said slowly, the authority in his voice making her back snap straight. She turned around and went to her chair. "Good girl."

Rayma and Jordan's mouths dropped open until they looked like twin cod-fish who'd just been electrocuted.

"Something strange is going on," Rayma said after a moment. "Something really fucking strange."

"You're telling me," Jordan murmured, his gaze bouncing curiously between Aiden and Oona.

"I'll tell you what's weird," Aiden said, slicing into the dessert and plating it on four plates. "What is with all the pineapples?"

Chapter Thirteen

He made sure to lock the door this time, but he did keep the light off in the bathroom when he went back in there later that night once everyone had fallen asleep. The way Oona had just snapped to attention and done as he said, then her reaction when he called her a good girl ... he nearly came in his fucking jeans right there while dishing up the tiramisu.

But, fuck her, too.

That little stunt she pulled with the cash—offering to pay their groceries and utilities, that was fucking weird and so ... out of character.

And yet, despite the way the woman irritated him to no-end, he found himself tossing and turning again, with a steel pipe in his boxers and thoughts of going into her room and sliding between her thighs at the forefront of his mind.

No. Fucking. Way.

So, he did the next best thing. He went into the bathroom, stood over the toilet, and jerked off while watching videos of Oona pole dancing online. The company she did the dancing with posted it to their social media and on their website. It'd been easy enough to find, and over the last week and a bit, he'd gone through every one of her videos more than once.

The Luna Love on stage was so different from the Oona Young he was forced to sleep under the same roof with. Luna Love was fun and confident, sassy and bold. She owned the stage, drew in the audience, and made them feel like she was giving each and every one of them their own private show. She commanded their attention with the shimmy of her hips, the flick of her ass, and the way she wrapped her leg around the pole and hung from it like a fucking flag.

But Oona ... Oona was rigid and had a giant stick up her ass.

He kept telling himself that he was jerking it to Luna and that was okay, but he knew that they were the same person, which meant he was having all the wrong thoughts and feelings for entirely the wrong person.

He knew an addictive personality could be hereditary, it was one of the reasons he'd never touched alcohol or any hard drugs. If his father could so easily become a drunk, then maybe Aiden could, too. But just because he didn't have drugs or alcohol to get addicted to, didn't mean he couldn't still get addicted to something else. And the more time he spent avoiding her, the more he started to worry that Luna or Oona or both were his addiction. He couldn't get the woman out of his head.

She infuriated him. Was like poison. And yet, he wanted her so fucking badly, it made his gut hurt.

He finished himself off just as Luna Love finished her set on stage, doing the splits on the pole, then almost slithering down it head first, only to land on the ground on her belly, stick her ass in the air, and wink at the crowd. Yeah, that made him blow his load, hard.

He cleaned up his mess—not that he really made one—and exited the bathroom, praying that Luna Love's alter ego wasn't lurking beyond the bathroom door just waiting to catch him again.

The coast was clear.

He took one step, then another, out of the bathroom, only to stop in his tracks at the moan that came from the guest room.

That was no ordinary moan.

That was a sex moan.

And he'd absolutely heard her make those noises before.

Just like last night, when he'd had to get up to yank it because she was making those noises, she was making them again. He leaned in closer to the door until his ear was against it, listening to the soft whimpers, heavy breathing, and sharp inhales.

Was she touching herself? Or was she sleeping?

He'd never been with a woman who actively had sex dreams to the point where she was vocal about it while sleeping. Not that he didn't know it was a thing, he'd just never witnessed it himself in person before.

His hand fell to the knob, and for the briefest of moments, he considered going into her room to find out for himself. But he released it like he'd touched a hot coal.

No. That would be a serious invasion of privacy, and unlike the bathroom, the guest room was *her* space.

But his curiosity burned so hot, his palms itched.

"Oh, Aiden," she crooned softly.

What the fuck?

Okay, first of all, holy fuck.

Second of all, she had to be sleeping, because even if she was awake and in the throes of her orgasm, or on the cusp of it, she wasn't dumb enough to utter his name out loud. The apartment was small and the walls had been proven thin.

Third of all, she was having a sex dream about him. Him.

That last revelation couldn't be ignored.

Holy fuck.

He stayed beside her door a little longer, hoping to hear his name again, to hear her find her release, but the sounds of climax never came. His name was never murmured again and eventually, he was forced to give up.

But, of course, his cock heard everything and perked up in anticipation, just in case he may be needed.

163

Which meant, Aiden couldn't just go back to sleep.

So, like a teenage boy having found a stash of old porno mags, he went back into the bathroom and locked the door, all so he could hopefully, eventually, just maybe get some fucking sleep.

"It's time to par-tay!" Mieka cheered as Rayma and Oona piled into the stretch Escalade they'd rented for the bachelorette party. They were the last to be picked up, so everyone who was invited was already inside. Pasha's sister in-laws, Krista, Stacey, and Lydia, as well as Rayma's best friend Peyton and three other women: Bella, Denise, and Chelsea. Everyone whooped and hollered when Rayma and Oona climbed into the luxury car.

"This is Andre, he'll be our driver for the evening," Mieka announced, pointing to the man in the chauffeur's hat at the front of the Escalade. Andre gave a wave without turning around. "His wife is due any minute with baby number four, so let's send that baby some stay-in-the-womb vibes, okay?"

"Stay in the womb, baby. Come out tomorrow," Oona said, pressing her fingers to her temples.

Andre chuckled. "Thanks."

"And of course, we can't forget about the bride-to-be's tiara, sash, penis necklace, tutu and penis earrings," Pasha said, leaning forward to deck out their grinning baby sister in all the tacky shit they'd purchased the day before. She pretended to sniffle. "You've never looked more beautiful or grown up, kiddo."

Rayma was all smiles. "It's time to party, bitches! Because I'm getting MAR-RIED! Someone hand me the bottle of champagne. I need to catch up." Denise handed her the bottle and Rayma drank straight from it. Everyone watched her with wide eyes.

When she finally came up for air, she let out a big "Whooooo!" which prompted everyone else to echo her. "Tally-ho, driver-man! To the first stop!" Rayma sat next to Oona and leaned over to whisper into her ear. "This is going to be a great night." Then she kissed Oona on the cheek, only to go "Whooooo" again.

The bride was in all white, along with her tacky crap, while the rest of the bachelorette party was in black. It was just another way to bring attention to Rayma and keep it off the rest of them.

Oona was wearing one of her favorite little black dresses. She couldn't even remember how many times it had come to her rescue when she needed something classy but also sexy to wear, and drew a blank the moment she opened her closet door.

The dress had a slight wave at the bottom hem that hit her mid-thigh, a deep V, and the same kind of fluttery wave or ruffle in the cap sleeve. It was made out of soft and sexy jersey fabric and could be rocked day or night, depending on the makeup, jewelry, and shoes. Since it was winter time, she was sporting black boots with a spiked heel that hit her upper calf, no jewelry besides her long dangly earrings with fake diamonds on the pendant, and she kept her hair long and wavy. Then, because she didn't want to catch pneumonia, she tossed on her black leather jacket. She let Rayma do her makeup, and her baby sister convinced her to go with a dark wine-colored lip stain. Even she had to admit that she looked pretty damn good. Finally, of course, she layered on half a dozen plastic penis necklaces of various glow-in-the-dark colors.

Jordan had been picked up earlier that day for his party, meanwhile Oona treated Rayma to a mani-pedi at a salon, just the two of them. She would have loved to invited her other sisters, but they were busy doing something and it was also just really nice to spend some more one-on-one time with Rayma.

But Rayma's party started a little later than Jordan's. It was just after six o'clock, so first they were going out for dinner to Vista 18, which was a swanky restaurant and lounge on the top floor of the Chateau Victoria Hotel. Of course,

Oona and her sisters were covering the tab for Rayma, which they had no problem doing. Rayma was worth it.

When it came to picking her maid of honor, Rayma said she couldn't choose between her four sisters, so she asked them all to be her maids and matrons of honor. Her best friend, Peyton, was a bridesmaid. It was a little uneven, considering that Jordan only had Aiden and Jace on his side, but Rayma didn't seem to care about the lack of balance. She said she wanted who she wanted and Jordan wanted who he wanted and that was that.

They drank and sang like tone-deaf sorority girls all the way downtown to the Chateau. They had a reservation and a few decorations had been covertly dropped off for the staff to set up ahead of time.

Rayma squealed when the Escalade pulled up the Chateau. "Are we going to Vista 18?"

"It was on your list of approved places, you little control freak," Pasha said dryly as they all piled out of the limo.

Rayma beamed. "And you listened." She patted Pasha on the head. "Good, big sister."

Pasha rolled her soft brown eyes, then swatted Rayma on the butt playfully. "Get moving, kiddo."

Heels clicking across the cobblestone, they all giggled and gossiped as they made their way to the front door of the hotel. A man in a uniform and a big smile held it open for them and Rayma did a little twirl as she stepped through. "I'm getting married!"

"He's a lucky man," the hotel employee said.

"He sure is," Rayma cheered, heading to the elevator.

Oona fell in line with Triss and by the time they approached the elevator, it was too full. "We'll grab the next one," Oona said.

Rayma's face fell. "No, we can cram in. I can ride on Pasha's shoulders." She tried to climb Pasha like a tree, but Pasha gently shoved her off.

"I'd rather not put my back out, thanks," Pasha said with an eye roll.

"It's all good, kiddo. We'll meet you at the top," Triss said as the doors closed.

Oona snickered while Triss yawned.

"How's my nephew?" she asked, leaning over and rubbing her older sister's perfect baby bump. Triss was in her final trimester and just a month away from delivering. She was waddling more than she was walking—her words, not Oona's—and sleeping a lot. Oona thought she looked radiant and like she was trying to smuggle a watermelon under her dress.

"I think he's going to come out with a full head of hair. I have such bad heart burn. Pasha had to write me a prescription for something because Rolaids just weren't cutting it. I couldn't even sleep the other night."

Oona pouted and the elevator door opened. They waited for the people inside to exit, then stepped in. "That sucks. I'm sorry my beautiful little nephew is making you uncomfortable."

Triss smiled and rubbed her belly. "He's worth it, though." She yawned again. "How are you doing? Rayma texted us last night to say there's a weird vibe going on between you and Jordan's brother. What's going on?"

Heat raced up Oona's face and spread across her chest, and into her armpits, making them suddenly very sweaty.

"Come on, Oons. You can't keep anything from me. What's going on?"

She'd been dying to tell someone. The secret had been eating away at her since she turned around at the airport and saw Aiden greeting Jordan and calling him *brother*.

But she didn't want to take attention away from Rayma or make things awkward for her sister's wedding. This was ten days. She could endure the man she was stupidly attracted to, but also couldn't stand for ten days. She'd already endured it for three and they'd only slipped up and had sex once. Which would *definitely* not be happening again. Ever.

"We um ..."

Triss's brown eyes went wide. "You what?"

"We met a few weeks ago and I was Luna, he was Caden, and we spent the night together. Then the next day he comes in and he's my new patient. I refuse him treatment. Things turn ugly. He leaves. Then we're on the same flight out of Montreal and end up sitting next to each other. It was awful. Horrible. Terrible. No good. Not at all. Then in the airport, I find out he's Jordan brother and things get even worse, since now we hate each other. But then we accidentally hate-fucked the other day. And things are *so* messy. I just need to stay away from him. Stop letting things happen to me, and start *making* them happen. And that means avoiding Aiden and making sure this wedding goes off without a hitch." She exhaled and her chest heaved. She'd said all of that so fast, and without taking a breath. She turned to Triss and grabbed her sister's hands hard. "You can't say *anything*. I mean it, Triss. Not a word to anyone. This is Rayma's day. Rayma's week. I don't want to take any attention away from her or make things awkward or weird. She deserves every bit of awesome and I will not be the one to ruin it for her."

Triss's mouth had dropped open mid speed-diatribe, and it had remained that way. She was blinking, but otherwise hadn't moved.

The elevator chimed and the doors opened, spitting them out onto the eighteenth floor. "Promise me," Oona murmured, releasing her sister's hands and holding up her pinky finger, waiting for Triss to loop her pinky through it.

Finally, Triss snapped out of it and nodded, though she still seemed a little shell-shocked. She slowly linked her pinky around Oona's.

"You're bound by the pinky promise, now," Oona said. "Punishable by death."

That cracked Triss's stunned face and she smiled and rolled her eyes. "Taking a page from Rayma's dramatic playbook, are you?'

"If I have to."

They headed toward the party room they'd reserved.

She knew she could trust Triss.

To be honest, she could trust any of her sisters to keep a secret like this. But Triss was a speech pathologist and she knew the meaning of confidentiality. Pasha was a doctor and knew it, too. So if it'd been Pasha in that elevator with her and pumping her for information, Oona probably would have broken the seal on her secret to her, too. She was just desperate to tell someone. And the relief she felt at finally sharing her secret with another person was monumental. It was like a weight had been lifted off her shoulders. And not necessarily transferred to Triss, but now she had someone on her side. Someone to help her fend off questions about Aiden and help her manage the situation. She wasn't alone navigating this sludge-filled river of awkwardness and sexual tension.

She could tell Triss was still processing the news from the elevator, but to the untrained eye, her sister looked normal.

But the Young sisters were not untrained eyes and Pasha, Rayma and Mieka all zeroed in on Triss's face.

Shit. Maybe Oona told the wrong sister. Triss could be a bit of a glass house sometimes. And with the pregnancy hormones, she was probably even more transparent than normal.

"You okay?" Pasha asked from her seat between the redheaded Krista and the strawberry blonde Stacey.

Triss nodded and rubbed her belly. "Just a little indigestion."

"I'll order you a ginger ale," Mieka said, turning to the server who was taking drink orders. "Can my pregnant sister get a ginger ale, please?"

The server nodded.

"That's all it is?" Pasha asked, apparently not convinced at all. "I *am* a doctor, you know. And I've been pregnant." She looked to her three sister in-laws. "We all have. So you don't have to hide anything from us."

Triss's gaze shot to Oona across the long table.

Oh shit.

"Did you fart in a crowded elevator?" Lydia asked. "Because I've been there."

Stacey snorted, but then nodded. "Me, too."

169

"It's time for shots!" Rayma announced, redirecting everyone's attention as another server came around the corner with a big tray of shot glasses brimming with some pink and blue ombre-colored concoction.

"What are *those*?" Lydia asked, her eyes wide. "They look like—"

"They're porn stars," Rayma said, grabbing one off the tray and downing it, then grabbing another. "They taste like my childhood."

The server made a choking noise in his throat.

"Not my *childhood*," Rayma corrected. "I mean my youth. Like my rebellious teenage years."

"So sugar and regret?" Krista said, reluctantly taking one as it was passed down to her.

"Yep," Rayma said. "Bottoms up, ladies!"

They all lifted their tiny glasses toward the center of the table, everyone but Triss that is.

"To Rayma," Pasha said. "All grown up, and keeping it classy draped in dick."

"As one should be," Rayma added.

"To Rayma, draped in dick," they cheered before tipping back their shots.

It was way too sweet and Oona's brain instantly buzzed. Her partying time in college was brief, but she'd always stuck to shots of tequila or Jägermeister when she went out. None of these fancy sugary shots that made your glucose levels spike off the charts in seconds.

"Okay, I need something tart to cleanse my palate of that liquid Fun Dip," Krista said, shaking her head and going, "Gah." She turned to the server who had delivered the shots. "I'll get a gin—like a really good gin—on ice with a lime, please."

The server nodded, then disappeared.

Krista was married to the oldest Harty boy. She was also a sergeant with the Royal Canadian Mounted Police or RCMP, though apparently not the same municipality as Jordan. From what Jordan had explained the other day, the Greater Victoria Area was made up of thirteen municipalities and each municipality had its own police force. And to make things even more complicated, some municipalities had RCMP, while others had city police. At one point they had been in the same department, which was how they met and how Rayma and Jordan were introduced, but Jordan had since been transferred a few times.

Oona—always psychoanalyzing everyone—got that Krista was no-nonsense, but probably had a very gentle underbelly. She was scanning the area like any cop would, assessing threats and probably wouldn't allow herself to have more than a couple of drinks, so that she remained alert and ready for anything.

They ordered food and drinks, and Rayma pumped them for information about the evening, but this was one secret that Oona was okay keeping. Everyone *but* Rayma knew what was going on. They had all agreed and paid their fees ahead of time.

Oona was a little nervous for her part in it, but she also knew this was something her little sister had wanted to do for a long time, and just like when they were kids, Oona would do anything to make Rayma smile.

"I wonder what Jordan and the guys are up to," Rayma mused as she ate her cashew chicken lettuce wraps. She'd smartly, and without a care how it looked, draped herself in napkins, tucking them everywhere and hovering over her plate in a weird position so that she didn't accidentally get sauce on her dress. For someone who had consumed twice as much alcohol as the rest of them, she was surprisingly adept at eating and not making a mess.

Krista, Stacey, Pasha and Lydia all checked their phones. "They're at axe throwing."

"Really?" Rayma squeaked. "That sounds like fun."

"They did rock climbing, then the gun range earlier," Krista said. "It takes a lot for my husband to smile—basically just boobs, bacon and beer make that happen—but I bet he's enjoying himself right now."

"Heath already knows he's to snap any pictures of Brock smiling that he can," Pasha said. "He and Rex are both on smile duty."

Lydia snorted, then turned her phone around to show a photo. "Almost."

It was a picture of a very handsome, very beefy, green-eyed man probably in his late forties or early fifties, with one corner of his mouth lifted, while the other corner was turned down.

"How is that even possible?" Peyton, Rayma's best friend asked. "He's frowning and smiling."

Then they all tried to imitate Brock's expression until everyone around the table was cracking up.

It was after eight o'clock when they finally left Vista 18 and headed back down to the Escalade.

"Where are we off to now?" Rayma asked, still holding her own pretty well, despite what her blood alcohol level probably was.

Oona looped her arm through Rayma's. "I think you're going to like this next event, kiddo. After all, you *have* been begging me to teach you for quite some time."

Rayma gasped, skidded to a stop in her heels, turned to face Oona and gripped her by the shoulders. "Are we ...?" Her eyes wide in anticipation and excitement.

Oona smiled. "Be prepared to do some squats."

Chapter Fourteen

"So, I just got a text from Rayma," Jordan said, glancing up from his phone as they all stood around a high-top table at a bar on their pub crawl. "She told me to *get my ass to* the Fort Street Hype Studio by eleven or she'll never give me a blowjob again."

Several of the guys at the table chuckled and rolled their eyes.

"Not sure how serious she is, but I wouldn't risk it," Jace said, sipping his festive cranberry wheat ale. They were downtown at a place called The Harbor Club. It was right on the water, loud, and busy.

But when Aiden did his research about best places to go on a Victoria pub crawl, The Harbor Club had popped up on more than one website, so he knew he needed to add it to the list. It was their second bar after rock climbing, the gun range, axe throwing and dinner at the steak house.

Set in a large, old, brick building with an industrial feel, the interior boasted high exposed ceilings, with wooden beams, and the original brick interior. There seemed to be multiple levels and different areas for drinking, eating, and socializing. They had to all walk through the crowd single file because it was shoulder-to-shoulder busy.

Jordan seemed to be having a great time, and Aiden had to say, the company his brother kept was pretty decent.

There wasn't one guy there that Aiden was struggling to find tolerable. And just as he figured, Jace was a great guy. The bags under his blue-hazel eyes spoke of his intense training regime, and the fact that his biceps were practically bursting out of his tight black T-shirt, and his traps were swol as fuck, said he was going extra hard as the tryout day grew nearer. He'd yawned more than once since the old person bus picked him up, but he kept up with everyone and put away an impressive ribeye the size of Aiden's size-thirteen shoe. Then he had two baked potatoes, a side salad and French bread with butter. And as they stood at their table drinking beer, Jace was perusing the menu because he was "feeling peckish."

"Are the women going to be there?" Chase asked. He was bald, beefy, and hardly cracked a smile. Which didn't bother Aiden. Neither Chase, or his older brother Brock seemed to be enjoying themselves, at least not if you went by their facial expressions, but then when they left the gun range and axe throwing, they both independently clapped Aiden on the back and said he did a great job and how much fun they had.

Rex and Heath, the younger two Harty boys, who were still either closing in on forty or in their early forties, seemed less serious and smiled and joked a fair bit. Heath reminded Aiden a lot of his old He-Man action figure, with his enormous arms and shaggy blonde hair that nearly reached his shoulders.

All four men were enormous, though. Bigger than Jace in both size and breadth. Aiden felt like a wilting flower between all the redwoods. Even though he was over six-feet-tall and worked out, these guys just had an enormous presence about them that made everyone in the bar take notice.

Jordan and his other cop friends weren't slouches, either, but between the Harty boys and Jace, they *looked* small.

"Well, it's nine-thirty now, so we have some time to kill before eleven," Rex said, finishing his beer, the overhead track lighting gleaming off his shiny bald head. Chase and Rex were bald, while Brock kept his hair trimmed short, military-style, and Heath wore his all blonde and rebellious.

"I just ordered food," Jace said, having turned away for a moment to speak with a server. "Nachos for the table and a Thai chicken wrap with onion rings for myself."

"Do you *ever* get full?" Tyler, one of Jordan's cop buddies, asked.

Jace shook his head and sipped his beer. "Not while I'm training."

The two other cops there—Matt and Patrick—shook their heads. "My wife would kill me if I went out for ERT," Matt said. Patrick nodded. "The training time, always being on call. I mentioned it once in passing and she flat out told me she'd divorce me if I ever did it. That it's no way to raise a family or have a decent relationship. It's for single people."

"There's a reason people don't last more than a few years on ERT," Jordan said. "The demand on your time and body is a lot."

"I'm happy being a regular ol' beat cop for now," Patrick said, which earned him confirming nods from Jordan and Matt.

"Well, I'm currently single and in the best health of my life," said Jace, seemingly unaffected by their comments. "So, now's the time to do it. No kids, no woman. Not even a damn houseplant to neglect." He scratched at his dark scruff that clung perfectly trimmed to his chin. "Thinking I might take the bomb tech training course if I make ERT."

They ordered another pitcher and chatted while some of them watched the games overhead on the screens.

A pool table opened up, so they divided into teams and played a few rounds while snacking on the nachos Jace ordered and drinking more beer.

Aiden, of course, stuck with his club soda and kept a watchful eye on his little brother and how much he consumed.

By the time ten forty-five rolled around, they were at The Bard and Banker, an English-style pub with mood-lighting, plush fabrics, dark woods, and brass fixtures. It had fancy chandeliers hanging from the ceiling and was set in what had to be a building almost two centuries old. Like The Harbor Club, it had a few different levels, and lots of seating, but since it was Saturday night, it was packed and they found themselves having to almost yell over the music and boisterous laughter of the people around them.

They'd managed to find a table with chairs this time, which was a good thing, because Jordan was almost falling over, he was so drunk. Aiden was getting worried.

"Can I get some water, please?" Aiden asked the server when she came around to check on their drinks. "This guy needs some water."

"I'm fine," Jordan slurred.

"You're drunk," Aiden said.

"So? It's my bachelor party. Aren't I sssssupposed to be drunk?" Jordan leaned over into Aiden and got right up in his face, his beer and nacho breath making Aiden blanche. "I'm glad you're here."

Aiden smiled with his mouth closed and patted his brother on the back. "Me, too." The server brought the water and Aiden thanked her for it. "Here. You need this."

Jordan smiled sloppily. "I've learned that it wasn't our fault, you know." He glanced at Brock, then the other three Harty Boys. "Their mum taught me that. That it wasn't our fault and we need to stop carrying around this guilt."

Heat flooded Aiden's chest and he gently—or so he thought—pushed Jordan away, so he would stop breathing on him. But apparently, it was more of a shove, and hard enough that Jordan's drunk ass fell off his chair.

"Whoa!" Jace and Heath both said, while Chase helped Jordan up. He didn't fall to his back or ass, but he was struggling to stand up straight.

"What the hell, man?" Patrick said, turning to Aiden.

Aiden swallowed and his eyes darted across the faces of the other men. "I—I didn't mean to push him that hard. I swear." Though, he wasn't going to lie and say that he wasn't glad Jordan falling off his chair also shut him up. Maybe Aiden did mean to push him that hard? Was it a fear response?

Fear of other people finding out what happened?

"It's okay," Jordan said, still slurring his words. "He's still working through shit." He focused on Aiden. "I'm sorry. I should ... I shouldn't have said anything."

"What's he talking about?" Heath asked.

Jordan glanced at Heath. "Family shit, man. Just sssstupid Lassiter family shit. Our family is stupid. Our mom was stupid. Or *is* stupid. I think she's still alive. Our dad is stupid." He rolled his eyes. "How that motherfucker is still alive boggles my damn mind. And all the rest of our family that cast us aside is stupid. We're from stupid, stupid heads." He focused back on Aiden. "But we're not stupid, stupid heads. *You're* not a stupid, stupid head, Aiden. You're my brother. The only family ... the only Lassie I have. You're *Big* Lassie." He turned to his friends. "That's what Rayma calls him. Big Lassie, and now I'm Little Lassie." He dropped his voice to a whisper that wasn't a whisper at all. "But in the bedroom, I'm still Big Lassie."

Several of the men snorted and laughed.

But Jordan remained serious. "But you're my only Lassie, Big Lassie. And you're not a stupid, stupid head at all. You're my brother. And I've really missed you. We let our grief over what happened come between us. When it should have brought us closer." He looped his arm over Aiden's shoulder, but it ended up being more like Aiden's neck. "And you're my best man."

Aiden tried to smile, but his lips ended up just twisting around his face. The heat of everyone's curiosity burned into his forehead, as they all stared at him and he did his very best to stare at the scratches of the wooden table.

Brock checked his phone. "Grant's outside to drive us to Hype."

"I'll take care of the tab," Aiden said, unraveling himself from Jordan's embrace, but facing his brother. "Please drink this water."

Jordan nodded and chugged it, but a fair bit ran down his chin he drank it so fast. "Ah!" He plunked the glass on the table. "I feel soberer already."

"There's more water in the bus," Heath said, taking Jordan by the shoulder and giving Aiden a weird look. "We'll meet you out there."

Aiden nodded and went up to the bar to settle their tab.

After he finished paying, he spun around only to nearly run smack-dab into the barrel chest of Brock. "Care to tell me what that shove was about?"

Aiden was actually as tall as Brock and delighted in the fact that he could look the man in the eye. He still felt like Brock was staring *down* at him, though. "I didn't think I pushed him that hard."

"Well, you did. What was it about?"

"Family shit. Just as Jordan told you." Aiden waved his hand to dismiss the mountain of a man. He might not have any issues with these guys, but he also hardly knew them, and just because his brother was seeing their mother as a therapist, didn't mean that extended to Aiden in any way, and he wasn't about to pour out his tattered heart to the bulldozer with a scowl.

Brock nodded slowly, then grunted. "As long as we don't have anything to worry about."

"Nothing. Don't forget, I'm stone-cold sober."

"Haven't forgotten. Just makes it all the more curious why *you're* the one unable to control himself."

That wave of heat from earlier was back and flushed right up Aiden's chest and cheeks. "Didn't mean to shove him so hard. He was just a little close. And his breath stunk."

Brock grunted again and stepped to the side so Aiden could go ahead of him to the door.

Grant, Joy's husband, had pulled the black shuttle bus right up to the curb so all they had to do was climb in.

There was only the faintest scent of moth balls and what Aiden could only describe as *old person* in the bus, but otherwise, you'd never know the vehicle was used to shuttle great grandparents around the city from their retirement home.

"Could have probably walked there," Rex said, staring out the window as Grant wove them through traffic. "It's close enough."

"Yeah, but then we'd be late and our man here runs the risk of never getting a blowie again," Patrick said, chuckling as he slapped Jordan on the back from where he sat behind him.

"Why am I driving you here?" Grant asked.

"No idea. Just got a text from Rayma that said we needed to be at Hype at eleven," Jordan said with a slight slur before taking a pull off his water bottle. "And I do what my lady asks of me."

"Well, we're here," Grant said.

"That was fast," Jace said with delight, standing up and suppressing a belch. "That Thai chicken wrap is coming back on me, anybody got any Tums or Rolaids or anything?"

"Glove compartment." Grant pointed to the front dash of the bus.

"Score," Jace said, opening the glove compartment and holding up everyone else on the bus. He glanced behind him and said, "Sorry," as he popped half a dozen Tums into his mouth before bounding down the steps, out of the bus, and heaving open the door for the rest of them.

A woman with extremely short, extremely white-blonde hair stood behind the counter. "Right this way." Her smile was cunning and it was if she was holding in a secret, she was struggling to keep to herself.

They funneled down the narrow hallway and into a room, it had a window and seats behind the window, but beyond the window everything was black.

"Is this an escape room?" Matt asked. "Because I suck at those."

"Ladies and gentlemen, for one night only," a familiar feminine voice announced, her voice coming through speakers in the room they were in, "the beautiful, the talented, the salacious—Angel Eyed Dolls!" Then the lights beyond the window came on to reveal all the women who were at the bachelorette party decked out in lingerie, feathers and with one high-heeled foot propped up on a chair.

"Holy shit," Jordan said.

Aiden zoomed in on Oona who looked hotter than the fucking sun as she stood there with her Luna Love face on, pure sex in her eyes, front and center, getting ready to lead the group.

Holy shit, indeed.

The song "Buttons" by the Pussycat Dolls started up and Oona and the women behind her began to dance.

Rayma had been bugging Oona for ages to teach her burlesque.

But how could Oona do that when they lived thousands of miles from each other?

Oona wasn't sure, but now, she was fulfilling her little sister's wish.

And since Mieka was a professional dancer, and could pretty much do any move to any song ever, between the two of them, they made it happen.

She and her sisters set up the evening with the dance studio, which taught burlesque classes and had all the costumes on hand, all they had to do was pay and show up. Then they had the space until eleven-thirty to do what they needed to do. Rayma squealed with delight when she realized what they were doing, hugging Oona hard enough to bruise her ribs.

Of course, they all had to sober up a little to practice, since they were dancing in high heels, but everyone was a good sport about it. Triss—feeling big, awkward and gassy—decided to sit out the dancing, but cheered them on from her comfy chair in the corner.

Oona and Mieka had prepared a simple but sexy routine, which they taught to the rest of the women, and at eleven, Triss was going to film it.

There was a big mirror in front of them, and Oona kept reminding all the women to keep their sexy faces on. To pretend that it wasn't a mirror, that it was their man sitting there in a chair and they were giving him a private dance.

That prompted Peyton to speak up and say with an embellished pout that she didn't have a man.

"You can just dance for a pretend man," Rayma offered.

"That seems so pathetic," Peyton said, deepening her pout even more so that her bottom lip curled and pushed outward. "I'll just dance for an empty chair. At least it can't dump me." Then she grabbed the bottle of tequila that Mieka had smuggled in her purse and took a pull, then made a face of instant regret.

For only a few hours of training and practice, the women did exceptionally well. Krista was a little rigid and awkward at first, and she said that her outfit was riding up and chafing funny, so they switched her costume and she relaxed and got right into it. Lydia and Stacey couldn't stop giggling, and Pasha, Rayma, and Mieka broke formation and had a twerking contest in front of the mirror.

They were all laughing until their sides and faces hurt, but eventually, they rallied and finished their routine.

Even though they had no audience, Oona wanted everyone to perform like they did. Which was why she asked Triss to film it. So all the women could take home their keepsake and watch it later, or show their partner, but not have to worry about actually performing in front of anyone. Because even though Oona performed all the time, it still spun her gut like the tea cup ride at an amusement park right before she went on stage.

They did a similar routine to the one she performed on stage with her crew the night she met Aiden. They had black folding chairs that they danced on and around, stuck their butts in the air, ran their hands down their torsos provocatively, bit their bottom lips and shimmied their hips and butts. They did the splits as best they could, rocked their curves and jostled all the bits their mamas gave them.

Then each woman got a few seconds to move to the center and do her own freestyle dance, while giving the camera fuck-me eyes, and feeling sexier than ever.

It was all about female empowerment and feeling confident and sexy in your own skin. They were all different sizes, shapes, and colors, but every single one of them was sexy, beautiful, and a bad ass bitch.

By the time the song was over, they were all exhausted and breathing heavily.

But what they hadn't anticipated, as their chests heaved and they remained in their end pose, was for the sudden burst of cheering, whooping, *whistling*, and clapping from just beyond the mirror.

Then a light flicked on and the mirror was revealed to not just be a mirror at all, but a *two*-way mirror, and on the other side of it was the bachelor party.

No wonder she recognized that whistle.

Every woman's mouth dropped open, but the men just kept cheering.

The only person who didn't looked stunned and slowly growing redder in the cheeks by the second, was Rayma. She was all smiles and waving.

"I texted Little Lassie and told them to come at eleven," she said, so proud of herself. "I wanted him to see this. And I figured all the guys would want to watch."

As it turned out, Bella, Denise, and Chelsea were actually married or dating three of the police officers at the bachelor party—Tyler, Matt, and Patrick. So besides Mieka and Triss, whose men were still ranching it up in Colorado, everyone but Peyton and Oona were attached.

Slowly, the women who could see their partners, started to break formation and the color fled their cheeks. Then the men rushed in and those whose partners were there found their woman and scooped them up. Or at least Jordan, Heath, Rex, Patrick, Matt, and Tyler did. Brock, who was with Krista and Chase who was with Stacey, were a little more reserved, simply walking up to their wives with big, smitten smiles on their faces.

Jordan spun Rayma around while her feet dangled in the air and she giggled. "Glad you came, Little Lassie?" she asked.

"Absolutely." He beamed.

"And now you still get blowjobs," she added.

Oona's eyes found Aiden. He was watching her like a bird of prey. Laser-focused, barely blinking. She squirmed and heat rushed through her. His lids were hooded and his nostrils flared.

Rayma turned to the group. "I hope you don't mind that I messaged Little Lassie. I just missed him."

Heads shook and chatter echoed around them.

"We only have the place until eleven-thirty," Triss reminded everyone from her chair in the corner.

"Does that mean we have to go home?" Rayma asked, her expression similar to the one she used to make when they were kids and Oona said Rayma had to sleep in her own bed and not in Oona's.

"No," Pasha said quickly, then stifled a yawn. "We just have the studio until eleven-thirty."

"We could go to an after-hours lounge," Jace offered, his eyes roaming Peyton appreciatively.

The majority of the group nodded, then the women took off to go change.

Rayma found Oona in the change room. "You're not mad I invited them?"

Oona sat down on the wooden bench that ran along one wall so she could remove her fishnet stockings. "No, kiddo, I'm not. This is your party and if you wanted your fiancé there, then that's your choice. I *do* think a heads up would have been appropriate, though. Since some people get stage fright and didn't sign up to perform in front of other people's husbands."

The corners of Rayma's mouth curled down and she nodded. "Yeah, I know. I just thought if I asked, they'd say no, then their men would never get to see them. And everyone rocked it."

"I don't think there are any hard feelings. We all love you, and you're right, every woman in here rocked that dance."

Rayma bent down and kissed Oona on the cheek. "Thank you, Oons, this was more than I ever expected."

"You're welcome, kiddo. And you're worth it."

Triss entered the change room. "Uh ... we have a bit of an issue."

Everyone stopped what they were doing and looked up.

"Our limo driver's wife's water just broke, and she is already eight centimeters dilated. She's having a home birth and the midwife is with his wife and telling Andre he needs to haul ass home." Triss's lips twisted in resignation.

"Oh shit," Pasha said, pulling her black shift dress over her black bra and panties. "He might not make it, depending on where he lives."

Triss nodded. "And we're also without a ride."

"Oh, I didn't even think of that," Pasha said.

"Brock says that there's enough room on the guy's bus, though, so if we're okay making this a joint party, we don't need to worry about securing cabs home." Triss scanned everyone in the change room.

All the women shrugged and nodded.

"Okay, I'll go tell the guys to pick up their dirty socks and put the toilet seat down." Then Triss disappeared back into the studio.

"I hope Andre gets home in time," Rayma said, then she turned to Pasha. "How many centimeters do you need to get to, to have a baby?"

"Ten," Pasha said.

"Shit, he better floor it then."

They got re-dressed in their black outfits—all but Rayma who wore white—and joined the men in the studio.

Rayma gave Oona a brief bio on everyone the other day, so even though she hadn't been introduced to all the guys, she knew who each of them was based on Rayma's very accurate descriptions.

Jace, the beefy best-friend of Jordan was on his phone when they joined the men, but he quickly ended his call and stowed his cell in the back pocket of his dark jeans, which hugged his very nice butt to perfection. "Got us a VIP table at Dark River."

"How'd you swing that?" Jordan asked as they all walked through the studio hallway toward the front door.

Pasha stayed behind to thank the girl at the front desk.

"The owner is my sister's brother in-law. I just called up Florian and told him what we needed. He said he'd make it happen."

"Cool," Jordan said, smacking Jace on the back. "Always good to have friends with connections."

Everyone piled into the bus, which was being driven by a handsome older gentleman with more salt than pepper in his hair, stormy gray eyes and a very nice smile. Oona knew this was Grant, Joy's husband, but despite the fact he was probably old enough to be Oona's father, it was impossible not to appreciate how attractive he was. She also knew that Rayma teased Grant relentlessly about how good looking he was. Called him a Zaddy and other things that apparently made Grant roll his eyes and go pink in the cheeks.

"Where to?" Grant asked, once they were all seated.

"Dark River which is off Humboldt," Jace said, sliding in beside Peyton on the bus. She glanced up at him and blushed as she smiled, her grays eyes taking in his big arms. The man was not wearing a jacket, and the cords in his forearms stuck out as if someone had wrapped his limbs in twine. She licked her lips at the same time Jace glanced down at her. "Hi."

"Hi," she said breathlessly, tucking a strand of her wavy brick-red hair behind her ear.

He offered her his hand. She took it. "Jace."

"Peyton."

His eyes went wide. "Oh! You're Peyton? I've been looking forward to meeting you. Apparently, we are walking down the aisle together."

"Wh-what?" she stammered.

"I'm a groomsman, and you're a bridesmaid, right?"

"Oh! Haha. Yeah. Sorry. I thought ..."

His grin was sexy and full of sin. "I'm surprised we haven't met already, since you're Rayma's best friend and Jordan is mine."

"Yeah ..." Peyton said. Oona could practically hear the woman's heart hammering against her ribcage.

"Then again, I'm training for ERT, so I haven't been around much."

"Right ..." Peyton scraped her top teeth over her bottom lip and nodded. "Y-your arms are huge," she blurted out.

Jace was all smiles.

A snort behind Oona had her spinning around to find Aiden rolling his eyes and shaking his head. "What the fuck is your problem?" she hissed under her breath. She was sitting in a seat by herself, and so was he. Everyone else on the bus was paired up.

"No problem," he said.

"Liar."

"What did you just call me, *Luna*?"

"Nothing, *Caden*. Oh wait, I did. I called you a *liar*. Because you obviously have a problem, but like everything else in your life, you're in fucking denial about it."

Anger flared in his eyes, which wasn't easy to see given how dark the bus was now that they were driving. "Are we discussing each others faults right now? Is that what we're doing? Should we discuss your little performance last night at dinner? Laying cash on the table to pay for their fucking hot water bill? Could you be anymore pathetic?"

"Me? What about you? Rubbing it in that you were just pulling your weight and not being a freeloader? Insinuating that I *was* being one because I didn't cook some elaborate five-course meal."

"I insinuated nothing. You obviously inferred it because you're so insecure."

186

Her jaw dropped and she spun around more to face him, her voice rising. "Are you fucking kidding me?"

"Not kidding anything. Just making an observation."

"Would you like *me* to articulate some of *my* observations, *Officer* Lassiter?"

His nostrils flared and a tight scowl slashed across his face. They stared at each other in the dark of the bus while conversations and laughter filtered around them.

The bus came to a stop. "We're here," Grant announced.

"Sweet," Rayma said, standing up first and heading to the door of the bus, Jordan behind her.

They filed out and followed Jace down the stairs to the underground lounge in an old brick building. There was no signage for Dark River and if Jace wasn't a cop, Oona would have probably said, "No, thanks, this screams horror movie."

Once the door to the lounge opened, music pumped out, calling them in from the cold like a bard's lute in the belly of a castle, to come warm themselves by the hearth and drink mead with the lord.

Jace stalked his big frame forward, being led by a short man with an expensive suit and a comb-over. A velvet rope was opened allowing them to step up into a big booth area.

"I've never been here before," Rayma said, snuggling into Jordan's arm. "It's pretty cool."

And it was. With dark velvet booths, dimmed bedroom lighting, and swaths of gauzy fabric in rich jewel-tones draping the walls and hanging from the ceiling. There were even some four-post canopy beds scattered around, while women dressed in very little did erotic acrobatics in aerial silks fastened to the exposed wooden rafters. The whole vibe of the place was—seductive relaxation with just a splash of the forbidden.

A few bottles of champagne were brought over and the Harty boys took to deploying the corks and pouring the bubbly.

Thank God, Aiden was on the opposite side of the booth, because if he'd been in kicking distance, Oona wasn't sure she could have restrained herself.

However, being on the opposite side of the over-stuffed velvet seating, meant he was directly in her line of sight and she was forced to look at him no matter what.

And of course, that asshole was staring right at her. Daring her to say something. To reveal something she'd analyzed about him.

"You okay?" Triss asked, whispering into her ear. "I saw you two arguing on the bus." They were side-by-side on the booth, with Mieka on the other side of Oona.

Mieka leaned in. "What's wrong?"

Oona flicked her gaze between her sisters.

"Who were you arguing with?" Mieka asked. "I saw you talking with Aiden. Were you arguing with him?"

Oona's mouth twisted.

Mieka's gaze darted to Aiden, who was still watching them.

Then her eyes went wide and she pivoted back to face Oona. "Did you hook up with Jordan's brother?"

"I didn't say a word," Triss said quickly. "Swear to God." She held up her pinky.

"You just did," Oona scolded, which made Triss's cheeks grow pink.

Mieka's mouth formed a surprised *O* shape. "You did! You hooked up with him?"

Mieka used to dance for the cruise ships until she broke her arm and they took that as an opportunity not to renew her contract. Devastated, and lost, feeling as though she no longer had a life's purpose, she fled to the ranch in Colorado to visit Triss, which was where she fell in love with Triss's brother in-law Nate. Now, Nate was building Mieka a dance studio on the ranch and she was going to teach lessons to all the rural kids. She was also the most like Rayma. Not *as* filter-free, but damn close. She was also the next wildest of all the sisters. She didn't put their parents through the wringer like Rayma did, but she snuck out a lot and lied about her whereabouts more than Pasha, Triss, and Oona.

"When?" Mieka asked, unable to keep herself from looking back over to Aiden.

"Long story," Oona said. "Regardless, we do *not* get along. Despite our *brief—*"

"Horizontal flamenco?" Mieka cut in.

Oona rolled her eyes and sipped her champagne. "I was going to say *encounter.*"

"Of the naked kind," Mieka added cheekily, taking a small nip of bubbly from her flute.

"Regardless. It won't be happening again, and we need to keep it under wraps for Rayma's sake. I don't want my folly to affect our baby sister's wedding at all. We're trying not to be awkward."

"But the sexual tension and the fact that you've probably had his dick in your mouth is making it difficult and all kinds of awkward, right?" Mieka asked.

Oona growled. Triss leaned over and shoved Mieka in the shoulder.

"I'm just making an observation. And what I *observed* when you two were talking on the bus was a whole lot of pent up ... *heat*, but no where to vent it."

"Shots!" Rayma cheered as a server brought over a tray of shots, this time with a clear liquid inside.

Oona exhaled in relief from the distraction and change of subject. She reached over and grabbed one off the tray, then slammed it back before even asking what it was.

"Thank God they're not those porn star things again," Krista murmured, taking a shot off the tray as she snuggled into Brock's big embrace.

He, on the other hand, eyed the liquid in the shot glass suspiciously, took his wife's from her and gave it a sniff. Then he shook his head. "Smells like pie."

"What is this?" Krista asked, turning to Rayma who just grabbed her shot glass off the tray.

"It's an apple cake."

"Which is?" Stacey probed, eyeing the tray as it came to her like it was a dog that might bite her, or in the steaming pie that might burn her tongue.

"Apple liqueur and vanilla vodka," Rayma said plainly before downing hers like it was no big deal.

Several others followed and they all made faces. Some expressions conveyed delight and relief, while others cringed at how sweet it was.

It hadn't been terrible, a little sweet, but it was better than the porn star. Oona shrugged, grabbed another one off the tray, clinked her shooter against Mieka's, then the two of them linked arms like married people do and downed their apple cakes.

Then she sipped the dry champagne to cleanse her palate, all the while the heat of Aiden's gaze on her was enough to make sweat form between her breasts.

The man had some intense stares, that was for sure. And in her slightly boozy state, she was having a hard time discerning his lusty looks from his judgmental ones.

She knew all about resting bitch face.

Did Aiden have resting aroused and disgruntled face?

She snickered inwardly at the word *disgruntled*. It was a funny word.

The two parties continued to drink and socialize. More champagne bottles came out, along with trays and trays of shots that Rayma kept ordering.

It was nearly one-thirty by the time they all decided to pack it in and head home.

Both Jordan and Rayma were sufficiently plastered, hanging off each other and stumbling their way up the stairs from the lounge to the waiting bus.

Oona was also drunker than she'd been in a long time—possibly ever.

It was just easier to distract herself with drinking, than allow the frustration and confusion she felt about Aiden fester like an untreated wound. That of course, didn't stop Mieka from making more than one comment about how sisters marrying brothers was the best and that she highly recommended it.

But she didn't know the whole story.

She just knew that Oona and Aiden had slept together and that the possibility of that happening again was less than zero.

"I thought you didn't drink," came a dark and husky voice right next to her ear as she made her way up the brick stairs from the lounge to the sidewalk. The air was freeze-your-nipples cold, and she shivered as she wrapped her leather jacket tighter around herself.

Obviously, it was Aiden.

Everyone else there—besides Triss who had an obvious reason to stay sober—was drinking.

She ignored him.

His growl made her nipples pebble harder than they already were from that frigid wind whipping off the water like it had something to prove. Like it was reminding the east coasters that just because the thermostat might not read low double-digits, didn't mean the weather couldn't freeze the balls off a prize bull.

They were the last to climb onto the bus and she gasped when his hand grazed her calf behind her as she took the top step.

"You okay?" Grant asked her, his expression creased with fatherly concern.

Oona flashed him a drunken smile. "Yeah, just almost tripped." Then she kicked backward, hoping to make contact with the man behind her, only she didn't and she had to reach out and grip the railing and dash for support.

"Careful," Grant said, reaching out to steady her.

"Thanks." She gave him another big smile, then found her seat.

Even though there were empty seats, Aiden chose to cram in beside her, squishing her into the window.

She glared at him just as the bus pulled away from the curb. "What the fuck? Go sit somewhere else."

"I thought you didn't drink," he repeated, the hooded lids of his eyes and the glare in his irises making her squeeze her thighs together and saliva fill her mouth.

Why did this asshole turn her on so much? She hated that she wanted him as much as she loathed him. That the dimples in his cheeks made her pussy flutter.

"That's not what I said," she bit back. "I never said I didn't drink. I said, *I don't drink very often.*"

"You also said you don't drink when you're out. Only home or with friends and maybe one or two glasses of wine," he countered, his smile smug and something she desperately wanted to punch—or kiss—off his face.

Oooh, please let it be the former.

She'd never forgive herself if it was the latter.

"This is an extenuating circumstance. And I'm not so rigid with my life that I don't allow for those. It's my baby sister's bachelorette party. A one-off. And, I happen to think I could not be around a safer crowd of people to over-imbibe. My sister is a doctor, and her husband and his brothers are like formers SEALs or something, then there are like seven cops here, too. If that's not a safe group to let down my hair around, well then, I may as well go live in a cave in Belize or something because the world has obviously gone to shit."

For how drunk she felt and how fast her head was spinning, she articulated all of that pretty well. But she resisted the urge to give herself a high five. She did mentally, though.

"Or it's called no self-control."

Her mouth dropped open and she gaped at him. "Are you fucking kidding me?" Oh, crap. Her voice was a lot louder than she expected it to be.

Conversation came to a stand-still in the bus and everyone turned to face them.

"What's happening?" Rayma asked, sitting on Jordan's lap in their seat. "Is Big Lassie still claiming he wasn't yanking it in the bathroom the other night?"

Oona sneered at Aiden before addressing her sister. "No. He just told me that I have no self-control when it comes to alcohol."

Chapter Fifteen

Aiden knew the moment it came out of his mouth that he'd have been better off sticking his foot directly into his pie-hole. The look on Oona's face had him feeling instant regret.

Then her expression changed from one of horror, to one of revenge.

"Bro," Jordan said. "Not cool. You hardly know Oona, why would you say something like that?"

"Because when we met, I told him I didn't drink very much," Oona said.

"When you met the other night?" Jordan asked, completely oblivious.

Oona shook her head. "No. When we met back in Montreal. It was after one of my shows and we met in the bar. I told him I didn't drink very often. I ordered a Shirley Temple. Now, he's throwing it in my face that I over-indulged tonight and is calling me a liar."

"I never said—"

"So wait, you two met before we introduced you?" Jordan asked. "But you acted like strangers." He scratched his head. "Am I just that drunk? Or is everyone else really confused, too?"

"Confused," several people said, nodding, and murmuring.

"We met at the bar and then—" Oona swallowed, but avoided looking at Aiden, "then we slept together."

"You WHAT?" Rayma exclaimed, her brown eyes wide as she tried to scramble off Jordan's lap. "Why didn't you tell me?"

"Because it did not end well," Oona said. "The next day, it turns out that Aiden was to be my next patient. When we met at the bar, I was Luna and he was *Caden*. We never exchanged last names."

"Oh shit," Grant murmured from the front.

"I obviously said no to treating him, because of a conflict of interest. And he got mad. Said I was holding his job hostage and making our night together a bigger deal than it was."

"Bro," Jace said, his arm draped around the backseat behind Peyton. "Not cool."

Heat spun through Aiden and his gut churned like he was the one who'd had one-too-many shots and needed a garbage bin or for the bus to pull over. He was in the hot seat, and it was of his own making.

Oona was on a tirade now. A revenge tirade and he had no idea how to stop her.

It would probably be worse for him if he did.

He braced for the impact and kept his mouth shut.

"I apologized, but that wasn't good enough. He didn't see the problem, he stormed out and said I was bad in bed just before he left."

"Whoa!" several people in the bus said.

Jace shook his big block head. "Not cool, man. Not cool."

Rayma looked ready to explode as she glared at Aiden. Then she shifted her gaze back to Jordan. "Did you know this?"

Jordan blinked several times at his fiancée. "This is the first time I am hearing it just like you. I thought they met in the airport."

Rayma's brows relaxed, then she faced Aiden again. "What the fuck is your deal, buddy? Hmm? I can tell you right now that even though I have no personal

194

experience—because *ew*—I know that my sister is not bad in bed. You've seen her dance. Can somebody who dances like that be bad in bed?"

No. No, they couldn't.

And Aiden knew first hand that Oona was not bad in bed at all.

She'd been incredible the two times they'd been together.

But he reacted out of anger and said the first thing he knew would strike the bullseye and do the most amount of damage. His first instinct had been to go on the offense. A form of self-preservation that landed him in hot water more often than not.

"So, you two have been silently feuding in our house for the past several days?" Jordan asked, drunk and bewildered and looking at Aiden in a way that made a crippling ache form in Aiden's chest. They'd made significant strides in their relationship over the last few days, and all of that seemed to be crumbling like a gingerbread house out in the rain.

Oona nodded, then turned to Rayma. "I wanted to keep it a secret. I tried so hard to just act like nothing happened. To pretend this *asshole* was just a stranger and that we could co-exist in your apartment until the wedding was over. For you, kiddo, I would do anything. I don't want my drama to affect your special day." Her last few words came out choked and she sniffled.

The hot and hateful glares coming at Aiden from everyone in the bus had him squirming in his seat.

How much more was Oona going to tell them?

Was she going to let them know that he was suspended from work? Would she tell them why? With all the cops on the bus, he already knew the kind of judgment they'd strike him with. The way they'd look at him.

Everyone already hated him. But they could hate him harder.

"I can swap places with Oona," Mieka said. "I can go stay with Rayma and Jordan and she can move into the basement suite with Triss and Asher when he gets here."

Oona waved her hand. "No, it's fine. Honestly. The only reason any of this came out is because I apparently turn into Rayma when I'm drunk and have no filter," Oona said. "I can handle *him*."

"But you shouldn't have to," Pasha said, giving Aiden the stink-eye.

Aiden exhaled and hung his head. "I can go stay at a hotel."

"Now he speaks," Mieka sneered. "Not a bad idea."

"First stop," Grant said. "Patrick and Bella, I believe."

Patrick and Bella got up from their seats near the back of the bus, both of them casting Aiden harsh looks, while softening their eyes and smiling when they glanced at Oona. "Thanks, Grant," Patrick said, before stepping out of the bus.

"Saying someone is bad in bed is like the lowest of the low, man," Rayma said. "Like who even does that?"

"Were you just pissed off she wasn't the pole and burlesque dancer you met at the hotel? That she has a good job and brains and is probably a hell of a lot smarter than you?" Mieka asked. "That she didn't want to compromise her career and see you as a patient given the conflict of interest?"

"She's like two different people," Aiden blurted out.

"How?" Pasha asked. "How is she two different people?"

"Luna the performer and Oona the ..."

"Stuck up bitch?" Mieka asked.

"I didn't say that!" Aiden quickly said.

"Didn't have to, *bruh*," Rayma said, crossing her arms over her chest and staring laser beams at Aiden, her head shaking in disbelief. "I just ... how could I be so wrong about you ... *Aiden*? Because you're sure as hell not Big Lassie anymore. You're just *Aiden*. Probably bad in bed, decent in the kitchen and terrible on a bus." Then she made a raspberry with her tongue and folded herself into a pout.

After that, the bus went quiet as Grant drove around the city dropping people off.

196

Rayma, Jordan, Oona and Aiden weren't the last people to be dropped off, but they were close.

Aiden let the three of them go ahead of him as they exited the bus, and he could feel the glares from the rest of the remaining passengers boring into his back. A hand landed on his arm as he was about to take the first step down. "Something far bigger is going on and you need to fix it," Grant said, his voice even and not without kindness. "I don't know you from a hole in the wall, but I love Rayma *and* Jordan like they're my own, so if you do anything to ruin their day, you will have an entire family coming after you."

Aiden clenched his molars together and appraised the older man before nodding and turning to face the apartment building. He climbed down the steps and didn't look behind him as the bus pulled away. He followed Jordan inside, where Rayma and Oona were already pulling off their boots.

"Oons, you go shower first," Rayma said, her eyes glassy and having a hard time focusing. She swayed a little.

Oona didn't say a word. She just nodded and went to the guest room, returning a moment later, her arms loaded with her towels, pajamas and toiletries.

Once the bathroom door closed and the shower started, Rayma rounded on Aiden, her finger pointed at him as she stalked forward. "You sssonofabitch," she slurred, poking him hard in the chest. "How dare you hurt her. How *dare* you."

Jordan stood behind the kitchen island drinking a glass of water and watching his fiancée with veiled interest.

"You better do some hardcore fucking grovelling, *bruh*," Rayma started. "Apologize and make amends. I don't care how. But Oona Young is the salt of the motherfucking earth and the fact that you hurt her just makes me want to yank out all your hair, and shove it down your throat until you choke on it."

Rayma wasn't super short, but she was definitely shorter than Aiden, but what the woman lacked in height, she made up for in presence and spirit. She kept poking his chest with her finger, glaring up at him, a harsh and unforgiving sneer on her face as her eye makeup, which had smudged and fallen below her eyes a bit throughout the night, just gave her a bit of a deranged and almost terrorizing look.

"She might have been trying to keep your ... *whatever the fuck it is*, a secret to protect my special day, but it will be special no matter what." She rose up onto her tippy toes, which brought her eye level with Aiden's neck. "Whether you're there or not. We Young sisters protect our own and if you don't fix this, be prepared for four sisters to come after you with their claws out." She pulled her finger away, then bent the fingers on both hands like they were claws and hissed at him like some kind of feral honey badger or mongoose. Then she flicked her gaze to Jordan. "I'm going to bed. Too tired for sex, though. Sorry, Lassie. Love you."

She gave one final hard, warning glare to Aiden before spinning on her heels and stalking off to their bedroom, where she closed the door.

Jordan had remained quiet since they got into the apartment.

Aiden didn't say a word. He didn't know what to say. So he just went about making up the pullout couch.

Jordan remained in the kitchen, drinking water and watching Aiden.

Oona exited the bathroom but didn't say anything to either of them. She just skittered around the corner into the guest room and closed the door.

Once the door *snicked* shut, Jordan came around the island and into the living room. He sat down in the La-Z-Boy and lifted his brows at Aiden who was just finishing up his bed. "You know who you reminded me of tonight?" Jordan said, his words slow and deliberate, like he was tasting each syllable on his tongue as he said them.

Aiden's heart started to hammer.

"Like Dad," Jordan said.

Aiden rounded on him.

Jordan's brows hiked up nearly to his hairline, challenging Aiden to contradict him. "You might not have been a raging drunk like him, but you played the belligerent asshole card as if he'd handed it to you himself."

Aiden stopped what he was doing and gaped at his brother. "What the fuck? I am not. I'm nothing like him."

"You don't think so?" Jordan asked, remaining calm. "Because the dad I remember always rustled up an excuse for his behavior. Always justified his anger in some way. Deflected the blame. Made it *our* fault. Or Mom's fault. *We* made him mad. *We* were the reason he drank. The reason he lost his temper. The reason he was unable to control his emotions or his addiction."

"I ..."

"Now is your chance to tell me exactly what happened. Leave nothing out, so I can have both sides of the story and *then* cast my judgment. Because right now, Aiden, everyone is out for your jugular. I am the only hope you have of even remaining invited to this wedding." He swallowed. "And fucking hell, I want my brother there beside me. But if my fiancée says you're not welcome, then you're not welcome."

Aiden held Jordan's gaze for a long moment. Probably longer than a minute before he let his eyes close, his shoulders drop, and his chin fall to his chest.

"Have a seat," Jordan said, indicating Aiden should climb onto his bed and prop himself up on the back of the couch.

Aiden did that but he didn't say anything.

"Can't help you if you don't talk," Jordan said, impatience creeping into his voice, along with his weariness.

"Got suspended," Aiden murmured. "'bout five months ago."

He couldn't bring himself to look at his brother, but he could tell out of the corner of his eye that Jordan's mouth dropped open.

"Pulled a guy over, he'd been drinking, had his kid in the car and I punched him. The driver, not the kid."

Jordan shoved his fingers into his hair, and made a loud exhale accompanied by a, "Fuck."

"Wasn't the first time I got *overly invested* in a DUI and they suspended me this time. Other times were just warnings. But someone videotaped me punching the guy and it went a little viral. CCRC did an investigation, I went to court and the judge ruled that I have to go to anger management and counseling before I can return to the force. And even then, I'll be on probation and not allowed to ride alone for up to a year."

"Let me guess, Oona was supposed to be your therapist?"

Aiden nodded. "After being on a waitlist for months."

"So you figured you'd be stuck on a waitlist again—kept from going back to work even longer—because she declined treating you, given your ... new kind of a relationship."

Aiden grunted and nodded. "Just felt like she was holding my career hostage, while only looking out for her own. Didn't give a shit what this would do to me. How long I'd been waiting to see her. They say she's the best for PTSD and shit. I could separate what happened the night before, why couldn't she?"

"So when she declined, you—"

"Retaliated with anger."

"I see."

"We've, um, also—" Fuck, he felt like a teenager, confessing his sins to the pastor or something. Not that they were a religious family—though his mother did try to get them to go to church for special occasions like Christmas and Easter. "We slept together again, since we've been here in Victoria."

Jordan grumbled something, then pried himself out of his chair. "I need a fucking beer."

Aiden resisted the urge to say anything snarky about needing alcohol to cope, though it sat hot and bouncy on his tongue. But he was trying to be better. He was already in a scalding kettle of trouble, and the last thing he needed to do was offend his remaining lifeline—his brother.

Jordan returned to the La-Z-Boy with a beer and took a pull from the bottle. "When did this happen?"

"A couple of mornings ago. You and Rayma were at work. Oona slept in, I went for a run, came back, had a shower, she was making a smoothie and ..." He tossed his hands up. "We hate fucked."

"Hate fucked?"

"I don't know what else to call it. We certainly don't *like* each other."

"Right."

"That was the only time?"

Aiden nodded. "We've argued a lot since arriving here, though."

"Yeah, that display at dinner the other night when you cooked was fucking weird. Rayma and I talked about it in bed later and couldn't figure out what was going on. Rayma thought it was sexual tension, but I said *no way*."

Aiden snorted. Oh, there was definitely sexual tension. Along with a myriad of other complicated things.

"Neither of us guessed it was this messy, though," Jordan went on. "Thought maybe things were just awkward since Rayma said she could set you guys up and you both knew she was attempting it."

"No, it goes a lot deeper than that."

"Clearly."

"So, have you seen another therapist?"

Aiden shook his head. "I got expedited to the top of another list and I start seeing a different therapist shortly after the new year."

"I'm sure Oona had a hand in making that happen."

Yeah, Aiden was sure of it, too.

"She's just ..."

Jordan's brows hiked.

"She's like two different people."

"You said that earlier."

"The Luna Love I met the night at the bar was fun and playful, bold, and intriguing. She was the perfect combination of sweet and sexy. But Oona Young is closed-off and pretentious, rigid, and all business. It was like getting whiplash when I walked into her office and saw her."

"You think Rayma is the same at home as she is at work? That she's as outspoken, filter-free, and," he brought his voice down to a whisper, "bat shit crazy in the best kind of way, with her social work clients as she is here in the comfort of her own home?"

Aiden shook his head.

"No. Of course not. We all adopt different forms of ourselves depending on our environment and the situation. Just like, I'm going to be more candid with you than I would be with say Krista. She might be family, but she's still a superior officer and I have to maintain that level of respect and distance. I'm also not going to be as playful with you as I am my fiancée. Don't expect me to pinch your nipple or slap your ass anytime soon."

Aiden rolled his eyes.

But Jordan remained serious. "Oona is also *a performer,* so much so that she adopts a different name and probably a different personality. Did you tell her you were Police Officer Aiden, when you met?"

"No. I told her I was Caden and a first responder. She told me she was Luna and in healthcare."

"Lies veiled in truth. And I'm sure you were a little different than your authentic self because the freedom of anonymity allowed you to step outside your comfort zone."

Aiden hadn't really thought about it like that, but he had to agree. He hadn't been so different from who he really was, but maybe a little. Maybe enough.

"Oona just stayed in character a little longer once the curtain closed. You can't fault her for that. It might be a safe place for her to be. She may know that she's rigid as Oona, but playful as Luna, and that you responded positively to Luna, so she gave you what you responded to."

Aiden's head was going to explode.

He'd really fucked up.

"I don't know her *that* well, but I think Oona is great. Rayma has nothing but amazing things to say about her, and seems to idolize her. And that's saying a lot. So, if she gets the Rayma stamp of approval, then she has mine, as well."

"How do I fix this?" Aiden asked.

"Start by apologizing, then see what else you can do?" Jordan shrugged. "The Young sisters might be fierce, but their hearts are enormous. If Rayma can forgive me for ghosting her for three years, then maybe Oona can forgive you for lashing out."

"And if she doesn't?" Aiden asked, his body achy from how much his gut spun and his heart hurt.

Jordan shrugged, finished his beer, and got up from his La-Z-Boy with a grunt. "Won't know until you try."

Chapter Sixteen

The next morning, Aiden got up before anyone else in the house and went out for a run. Thankfully, the clouds rolled in sometime during the night and it started to rain, which meant it wasn't cold enough to freeze, and he didn't have to worry about black ice patches trying to kill him.

By the time he got back from his run, the house was quiet.

He knew he wasn't alone, but he also knew there was only one other person there.

Rayma.

Her car was parked out front on the street, while Jordan's truck was gone.

Aiden couldn't smell Oona's unique floral-nutty scent, so he knew she wasn't there, either.

"Ah, you're home," came Rayma's voice as she opened her bedroom door. "Good. Shower, get dressed, then we have an appointment."

Aiden scrunched his brows. "Huh? We already did the serge fitting."

"I know." Her cool disinterest was muddling. He didn't know Rayma very well, but what he did know was that the woman exuded warmth and bubbliness. Right now, she was flat, cold, and regarding him with lightly veiled disdain.

Not that he didn't deserve it, but the contrast in demeanor was still jarring.

He didn't ask anymore questions, because Rayma left him no room to ask them. So he did as he was told and showered, then got dressed.

He barely had on his shirt and she was standing by their front door with her keys in her hand, tapping her foot. "Don't have all day, *bruh*. I *do* have a wedding to plan, you know."

"Right. Sorry." He tossed on his dark gray winter jacket and slid into his boots, then followed her out to her car. "You're taking me out to the woods to kill me, aren't you?" he asked, adding an uncomfortable chuckle to the end of that sentence.

She shot him a look over her shoulder that said, "Don't tempt me."

They drove in silence for about fifteen minutes, then pulled up to a well-maintained red brick bungalow with a big shop on one side, a white sedan and a gray SUV parked in the driveway. Although it was winter, the yard was immaculate and probably boasted candy-colored flowers in the spring. Twin hooks were drilled into the beams of the garage overhang where hanging baskets overflowing with life probably hung like earrings during the summer.

But for now, there was a green wreath with red and silver accents on the door, some tastefully hung Christmas lights, and a welcome mat with a Christmas tree on it that had two giant gift boxes below it. "Is that—"

"Yes, it's a dick and balls on the welcome mat," Rayma said, not bothering to knock, but going right in. "Nana! Grantpa! I'm here. Put your clothes back on, you horny old buggers."

"We're in the kitchen," a man's voice called.

"Doing the nasty where you make our Christmas turkey?" Rayma said, kicking off her boots at the front door, then making her way into the house. The place was warm and cozy. An enormous Christmas tree sat in one corner of the living room, bedazzled to within an inch of its life with ornaments and warm white lights, while heaps of gifts sat below glittering with festive wrapping paper and bows.

Rayma entered the kitchen, Aiden on her heels. There, they found Grant, their driver from last night, sitting at the kitchen table sipping from a coffee cup, while a tiny woman who was probably not even five-feet-tall with her gray hair up in a tight ballerina bun fussed over a stove with simmering pots. She wore a frilly apron with daisies on it and dark jeans and a long-sleeve button-up shirt in a soft pink. Her blue eyes lit up like birthday candles when she saw Rayma.

"Hello, my darling," she said, embracing Rayma. "Am I talking too loud for you?"

Rayma hugged the woman back, giving her a real, genuine squeeze. "I can handle my liquor, Nana, you know that."

"How's your husband-to-be fairing this morning?" Grant asked.

"A little less raring to go, he said his head hurt when he woke up, but he's functioning on most of his cylinders. He got a call early this morning about a case he was working on. Needed to pop down to the station to help with a report. Dropped Oona off at Pasha's on the way."

Aiden knew she was giving the information to her and Grant in a way that was also educating him of his brother and Oona's whereabouts, since he hadn't asked, but had been crazy-curious.

"And this must be Aiden," the woman said, her gaze roaming Aiden for a moment with carefully cloaked judgment.

Aiden cleared his throat and stuck out his hand. "Nice to meet you ... Mrs. Hart? Mrs. ...?" He glanced at Grant. Grant wasn't the Harty Boys father, he knew that. They'd all called him by his first name last night, so he was probably her second husband, and therefore didn't share the same last name as his stepsons. But did she keep her former last name, the one she shared with her sons? Or did she take Grant's? Or did she keep her maiden name?

"You can just call me Joy, honey," she said, taking his hand and giving it a firm shake. "Can I get you two some coffee?"

"None for me, Nana," Rayma said. "I have to go to the florists, then pick up the flower girl dresses from the seamstress and—" Her phone started to warble in her pocket and she grabbed it. "It's Pasha." She put it to her ear. "Hey, what's up?" They all watched as Rayma's happy, carefree expression fell from her face, as if someone had strapped anvils to it and tossed it off the side of a bridge. Her eyes went wide in horror and her blinking became deliberate and frequent. "Why? Why? Why?"

Joy rested a hand on Rayma's shoulder. "Put it on speaker, sweetie."

Rayma nodded, but her hands shook as she tried. Joy ended up having to take the phone from her and do it. "Pasha, my love, it's Joy, you're on speakerphone now. What has Rayma so upset?"

Pasha exhaled into the phone. "Mom and Dad caught an earlier flight."

Joy's dark blue eyes widened, so did Grant's.

It appeared that Aiden was the only one left in the dark.

"They're en route now," Pasha said.

"But that's days earlier than scheduled," Grant said. "They weren't supposed to arrive until the day of the wedding. That was the plan. Rayma didn't want them here any earlier than necessary."

"Apparently a big storm is forecasted for that time and they didn't want to risk being snowed in. They have booked a hotel and arrive tonight. I woke up to the email from Dad, along with their flight itinerary." Her voice was sad. "I'm sorry, Rayma. Just know that we are *all* here for you and will not let them ruin your wedding."

Rayma's bottom lip trembled and she swallowed, but then she looked at Joy and seemed to inflate like a balloon right before their eyes. She puffed out her chest, lifted her chin, and clenched her jaw tight. "I can do this."

Joy smiled at her and nodded. "Absolutely, you can, angel."

"*We* can do this," Pasha said. "We're all here."

"That's right, kiddo. We're all here for you," said another woman's voice on the phone. It took Aiden less than a second to realize it was Oona's voice and his belly fluttered. "You don't have to brave them alone."

"I've already texted Jordan and told him," Pasha said. "And Heath and I will go and pick them up from the airport. You don't even have to see them tonight. Their flight doesn't get in until late, so we'll just take them straight to the Howard Johnson, which is where they're staying. You never have to be alone with them, Rayma. We will always have someone there with you."

Rayma nodded. But her strength had returned. "I'm not afraid of them. They can't hurt me anymore."

"No, they can't," came another voice, which sounded like Triss.

"Them sending me to Pasha was the best thing that ever happened to me. I never would have met Joy, or this amazing family, or Jordan," Rayma went on. "I'm not going to let them ruin this day for me."

"That's our girl," Mieka said. "We have your back. Always."

At this point, Joy had wrapped her arm around Rayma and was still holding her phone, nodding at everything the women on the other end said.

Aiden, however, was confused as fuck. What on earth had Rayma's parents done to her to elicit such a terrified response? And why, if they had done something so horrible, were they still invited to the wedding?

"We'll get through this," Pasha said. "That's what bridesmaids and maids of honors do. We take care of the bullshit, so the bride can have a drama-free day."

"And days leading up to the wedding," Triss added.

"Thank you," Rayma said softly.

"I'll call you later, kiddo," Pasha said. Then the call disconnected.

Rayma exhaled and her shoulders slumped and rounded as she accepted her phone back from Joy. "Maybe I will have that coffee now, Nana. Take it to go." Joy nodded, disengaged herself from Rayma, and went about pouring two to-go coffee from the French press. Then she set the electric kettle on to boil again, emptied the old grounds into the compost, and filled the carafe with fresh ones.

"Need someone to drive you around today?" Grant offered. "If you're worked up, I don't want you behind the wheel. Happy to run errands with you."

Rayma smiled and was about to shake her head, but then she stopped herself and nodded. "Actually, that would be really great. I could use the company and all the crazy holiday weekend drivers will just give me road rage."

Grant grinned. "Just let me brush my teeth and grab my coat." Then he was up and out of his seat, pausing only for a second in the kitchen to kiss Joy on the cheek. She handed him the two to-go mugs. Like she knew all along that Grant was going to go with Rayma. Cradling one mug in his elbow, he rested a hand on Aiden's shoulder and gave it a squeeze before exiting the room.

Aiden's mind reeled. He couldn't understand why he was there, or why he was being left alone with Joy. And he really wanted to know what the drama and history was behind Rayma's reaction to her parents' early arrival.

Until now, it was like Rayma had almost forgotten he was there. But she shook her head like she was trying to shake off a fly and faced him. "Jordan will pick you up here after he's done." Then she kissed Joy on her forehead, spun on her heel, and left.

"What do you take in your coffee?" Joy asked him, pouring boiling water from the kettle over the fresh coffee grounds in the carafe.

"Just black," Aiden said, his bewilderment still front and center.

Joy nodded. "Would you like to sit in here? The living room? Or we can go to my office. I'm flexible."

"Uh ... sorry, it's very nice to finally meet you, but what am I doing here?"

Joy chuckled to herself, which made the lines beside her eyes crinkle. She was a very nice-looking woman who took care of herself. Petite and even though she was probably pushing seventy, given the ages of her sons, she didn't look it. Also, how such a tiny woman had managed to raise such behemoths as her sons boggled Aiden's mind. They couldn't have been small babies. "Ah, so this was an ambush, then?" she finally asked, taking a mug down from the cupboard. She already had one down for herself. She stirred the grounds in the carafe, then put on the press, and pushed down.

"I think so. But what is *this*, exactly?"

"Well, Rayma called me early this morning and asked if I had room for a therapy session. I thought it was for her at first, to discuss last-minute concerns or issues regarding the wedding and her parents, which is totally understandable." Was it? Why was it understandable? What did her parents do to her? "But it was for you."

Aiden's jaw dropped.

"I heard about last night," Joy said. "Sounds like things are *pretty* messy."

He was there for therapy?

His head swiveled in the direction of the front door, but Rayma and Grant had already left. Did Jordan know about this? Was it his idea?

She poured the coffee from the French press into both mugs, added a splash of almond milk for herself, then passed his mug to him. "Let's go sit in the living room. I can turn on the fireplace."

Struck dumb, he followed her. She flicked on the electric fireplace, then took a seat in a comfortable-looking recliner, indicating he should find a spot on the couch or love seat.

"I ... I'm sorry ... Joy, but I don't know if this is appropriate. I don't know you."

"And you're well acquainted with your other therapists?"

He swallowed. "Well ... no. I actually haven't started seeing my therapist yet. I was supposed to—" He stopped himself and narrowed his gaze at her. "How much do you know?"

"Whatever was said in the bus last night."

He nodded and dropped his focus to his lap. "Right. So you know about Oona and me."

"Yes."

He huffed out a deep breath. "And you think I'm a total dick, too?"

Joy shrugged. "Have I called you a *total dick*?"

"Well, no."

"Then I don't think you're a total dick. If I thought you were a total dick, then I'd say it to your face."

No wonder Rayma and Joy got along so well. It was like talking to Rayma all grown up with a silver ballerina bun.

Joy sipped her coffee. "I'm just here if you want to talk."

Did he want to talk?

He knew he *needed* to talk, but he sure as hell didn't want to. Not about the trauma that triggered him. That made him lash out at drunk drivers and have no mercy. He'd tried so hard to bury that day. To bury that part of his life and the aftermath of what happened. But no matter how much dirt he piled onto it, it just kept eroding away at him. Just kept rising to the surface and ruling his life. His job.

Then a lightbulb went on in his head. "Jordan told me you counsel him, right?"

Joy slowly nodded. "I do."

"So you ... like you know, right?"

"I know a lot of things."

"But like, you *know* about ... about Dallas and our dad and what happened? Why Jordan and I are or *were* estranged? Why I'm the only member of the family he invited to the wedding? You know already. I don't have to tell you. I don't have to dredge all that up, because you know."

"I only know Jordan's version of things and how it impacted him. I know how Jordan feels about the situation."

"Which is probably the same as me. So—"

"So, what? You think you can just shake your brother's hand and receive therapy via osmosis?"

"No!" Aiden's back went straight. "I just ... I don't have to tell you the details of what happened. You already know."

"I don't know your recount of what happened."

"Same thing. I'd tell you the same story."

"Would you?"

He growled. "Oh fuck, lady, come on. Don't do this to me. You know what happened."

"I do."

"So … whatever advice you've given to Jordan to fix him, give to me, too."

Joy smiled. "Talk about it. That's the advice I give to all my patients. Talk about what happened. Open up. Get it out so it's not eating away at you inside."

White-hot heat raced through Aiden's limbs, and it wasn't just because he was cradling his coffee mug which steamed like a locomotive. "I can't."

"Okay."

She sipped her coffee and blinked.

"When Jordan got super drunk last night, he started saying how it wasn't our fault and that we need to stop carrying around this guilt."

"That's good."

"No, it's not."

"No?"

"He said it in front of a bunch of other people. A bunch of guys. Like your sons, and the guys he works with. Then they all started asking questions. Like what did he mean?"

"And did he explain?"

"No. Fuck no. I shut him down." And shoved him, which sent him flying backward. But Aiden left that part out of his explanation.

"Why?"

Aiden scoffed. "Because it's nobody else's business what happened."

"But wasn't it in the papers and all over the news? It became everyone's business. Your town was rocked by what happened to that child. By what happened to that family. To his mother."

"Years ago." He rolled his eyes, struggling to tamp down the bile that rose up his throat, and coated the back of his tongue. "Why do we need to dredge that shit up now?"

"Because it's obviously still impacting your life. Nobody else is dredging it up but you. You're dredging it up because you're allowing your trauma to trigger you. To *still* trigger you and impact your life. Because you're not dealing with the trauma in a constructive way."

Aiden shook his head. "No. I—"

Joy twisted her lips and cocked her head to the side. "You took a fair bit of time off work to come here. I was married to a cop. I know it's not easy to get this time of year off work."

Did she know he was on suspension?

"Have you talked to Jordan?" he asked.

"I talk to Jordan all the time. But right now, I'm talking to you."

Oh, she was starting to frustrate him. "Did you talk to Jordan about what I told him last night?"

"No. I haven't spoken to Jordan today."

"So you don't know that I'm suspended from work for punching a person I pulled over for drunk driving. That it was videotaped, went viral, and anger management, and therapy are a condition of returning to active duty?"

"I do now," she said blandly. "That must be really hard."

His fingers curled around the handle of the mug, and the other hand bunched into a tight fist on his thigh. Joy's eyes drifted down to his fist. "It wasn't the first time you over reacted to a drunk driver, either, was it?"

"No."

"But because it was videotaped and you had previous warnings, they suspended you."

"Yes."

"And Oona was your designated therapist, but because you slept together, it became a conflict of interest and unethical."

"Yes."

"Which also meant pushing back your return to work because you need to wait until another therapist becomes available."

"Yes."

"And you reacted poorly when she declined seeing you. You lashed out."

"Yes."

Joy nodded. Then she hummed. Then she sipped her coffee, all while maintaining eye contact with Aiden. It wasn't alarming eye contact, but it was constant. She was ... figuring him out. Finally, she spoke and Aiden exhaled deeply through his nose. "Have you tried apologizing?"

He shook his head. "No. We've slept together again, though."

Her brows rose. "And how did that go over?"

"Not well. I'm like deliberately doing things to incite her, to push her buttons, piss her off and make her mad, and I don't know why. She infuriates me, and yet—she's also this fucking addiction. I can't stop thinking about her. I want to piss her off. But I also want her."

Whoa! Where did that come from? He had been doing all of that, but he'd never acknowledged that was what he was doing. Never actually made himself consciously aware of it until now.

Joy seemed to see his revelation because her brows hiked up even higher on her forehead. She remained quiet.

"I met her as Luna. Luna Love is her stage name and that's when we met. Right after she did a show. She remained Luna when we got a hotel room. And I liked Luna. But then the next day when I met *Oona*, she was just different."

"No longer in character. She was also in her professional workspace. And for you, the spell was broken."

"Yeah. No. No, wait, no it wasn't *broken*. It was just ... she was just not the Luna Love I met the night before."

"Because she was professional, ethical, and looking out for not only her career, but yours, as well."

"I didn't see it like that at the time. And even now, here, she's ... *not* Luna."

"Because she's not on stage. Because you know both sides of her now and she doesn't have to pretend to be someone she's not to get you to like her. Because she doesn't *care* if you like her."

"But she does."

At that comment Joy's head reared back. "How do you know?"

"Because she propositioned me in her office. After she declined seeing me as a patient, she told me that she felt a connection with me and would like to see me on a personal level again if I was willing. That she couldn't see me as a patient, but would like to know if I wanted to go out."

"Wow. That's ..." Joy blinked. "That's a bold and brave move on her part."

"I was fuming. I shut her down."

"Yes. And?"

"And told her she was bad in bed."

"I heard about that. And you still think she wants you to like her after that? After your behavior since then?"

Aiden scratched at his jaw. "I don't know. Probably not."

"And yet, you keep pushing her buttons."

"Because she already thinks I'm an asshole. Might as well just play into the role, right?"

"I don't know. Is that what you think should be happening? That you *need* to be an asshole, that you *need* to make her angry?"

Aiden lifted a shoulder.

"What happens when she gets angry?"

"I get angry."

Joy nodded.

A knock at the door had them both looking up.

Aiden cleared his throat as Joy set down her coffee mug and pried herself out of her chair to go answer the door. "Hello, honey, come on in."

Aiden swallowed, though it ended up being harder than he thought given the sudden knot at the top of his throat. He took a sip of his coffee—Joy made a strong brew—and slowly swallowed, allowing it to massage his esophagus.

Jordan came around the corner behind Joy, his expression hesitant but also curious. "I can come back if—"

"It's all good," Aiden said quickly, standing up. He maneuvered around the coffee table, draining his mug on his way to the kitchen where he rinsed it out with soapy water, then set it in the drying rack before returning to the living room. Joy was watching him with a smile in her eyes.

Jordan focused on Joy. "Have you talked to Rayma? I'm worried about her."

"She's out running errands with Grant. He offered to drive her around after she got the news from Pasha about her parents flying out early. He didn't want her driving in this nutty Christmas weekend traffic with that on her mind. A recipe for an accident."

Jordan blew out a breath of relief. "Oh, I'm glad he's with her."

Joy smiled. "They always have fun together. I think she's okay. She had a little bit of a panic at first, but then she held her head up high and resolved that she wasn't going to let them ruin anything. That she's come too far. She had that Rayma strength that we all love."

"That's my woman," Jordan said with pride.

Joy patted him on the arm. "I do like Pasha's plan to not let her be alone with them at all, though. She's a strong woman, but she needs people to have her back."

"I agree," Jordan said. "We'll all make sure of it." Then he faced Aiden. "You okay?"

Aiden nodded. "Yeah." He turned to Joy, his brain firing in a million different directions. "Uh ... thanks."

Joy grinned. "Anytime, honey. If you want to talk in a professional or personal manner, I'm here. But I'm sure we'll see each other again before the wedding."

Then she leaned in and up onto her tip toes and gave each of the boys a hug. "You two behave, okay?"

"Always, Nana," Jordan said teasingly as he opened the front door and the two of them headed back outside.

Once the front door closed and they were in Jordan's truck, Aiden turned to his brother. "What's wrong with Rayma and Oona's parents? I was there when Rayma got the call from Pasha and she nearly had an anxiety attack."

Jordan started up the engine of his truck and backed out of the driveway. "Come on, I've been tasked with picking up the wine for the tables. I'll fill you in."

Chapter Seventeen

After running her errands with Grant and cooling off, Rayma joined Oona and her sisters at Pasha's house for a much-needed *bitch-fest*.

"Since it's the middle of the day and I'm driving, I brought carbs instead of booze," Rayma said, entering Pasha's house and announcing herself by holding up a box of donuts from the gourmet donut shop downtown.

They were all sitting around Pasha's dining room table writing names for the place-settings, and doing other menial wedding day décor tasks while Pasha's seven-year-old son Raze and five-year-old daughter Eve played Legos on the floor in the living room.

Oona loved her oldest sister's home. It was impeccably decorated while not coming across as pretentious or trendy. Right now, in all of the magazines and on every social media site people were decorating their homes in whites and beiges. And while beautiful, that could look cookie-cutter and boring. It also didn't seem practical for a house with children.

Pasha had never been one to conform, though. One wall was a rich café latte color, while the others were a warm white. Her color scheme was beige and brown with pops of deep forest green and the perfect amount of black accent pieces, like a throw pillow or picture frame. It was like walking into a hunting lodge but without the log walls and all the animal heads everywhere.

The brown leather couch was softer than butter, and the area rug was a nifty beige with a pattern of dark green leaves.

And house plants were everywhere. Big and small, short and tall. Heath said he felt like he lived in a jungle, but Pasha just kept saying they had the purest, cleanest air in the city.

Oona loved it. Even though she was just starting on her houseplant collection with Harmonia, now that she'd seen how you could use plants as décor and art—as her sister did—she was eager to build her own clean air jungle in her condo. Harmonia didn't just need *one* friend, she needed dozens.

An enormous live Christmas tree sat in the corner opposite the big screen television mounted to the wall, and it glittered with warm white lights, paper chains made by the kids and various ornaments both bought, and handmade at school. Other tastefully placed holiday decorations were scattered throughout the house, and a beautiful handmade (by Pasha) wreath made out of cedar boughs and holly welcomed you into their home at the front door.

Just like Pasha, her home was warm, inviting, and not the least bit pretentious.

Oona got up from her spot at the table and went into the kitchen to grab plates for the donuts and put the kettle on again for more tea. They'd been drinking a lot of tea.

"Donuts!" Raze cheered, having spied what was probably a familiar box, and getting up from the floor, running to Rayma.

"Can we have one, please, Auntie Rayma?" Eve asked, following her brother and gazing up at the box with her big blue eyes.

You'd never know either child came from Pasha at all. They were both spitting images of Heath. Blond hair and big blue eyes. Gorgeous children, but the Young genes were no match for the Hart genes when it came to making babies.

"You'll have to ask your mom," Rayma said. Then she brought her voice down. "But cool Auntie Rayma made sure to get your favorites."

"Yay!" The kids cheered.

"Ask Auntie Rayma to cut them in half and you can each have half of one for now," Pasha said. "You don't need that much sugar in your system in one go."

"Yay!" The kids cheered again, following Rayma into the kitchen where Oona was getting out a knife and cutting board.

"How are you doing, kiddo?" Oona asked her sister, setting down the knife on the cutting board and pulling her little sister in for a hug.

Rayma put the donut box on the counter and embraced her sister. "I've been better, obviously. But, it is what it is, and I need to figure it out. I won't let them ruin my wedding."

"*We* won't let them ruin your wedding," Oona said, squeezing Rayma tighter, then smiling when Rayma did it back. They kept squeezing each other harder and harder until Oona finally caved and said uncle.

Raze and Eve were watching them curiously.

Oona cleared her throat and released Rayma, then grabbed the donut box and opened it. "Which ones are your favorites?"

"I like the salted caramel one," Raze said, sidling right up next to Oona and leaning over so he could look into the box. He was taller than your average seven-year-old. Which probably meant he was going to be a mountain like his father one day. His head already brushed Oona's shoulder. It would be no time before he was taller than her. Before he was taller than all of them.

"I can't see!" Eve protested.

"Here." Raze bent down and she climbed onto his back in a piggyback, then maneuvered his body so she could see into the box, too. Oona would have just brought the box down to her level, but she enjoyed watching her niece and nephew interact and the way Raze doted on his little sister.

Eve's eyes went wide and she licked her lips. "I like the apple pie one the best. No, wait. The lemon. No, the strawberry cheesecake. No ... ahhhh! I can't decide."

"I thought the maple bacon ones were your favorite?" Rayma said with a chuckle. "That's why I grabbed that one."

"Oohhh right!" Eve gently smacked her palm to her forehead. "I totally forgot. Yep. That's my favorite. Thanks, Auntie Rayma."

"Maple bacon?" Oona asked, wrinkling her nose at the thought of bacon on a donut.

"Don't knock it until you try it," Eve said, sliding off her brother's back and plopping her hands on her hips in a sassy way that reminded Oona so much of Rayma.

"I guess I'll have to try it then," Oona said.

"I'll share a bite with you." Eve beamed.

Oona grabbed the two donuts the kids selected then cut them in half, putting a half on a plate for each of them.

"Eat them at the island, please," Pasha said from the dining room.

The kids took their bounty to the big white quartz kitchen island and pulled up bar stools.

"Want a bite of my donut?" Eve asked Oona before she even took a bite.

"I'll just try a sliver off this piece," Oona said. "But thank you, sweetheart." She sliced off an almost see-through piece of the donut and popped it into her mouth. Eve watched her like a hawk.

And, surprisingly, it wasn't half bad. She made sure to get a small piece of crumbled bacon and maple drizzle for the full affect.

"What do you think?" Eve asked, hopeful.

"Not half bad," Oona agree, delighting her niece, who then proceeded to cram her whole piece into her mouth.

"It's my favorite," Eve said with her mouth full, crumbs flying out of her face.

"Eve! Mouth closed," Pasha scolded.

"Well, I'm going to eat my feelings," Rayma said, leaning over and grabbing a donut decorated with dried purple flowers and taking a giant bite. "Mmmmm, Earl Grey and lavender." She tipped her chin to Oona. "I grabbed two of these because I thought you'd like the Earl Grey."

Oona wasn't normally one for such sweets or even donuts, but she had to admit an Earl Grey lavender donut sounded pretty delicious. She cut the other one in half and picked up one piece, taking a bite. An explosion of flavor caressed her tongue. The subtle notes of bergamot and the floral hints of lavender had her closing her eyes and humming in delight.

"Told you," Rayma said, playfully elbowing Oona, which prompted her to open her eyes.

"Well, don't hog them all for yourselves," Mieka said. "Share the mouthgasms this way. We've got a grumpy preggo over here."

"Hey!" Triss said. "I'm not grumpy. I'm just achy. This little man has decided my pelvis is his new playground and my bladder is a trampoline."

Oona brought the box, along with plates and napkins over to the table and set it in the center, while Rayma finished off making the tea in the kitchen.

Even though the sisters didn't spend a lot of time together, the five of them, now that they were all adults and working hard at improving their relationships and bond, there was no awkwardness between them. One finished off where the other started without even thinking about it. It helped that Triss and Mieka lived on the same ranch in Colorado and that Rayma and Pasha lived in the same city. Their proximity had definitely aided in their closeness.

Oona often felt left out. She wanted to be as close as the others were. Both in proximity and relationship, but being in Montreal made it hard.

The door leading down to the basement opened and Heath's enormous frame filled the doorjamb. He smiled at Rayma. "How you doing, kiddo?"

Rayma reached for another donut. "Eating my feelings, one donut at a time."

Heath's eyes widened when he spied the box. "Are there enough to share?"

"Bought two dozen because I knew I was coming to your house, big man, there's enough."

Heath's blue eyes twinkled as he reached over his wife's head and grabbed a chocolate-covered one. "Bathroom sink is fixed. It was just a loose coupling nut that was causing the leak." He took a bite of the donut and moaned before addressing his wife. "Was gonna take the kids shopping, unless you'd prefer that I leave them here for the sugar to kick in." His grin was cheeky and teasing as he chewed. For a behemoth of a man with blond hair nearly down to his shoulders, and a way about him that sort of screamed killing machine, Heath was just a big teddy bear. Not to mention how he clearly worshipped Pasha, and was such a hands-on, amazing dad, there was no doubt in Oona's mind that her sister had hit the absolute jackpot. All her sisters had.

Did that mean all the good men were taken? Or just the good men for the Young women?

"No, no, you can take them," Pasha said, finishing off another name card and adding it to the stack. "Remember, Mommy likes wine, cheese and wine."

Eve hopped down from the island. "And not the crap wine, either, right, Mama? It's pinot or malbec or get the heck out."

Mieka and Triss snorted.

"Who told you that?" Oona asked.

"Auntie Rayma."

"Just training them young," Rayma said, reaching for another donut. "No sense letting them buy something we'll never drink like a chardonnay or shiraz, right?"

"Well, I need to know what all the hype is about." Triss grabbed a donut covered in streusel and took a bite. "Mmmm."

Heath pecked his wife on the cheek, then corralled his children and moments later they were dressed for a snow storm and out the door.

Mieka grabbed a donut, too. Hers was decked out with what appeared to be some kind of crumbled breakfast cereal on top.

"That's the Froot Loops one," Rayma said, licking sugar crystals off her thumb.

Mieka's dark brows bunched as she took a bite. But she appeared pleasantly surprised, nodded and kept chewing. "Sweet, but better than I thought."

They eventually moved on from name cards to center pieces, then other decorations.

It was closing in on five o'clock by the time they were done, all of them stuffed from donuts and needing to constantly get up to pee because of all the tea.

Heath texted earlier to say he was going to take the kids over to his brother, Rex's, for pizza for dinner, so the women had the house to themselves for longer.

"Takeout sounds like a great idea to me," Pasha said. "I don't feel like cooking."

"How about Indian?" Mieka suggested, glancing at her phone as she lounged on the overstuffed brown leather couch in Pasha's living room, a plush cream-colored microfleece throw draped over her body. "This place has great reviews and we can use a delivery app."

"Baby wants peshwari naan and aloo methi," Triss said, her eyes closed as she kicked up the footrest in the black La-Z-Boy recliner that faced the huge wall-mounted television. "Oh, and vegetable pakoras, too."

"That's definitely one thing I miss living out in the country," Mieka said. "The lack of ethnic restaurants. And Nate just wants to grab burgers whenever we go to Denver. I mean the burgers are good, but sometimes I want Tibetan or Moroccan or Ethiopian."

Triss didn't bother to open her eyes, but nodded. "Baby also wants paneer spinach, please."

"Does baby just want the whole damn menu?" Mieka asked, giving Triss a playful side-eye.

"Baby wants *allll* the food," Triss said sleepily, rubbing her belly. "He says if we forget the samosas, he'll give me heartburn for the remainder of the pregnancy."

Mieka snorted. "Don't you already have heartburn?"

"Don't remind me," Triss said with a wince. "But don't forget the samosas. Veggie and chicken ones."

Rayma came to sit next to Oona on the love seat. Oona wrapped her arm around her. "Pasha has wine. I'm happy driving home if you need a glass."

"Or six?" Rayma asked wearily.

"Or six."

"Thanks." She glanced up at Pasha in the kitchen since the living room and kitchen were open concept. "I'll make sure that wine on your counter isn't poisoned, Pash. Do an official taste-test. Would hate for my big sister to get sick."

Pasha's lip lifted on one side and she nodded. "Mieks? Oons?"

"None for me," Oona said.

"Does a horse eat hay?" Mieka replied. All their phones buzzed. "I just sent you all the menu for the Indian restaurant. Text me what you want and I'll place the order.

Within an hour they were all sitting around Pasha's cozy, stylish living room with the gas fireplace going, soft music in the background and the coffee table covered in takeout boxes. Rayma was on her third glass of wine and they were all giggling. Triss kept dozing in her recliner, waking up when someone laughed, only to demand they fill her in on what was so funny.

"I needed this," Rayma said, smiling like a cute little drunk. "So badly. Thank you."

"Kiddo, what Mom and Dad did to you was so wrong, and we will never forgive them for it," Triss said. "Sending you off to live with Pasha without even telling her, simply because you became *too wild and out of control*. No, they just refused to adapt their parenting. You needed love and structure, realistic boundaries, and support. Not their constant belittling and shaming."

"And certainly not their abandonment," Oona added.

Rayma sipped her wine and nodded gently.

"I'll never forget the way they made me feel after I cut the sleeves off my prom dress. Because let's all be honest here, a long-sleeved prom dress was stupid," Mieka said. "Mom said I was showing way too much skin and dressed inappropriately. Wouldn't let me leave the house until I put on a cardigan—which I tossed the moment I left with my date. Fuck that noise. It was way more conservative than all the other dresses there. Sadie Fitzwilliam wore a literal bra and a tutu as her prom dress."

"Or the way they'd shame the neighbor girls for what they wore—jeans, ballet flats and tank tops. Judging their parents for letting them go to parties and have friends over." Pasha sipped her wine. "Friends asked to come over, but I said no after a while. And it wasn't because Mom and Dad said no, even though they did, it was because I was too embarrassed to introduce my friends to my weirdo parents."

"Remember how we had to jump over the vacuum lines on the carpet in the living room?" Oona added. "And if we messed up the lines we got in trouble."

"I wasn't even allowed in the living room," Rayma said. "At least not without an adult present and then I had to tippy toe over those vacuum lines, and I was only allowed to sit on the floor. Never the furniture. Do you know how hard it is to sit on a carpet but not mess up the vacuum lines? It's impossible!"

"Let's talk about the furniture for a moment," Triss added. "Plastic on it, and we still weren't allowed to sit down on it." She made a face of disbelief. "You know they still have it on there, right? Like even now that there are no children around to make a mess, they still have the plastic."

All the sisters shook their heads.

"I just never felt like I was good enough in their eyes, you know?" Rayma said. "I knew that I was an oopsie baby. And I felt like that everyday. Knew I wasn't actually wanted, that I was an inconvenience and an extra mouth to feed. And I know that's why I acted out. Because as our therapist sister can agree, even negative attention is better than no attention."

Oona nodded solemnly. "I was an oopsie baby, too."

"Yeah, but you were close enough in age to Mieka that it wasn't *as* big of a deal. You're only three years apart. You and I are *five* years. Like they were done having kids, then I came along."

"Thank God Dad finally got snipped," Pasha said shaking her head.

"People are stupid," Rayma said. "And that includes our parents." She sighed. "I don't even know why they're coming. I've never felt like they really loved me. And the fact that they're spending money to come out here just boggles my mind. Royce and Yanna don't spend money."

No, they sure didn't.

Their parents were penny-pinchers to an embarrassing degree. Their mother used to send letters to people on the back of receipts rather than paper, using a Sharpie to block out her purchases, but then utilizing the blank back of the receipt for full-on letters to family members. And it wasn't that they couldn't afford it, it was that their parents just didn't want to spend the money. They weren't rich, but they weren't destitute, either.

Their mother Yanna's family immigrated to the United States as refugees during the Kosovo war when she was just a child. In high school, Yanna met the girls' dad, Royce, and they had been together ever since. Their mother's family had always been pacifists. Trouble duckers to the nth degree. The last thing they wanted to do was draw any undo attention to themselves and risk deportation. And that ideology followed their mother into her adult life with their father and their family. They were reserved, quiet, and conservative. Shaming their daughters for any kind of bold personality traits they might have. The girls had to be quiet, perfect, and well-behaved at all times. Laughter and excitement were even scolded. Clothing needed to be neutral and boring, hair in a braid. Children should be seen and not heard.

So, the fact that all of them had left home as soon as they could was no surprise.

Pasha toed the line and was the perfect child. Triss was pretty similar. Mieka rebelled a little, but her life revolved around dance, so she also had to be disciplined and was gone a lot. But she snuck out a bit, lied about where she was, and to Oona's knowledge never got caught.

Oona emulated Triss and Pasha since she idolized both of them and wanted to set a good example for Rayma.

But Rayma—the baby—was the wild one. She went against the grain of their upbringing with every fiber of her being and that just confused and devastated their parents. They couldn't understand *where they went wrong*. So they gave up when she was seventeen, bought her a one-way ticket from Baltimore to see Pasha in Seattle and told Pasha to fix her. That they'd done everything they knew how to do and Rayma was Pasha's problem now.

It was no wonder Rayma was as triggered as she was with the news of their parents coming. Oona figured in some way they were all probably experiencing some triggers.

A tear slid down Rayma's cheek, but when Oona tried to comfort her, Rayma shook her head and smiled. "I'm okay. You know, I asked Heath to walk me down the aisle, not Dad."

Mieka, Triss and Oona's eyes all went wide. Pasha, of course, already knew.

"Dad hasn't been there for me, hasn't loved me or cared for me the way Heath has. Heath was—is—my benchmark for a good man. For the perfect partner and I think I came pretty close."

"You definitely found a keeper," Pasha said. "We all adore Jordan."

"And Heath approves of him. Which is all I need."

"How did Dad take it?" Triss asked.

Rayma shrugged. "I haven't told him. They never call me. When I called and told them in October that I was engaged, their response was, 'That's nice'. That was it. Not, 'How can we help?' or 'What do you need?' or anything. Just, 'That's nice'. Dad never even asked if he could walk me down the aisle. And yet, when I told Pasha and Heath, Heath immediately asked what I needed and how he could help. He even offered to help pay for it—not that we took him up on it. The same with Joy and Grant. The same with everyone. And yet my own parents couldn't even find it in their hearts to be excited for me."

"Excitement will kill them, you know that," Mieka said dryly. "The same with bright colors, alcohol, boy bands, black eyeliner, sleeveless shirts and let's not forget, paying anybody a fucking compliment. That'll make them drop dead on the freaking spot."

They all snorted.

"When I told them that we wanted to get married on Christmas, which was when we met, and only two months after we got engaged, they gave me shit for taking the specialness away from the holiday and making it about myself."

"Oh, for fuck's sake," Mieka said, draining her wine glass and reaching for the bottle on the table to top herself up. "I think it's magical. And you met on Christmas day, but are getting married on Christmas Eve in order to *not* take away from the specialness. Mom and Dad can fuck right off." She grabbed a piece of garlic naan and sat back against the couch, ripping off pieces with a splash of angry vigor before popping them into her mouth.

"Also gave me shit for planning a wedding at a time when flights are so expensive," Rayma added. "Said I was being inconsiderate since they're the ones flying the farthest."

Oona cleared her throat. "Excuse me? I'm flying the same fucking distance. So did Aiden."

Oh wow, that was the first time she'd thought of Aiden all day.

"And I'm dealing with student loan debt, meanwhile Royce and Yanna are sitting pretty with their house paid off and their 401Ks intact," Oona added. "Not that you and Jordan aren't worth it. I have my loan payment plan in place. I'm not hurting for money. All I'm saying is that money woes are rich coming from two people who are retired, with their house paid off and who rationed our food out as kids like we lived in a refugee camp."

Everyone's heads bobbed in agreement.

Mieka licked her lips, and her eyes focused on Triss, then Pasha and finally Oona and Rayma. "You know, um, I never told you two, but um ... I got pregnant the night of Triss's wedding. It was Nate's."

"Was?" Oona asked, shock rippling through her.

Mieka nodded. "Yeah. I terminated it. Pasha set it up for me in Seattle, but couldn't come because the kids were sick. Nate came, though. He was great." She exhaled and broke eye contact, swirling her index finger around the rim of her wine glass. "I found out too late to take the morning after pill. You know how bad I am with taking the pill—my ADHD made me constantly forget. I have an IUD now. But, I just wasn't ready to be a mom. And I didn't think I'd ever end up living on the ranch or with Nate. I was still dancing on the ships, thought I would be for long time. And we're honestly not even sure if we'll have kids. Or maybe we'll adopt. We don't know. But we're in a really good place now and he supported me when it happened."

"Wow," Rayma said. "You were so brave."

"That couldn't have been an easy decision. I'm sorry you were faced with it at all," Oona said, her heart hurting for her sister and the pain she must have experienced having to make that choice.

Mieka's smile was small and she still didn't look up. "I don't know why I didn't tell you guys. I only told Triss earlier this year when I came back to Colorado to visit. I guess I just ..."

"Shame runs deep in our family. It's hard to get away from it, even if we've gotten away from *them*," Oona said softly.

Mieka nodded. "Yeah."

"Even after becoming a doctor, marrying a great man like Heath, and building this amazing life, Mom and Dad have never told me they're proud of me," Pasha said. "Never."

Mieka and Triss both nodded. Oona did, too.

Rayma made an amused noise in her throat and tossed her hand in the air. "Who here's got a praise kink now?"

They all exchanged looks and coy smiles crept onto their faces. Slowly, they each raised a hand and nodded.

"It's messed up how badly I like being called a good girl," Oona confessed. "Like really messed up."

"Oh, I fucking love it, too," Rayma agreed. "Like, pull my hair and call me a good girl when I'm choking on your dick, and I'll cream my goddamn panties so hard."

Mieka snorted a laugh, but nodded, as did Triss and Pasha.

"Thanks for that, Mom and Dad," Triss said, stifling a yawn.

"Praise and compliments are not the Young way," Rayma said with a shrug and sip of her wine. "Never has been. Never will be."

They were bonding, sharing, and pouring out their secrets. Preparing for their own kind of cold war with their parents.

And by sharing these secrets, it only strengthened their unity. Their bond. Their sisterhood. Knowing all the dirty grit about one another, abandoning the shame that had been ingrained in them since childhood, was their way of preparing for battle. Of armoring each other.

"Even though they got me the help I needed, I knew they were ashamed of my dyslexia," Triss said. "Never wanted me to tell anybody. Nobody in the family outside of the seven of us was to ever know I had a learning disability. I felt like I had this dirty secret. Like there was something wrong with me."

Mieka's head bobbed emphatically. "The same with my ADHD. I got the help. Got on the right med concoction, but heaven forbid I ever told anyone I had ADHD. Mom got so mad at me one time when I almost blurted it out at a family dinner at Uncle Raffi's house. I've never seen her face get so tight or so red."

"I remember that," Triss said.

"We'll never be more than five disappointing embarrassments," Rayma said. "I acknowledged that a long time ago. Still having a hard time making peace with it, but I'm working on it."

Oona took a deep breath and stared down at her entwined fingers in her lap. "Oons?" Mieka said. "You okay?"

Oona's lips twisted. "Since we're, you know ... sharing, I may as well tell you guys that Russell used to beat me."

A few gasps echoed around her, but she didn't look up from her lap.

"He liked to drink, and he used to hit me when he'd had too much. Then he started to do it even when he was sober. So ... you know, it wasn't just the disease that made him a shitty person." She swallowed hard and took another deep breath before speaking again. "It took a lot for me to get away from him. I had to have a plan. An exit strategy, because he had moved himself into my apartment. Into my life. He was controlling and belittling. He stole from me and cut me off from my friends. I stopped sleeping with him and he didn't take that well." She licked her lips, not ready to meet the gazes of her sisters, so she focused on the sleeves of her cardigan and bunched them in her fists. "So then he started cheating. Which I was fine with. Honestly." She risked a glance up and made brief eye-contact with each of her sisters. "I videotaped one of his attacks and that was what finally landed him in prison. He's out on parole now, though."

"Oons," Rayma said beside her, inching closer and wrapping an arm around her shoulder. "You've never said a word about this before."

Oona huffed a mirthless laugh. "There's that shame again. Mom's voice in the back of my mind asking me what I did to provoke him. What could I do to *not* upset him." She snorted. "*Breathe* was the only answer I could come up with. If I stopped breathing, if I stopped existing, that would not upset him."

"Did you ..." Triss started to ask, but Oona cut her off with a head shake.

"No, I never attempted to take my own life." She laughed humorlessly again. "And the reason behind that, and this sounds so wrong, was that I figured I had spent way too much time and money on my education to just throw it all away."

"And there are people who love you and would miss you," Pasha added.

Oona nodded solemnly but didn't look up. "I never thought of that. How fucked up, huh?"

Rayma squeezed her tighter. "We get it, though. And holy fuck do I ever hear that voice in my head. All the victim blaming. The shaming and chastising." She made a derisive noise in her throat. "You know when I was kidnapped, bound, and gagged, and fearing for my life, all I heard in my head was my internal voice blaming me and saying, 'You should have done this ... Why didn't you do this?' It was an endless shame loop. And I still hear it when I do something dumb. Even drop a vase or a plate and it smashes. And I know Mom's disappointment in me put that voice there."

Glancing up at her sisters again from where she'd been studying her jean-clad lap, Oona spied damp eyes and small drops rolling unchecked down Triss and Pasha's cheeks.

"You know, since we're sharing our deepest darkest secrets, I figured I might as well jump on the bandwagon." Oona tried to laugh it off, but Rayma just squeezed her tighter and leaned her head against Oona's.

"I'm sorry that happened to you," Rayma said.

"Me, too," Triss whispered, swiping at her cheeks with her palm.

Mieka's lip trembled and she nodded. "So sorry."

"I'll have Heath and Chase look into Russell, keep tabs on him. Get some eyes on him in Montreal. Now that we know what he's capable of and that he's out, he'll never really be a free man." The resolve in Pasha's voice was laced with both anger and pain. Pain she probably felt for Oona, pain in not knowing about Oona's suffering until now, and pain for their family that the shame their parents projected onto them ran so deep that Oona didn't even feel like she could tell her own sisters what was happening to her.

Well, not anymore.

"No more hiding," Triss said. "No more secrets. Not from each other. I will never shame any of you. I will never judge you. I will only support, love, and lift you up. No more hiding." More tears slid down her cheeks and before they knew it, they were all crying.

Pasha's lips twisted and she glanced at Rayma. Rayma nodded in encouragement. "It's okay."

Swallowing, Pasha sucked in a deep breath through her nose, then glanced at Triss. "I'm not trying to spook you, but it's something to be aware of, since your due date is coming up."

Triss cocked her head to the side.

"A few months after Eve was born, the postpartum depression hit me really hard. Along with the postpartum anxiety. I'm talking *dark,* dark thoughts. My temper was out of control, and poor Raze and Heath got the brunt of it. There were some days I couldn't get out of bed. Other days where I refused to leave the house." Fresh tears slid down her cheeks. "But after we figured out what was wrong, I got medicated and spoke with Joy for a long time. The counseling sessions helped. I'm still on a low-dose anti-depressant, and I'm honestly not sure I'll ever go off it. I'm a better mom and wife because of it. I have coping tools. I have patience and I can recognize when things are tough, and I use my tools to keep myself from spiraling." Her gaze flicked between all of them. "But it was bad. Like *really,* really bad for a while."

Rayma nodded. "I was scared I was going to get a call from Heath that you'd—"

"I know," Pasha said quickly. "I was scared about that, too. That I'd go that far. I certainly had thoughts about it."

Besides Rayma, who obviously knew about Pasha's depression, the rest of them had slack jaws.

"I'm so sorry, Pash" Oona finally said. "So sorry you went through that."

Pasha nodded and another tear fell. Then she focused on Triss again. "Please, talk to me. Talk to someone if you start to feel lost and hopeless. It's not uncommon. It's nothing to be ashamed of. So many women experience it, and there is a way out of the darkness."

Triss's head bobbed and her eyes grew watery. "I will. And I'm so sorry, Pash."

"No more hiding. No more secrets," Rayma reiterated.

They all agreed.

Since Triss was pregnant and had a hard time getting out of her chair, they all went to her and they wrapped each other up in a weird group-hug, four of them kneeling beside the La-Z-Boy, tears flowing, arms around each other.

"I'm so lucky to have you as my sisters," Rayma said, her words coming out choppy and breathy as she spoke through the tears.

They all nodded and murmured similar sentiments.

Oona was the first to pull away. She was closest to Rayma, turned to her, took her by the shoulders, looked her in the eyes and said, "Kiddo, I am so freaking proud of you. You are an amazing person and I am so honored to be your sister and know you."

A tear slid down Rayma's cheek. "I'm so proud of you, too, Oons. I mean, *Dr.* Oons."

Oona laughed through her sob.

Then, one-by-one, they all turned to each other and said how proud they were. They armed themselves. They prepared for battle, but most of all, they bonded like sisters should. Like the sisters they should have always been. They didn't need their parents' approval, praise, or love. They had more than enough to go around between the five of them.

And by the time Oona drove her and Rayma home in the dark, Oona's heart felt lighter than it had in ages. Possibly ever. Rayma was dozy in the passenger seat, but she had a smile on her face and the stress creases that had been on her forehead earlier were gone.

"I love you, Oons," Rayma said sleepily.

"I love you, too, kiddo."

"Aiden had a therapy session with Joy today."

Oona nearly drove off the road. "Wait, what?"

Chapter Eighteen

The women didn't get home until later. Well past dinner. Jordan and Aiden picked up burgers after they ran some errands, then put a hockey game on in the living room while they filled their arteries with delicious grease and salt.

They didn't say much to each other, but Aiden could tell Jordan was curious about how Aiden's visit went with Joy.

Aiden, on the other hand, was still processing everything he'd learned about Rayma. About her and Oona's parents and why Rayma had reacted the way she did when she found out they were arriving early.

Jordan didn't really leave out any details, either. He said that Rayma was an open book about it now, having kept it all a secret for so long, but realized that it was healthier for her healing process if the people around her knew what she was dealing with.

Apparently, when Rayma was seventeen, she'd been a bit of wild child. Fraternizing with the wrong crowd. And wrong crowd didn't mean the stoners and class-skippers in high school. Wrong crowd in this case was an outlaw biker gang called the True Destroyers. She spent time at their club house, went to parties, did drugs, and who knows what else.

Her parents didn't know what to do with her. Their other four daughters hadn't acted like this, so they were at a loss and also not willing to adapt their parenting style, so they just gave up on her. And without consulting Pasha, they bought Rayma a one-way ticket to Seattle from Baltimore and told Pasha that Rayma was her problem. Meanwhile, Pasha was busy with her pediatric residency and had no time to raise a seventeen-year-old.

Being seventeen and feeling unwanted by everyone around her, Rayma rebelled and took off to go meet with a talent agent or something. She was trying to make it big in the influencer world and had been chatting with someone who claimed to be important and could help her career.

Well, obviously, that was a big scam and Rayma was kidnapped by human traffickers and shipped down to Nevada, which was where Heath and Pasha found her and rescued her, with the help of Heath's brothers.

After that, Rayma moved to Canada and lived with Joy, who set her on the right path and gave her the parental love she so desperately craved. Rayma finished high school in Victoria while living with Joy, then attended college and eventually decided to call Victoria home for good and get her Canadian citizenship, much like Pasha.

Aiden was just floored.

He had no idea, and after Jordan educated him a bit more on just how belittling and shaming Yanna and Royce could be, it was no wonder Rayma reacted the way she did when she found out they were arriving days earlier. In Aiden's opinion, Rayma had kept it together like a pro. He'd have probably been losing his shit if he'd been in her shoes.

He also had newfound respect for Rayma. For all the Young sisters. They got out from under their parents' controlling thumbs and made enormous successes of themselves.

The sound of a key sliding into a lock made both of them turn toward the entryway. Jordan was up out of his seat and opened the door for them, his eyes wide as he took in the disheveled, but smiling and puffy-eyed state of his future bride. "What happened over there?"

"A lot of bonding. A lot of crying. A lot of wine, a lot of donuts, a lot of Indian food, a lot of ... sisterliness," Rayma said, stepping into Jordan's arms. "I'm going to have a shower then crawl into bed. I'm not that drunk, but I am pretty tired from all the crying."

Jordan turned a worried eye to Oona. "Why was everyone crying?"

"It was good crying," Oona assured him. "Catharsis. Therapeutic. Trust me, it needed to happen."

"Okay," he said, still unconvinced and returning his gaze to Rayma, regarding her carefully. The love and concern in his eyes as he watched his future wife was practically tangible. Aiden had never felt that kind of love from someone before, and he wasn't sure he'd ever felt it *for* someone, either.

Jordan and Rayma were something to strive for.

He just wasn't sure he was worthy, or if he'd ever be.

"I'm not going to let my parents ruin my wedding day, Lassie. I'm just not." Rayma ditched her boots and hung up her coat. She spied the bowl of salt and vinegar chips on the coffee table and walked over to grab a handful, dropping her gaze to Aiden. "How did your chat go with Joy?"

Aiden swallowed. "It went well, I think."

"Yeah? Did she fix you?"

"Rayma," Jordan said slowly.

Rayma swatted her hand toward her fiancé. "I know. I know. One therapy session does not fix a person. But it's the drop of Elmer's glue needed to start putting the pieces back together, right?"

All Aiden could do was nod.

Rayma popped a chip into her mouth. "We ate so many donuts and so much Indian food. My butthole will probably be angry with me tomorrow, but my tastebuds were so happy with me today."

Oona snorted and rolled her eyes from where she stood in the kitchen.

Aiden's gaze pivoted toward her.

He saw her differently now, too.

Stronger. More resilient. And he understood a bit better why she was so reserved and cold in certain circumstances. It was a product of her upbringing. A form of self-preservation. But also, an ingrained conservativism she was probably fighting tooth and nail by adopting her alter ego, *Luna*.

"Come snuggle me in bed, Lassie. I can't guarantee sex, but maybe."

Jordan rolled his eyes and turned to Aiden. "You gonna be okay out here? Or do I need to put a strip of tape down the center of the apartment, you each get a side."

"We're adults," Oona said. "I think we can manage."

Aiden nodded. "Not going to do anything to ruin your special day, bro. I promise."

Jordan yawned and bobbed his head, then followed his fiancée into their bedroom and shut the door.

Aiden glanced back up at Oona who was standing on the far side of the island watching him.

He stood up and cleared his throat. "I uh ... I owe you an apology."

All that shifted was the height of her brows on her forehead. She hiked them up ever so slightly, but otherwise, her facial expression never changed.

"I'm sorry for the way I reacted when you declined seeing me as a patient. I understand why you had to. It was for reasons greater than just what happened between us. And I get that now." He was staring down at the granite island, gripping it tight enough to make the tips of his fingers turn white. He released it and cleared his throat again, lifting his gaze to her face. "I also never should have said that you were bad in bed. You're not, for the record, and that was just mean."

She was quiet for a very long minute.

Aiden shifted back and forth awkwardly on his feet, alternating between staring at the counter and her. Was he supposed to say something else?

He did what he was supposed to do. What Joy told him to do and that was apologize.

Did he deserve a second chance?

She finally nodded, though her jaw remained tight. "Thank you. I appreciate that." Then she smiled tightly and headed to her bedroom, then the bathroom, closing the door behind her. The shower started shortly after.

His jaw dropped.

That was it?

What else were you expecting?

He couldn't answer that, but he was certainly expecting more of ... something. More discussion between them. Perhaps an apology from her for ...

What? What has she done? Everything she's done has been in retaliation to your behavior. She's never instigated anything.

That was true.

She remained classy as much as she could—until alcohol got involved at least—but either way, she was never the one to start a battle. But she didn't shy away from joining it, either.

However, since the moment she found out he was her patient and said she couldn't treat him, he'd been a colossal prick.

He said she was bad in bed.

He'd done nothing but make her life miserable. Because *he* was miserable.

If the shoe was on the other foot, he'd be mighty hesitant to give himself a second chance.

And even though he still didn't know even half the story regarding Oona's ex, it didn't take a person with a PhD to recognize that his behavior had probably been pretty damn triggering for her.

His stomach spun as the shame he felt for even being remotely like her ex gutted him to the spine.

Eventually, he left his post, standing there staring at the door, and put the chips away, then started turning down his bed for the night. It was only ten o'clock, but he could put in his earbuds and listen to an audiobook for a while or scroll on his phone.

He was just tearing off his jeans when the bathroom door opened. He wanted to look up, to watch her walk away, but he restrained himself and remained focused on getting dressed.

The sear of her eyes on him made him look up, though. He was down to his boxers and long-sleeve shirt.

She was in nothing but a towel.

"Goodnight," he said, not sure what else to say.

Her head cocked to the side and she blinked a few times.

He was like a bug under a microscope and she was deciding whether to set him free or squish him.

"Let's fuck," she finally said, turning to head to her room.

"What?"

She turned around. "You heard me."

He scrambled around the pull-out bed after her and into the guest room. "Are you serious?"

She dropped her towel. "This doesn't change a thing. But ... I need it. Tonight was good, but it was hard. I just ... I need the distraction. I need the dopamine and oxytocin. Need to get rid of the cortisol build-up." She shrugged and climbed onto the bed. "I can get it from you, or I can do it myself."

He shut the door, turned off the light and crawled onto the bed and over her, pressing her into the pillows. "Oh no, I can help you."

"Good." Her arms came up around his neck as his lips found her throat. "This doesn't change anything, though."

"I know."

"And an apology after one therapy session isn't enough, either."

"Okay."

"Nobody needs to know about this."

"Stop talking, Oona." He took her mouth, wedging his tongue inside. She moaned and wrapped her legs around his waist, lifting her hips up to grind against his erection.

He certainly hadn't been expecting her to invite him into her bed. Not in a million years did he think that would ever happen again. Sure, they had chemistry and sexual tension that was so tight it was threatening to cut off circulation to certain parts of his body, but all of that constantly competed with the fact that they also couldn't stand each other.

He cupped her breast and broke their kiss, dropping his mouth to her jaw, her throat, her collarbone, and scraping his teeth down and over her breast until his lips encircled her nipple. It was already hard and pointed, but he captured it anyway and sucked, reveling in the groan that rumbled in Oona's chest and the way she arched her back and pressed her breast harder against his face. She reached between them and pushed her hand beneath the waistband of his boxers, wrapping her soft fingers around his cock and stroking him, using her thumb to swirl the precum around.

He bucked into her fist, fucking her hand and moving his mouth over to her other breast, biting that nipple and relishing the raspy gasp that scraped out of her throat.

But he wanted more.

He needed to taste her again.

He gave her nipple one final lave with his tongue, then slowly moved south, peppering her abdomen and hip bones, the tops of her thighs and inner thighs with kisses and gentle but deliberate nips.

She spread her legs for him and planted her feet on the mattress. The scent of her arousal was heady and had his mouth pooling with saliva.

It was dark in the room, but he could just imagine how her pink center glistened, plump, juicy, and just waiting for him.

With a flick of his tongue that involved a lot of fucking self-restraint, he hit her clit.

She sucked in a sharp breath.

He did it again.

Her hips lifted.

All he wanted to do right now was dive face-first into her heat, up to his fucking ears and let her pussy drench his face, shove his tongue so far inside her he got a cramp and make her sensitive little clit quadruple in size and throb against his lips.

But he also didn't want this to be over too quickly.

Unlike last time, which had been sex fueled with contempt, and was over so fucking fast he blinked and it was done, this time, he wanted to savor her. Wanted to pour out his apology through his body. Let her feel how sorry he was.

Her hips churned as he continued to flick.

She growled and it was all he could do to keep his chuckle silent.

He circled her soaked center with one finger and slowly pushed it inside. She sighed and her hips leaped off the bed. Her pussy walls squeezed his finger and she pushed downward with her pelvis to take more of his finger inside her. He added another, curling the tips to press up on that special little button.

"Oh God," she gasped.

He was still just flicking her clit with his tongue. He wanted to suck it like a fucking lollipop, but the reaction he was getting from just the flick was pretty enticing.

Her hips bucked and churned without much of a rhythm. His eyes had adjusted to the darkness now and when he glanced up her body, he could see Oona pulling on her nipples. Her bottom lip was caught between her teeth, her eyes were closed, and she was rolling her nipples between her fingers, then tugging on them. And she wasn't being gentle about it, either. She pulled them out farther than he would have, then gave them a bit of a flick and twist between her thumb and index finger.

Enthralled in the way she pleasured herself, he was still pumping his fingers inside of her, but had forgotten about his tongue.

"Tongue," she breathed above him.

He grinned. *Yes, ma'am.*

But rather than give her exactly what she asked for, he put them both out of their misery and pulled her swollen clit into his mouth and sucked it hard.

Her hips jerked up. "Yessssss."

He smiled and sucked harder, pulling that tender nub deeper into his mouth, stretching it and feeling it swell against his tongue.

"Oh God," she sighed, squeezing her pussy around his fingers.

He continued to eat her this way. Sucking her clit and fucking her with his fingers. She was close, he could tell, but seemed to be holding off coming.

"You need to come," he said, his words muffled. "I can tell."

"I'm fine," she breathed.

"Come, Oona," he growled, slowly adding another finger inside of her. "Come for me."

He swirled his tongue around her clit, pumped his fingers and when her body gave a little shudder and she squeaked above him and opened her mouth, he pulled her clit to the back of his tongue and sucked as hard as he could.

She detonated.

Her pussy spasmed and pulsed around his fingers as he continued to move them, pressing up hard on her G-spot as it expanded and hardened against his fingertips. Her juices flowed out over his fingers and hand, dripping onto the bedsheet and coating his whiskers.

She kept going up though. Kept breathing heavy, kept coming.

Her clit swelled even more against his tongue, and he was forced to inhale a breath through his nose, but he never stopped sucking. Never stopped curling his fingers as her orgasm continued to unfold around them. She was making various noises, all of them quiet, all of them incoherent. No words, just sexy sounds, and breathy gasps that made his dick twitch beneath him and his balls tighten up against his taint.

He pressed even harder on her G-spot and more sweet honey flowed over his hand.

The woman just kept going.

Finally, he wasn't sure how long it took, but she started to slide down the backside of her climax. Her back returned to the mattress and her pussy released his fingers from it's vice grip.

He didn't realize until that moment that his fingers had started to cramp inside of her. But he also didn't care.

Releasing her clit, he gave it a playful lick and pulled his fingers free, turning his head and kissing her inner thighs, then her plump folds, and the top of her mound. He climbed back up her and was about to just slide inside, but she stopped him with a hand on his chest.

"Condom," she said, her voice hoarse, eyes slightly unfocused.

He nodded and sat back on his knees, but then he had a better idea and rolled over so he was on his back, yanking off his boxers in the process. "I want you on top," he said as she reached into her purse that was on the floor and pulled a condom off the strip, then handed it to him.

She nodded and waited for him to roll on the condom, then swung one long leg over his body and straddled him.

"Gonna stick a finger in your ass," he said as she lifted up, positioned him at her center and slowly dropped down. She nodded. Fuck, she was a snug fit. He loved it. The way her pussy hugged his cock like a fucking second skin was goddamn perfection.

Circling a finger around behind her, he dipped it between them and gathered some of her personal lube, then trailed it up between her crease. She puckered against his finger slightly, but then relaxed and let him inside.

Placing two hands on his chest, she started to lift up and down, riding him, letting her luscious tits bounce just inches from his face. Her nipples were still hard and he licked his lips. He wanted those perfectly ripe raspberries in his mouth.

"Hang on," he rasped, keeping his finger in her ass, but gripping the bed with his other hand. She lifted up, keeping just the tip of him inside her while he scooted up the bed until his back was against the headboard. "That's better," he said, leaning forward so he could take a nipple between his teeth again. He played with them harder, emulating what she did to herself earlier. Giving her that gentle, but deliberate snap of pain that she seemed to crave. And when he removed his mouth and raked his chin with it's wiry stubble across her bud, she squeezed her tight little cunt around him even harder.

His finger in her ass continued to pump, and the way she dropped hard onto his cock and finger said she didn't mind the breach one bit.

He was close in no time, loving the heat of her, her feminine noises and even just the smell. The smell of whatever floral and nutty body wash she used, her sweet and musky pussy, and their combined sweat mingling in the room. It was an intoxicating, drugging combination and he never wanted it to end.

Her hands fell to his shoulders and she increased the force and speed of her hip lifts and drops, taking the crown of his cock all the way out to her pussy lips, doing a little counter-clockwise swirl, then slamming back down, until he was all the way inside her.

"Fuck," he grunted when she did it again, only making sure to squeeze him extra tight with her hot, wet little cunt as she went.

She lifted up again, only this time, she paused when he was barely inside of her. He lifted his gaze, breaking his lip lock with her nipple, and found her watching him.

She bit her lip and slowly, like a sex kitten, or seductress or something, sunk back down, squeezing him even harder, but dropping half an inch at a time, torturing him. Torturing both of them.

She was only halfway down when she broke, tossed her head back and came again.

But the rippling of her pussy and the way she pressed her tits into his face was enough to give him a hard shove over the edge. Her long hair tickled the tops of his thighs. He stilled beneath her, stilled his finger inside her and blew his load.

Fuck, how he wished they could go condom-free and he could fill her up properly. Paint her fucking insides white with his cum. Claim her. Leave a part of himself behind.

The idea of knowing she would be walking around tomorrow with his cum inside of her was such a big fucking turn on.

But she was smarter than he was.

A condom was the right and responsible thing to do.

Even if it wasn't the most enjoyable.

Not that had he could really complain, though. Even with a rubber on, she still felt incredible. Still milked him dry with each squeeze, with each quiver of her walls.

Her orgasm wasn't as long this time, and before he was even done, she relaxed on top of him and sat up straight, watching him unravel.

His eyes were closed, but he could feel her gaze on him. Heated and curious, sated and aroused.

His balls twitched beneath them, and his cock gave a final jolt before he exhaled, and slumped heavily against the headboard.

She barely gave him a moment of calm before she climbed off him, wrapped a housecoat around her body from the back of the door and slipped out.

The toilet flushed, the sink ran and she returned a moment later, her gaze on him curious.

"So ... are we good?" he asked, leaning over to find his boxers.

She removed her housecoat and hung it back up, then went on the hunt for her pajamas.

"What do you mean?"

"Well, like, I apologized and then we just fucked, so ..."

"I said this doesn't change anything, Aiden. This was purely ... chemical. Yes, you apologized, but you need to do the work. As far as I'm concerned, they were just words with nothing to back them up."

A heat of embarrassment and frustration filled his chest, then began to worm its way up his neck and face. A sick feeling formed in his belly and he snapped the waistband of his boxers over his hips then stood up straight. "You just used me?"

She rolled her eyes and flicked on the bedside lamp. "I was upfront about what this was."

"You really think you're better than me, don't you?"

Oh my God! Stop fucking talking. Just stop.

Her lips twisted, but then she smiled. "I'm not doing this again."

"Not doing what?"

"I know what you're doing. You're trying to incite me. You're pushing my buttons because you *want* to fight. You want me to call you an asshole, a jerk, a fucked-up piece of shit. Because then your own feelings about yourself are validated."

"Fuck off."

His brain was telling him to shut up. That he was undoing everything he'd accomplished, but apparently, his mouth had gone rogue. He was going to ruin all his progress. Fuck. Fuck. Fuck.

She lifted a shoulder and shook her head. "I'm not going to be the whip you use to beat yourself with anymore. I'm not going to bite the bait you're dangling. I have too much other shit on my plate to deal with. I am not going to continue to butt heads with you just so you can dig yourself deeper into this trench of loneliness, anger, and despair." She glanced at the rumpled bed sheets. "This was a bad idea."

"Already regret it, huh?"

The door to the rational part of his brain slammed shut.

"I wish I didn't."

He scoffed. "Hey, you propositioned me, remember?"

"I did."

"So ..."

She shrugged again. "So what? It's the twenty-first century. Women are allowed to ask for sex. They are allowed to make mistakes. *All* people are."

"And I've apologized for mine, and yet that doesn't seem to be enough. Who's the hypocrite?"

"I'm *not* doing this. Just because you don't drink, doesn't mean you're not self-destructive. There are other ways to destroy yourself other than substances. You make me mad so that I retaliate, which makes you mad. It reinforces your anger and self-loathing. It amplifies the guilt and the denial you're drowning in. You need help, Aiden. An apology is a good start, but it's just a Band-Aid on a gunshot." Her eyes flicked to the door. "Goodnight."

Then she slid into bed, pulled the covers over her body, and turned off the bedside lamp, rolling over onto her side to show him her back.

He stood there like a buffoon for a hot minute staring at her, waiting for her to roll back over and get mad at him, tell him to leave or say something snarky. But she didn't.

Eventually, he had no other choice but to leave, closing the door behind him.

In her room he had removed the condom, tied it and stuffed it into a Kleenex. But when he went to the bathroom, he rolled it up in more toilet paper before tossing it into the bathroom garbage. Then he washed his face, brushed his teeth and went to bed.

You'd think he'd be able to sleep like a baby after draining his balls, but that wasn't the fucking case.

Oona's words cut him deep.

They cut right through him if he was being honest.

But the longer he thought about it, the more he realized she was right.

His anger faded and his epiphany, though slow to develop, came. He'd said as much to Joy earlier that day. That he was constantly trying to push Oona's buttons and yet he didn't know why.

But Oona had figured it out.

Of course, she did, though. She was a brilliant therapist and had probably psychoanalyzed the shit out of him.

And even though that scared him half to death, he also knew she was right.

He needed to apologize with more than just words.

Actions, too.

Otherwise, he'd never make progress. He'd never get back on the force.

Tomorrow.

He didn't know how, but tomorrow he was going to start fixing things.

He just hoped it wasn't too late.

Chapter Nineteen

The next morning, it was too cold and icy to go for a run, even though the sky was blue and the sun was bright, which just felt like Mother Nature was mocking him. But Aiden decided not to let that get him down, so he asked Jordan to drop him off at a gym nearby. Jordan took him to his gym and the two of them worked out together. It was weird and kind of awesome pumping iron next to his brother, spotting him when he did bench presses and racing him on the adjacent treadmill. It brought back decade's old memories from when they were teenagers and would do the same thing in their small town in Quebec.

"I, uh, I need to apologize," Aiden started, as they lowered the speed on their treadmills after a ten-minute uphill sprint. His lungs burned, calves screamed, and quads trembled. It was a good, masochistic feeling that he found addictive.

"Yeah?" Jordan asked, squirting water into his mouth from his water bottle. "What'd you do now?"

"Just for everything. How I behaved at the bachelor party—at least the end of it on the bus. How I treated Oona. And even for what happened with us ... you know, back then. I'm your big brother. I shouldn't have let that tear us apart."

Jordan was quiet for a moment, his gaze on the screen of his treadmill, watching the numbers drop as his speed slowed for his cool down. "I appreciate that," he finally said. "It means a lot."

"You were younger than me and I should have protected you," Aiden went on.

"You're only two years older than me. And we're both adults now. I just as easily could have reached out sooner."

"But back then, I should have been the one to report Dad for hitting Dallas and driving off. I should have been the one to take the brunt of the family's anger. The lion's share of the town's hate."

"Charlet Heights is more like a cult than it is a town and we both know it," Jordan said. "The fact that nearly everyone backed Dad. That they turned on *us* after what he did, just goes to show you it wouldn't have mattered *who* turned him in, me or you. We both turned on him and for that, we're pariahs."

"I'm fine being a pariah to those lunatics. Defending a drunk. A child-killer, while going after the dead kid's mom until she throws herself off a bridge. Then turning on us. Teenagers, for doing what any sane person would say was the right thing. Don't need any of those Kool-Aid guzzling nutjobs in my life." Aiden blinked a few times.

It was surprising how easy it was to talk about what happened all those years ago. He hadn't murmured a word about it in decades because of how badly it hurt. How much hate and anger it stirred up inside of him. Like the silt on the bottom of a pond being disturbed after ages of just sitting there, piling up on to itself, becoming more like quicksand, so that when someone finally took a step, they got sucked in up to their waist, unable to break free.

But he didn't feel like he was being sucked into the depths of silt. His layers of hate and anger weren't nearly as disturbed as he anticipated.

Maybe it was because Jordan knew exactly how he was feeling that he could talk about it. But whatever it was, talking about it helped.

Go figure.

"I still think back to all the times I had to drive us home, starting at eight-years-old after Dad would get too drunk to drive when he'd take us out hunting with him," Aiden said. "And he was the fucking mayor."

"*Beloved* mayor," Jordan added. Their treadmills stopped, so they hopped off, cleaned their machines, and headed over to the leg press machine.

"Not gonna lie," Aiden started, spotting his brother as he flipped off the lock and started to bend his knees into his chest, "I've kept tabs on Dad and that judge that let him off so easily. Well, I did until the judge died a couple of years ago. But Dad is still kicking. Not sure how."

"He's pickled. Pickled shit lasts forever," Jordan said with a grunt, pushing the weights back up until his legs were almost completely straight. "What about Mom?"

"No fucking clue. Even though Dad was the one that hit Dallas, even though Dad was the drunk, I just—"

"Mom enabled him," Jordan finished.

"Yeah."

"She didn't have our backs. Said that we should be grateful that our father wasn't an abusive drunk like her father. That it could have been a lot worse. She abandoned us and enabled him."

Jordan nodded, grunted again, and switched the lock on the leg press for a break. "I just can't with either of them." He swallowed and looked up at Aiden, his face flush, beads of sweat dancing along his hairline. "Is that why you don't drink?"

Aiden nodded. "Yeah. I just can't bring myself to try it after seeing what it did to Dad. To our family. But I don't judge you for drinking, to each their own," he said quickly.

Jordan's lip twitched. "Bet you haven't always felt that way."

"No, I haven't. But I'm trying to change. It's hard, though. Dallas was only twelve."

Jordan shook his head, his jaw tight. "I know. A twelve-year-old boy with Downs Syndrome doing his first-ever solo walk to the corner store to get a hotdog. After weeks of planning and practicing it with his mom. And in the middle of the fucking day, our drunk father struck him with his car and fled the scene."

Aiden pulled in a deep breath through his nose. "I feel like if maybe I'd disabled the transmission somehow ... done more than just hide his keys."

"He would have taken Mom's car, or the neighbor's, or found another way. Or it would have been a different time when we didn't hide his keys, and he would have hit someone else's child. It's not our fault. We did what we could. We were still kids, too. And we had jobs. We couldn't just sit at home and babysit a grown-ass man. We had lives and jobs and our own shit going on. We did everything we could, aside from tying Dad down to the couch. What happened is ultimately on him." Jordan flicked off the lock on the leg press machine again and did more reps, grunting and sucking in air through clenched teeth.

Aiden spotted him, made sure he wasn't doing too much, then when Jordan nodded that this would be his final rep, Aiden helped him push the press up the last couple of inches so that they could flick the lock. Jordan had packed on a lot of weight and that couldn't have been an easy set.

Then it was Aiden's turn.

By the time they were finished at the gym, Aiden's legs were the consistency of Jell-O and his heart felt lighter.

They arrived home at Jordan and Rayma's apartment to find a rental car parked out front. "Oh fuck," Jordan murmured when they climbed out of his truck.

"What?" Aiden followed his brother to the front door.

"They're here."

"Who? Rayma and Oona's parents?"

"Yeah. I just hope that Oona's still here for Rayma's sake. Everyone has made a pact that she won't be left alone with them, particularly her mother, under any circumstances."

"Yeah, I heard that. Count me in there. I'll help anyway I can."

Jordan nodded and smiled half-heartedly in appreciation as he unlocked the door and opened it.

Voices drifted out from the direction of Rayma's closed bedroom door, two he recognized, one he didn't.

A man with gray hair and light brown eyes sat in Jordan's La-Z-Boy reading quietly from a book. He glanced up at them both. "I'm assuming one of you is Jordan?" he asked with a smile.

Jordan stepped forward. "I am, sir. It's nice to finally meet you, Mr. Young."

"Nice to meet you, too," Mr. Young said, closing his book and climbing out of the chair and taking Jordan's hand.

"This is my brother, Aiden," Jordan said, introducing Aiden, "he flew out here from Montreal." Aiden shook hands with Mr. Young and offered him a smile, but knowing what he knew about Rayma and Oona's parents now, made it hard for him to display any genuine joy about meeting these people.

"Yanna wanted to see Rayma's dress on her, so they're in the bedroom right now."

"Oona in there, too?" Jordan asked quickly.

Mr. Young nodded. "Yes."

Jordan relaxed a bit. So did Aiden.

"How is your hotel so far? And how was your flight?" Jordan asked.

"Nothing eventful getting here, which is what you want in a flight. And the hotel is fine. We're simple people. We don't need extravagance. Just a clean room with quiet neighbors is more than enough for me."

"Can I make you a coffee?" Jordan asked, circling behind the island and opening the cupboard to grab the tin of beans.

"Oh, none for me. I have one cup a day and that is more than enough."

"I'll have one if you're making it already," Aiden said. "Gonna pop into the shower first."

Jordan nodded at him, then Aiden gathered his stuff and made haste into the bathroom. He made sure not to take too long, since it was only a matter of time until Mrs. Young came out and reinforcements would be required.

Drying his hair, he opened the bathroom door only for Rayma to open her bedroom door at the same time, her face flushed, eyes close to spilling over with tears. She stalked into the kitchen, opened a cupboard door, grabbed a bottle of tequila, unscrewed it and took a long sip straight from the bottle.

Slowly, Aiden wandered into the living room only to find it empty. Where were Jordan and Mr. Young?

Oona came out of the bedroom after Rayma and dropped her voice low. "Ignore her."

Rayma took another swig of the bottle then clenched her jaw and flared her nostrils at the same time a tear slipped down her cheek.

"That's not going to fix things," Aiden said, "It's not even noon." The look on Oona's face as she spun around and glared at him had him instantly regretting his words. Fuck, he should know better by now.

Too late.

She left her sister and rounded on Aiden, her finger out and poking hard into his chest as she brought her voice down low and gritted out, "Go. Now."

"I—" Aiden sighed. "I'm sorry, Rayma. I spoke before I thought."

"No shit," Oona said. Her eyes softened, but they weren't because of Aiden, she turned back to her sister. "Your dress is gorgeous, Rayma. You do not have to make any changes. Ignore her."

A beautiful woman with dark hair, and brown eyes flecked with gold came out of the bedroom. Even if Aiden didn't know that this woman was Rayma and Oona's mother, Yanna, it would be easy enough to discern since her daughters were her doppelgangers. She regarded Aiden with blatant, irritated curiosity. "And you are?"

Aiden cleared his throat and stuck out his hand. "Aiden Lassiter, Mrs. Young. I'm Jordan's brother."

Mrs. Young nodded and took his hand in her soft papery one. "Nice to meet you."

The front door opened and Jordan and Mr. Young returned.

"Well, I'm glad that's all it was," Mr. Young said, removing his gloves. "Hate to have to take the rental car back so soon. Don't know why they gave us such a fancy one. A simple sedan is more than enough for me."

"Just a loose spark plug. All better now. And I don't think Camrys are fancy, sir. Just reliable." Jordan zeroed in on Rayma's sad face and the tequila bottle which she'd hidden behind herself on the counter, away from the eyes of their parents. His eyes widened, then he shifted his gaze to Oona who shook her head stiffly.

"I've got an idea," Aiden piped up. He turned to Mrs. Young. "I'm new to town and would really like to explore it a bit more. It's a lovely day, why don't the three of us go explore? I've read about Butchart Gardens, Craigdarroch Castle, there's a gingerbread house exhibit somewhere and a Christmas tree exhibit somewhere else. What do you say?"

Mr. and Mrs. Young exchanged looks with each other.

"Well, I thought Rayma would need more help, but—"

"I'm pretty much set," Rayma said quickly, cutting off her mother. "It's all good. You guys should go. Explore. Experience the magic and wonder of Victoria at Christmas. You'll never get a more beautiful day to do it."

Mr. Young shrugged and nodded. "I've heard there is a miniature world in town somewhere, maybe we can go check that out? Seeing that would be more than enough for me."

"You bet," Aiden said, flashing a smile to Rayma, to which she mouthed the words, "Thank you," back.

In just a few minutes, Aiden and the Youngs were out the door and in the rental car.

Even though he didn't necessarily want to spend any time with these people since he knew what kind of crappy parents they were, he looked at this as killing two birds with one stone. Or maybe even three birds. He was helping Rayma. He was showing Oona that he was capable of change, and he was proving to himself that he could be professional and courteous even toward people he didn't care for.

Now, he just needed to find enough things to do with them to fill the day and keep them away from Rayma.

Maybe they could just go to the IMAX and watch back-to-back documentaries all day. Then he wouldn't have to talk to them, they'd all learn something, and it'd pass the time.

He'd leave that as a backup plan. But first, to the castle! With any luck they would have an old timey stockade he could put Mrs. Young in for a little bit after how she made Rayma feel.

It was dark and well-past the dinner hour by the time Aiden and Rayma and Oona's parents finished their day. They visited the tourist center and grabbed pamphlets to make sure they didn't miss out on anything, then they went everywhere. Butterfly World, the Aquarium, Butchart Gardens, Craigdarroch Castle, Miniature World, the museum, the bug zoo and finished it off with the IMAX.

He was exhausted by the end of it. But so were Rayma and Oona's parents. They even suggested that Aiden take their car home. That he just drop them off and pick them up tomorrow, considering that their hotel was only a ten minute drive from Rayma and Jordan's apartment anyway.

He protested at first, but they were both yawning so much with weary looks about them, he didn't think it'd be such a great idea to put either of them behind the wheel to drive home after dropping him off. So he agreed.

"I will text you tomorrow and we will coordinate a pickup time," Mrs. Young said, stifling another yawn behind her hand. "Thank you for a very nice day, Aiden."

"My pleasure, Mrs. Young. Mr. Young. You two have a wonderful night and we'll see you tomorrow."

They waved at him as they made their way to the front door of their hotel.

He pulled out of the hotel parking lot and stopped at the entrance onto the road to get his bearings.

All things considered, it hadn't been a horrible day, but he could see flickerings of judgment and ridicule in Mrs. Young's eyes. And the way she commented on children at the aquarium and Butterfly World who were not misbehaving but just having fun, spoke volumes of what kind of a controlling and unfun parent she must have been. She was the queen of dirty looks. And, unfortunately, quite a few weary-eyed parents who were just trying to get their kids out of the house for a little fun were the recipients of Yanna Young's judgment-filled glare.

Mr. Young wasn't so bad. He was pretty quiet for the most part and very plain. He wore brown and beige and a tweed brown pageboy hat, and by noon, Aiden had started a mental tally of how many times Mr. Young said, "More than enough for me."

At the time he dropped them off at their hotel, Royce Young had said—and only since noon—"More than enough for me" twenty-three times.

When they had lunch and he ordered a cup of soup and half a sandwich, even though Aiden said he was paying and that Mr. Young should order the bowl of soup and full sandwich if he wanted it, Mr. Young said, "Oh no. I'll be fine. Half a sandwich and a small cup of broth is more than enough for me."

It was weird and something Aiden was dying to speak to his sister in-law and Oona about.

The GPS on his phone said he was only about ten minutes from Rayma and Jordan's house, so he put on his indicator and was about to pull out, intending to head right and proceed to the highway on ramp when an SUV went zooming past him, going way, way over the speed limit.

"Jesus Christ," he murmured, shaking his head.

If he were on duty and in a patrol car, his lights would be on so fucking fast and he'd be after that chump, chasing him down and issuing him a ticket.

But he wasn't.

So he couldn't.

He pulled out and sped up a little, catching up with the gray Chevy Equinox. Then the motherfucker behind the wheel ran a goddamn red light. Cars honked and skidded to avoid a collision, several of them swerving out into the middle of the convoluted intersection.

Fucking hell.

It wasn't even that late at night and there was already a fucking drunk driver on the road.

Your dad was wasted mid day and hit a kid. Time of day means nothing to an addict.

Right. It didn't.

It was also the holiday season, which meant people were drinking at all hours of the day at get togethers and company parties. And some people had a very low tolerance and were inebriated after only a couple of drinks.

Clearly, this person had tied on a few too many and was now putting everyone else on the road in peril with their selfishness.

He might not be on duty, or even from Victoria, but that didn't mean he couldn't do something. He was still a police officer. Still a sworn-in member of the Royal Canadian Mounted Police and with that oath, he would serve and protect the people of Canada until his dying breath.

The light turned green and Aiden gunned it through the now clear intersection in the direction of the perpetrator. It didn't take long for him to catch up to the SUV. It was on the highway now, having taken the on ramp, and now it wasn't just speeding but it was zigzagging all over the road, too. Into both lanes, eliciting honks and emergency braking from other drivers, then over onto the shoulder and nearly into the ditch that made up the median between the four-lane highway.

Aiden wove through traffic and pulled up beside the Chevy. He memorized the license plate. *G5P 4T8*. When he had a minute where he wasn't distracted, he'd call 911 and report the driver. But right now, he needed to make sure the driver didn't cause an accident and hurt someone.

It was in the left lane, so he pulled up on the right and rolled down his window preparing to tell the driver to pull over. Only, when he looked through the passenger window into the dark interior of the vehicle, he saw that the man behind the wheel was unconscious. Or about to be.

His head fell back against the headrest and his eyes were drooping closed. Yet, the vehicle was still going. His foot was still on the accelerator.

It appeared to be a man in his mid to late fifties. Of Asian ethnicity and upper middle class, based on his watch and the leather interior of the vehicle. The man's hands fell away from thesteering wheel and his body slumped sideways into the driver side door.

The Chevy veered to the left even more.

"Oh fuck!" Aiden cried when he realized the car was going into the ditch at fucking ninety kilometers an hour.

He checked behind him to make sure there wasn't anybody riding his ass and about to rear end him, then he slammed on his brakes, knowing that it would take him a moment to actually come to a complete stop. He maneuvered the rental car onto the left shoulder and watched in horror as the Chevy drove right into the ditch at full speed and rolled over onto its side, then roof, the wheels still spinning in the air.

Aiden put the Young's rental car into park, put on his hazard lights and jumped out, racing down into the ditch to the driver's side door.

It wasn't crunched in too badly, so he was able to open it, but that caused the man to fall out of the Chevy, since he wasn't wearing a seatbelt, and he crumpled to the grass in a heap at Aiden's feet.

Aiden crouched down and gently rolled the man over onto his back. "Sir. Sir, can you hear me? Are you okay?"

Another driver stopped and came down. "Everything okay?"

"Call 911. I don't want to move him. I think he was drinking and driving," Aiden replied, the sizzling sound of rubber tires on wet pavement a deafening buzz around him.

The young man nodded and pulled his phone out of his pocket.

Aiden returned to the man on the ground. "Sir. My name is Aiden and I'm a police officer from Montreal. Can you hear me?"

The man made a noise, then his head lolled to the side. Aiden returned to the vehicle, reached in, put it into park and turned off the ignition before dropping back to his knees beside the unconscious man. That's when he noticed that the left side of the man's face was severely drooping. He got back up and went to the Chevy, taking a big inhale of the interior. Then he dropped to his knees once more and brought his nose right down to the man's face.

There was no smell of alcohol. Not on the man's breath or in the vehicle. Normally if someone was intoxicated enough to pass out and roll their vehicle, they smelled like the inside of a rum bottle.

He checked to see if the man was breathing.

He wasn't.

So immediately, Aiden started to administer CPR. Hand-over-hand, to the beat of *Staying Alive*, he did chest compressions. Then he plugged the man's nose and performed mouth-to-mouth, then resumed the chest compressions.

Already the peel of an ambulance echoed in the background along with more headlights shining down on them from both sides of the highway where people had stopped to either spectate or offer help.

Aiden knew better than to try to move the man from his seat in case of a spinal injury, but the guy just fell out of the vehicle when Aiden opened the door, there wasn't much he could do. He kept checking the guy's pulse, checked his limbs and neck for any noticeable injuries, but it didn't seem like there were any.

He resumed chest compressions when he couldn't locate a pulse.

The ambulance siren drew closer and soon the white and red flashing lights had Aiden squinting and shielding his eyes. Three paramedics came bounding down into the ditch. Aiden checked the man's pulse again. It was faint, but it was there.

A firetruck siren started in the background, too, and Aiden could already see their lights approaching.

He stepped out of the way so paramedics could take over CPR, but started to recount what happened to the first paramedic that approached him. "Guy was speeding like a maniac. Ran a red, then started swerving all over the road. I pulled up beside him to see what was going on and get him to pull over, that's when he passed out and went into the ditch."

"Why would you do that?" the paramedic asked.

"I'm a cop back in Montreal. I thought he was drunk."

"And you don't think that now?"

"I think he had a stroke," Aiden said. "I don't smell alcohol and the left side of his face is drooping."

The paramedic nodded. They managed to get the guy breathing again—thank God—then they went about getting the man onto a stretcher board.

The firetruck rolled up and a few firefighters bailed out to survey the scene, as well.

Aiden stayed to answer anymore questions, but he knew from experience that he wasn't of very much help. He gave them his phone number and name in case they had anymore questions, then eventually, like the rest of the lookie loos, he got back into the Camry and drove off like nothing had happened.

Only so much had happened.

And it wasn't just the accident and the man nearly dying.

Aiden's assumptions about the guy were wrong.

He'd been wrong about a lot of things.

For a very long time.

Chapter Twenty

Yanna Young hadn't changed one bit.

Oona didn't know why she thought that their mother would change. Would soften and become less ashamed of her daughters. Less judgmental.

But if she didn't think her behavior was problematic, what reason did she have to try to augment it? However, Oona allowed her optimism to rise to the surface, hoping that maybe a Christmas miracle would occur and their mother would become a tolerable version of herself for the sake of Rayma's wedding and the family all being together.

But nope. Oona should have known better.

The moment their mother walked into Rayma's house, she had comments.

She had judgment.

She had her shame shadow to cast on every corner and cranny she made eye contact with.

She vehemently disagreed with the idea that Rayma and Jordan were living together before they were married, and when she found out that there was going to be an open bar—let alone alcohol served at the wedding at all—she made Rayma feel like she was hosting a rave rather than a tasteful winter wedding for all her nearest and dearest. The same thing happened at Triss's wedding, so her comments about that barely fazed them.

But the straw that broke the camel's back, or the words that drove Rayma to day drink more accurately, were when Rayma tried on her dress and all their mother did was cluck her tongue and shake her head.

"I don't understand the need to show so much skin," their mother said. "What ever happened to modesty? To humility. Less is more, don't you think? If you insist on having this *party* at Christmas, in the winter, why not wear something a little more appropriate, with sleeves at the very least?"

Rayma's eyes met Oona's in the mirror, and her chin wobbled. "It's not a *party*, Mom. It's my wedding."

Their mother just rolled her eyes and looked away, clucking her tongue again, and taking in Rayma and Jordan's bedroom with complete disapproval. "I mean, you already know that I totally disapprove of the idea of you marrying a police officer. It's as if you girls are doing this deliberately to defy me. To keep me up at night with worry. First, Pasha marries a SEAL or whatever Heath is, and now you're marrying a police officer. Their jobs are dangerous. He may not come home one day, you know? Then what? Then you'll be alone. And God forbid you have children and they end up fatherless because you couldn't marry a man with a safe job like an accountant or lawyer."

Oona swallowed. "We can't control who we fall in love with, Mom. Jordan is a good guy, with an honorable job."

Rayma ground her teeth loud enough, the upstairs neighbors probably thought there were mice in the walls.

"At least Triss and Mieka are with men who left their dangerous lives behind and work with horses. Though Mieka *is* living in sin with Nate." Their mother shook her head, brown eyes filled to the brim with disapproval. "And horses can be unpredictable. You can die falling off one. I just don't understand why my daughters couldn't find men with safe careers. Careers that didn't perpetually put them in harm's way."

She picked up an object off Rayma's nightstand and scrunched her nose as she stared at it trying to figure out what it was. She couldn't figure it out, then set it back down, turning toward Rayma who stood in front of the full-length mirror.

"And why the low back? It just feels completely unnecessary and as if you're trying to show off your body. Nobody needs to know what your bare back looks like besides your husband. And there are going to be *other* people's husbands there. How do you think their wives are going to feel with you parading your body around like that, making their men look at you? What are you trying to prove, Rayma? Really?" Her head shook some more. "You really haven't changed, have you? It's always all about Rayma. What Rayma wants. Nobody else matters."

Rayma's dress happened to be an absolute work of art. It was tasteful and gorgeous and suited Rayma to utter perfection. With frilly cap sleeves, a sweetheart neckline and a low back that had just a small delicate lace tie at the nape of her neck, the dress was a fitted off-white lace gown that pooled at her feet and had a small three-foot train. There was nothing overly provocative or unnecessary about it and up until the moment Rayma put it on for their mother, she'd positively glowed when she wore the dress. Now, she was deflating like a balloon with a pin prick and the light around her was fading.

Oona walked up behind her and untied the small lace tie at her neck, then started to unzip the zipper at Rayma's bum. "Let's get you out of this, kiddo," she whispered.

Rayma stepped out of the dress and immediately covered her breasts until Oona quickly passed her her bra.

Rayma and Oona had no nudity issues with each other, but like hell would they ever let their mother see them naked.

Not only because she would probably find something to pick them apart for like boney hips or a bit of tummy fat, but also because all of the Young sisters had tattoos and their parents absolutely loathed tattoos.

Rayma made sure that her underwear hid the tattoo on her hipbone, the matching one that all the sisters had, but she needed to get dressed fast if she wanted to keep her belly button piercing a secret from their mother.

But Yanna Young wasn't even paying attention as Rayma got dressed, she was too busy laying Rayma's dress out on the bed and trying to burn it to a pile of ash with her laser vision of judgment.

Not that she liked him, but thank God for Aiden taking their mother away, because if she'd stayed around Rayma any longer, Oona probably would be up on charges for murder by now.

Oona, Rayma, and Jordan were still up and in the living room chatting, with wine and potato chips fulfilling their evening peckishness when Aiden knocked on the door later that night, and Jordan let him in.

The man looked like he'd been in a car accident.

Which made sense considering he'd just spent the entire day with Rayma and Oona's parents. Oona often felt like she'd been side-swiped by an eighteen-wheeler after spending more than a few hours with her mother.

But a part of her also snickered on the inside that Aiden had gone through it.

Served him right after his comment to Rayma earlier that day about taking a shot of tequila to calm her nerves.

Karma could be a bitch.

"Dude," Jordan said, stepping out of the way, "what happened?"

"Our mother happened," Rayma said, a little tipsy from the wine. "I'd say he's in pretty decent shape, all things considered."

"Need some tequila?" Oona asked with a smirk.

Jordan and Rayma both snorted.

Aiden blinked a bunch of times, but he didn't say anything as he toed out of his boots and sloughed off his jacket. Jordan hung it up for him.

Rayma seemed to realize at the same time as Oona that something more than just an afternoon with their parents had Aiden looking like he'd seen a ghost, then been run over by a van full of them.

Rayma got up from her seat. "What happened?"

Aiden was still doing that weird, deliberate blinking thing, then he started to shake his head. "Just watched a guy break a bunch of speed laws, run a red, swerve all over the road and roll his SUV into a ditch."

"Fuck," Rayma and Jordan said at the same time.

"Is he okay?" Oona asked.

Aiden shrugged. "I don't know. I got out of the rental car, went to check on him, stayed with him and did CPR until the paramedics arrived, but he was in rough shape when they took him away."

"Fucking drunk drivers," Jordan murmured, shaking his head. "When are they going to learn?"

"I thought so, too," Aiden said slowly. "But ... I think the guy had a stroke. I don't think he was drunk."

"How do you know?" Rayma asked.

Licking his lips, Aiden pulled out a bar stool at the island and sat down. Jordan went into the kitchen, opened the fridge and grabbed a can of flavored sparkling water, then passed it to his brother. "I chased the guy down, got right up beside him, thinking I could make him pull over. But when I got up beside him, I saw that he was already unconscious. Then his hands fell from the wheel and he rolled into the ditch."

"Was that what all the sirens were for earlier?" Rayma asked. "Was it just up here on the Pat Bay Highway?"

"If that's the one that takes you to your parents' hotel, then, yeah."

"Holy shit," Jordan murmured, shoving his fingers into his brown hair and shaking his head. "How old of a guy?"

"Fifties maybe?" Aiden said with another shrug. "Not very old. But I didn't smell alcohol on him or in the vehicle and his face was droopy on the left side."

They all stared at Aiden in bewilderment. But it was what he wasn't saying, rather how he looked that was hitting Oona in a strange way. He hadn't been part of the accident, not literally anyway, so his haggard appearance was from something else.

The mental toll of an epiphany, perhaps?

Because he sure did look like a man who'd come to Jesus on his freaking hands and knees.

His eyes lasered in on Oona's and still, without saying a word, he told her that what she was thinking was true. He was different.

Curiosity made hot ribbons dance through her. What revelation did he have?

About what?

About who?

"I need to thank you, Aiden," Rayma said, sipping her pinot. "You've pissed me off more than once since arriving here, but you're well on your road to redemption after coming to my rescue today. An entire day with Yanna and Royce couldn't have been easy and the fact that you're still standing and I'm assuming my parents are still alive, says a lot about your strength of character." She pointed her finger at him though. "But consider yourself right back in the doghouse if you open your mouth and say they're really not that bad, and that you have no idea what we're all so frustrated about."

Aiden's lips twitched like he thought about saying it just to tease Rayma, but then he sobered and nodded. "Happy to help. I'm really sorry again for what I said earlier today. I didn't mean it."

Rayma waved her hand in dismissal. "You were right. I'm not going to solve my problems at the bottom of a bottle, but a few nips of what's in that bottle certainly takes off the edge of dealing with Yanna the Super Shamer. I also don't normally drink like this." She glanced at Jordan. "Right?"

"The Young sisters *do* seem to bring out the binge-drinkers in each other."

Oona and Rayma snorted.

"We like wine, what can we say?" Rayma shrugged. "But I *do* drink a fair bit of it when I'm with my sisters." She glanced at Oona. "Maybe we need to consider sober January?" Her eyes went wide. "Or sober February. My honeymoon is in January."

Oona rolled her eyes and smiled at her sister before turning her attention to Aiden. "What *did* the three of you get up to today?"

Delight filled his green eyes and he focused on her. "Everything. All kinds of mischief."

She snorted and smiled. "Bullshit. Yanna Young would have a heart attack if she even jay-walked."

He popped the tab on the sparkling water and took a sip. "The aquarium, Butterfly World, Butchart Gardens, Craigdarroch Castle, the bug zoo, your dad wanted to visit miniature world, because apparently that was more than enough for him."

Rayma had just taken a sip of her wine, but laughed as she had it in her mouth and snorted so hard it came out of her nose.

This only prompted Oona, Jordan, and Aiden to start laughing, too.

Jordan grabbed some paper towels and helped mop up his bride, meanwhile, Aiden's eyes—shimmering with amusement—found Oona's. His pain and shock from when he first arrived had mostly worn off, replaced by an almost tangible sense of peace and what Oona could only describe as glee. His eyes twinkled and his mouth curled up into a really sexy smile, causing the twin dimples to go into full-on attack mode.

"Sorry," Rayma said, a big grin on her face. "But we've always joked about how Dad says that. I can't believe you picked up on it."

"Started keeping track of it after lunch," Aiden said. "Got over twenty. So I'm sure it was well over thirty for the day."

"He's such a ... reductionist, is the best term I can come up with," Rayma said. "Reduces everything to being nothing." She waved her hand. "I don't know. Maybe that doesn't make any sense. I've had a couple of glasses of wine.

I'm feeling good and would rather not think too hard about my parents. Might kill my buzz."

Aiden nodded. "Fair enough. But yes, I understand what you're saying. He never asks for more. Not even when he should. Takes the bare minimum and believes that is all he deserves."

"Because he's a trouble ducker, and Mom's the fun police," Rayma said. "Let me guess, his lunch didn't come the way he ordered it, but he said it was more than enough for him and he never asked for a correction?"

Aiden continued to nod. "Yeah, how'd you know? He ordered a cup of soup, when I told him to get a bowl if he was hungry—which he said he was—and a half a sandwich, even when I said he should get a full one. I paid for lunch. Then his sandwich came on white when he ordered sourdough and I said I'd call over the waiter and ask for a fix but your dad's face went the color of a Roma tomato and he told me that white bread was fine. More than enough and he didn't want to cause trouble."

"Meanwhile, Mom probably ordered a small spring salad, no dressing, unseasoned chicken and she didn't finish it?" Oona asked.

Aiden's eyes widened. "Yeah."

"Booooorrrring," Rayma sung, shaking her head. "Ugh. They really haven't changed."

"Did you feel super judged when you ordered your meal and it came?" Oona asked.

"I did. I got the two-piece halibut and chips with coleslaw and their eyes were enormous when my plate came and as they watched me eat. I tried to offer them some, or for them to get something else off the menu, but they refused."

"Welcome to our life growing up," Rayma said. "Shamed about food, shamed about clothes, shamed about everything."

Oona simply nodded.

Rayma and Jordan both finished their wine and set the glasses in the sink. "I think I'm going to head to bed," Rayma said. "With all the wedding BS and now parent BS, I totally forgot to go Christmas shopping, so that is on the to-do list tomorrow."

"I'll go with you, kiddo," Oona said. "I already made sure that Pasha is on Mom and Dad duty. She's going to have them over and they're going to make a gingerbread house and bake and decorate Christmas cookies with Raze and Eve."

Rayma's shoulders left her ears and she smiled an exhausted smile. "Poor Raze and Eve."

Aiden and Jordan both snorted.

"Good night," Jordan said to Oona and Aiden, placing his hand at the small of Rayma's back and steering her to the bedroom. Their door closed.

The intensity of Aiden's eyes on her was an electrifying sizzle that she didn't altogether hate. It heated up that spot on her cheek where his gaze landed and created a blooming sensation that spread throughout the rest of her body, settling, of course, between her legs.

She turned to face him, her wine glass nearly empty. She finished it, maintaining eye contact with him, then took the glass to the sink to set it beside the other two. "You had an epiphany," she said, turning back to face him. It wasn't a question.

He nodded.

She frowned for a moment and her head slowly bobbed. "That's great." Oh, that curious cat inside her was scratching and meowing. Wanting to know what the epiphany was about. But it wasn't any of her business. Their relationship—or whatever it was—was strained and awkward, and she was absolutely NOT his therapist. She was a woman, who at a time, had been interested in him and now, unfortunately, found herself unable to stay off his dick no matter how much she knew he was bad for her.

At the thought of his dick, her gaze slithered down to his lap. She swallowed.

Oh, he was so wrong for her.

But it was her pattern.

She had a habit of falling for men she shouldn't. Whether they were actually bad boys, emotionally unavailable, or literally unavailable like that biologist Ben. More often than not, though, her pattern involved picking damaged men. Because as much as therapist Oona tried to tell herself that she couldn't fix them, soft-hearted Oona convinced herself that she could. That her love could put them back together and make them whole. Make them love her the way she loved them.

And even though Aiden wasn't Russell and wasn't self-destructive with alcohol, he was still self-destructive. He had trauma, triggers, and anger issues. He pushed her buttons until she lashed out, which made him lash out, and so the vortex of anger spun tighter and tighter until they were both so tangled, cutting off circulation, that they couldn't escape.

It was how he punished himself.

And she didn't want to be any part of it.

She didn't want to hurt or be hurt.

But the man had a masochistic side and he used her to hurt himself—or at least tried to—even if he wasn't aware of it. Deep down, she knew he was a good guy, he just needed some tools. He needed someone to talk to, to help him sort out his trauma and wrangle his demons.

That person wasn't her, though.

He stepped off the bar stool and slowly approached her.

Her heart threatened to bruise her ribs, it pounded so hard.

She licked her lips, but stood her ground.

He didn't stop until they were nearly toe-to-toe. She could smell his deodorant or laundry soap or whatever it was. It smelled good. Manly, woodsy, and delicious.

Lifting his hand, he reached up and gently tucked a strand of her hair behind her ear, letting his fingers graze her cheek.

Like an idiot with no willpower and intelligence, because her brain was not thinking right now, it was her clit running the show, she closed her eyes.

"I know you want this," he murmured, the hot puffs of his breath hitting her lips he was so close now.

Was he trying to push her into lashing out again? Make her mad so he could get mad? Did he want her to call him an asshole to validate how he felt about himself? Because she knew, he knew, he could be a jerk. She didn't see a lot of self-love when she looked at Aiden Lassiter. She saw a lot of pain. A lot of unresolved anger and a devastating amount of guilt.

He loathed himself for his past. His guilt for whatever happened when he and Jordan were teenagers would be a perpetual third wheel in any relationship unless he dealt with it properly.

And yet ...

She wanted him to kiss her.

She wanted to feel his lips press against hers. His hard body wrap around her and push her up against the wall. She wanted the bad boy, even if every part of her screamed that it was wrong.

Blinking open her eyes, she found him watching her. One side of his mouth hitched up into a lopsided smile that made her belly flutter. But it wasn't a cocky smile. He wasn't waiting for her to react negatively. Rather, there was guarded hope in his eyes that hit her in a part of her chest she hadn't been expecting.

She'd only had one glass of wine.

If she needed to drive, she could.

So it wasn't the wine talking.

She wasn't drunk.

Mind you, she'd never been drunk when she slept with Aiden. Not once.

Maybe if she had been drunk, she'd have made a better choice, because before she could let her brain talk her out of it, her clit took the reins and she threw her arms around his neck and kissed him.

He kissed her right back, fervently, moaning into her mouth and parting her lips to explore it with his tongue.

This is a bad, bad idea.

Shut up. It's my time for fun.

Oh great. Now her brain and clit were having an argument.

She ignored them both and allowed him to guide her to her bedroom, kicking the door closed with his heel. He had her on the bed, his big frame on top of her, large arms caging her in as his tongue plundered her mouth.

He peeled the neck of her sweater away from her shoulder and planted a warm wet kiss there, then scraped his teeth up her neck and along her jaw line, lifting the hem of her top with his hands as his mouth traveled down her body. She made quick work of her sweater, tossing it to the floor, so it was just her bra between them. But even that didn't last. She arched her back and removed her bra, letting it meet her sweater on the ground as he swirled his tongue around her belly button,

He climbed back up her body, dragging his tongue along her heated skin, creating gooseflesh in its wake until she trembled beneath him. He claimed her mouth once more, smiling against her lips when she reached for the hem of his shirt to peel it up his body.

He broke their kiss and sat up on his knees, pulling off his shirt to reveal those abs.

God damn those abs were perfection.

She bit her lip and reached for the button of his dark-wash jeans, unfastening it and then fumbling like a fool for the zipper.

His raspy chuckle made her nipples pearl as he slid off the bed and finished undressing.

She did the same with embarrassing speed, then reached for him as he climbed back on top of her, wedging his fingers between them to find her clit. He ran rough circles around it that had her hips bucking up, then his mouth dropped to her clavicle and he raked his teeth across it.

Her entire body quivered.

He slid one finger, then another into her channel and began to pump. She rocked her hips, taking his digits deeper and allowing his thumb to slide across her clit. His thumbnail scraped the clit hood and she gasped and bowed her back, tipping her head into the pillow, and her chin toward the ceiling.

He dragged his teeth across her jaw bone and to the corner of her mouth where he pulled at her bottom lip, and bit. She moaned from the snap of pain, then sighed when he slid his tongue across the bite to soothe it like a balm.

All the while, his fingers between her legs never stopped.

Her hips continued to swivel and lift, as her brain got closer and closer to short-circuiting. Her nipples were rock hard and achy, desperate for his mouth. For him to suck them, and roll them around on his tongue. She was becoming a wanton, sex-crazed, brainless animal when it came to Aiden. All she could think about when she saw him—besides how much he drove her crazy—was how badly she wanted him.

And he knew it.

He knew how she wanted him.

And that just frustrated her more.

He had the upper hand.

She'd shown him her cards that day in her office and each and every time they fell into bed together, she continued to give him more power.

And yet, when the sex was this good, she didn't particularly care.

She never had to see him again after they returned to Montreal.

They'd lived in the same city for years without ever crossing paths, they could do it again. But for now, she would bed the enemy to make him more tolerable. She would bed the enemy as a treat to herself. She would bed the enemy, but not try to fix him. Or change him. Or help him with his trauma and demons. She would simply ride him, get her orgasms and then go home.

If she stuck to her guns that way, and didn't feed into his self-harm, but rather, gave into her self-care, they could get through the rest of this wedding without hurting each other any more.

An orgasm threatened in her lower belly. Hammered on the door to be set free. But for some reason, she didn't want to come without him. She wanted them to come together.

She broke their kiss. "Condom," she breathed, still bucking up into his palm and grinding against his fingers.

He nodded and leaned over to open her nightstand drawer, which was where she'd moved the condoms from her purse after the first time they had sex. "Fuck."

Dread flashed through her. "What?"

"I uh ... I think we might have used the last one the other day."

"Impossible. I had five the night we met at the hotel."

"And we used two that night, but then one also had a hole in it that night. Which accounts for three."

Oh right.

"Then we used another one when I fucked you over the side of the couch, and another one when you invited me to your bed the other night. That makes five."

"Sonofabitch." Panic was quickly killing her impending climax. She looked up at him. "You don't have any?"

He shook his head. "I can go check in the bathroom."

"No. Rayma has an IUD. They don't use condoms." Then a lightbulb came on in her head. "I have an IUD. Are you clean?"

His head slowly bobbed. "You're the only person I've slept with in several months and I got checked after the woman before you."

She nodded. "Me, too."

"So ... we're going to go condom-free?" Excitement and worry ran neck-and-neck in his gaze.

"Unless you want to stop or just do oral?"

He shook his head and his green gaze darkened, his eyelids became hooded, as he pulled his fingers free of her and reached down to grab his cock, notching it at her center. "No. I want to come inside you." Then he surged forward with absolutely no warning, all the way to the hilt.

Oh, that stretch was divine. Almost enough to make her come right then and there.

He paused when he was fully seated and looked down at her. The magnitude of the fact that they were going condom-free was not lost on either of them. Neither was the symbolism.

As much as they didn't like each other, there was a new level of respect, of trust between them that neither person could deny.

They weren't friends.

They were family *adjacent* and not in a banjos playing in the background kind of way.

But they had chemistry and neither of them could deny that the sex between them was phenomenal. So rather than dwell on what they didn't have—which was any kind of a future or friendship—they chose to focus on what they *did* have, which was the next few days, an IUD, and a safe sex partner.

He took her mouth and kissed her, bracketing her in with his forearms on either side of her and cupping her head with his hands in a caring but possessive way. It was odd at first, but she kind of liked it. Then he started to move. Slow and deliberate. Long, languid pulls back, a pause when he was almost out, followed by an even slower, even more calculated slide back in.

Her hips leaped off the mattress to meet him and she ground her clit against his pubic bone as the climax in her lower belly started to flutter awake again.

He did this sexy little hip flick when he bottomed out and that just seemed to drive him even deeper, to hit her just right, making stars burst behind her closed eyelids and her limbs began to tingle.

They kissed passionately, as he continued to rock into her. Leaving one hand cupping her face, he brought the other one to her right calf, trailing the fingers down to her ankle and wrapping them around it, then he slowly guided her leg upward until it was beside her head and she was basically doing the splits. He knew she could bend this way, had seen her do it on stage.

That just allowed him to hit her even deeper. To rock even harder against her clit. She was more open for him, and for some weird reason, felt more exposed, which was bizarre considering that he'd seen every part of her, had his face, hands, and cock everywhere. But spreading her so wide elicited a new sense of vulnerability that excited her when it should have made her nervous.

But she didn't have the brain power to explore that strange feeling. She was so close she could practically taste the orgasm. It bubbled and frothed inside her, and her left leg that still was beneath him began to twitch. She could no longer match his rhythm and lift her hips to meet his accordingly.

She was on the precipice, staring down from the top of the cliff with nothing but clouds below, above, and beside her. The air was cool and crisp and she sucked in a deep breath, and when he brought his mouth down beside her ear and rasped, "Come," she leaped forward prepared to fall.

But she didn't fall at all.

She flew.

Her entire body trembled and shook as the orgasm rippled outward from her center, into every limb, up into her brain, her hair, the tips of her ears.

Her pussy tightened and pulsed around him, loving the feel of his heat and length inside of her without any kind of barrier. She'd never had sex without a condom before—not even with Russell—and the difference between with and without was unparalleled.

She refused to acknowledge the significance of her decision to go condom-free with Aiden—someone she barely tolerated—and chose to just ride out her climax and enjoy the moment. She could pick that decision apart later. At another time, and maybe with Teal. But for now, she had orgasms offered to her, so she was going to take them.

Her fingers dug deep trenches into his muscular shoulder blades as the sensations in her body continued to unravel. And when Aiden finally stilled above her, grunted and his cock started to pulse inside of her, she found another orgasm buried deep down in her belly and let that one fly free, as well.

They came together, bodies thrumming, chests heaving and a thick layer of sweat forming between their bare flesh.

He drove a little deeper and rocked against her clit again. She squeezed around him, dug her nails harder into his back, and let the last remaining of ripples of pleasure consume her.

When his release finally ended, he collapsed against her, allowing her to take all of his weight for just a moment. She liked that.

She retracted her nails from his back and sighed.

But he popped back up onto his forearms. "Sorry. Didn't mean to crush you."

She shook her head. "You weren't."

He cleared his throat and climbed off her, standing up beside the bed. "I'll uh ... go grab you a cloth."

She shook her head again. "Just hand me my underwear, I'm going to have a shower."

Scrunching his nose in confusion, he snatched her cute baby-blue briefs off the floor and handed them to her. She shoved them between her legs to catch what would have to come out, then stood up and walked to the back of the door where she grabbed the housecoat.

"I um ... I could use help scrubbing my back," she said, opening the bedroom door and glancing over her shoulder at him with a half-smile.

"You definitely could," he said, a smile in his voice. "It's a filthy back."

Then he followed her into the bathroom, closed the door and tackled her into the shower.

Chapter Twenty-One

"What in the ever-loving fuck is that white shit?" Rayma said, letting the drapes fall back down in front of the window and turning to face Oona, a terrified expression on her face.

"Snow?" Oona asked.

"Yeah, but what is it doing falling from the sky?"

"Ummm ... I don't know if this is meant to be a rhetorical question or ..."

"It's meant to be what the absolute fuck? It's the day before my ... sorry, *our,* wedding and it snowed seven inches overnight. And it's still fucking falling. Do you know what happens in this city when it snows like this? Everything shuts down. And I mean everything. Buses stop running, babies are told to stay in the womb, even the twenty-four-seven pizza places don't open. We don't have enough plows in the city to support this kind of bullshit weather. This is not good. Not good at all."

She was still in her pajamas—they all were—huddled up in the living room with coffee—Oona with her tea—as Rayma paced like a caged wildcat.

"Lassie, why aren't you freaking out?" she asked, her eyes wide and surprised as her tone grew harsh.

"Because we can't control the weather?" Jordan replied, but in the form of a question, glancing at Oona for help.

"I was an idiot for thinking we should get married in the winter. There is a reason weddings are mostly held in the spring and summer. Because you don't run into the wrath of Mother Nature nearly as much. Sure, she might throw a wild fire at you, or a freak rainstorm, but not *this!*" She pulled open the drapes again to reveal an absolute white-out. "This is fucked up. Mother Nature is a bitch and deserves global warming when she pulls this crap on us." Suddenly she spun around to face Oona, her eyes wide and wild. "What if *our* mother is Mother Nature and this is her way of telling me *I told you so?* What if she's doing this to smite me?"

"I don't think Mom is Mother Nature," Oona said. Though, Rayma did have a point. Mother Nature was behaving an awful lot like Yanna Young.

Aiden and Oona exchanges amused, yet sympathetic glances with each other across the apartment. Oona was curled up under a blanket on the couch sipping her tea, while Aiden was in the kitchen flipping pancakes on a griddle and making fresh whipped cream. He'd been awake before any of them and when they all woke up, he had coffee—and tea—ready, as well as pancake mix ready to go and frozen berries stewing on the stove.

They'd had sex again last night in the shower, and a few parts of her (her clit, vagina and the rest of her erogenous zones to be precise) wanted to invite him to stay in her bed, but her brain finally won the battle over her horny body parts, and made him return to his pull-out in the living room.

But those erogenous zones of hers still tingled from last night and the longer she stared at his mouth while he cooked, the more she wanted it back on her body.

She was pretty sure he knew what she was thinking because the sexy smirk that curled the corners of his mouth as he stared down into the bowl of whipping cream, he was hand whipping, was pure arrogance. And crap of craps it was turning her on.

"Now, I can't finish my Christmas shopping," Rayma said.

"What did you still have to buy?" Jordan asked her.

"Mostly just your stocking stuff, and a few things for Joy and Grant."

"I'm fine not having anything in my stocking," Jordan said. "Coupons for blowjobs are perfectly acceptable." He snorted, so did Aiden. Rayma gave him the middle finger. "And you know Joy and Grant are adamant that we not buy for them."

Rayma glared at him, and swatted her hand at an invisible fly. "And who listens to that?"

"Nobody," he conceded.

"Exactly."

"Either way, if that's all you have left to buy, I think it's okay if we stay inside today," Jordan went on. "I really don't need anything for my stocking, and Joy and Grant will understand."

Rayma huffed, then flopped dramatically onto the couch beside Oona, jostling Oona's tea. "This is a disaster."

Jordan brought up his phone and as he scrolled, his brows bunched tighter and tighter. Then he murmured, "Fuck," under his breath.

"What is it?" Rayma asked, not missing a beat and hinging up quickly from Oona's lap, once again nearly causing Oona's tea to spill.

"If you believe the Weather Network—"

"Which I don't," Rayma cut in. "Only job in the world where you can be wrong fifty-percent of the time and *not* get fired."

Aiden snorted.

"Anyway," Jordan went on, "*If* you believe the Weather Network, it's not supposed to stop snowing for two days. They're expecting an unprecedented amount. Up to two feet. Closer to three in Sooke, Langford and The Highlands."

Rayma's mouth created the most upside-down smile Oona had ever seen. It had to be a lot of work to hold her frown that tight. "Two feet?" She flopped back to Oona's lap, only this time, Oona was prepared and held her mug with two hands and well away from Rayma's dramatic, errant limbs.

Jordan swallowed. "But the Weather Network has been wrong before."

Rayma moaned and tossed her arms in the air, almost hitting Oona in the face. "What am I going to do?" She draped the back of her hand over her forehead. "Do we cancel the wedding? Postpone it? Live in sin for the rest of our lives? What if this is a sign? A sign we're not meant to be married."

"Now you're being ridiculous," Oona said. "Did you have a backup plan?"

"No!" Rayma exclaimed, her eyes wide. "Victoria doesn't usually get snow like this. I thought we'd be fine. The rest of the island gets hit like this sometimes, but we're in our own little tropical microclimate down here. I just assumed we were safe from Snowmaggedon."

Rayma's phone buzzed on the kitchen island. She whimpered and made gimme hands until Jordan rolled his eyes, got up from his La-Z-Boy, and retrieved her phone. Still with her head in Oona's lap, she answered her phone. "Hello?" She reached for Oona's hand and encouraged Oona to start petting her head.

Oona complied, but not without directing an amused eye roll at Aiden and Jordan. She ran her fingers through her sister's soft, thick hair, splaying it out across the blanket on her lap.

Oona could hear the other person on the phone.

"So what does that mean?" Rayma asked. "Like, no venue, either? Because at this point, I'll order pizza if it's just the food that's an issue. I'll boil hotdogs and serve Doritos."

"I'm afraid the leak is significant and the damage is too extensive. We're waiting on an insurance adjustor, but with the weather, we're not sure they will be able to make it until after Christmas. We've been advised to cancel all events."

"So ... like, what? I'm supposed to just *postpone* my wedding until Mother Nature decides to stop being a bitch?" Rayma asked, her words coming out choked. She swallowed and her chin wobbled.

"I'm so sorry, Ms. Young. My hands are tied. We were already very short-staffed because of it being Christmas Eve and now with the lack of food able to be delivered, and the extensive leak in the ball room, we must cancel."

"And my deposit?" Rayma asked. "What of that? Because I get if *I* was the one canceling because the groom took off with the best man, that I wouldn't get back my deposits."

Jordan and Aiden glanced at each other and made cringey faces at Rayma's incestuous insinuation.

She didn't even notice. "But *you're* canceling on me. I'm fine with the leak. We can bring towels and just shove them where the leak is until the reception is over. And if it's getting there that has you concerned, I have a truck. Everyone I know has a truck. My sister's husband has a plow he fixes to the front of his truck and could plow the entire road and parking lot. Getting to your resort is *not* a problem."

She was slipping into her Rayma panic spiral.

Oona kept playing with her sister's hair with one hand, which she knew would help keep her calm, then reached for the phone with the other hand, prying it out of Rayma's grip. "Hello, this is Oona Young, Rayma's sister. I'm up-to-date on things, and that is very unfortunate. But I believe my sister asked about a refund on her deposits."

"W-well," the woman on the other end sputtered, "we've never had to cancel because of weather before. And we have a no-refund policy." Oona cleared her throat and raised her brows at Jordan who was in the kitchen, on his phone pulling up the contract no doubt, given the way he nodded at her, and held up a finger for her to give him a minute.

His eyes darted across his phone screen quickly and his finger scrolled, then he smiled and nodded, bringing his phone over to Oona and pointing to the highlighted section.

Oona's head bobbed. "Yes, but the contract clearly states that if the *booking* party cancels less than three-months before the date, there will be no refund issued. It says nothing in this contract about the *hosting* party and their cancelation. So we will expect the food and venue deposit to be returned to Rayma Young and Jordan Lassiter in full."

"It's the day before Christmas Eve," the woman sputtered again. "This isn't even my department."

"And I'm really sorry you're the one dealing with this, truly. And of course, we're not expecting the refund to take place in the next thirty-seconds, or even in the next three days, but it will happen. We expect a full refund of the deposits by the first week of January, which I believe is more than reasonable."

"I-I'm not authorized to authorize refunds, I—"

"I understand that. Which is why I believe in two weeks, the person who *is* authorized will be able to take over. Again, we're disappointed and upset at the turn of events, but we also understand and certainly do not plan on crucifying the messenger."

"Speak for yourself," Rayma murmured.

"Life will go on." She glanced down at Rayma. "The wedding will happen and it will be magical and glorious and they will have more money for their honeymoon because they will receive their deposits back in full. Please reiterate this expectation to your superiors and those in accounting."

"I, uh ... o-okay."

"Thank you. You have a wonderful Christmas. Take care." Then Oona disconnected the call. She glanced up from her sister's teary face to find Aiden watching her with a gaping mouth and stunned look in his eyes. "What?" she asked before she could stop herself.

He sobered quickly and changed his face when Jordan spun around to look at him. Then he shook his head and stared down into the bowl of whipped cream like it was a Magic Eight Ball and held all the answers to the universe. "Nothing," he muttered.

"What are we going to do now?" Rayma asked, doing her whiny-voice thing again. She sat up and Jordan joined her on the couch, taking her in his arms.

"We'll figure it out," he said, rubbing her back. "I'll marry you right here, right now in our pajamas. I don't care."

Oona stood up, folded the dove-gray micro-fleece blanket that had been on her lap and inched past Rayma and Jordan's legs. "I'm going to get dressed and make some calls." She glanced back at her sister who had tears welling up in her eyes. "Don't worry about this, kiddo. We are going to give you an amazing wedding. It just might not be the wedding you anticipated, okay?"

Rayma's bottom lip stuck out and trembled.

"Okay?" Oona said more forcefully. "I'm not going to let this ruin my sister getting married. I promise."

Finally, Rayma managed a half-hearted nod. Jordan hugged her tighter.

Oona nodded curtly, then took off to her bedroom. The first person she called was Pasha.

"Fuck," Pasha said into the phone after Oona reiterated her conversation with the venue and catering person. "I had a feeling something like this was going to happen. Heath is going to go pick up Mom and Dad and bring them here since Jordan has their car and they wouldn't drive in this white shit anyway. They'll be here within the hour."

Oona glanced at the clock on her phone. It was nearly ten in the morning.

"Put the phone on speaker," Mieka said from the background. "I'm just glad that Nate and Asher's flights got in yesterday, otherwise they probably wouldn't have made it."

"So you must have a pretty full house now?" Oona asked, peeling out of her pajama pants and tank top and rummaging through her suitcase for her thick winter socks. She put the phone on speaker so she could search with both hands. She'd done a load of laundry yesterday, so she had more clothes to wear, considering that she'd packed pretty lightly.

"Yeah, full house. Both cowboys were up early and out shoveling the drive-way," Mieka said.

"Ranchers," came two gravely grumbles from the background.

"Made Heath feel like a slacker. Then all three of them were out there shoveling and snow-blowing the neighbors' driveways. But given the way its still coming down, they're going to have to get out there again soon," Pasha said.

"How is our sister doing?" Triss asked.

"As can be expected given that it's Rayma, her wedding, and it's Rayma," Oona said, which made the other three snort.

A knock at her bedroom door had her quickly tugging her navy-blue cashmere sweater over her head and slithering into her light gray yoga tights. She opened the door expecting Jordan. Rayma wouldn't have knocked. But instead, she found Aiden.

He cleared his throat. "I uh ... I have some ideas."

"Who is that?" Mieka asked.

"Aiden," Oona said, opening the door so he could step inside. She closed the door behind him and the room instantly felt smaller. Like she had to be smashed up against him because the walls were closing in.

She ignored that suffocating feeling and went to her nightstand to grab her stud diamond earrings and put them in. Then she sat on the edge of her bed and pulled on her thick winter socks. "Where is Rayma?" she asked him, chastising herself for letting her gaze wander down his body encased in a tight white tank top, and then getting glued to the front of his gray sweatpants.

"Jordan took her into their bedroom. She's crying."

"Ah, fuck," Mieka said. "Poor kiddo."

"The marriage commissioner also just called and he won't be able to make it. Apparently the only one they could get to work on Christmas Eve lives all the way out in Sooke and he's snowed in."

Oona hung her head and shook it. "Crap. Crap. Crap."

"You said you had ideas?" Pasha asked, her voice cold.

Aiden nodded, his tight body language indicating he could feel Pasha's icy demeanor through the phone. "Uh, yeah. Of your big, extended family, who has the biggest house and yard?"

"Well, Chase and Stacey, but they're way the fuck out by Prospect Lake and it snows like crazy out there. Roads are narrow and there is like no parking," Pasha said. "After that, it'd probably be us, then Krista and Brock, then Rex and Lydia. Joy and Grant have a bigger backyard than Rex and Brock, though. And better parking. Krista and Brock are on a cul-de-sac, and Rex and Lydia are on a private road with weird strata rules. So all things considered, I think we have the best set-up yard, house and parking. Why?"

"I thought that, together, we could set up tents, portable heaters, chairs, lights and do the ceremony outside. I doubt *all* the guests will be able to make it, anyway. Jordan said as much. So it'll probably be a smaller turnout. Could your house handle hosting a wedding?" he asked. "I'm happy to help out in any way. Cook, find tents, and heaters. I already called Canadian Tire and the one closest has four portable outdoor heaters in stock."

Oona's eyes were wide as she watched Aiden, who was staring at the phone on her unmade bed, rattle off his ideas.

"We could," Pasha said. "We have the patio, and the yard. Can move some furniture around inside so it's more functional for a crowd. And we have an outdoor heater. So do Chase and Stacey and Krista and Brock."

"And Mum has a heater, and a pop-up tent, so do we, and I think Brock, Chase and Rex each have one, too," Heath said, his voice starting out in the background and growing closer. "And between all of us and our lawn chairs, I'm sure we can make it work."

Oona started to nod. "Can we do this?"

"For Rayma, I'll walk across fucking glass," Pasha said, her voice warm again.

"Me, too," Triss and Mieka both said.

"I'll *eat* glass," Heath said, humor in his tone.

"Always have to one-up us, don't you?" Pasha said. Oona could practically hear her sister rolling her eyes.

"And so, what about booze?" Mieka asked.

290

"We picked up the wine the other day," Aiden said. "Dropped it off at Joy and Grant's in their garage."

"And I'm sure at least one liquor store in town is open. We can just go buy what we need. It was going to be an open bar, anyway," Triss said.

"I'm going to call the florist to see if they're open and what they have from the bouquets and arrangements available," Oona said. "And grocery stores usually have premade bouquets, too, if the florist is closed."

"What about food?" Heath asked.

Pasha and a few of the others snorted. It was well-known that Heath was a bottomless pit and could eat more than three average people, then say he was hungry an hour later.

"Happy to help there," Aiden said.

"I think we can all put together some dishes. Grocery stores aren't going to be shut down—not all of them, anyway. We can figure it out. Might not be what they had planned, but we'll make it work," Oona said, smiling at Aiden who smiled back.

"Okay, so we all have our jobs?" Pasha asked. "Heath, you reach out to your brothers about chairs, heaters, and tents. Also, twinkly lights. We need more twinkly lights than what we have. We're going to have the wedding here. Oona, you call the florist. Nate and Asher, I'm putting you on booze and snow shovel duty."

"Aye aye, Captain," said one of them, which was probably Nate, since Asher was broodier and quieter than his younger brother.

"And I'll talk to Mum about food, a tent, and heaters, too," Heath said. "And I bet you Grant would be willing to go online and get one of those quickie officiant licenses. He could marry Rayma and Aiden."

"I think he'd love that," Pasha said.

"I can start working on some appetizers," Aiden offered. Oona's heart fluttered. "And I'll call Jace," he added.

"Oh yeah, I guess someone should call the guests and let them know of the change," Pasha said.

"Mieka and I can do that," Triss said.

"Me, too," Oona said.

"All right, let's do this," Pasha said. "Operation: SNOW JOB FOR JOR-DAYMA is a-go."

"What the fuck kind of name is that?" Heath asked just before Pasha disconnected the call.

Oona snorted and faced Aiden. "Thank you."

He shrugged and one side of his mouth hitched up, revealing half a dimple. But even that half a dimple had her knees getting gelatinous. "Jordan's my brother. I want to see him happy just as much as you want to see Rayma happy."

Right. Jordan was Aiden's brother. For a second there when he was volunteering for things and coming up with ideas, she thought he was doing this all for Rayma. But he was doing it for his little brother, too. He was taking care of his younger brother just like Oona and her sisters were taking care of Rayma.

They held eye contact for a long time. Neither of them saying anything.

They didn't really talk last night. At least not in the conventional way. Their bodies talked. Their bodies talked a lot, and actually got along pretty well. But she was seeing a change in the man in front of her. He was evolving. She still wanted to know about his epiphany last night and the question sat on the back of her tongue like a petulant wad of peanut butter.

But it wasn't her place.

They were in a truce right now.

A weird, sex-truce, and she didn't want to rock the boat by asking him to open up. She'd shut that door when she declined seeing him as a client. She couldn't go and open it up now, not if she wanted things to remain amicable—and sexy—between them.

"I uh ... I think maybe we should talk about last night," he finally said.

Crap.

Exhaling through her nose, she busied herself by making the bed and tidying up her stuff. "Okay."

Was he going to say it was a mistake? Because she already knew that.

He was the last person she should be getting tangled up with, but it was temporary. She kept telling herself that. Temporary was okay.

She had no future with this man.

She was not falling back into old patterns. Not really.

She wasn't trying to fix him and she wasn't getting attached.

She just really liked parts of his body and the way they made parts of her body feel.

"I'd like to take you up on your offer," he started.

She paused with a hair elastic on her fingers, half her hair up as she was getting ready to put it in a ponytail. "What offer?"

"Back at your office. You said that you thought we had a connection and even though you couldn't see me as a client, you'd like to see me as ... *more*. I'd like that, too. I'd like for us to go on a proper date when we get back to Montreal."

Her bottom jaw went slack.

"I need to go to counseling. I understand that now. And I know it can't be you. And I'm going to anger management, too. But ... I like you. Even though we butt heads, I like you. You challenge me. You make me want to be a better person. A better version of myself. And I'd like to see where this goes. Beyond our time here."

She blinked at him, her arms and hair still paused as the shock had yet to wear off.

"I know I don't deserve a second chance," he went on. "I'm probably the last person in the world that deserves one, but ..." He shrugged. "I'm hoping in the spirit of Christmas, maybe you'll give me one, anyway?"

"Aiden ..." She exhaled and finished tying up her hair. "I don't understand."

"You and me. Let's do this," he said, excitement filling his voice.

She shook her head slowly, regret and guilt creating a sick lather in her belly. "No. I ... I thought we had an understanding? A truce. We're having fun right now, because we're finally—sort of—getting along. At least with our clothes off. But ..." If she told him this just felt like lip service, he'd probably lose his mind and they'd set themselves so far back. But that's exactly what it felt like.

She knew he was undergoing a transformation, had possibly crawled to Jesus on his hands and knees, but right now, she felt a desperation about him that didn't feel genuine. Like he was telling her what he thought she wanted to hear, not what she needed to hear.

And Russell had showed her on more than one occasion that saying you were going to get help and actually getting the help you needed were two different things. He paid her so much lip service it became white noise. He always promised he'd quit drinking, then he'd go to an AA meeting, be sober for a week, and fall right back off the wagon. He ran off any sponsor that tried to help him, and eventually just stopped trying altogether.

So she knew better than to believe before she saw. A promise was just words. Actions and doing the work was what made the difference.

But she was a smart enough woman, and knew this man well enough now, to tread carefully with her words. "Let's, uh, let's table this until after the wedding, okay? We're in a good place right now, getting along and working together for our siblings. Let's focus on them, okay? We can talk more about this later." She smiled, but it was one of those fake, closed-mouth, slightly flat smiles that stayed on only the lower half of her face.

Aiden was quiet for a long, awkward moment. He held her gaze, as well, which just made things even more agonizing and uncomfortable. But eventually, he broke focus, nodded, and smiled. "Pancakes are ready," he said softly, opening the door. "Whipped cream turned out really good, I think." Then he walked back out into the house, leaving her standing there stunned, confused, and just a little bit excited.

Even though the snow never stopped falling, there were still a few businesses that decided to open anyway. And thankfully, some of those businesses were grocery stores. The plows came through on the main roads, and luckily, Jordan and Rayma lived on a main road, so their street was clear-*ish*.

Though, Aiden still needed to dig his way out of the parking spot on the road, in order to get out Jordan's truck. Jordan stayed with Rayma to comfort her, while Oona was on phone duty, getting in touch with the florist and calling some of the guest list, as well.

So Aiden decided to go shopping to get ingredients for what he would make for the wedding.

The back cab of Jordan's truck was heaped with grocery bags and even though he knew he should head back to the apartment and start prepping, since the snow was still falling and being on the road unnecessarily was dangerous, he found himself driving in the opposite direction and suddenly in Joy and Grant's driveway.

Oona's reaction to his outpouring of his feelings wasn't what he expected. It was a bit like a kick in the nads, and he was struggling to make sense of it.

After last night and their time together, both in her bed and the shower, he thought they'd turned a corner. And then this morning, they were joining forces, working together to help their siblings. They were getting along. And he wanted to see where it could go—just like she did back in Montreal. Only now, she was throwing on the brakes.

It didn't make any sense.

Which was why he found himself on Joy and Grant's front stoop, with snow in his hair and on his jacket, knocking at the door.

Joy answered, her smile warm and welcoming. She immediately stepped to the side. "Come in, sweetheart. What brings you by?"

Aiden cleared his throat. "I, uh, I was hoping you had a couple of minutes to talk."

"Of course, of course. Grant is out in the garage gathering up all the things we need to bring over to Heath and Pasha's. And he's got an extra spring in his step now that he's the officiant for the wedding." She rolled her eyes and smiled playfully. "Would you like some coffee?"

"When you make it as strong as you do, it's impossible for me to refuse."

She beamed at him and he followed her into the kitchen where she turned on the electric kettle and went about dumping heaps of coffee grounds into the French press.

Just like last time, he took it black while Joy added a splash of almond milk to hers. Then they went into the living room and took the same seats they were in last time. "What's on your mind, honey?" she asked.

"Last night I followed a man who I thought was drunk driving. He was speeding, went through a red light, nearly caused a pile-up, then drove into the ditch."

Joy's blue eyes went wide. "Oh my. Was he all right?"

"I don't know. I performed CPR and stayed with him until the paramedics came, and I haven't heard anything since. There is nothing reported in the news, either. Jordan is looking into it, though. Putting out feelers to see if he can get some news on the condition of the man."

Joy nodded. "Well, I hope he's all right."

"Me, too." He exhaled loudly through his nose. "And ... I don't think he was drunk."

Understanding flashed in Joy's gaze. "No?"

"I didn't smell alcohol on him. Not on his breath, not in the vehicle. I think he had a stroke while driving."

"That is a very scary notion. And I'm sure probably caused him to go into panic, and become unable to control parts of his body necessary for driving safely."

Aiden nodded. "Yeah. And it just ... it just got me thinking, you know?"

"How so?"

"That I need to be smarter."

"Mhmm."

"Smarter about how I approach things. How I approach people. That I'm so quick to judge. To paint every person that I pull over with the same brush. Label them an alcoholic because of my own personal triggers. Because of my father. When yeah, some—probably most—are. But not all of them. I hated that guy last night. A part of me actually thought he deserved to get hurt when I first saw him roll into the ditch. That at least he was just hurting himself, but not others. But when I realized he probably wasn't drunk, I was so worried about him. I didn't want him to die, I didn't even want him to be hurt."

He glanced down at his lap.

"I'm ashamed that I even thought for a second that he deserved death if he was a drunk driver. But I did. His death would mean one less drunk driver on the road to hurt others. But I shouldn't think like that. We don't know what people are dealing with. What their background is."

Joy nodded. "No, we don't."

"We had a really fucked-up childhood. Dad was a drunk. Mum just ... she just existed. Didn't really show us any love, not really." He lobbed a humorless laugh. "I mean, she wasn't like Yanna, but she certainly wasn't warm and loving like you, either."

Joy smiled. "Everyone has a different idea of what it means to parent. And every parent loves their children in their own way. I'm sure your mother and father loved you and Jordan in their own ways, you just didn't feel it. Their love was misdirected. Misguided."

"She defended our father," Aiden blurted out. "Tried to keep Jordan and me out of his hair so he wouldn't get mad. But she always made it our fault that he got mad. Not that he was just an angry drunk asshole. But she also enjoyed the prestige that being the mayor's wife gave her. She worked a lot, too, so wasn't home much. I guess, I just never really saw what being part of a loving, supportive family was like until I saw the way Rayma and her sisters are with each other. How all of you Harts are. Banding together to take care of your own. Or even an extension of your own like Rayma."

"Rayma is a Hart as much as any of my sons. She is family," Joy said, her voice just barely clipped, but enough to drive home the point that there was no *extension* or *adjacentness* to Rayma. She was family through and through.

"I see that now. But just the way everyone had come together to help Rayma and Jordan, to protect Rayma, it's... Nobody in our family, on either side, the Lassiters or the Archambault side banded together to help us—ever. They all left Jordan and me to the wolves. Called us turncoats. *After* we did what was right. Because it was the right thing to do. Our father never should have gotten away with hitting Dallas."

"No, he shouldn't have. You're right. And the fact that your family all thought he should have is very concerning."

He sighed. "Anyway, seeing what a real family is like, combined with the guy last night, and I've been hit with a few epiphanies."

"I can see that."

"Oona and I have slept together again—twice. And although I think we've reached a truce, I think I want more. I watched her today as she took control of a situation that was quickly making Rayma spiral. Oona handled it with a cool, sexy confidence that just ... mesmerized me. I liked that Oona side of her. She was business-like, but also, patient, and kind. Understanding. She calmed down Rayma and the woman on the phone like a badass."

Joy simply smiled.

"I want to pursue something with Oona. I mean, there has to be a reason that this has all happened, right?" Wow, he said that out loud. He really was having some epiphanies. Normally, he would be the first to scoff at anything even remotely attributed to the fates or universe.

But the fact that he met Oona, that she was supposed to be his therapist, then they sat beside each other on the plane and were staying under the same roof, had to mean something. Add in the fact that the sex between them was explosive. He couldn't just ignore that, could he? She lived in Montreal for goodness sake. Of all places. And yet, there they were, working together to save a wedding and repeatedly falling into bed with each other.

Joy's smile slowly fell. She sipped her coffee. "Have you mentioned this to Oona?"

He nodded. "Yes. She said no. Or, at least she said no in the most roundabout way. Said we should table this discussion until after the wedding."

"She's a smart woman. I was going to tell you the same thing."

"But I think she'll say no afterward, too, and I don't understand why. She wanted this, too. Back in Montreal, in her office, she asked me out. So now that I'm asking her out, is she turning me down?"

"That's a question for Oona. *After* the wedding."

"I'm going to go to counseling and anger management."

"Good."

"If that's what she wants me to do. If that's what I need to do to be with her, I'll do it."

Joy nodded slowly and a cunning look of understanding fell across her fine features. "Ah. Did you say this to her?"

"Of course I did. I want her to know I'm serious."

"Maybe she wants to *see* it before she believes it. And, having a goal in order to power through challenges is great, but it needs to be more than just 'getting the girl.' You need to do the work for *you*. Not for her. Not for anybody else, but you. Otherwise, it won't stick."

He nodded. But he was impatient when it came to Oona. He'd fucked up so much, he just wanted to run to her, find her, and declare his feelings. Apologize and kiss her without any end date on when he could do that. Without any *truce* or cloaked-hate between them.

"I'm just worried that if I wait until *after* I've done the work, it'll be too late. That she'll be dating someone else, or be over me. Not interested or ... I dunno. Why can't I see her *and* do the work? I'm not *that* broken. I can still function."

Joy sipped her coffee and smiled. "I don't think you're broken at all, honey. Maybe a little banged up, disoriented perhaps, in need of a tune-up, but you're not broken. However, and I'm usually one to give facts and not pander to the fates, but, if it's meant to be, it's meant to be. And if it's not, it's not. And, if you like her that much, shouldn't you just want her to be happy, regardless of who that's with?"

Yes.

No.

Fuck.

"I think Oona is after peace, and seeing you do the work, before she makes herself vulnerable again. Remember the way you turned her down the first time?"

"Not a moment I'm particularly proud of ..."

"I know, honey." She offered him a small, understanding smile. "We can promise people things until we run out of oxygen, but that's just lip service. Following through for the right reasons is what sets us apart from the rest and makes the work long-lasting."

Her blue eyes twinkled and crinkled at the corners as her mouth curled up into a bigger, knowing, motherly smile. Even though he'd only just met Joy, he felt more *mothered* and cared for by this woman than he did his own mother. She was maternal instinct and love incarnate. An enormous heart in such a small package.

"I know it's hard," she went on. "And you want the feelings you have right now to stick around for as long as possible. But this isn't the real world. Not here. Not right now. Not for you two, anyway. The real world is back in Montreal, away from family, where you're not under the same roof, and she works and you *do* the work to get better. If this is meant to be, meant to last, it needs to happen there. Not in this winter fantasy vacation land where you are roommates and keep falling into bed with each other because of proximity and ease."

Aiden's chest rose and fell on a dramatic sigh. He sipped his coffee and stared at his lap. Of course, Joy was right. He wasn't sure this woman had ever been wrong about anything.

But the truth wasn't what he wanted to hear.

"Your epiphany about drunk drivers is a huge step," she said, interrupting his delicate emotional spiral as he focused on the ink-black coffee, steaming in his mug. "And realizing you have feelings for Oona and want more with her is another big step. But little steps are important, too. All the steps are. That's why they are there. One thing at a time."

He took another sip and nodded. "Thank you."

"Anytime, sweetheart. And I mean that. Even when you head home, you can call me anytime."

He lifted his gaze to hers.

She shrugged. "And for what it's worth, even though I don't know Oona all that well, from what I do know about her and having met her at Pasha's wedding, I think you guys make a pretty good fit. You just have to turn your puzzle pieces around a few times until it's the *right* fit."

He drank more of his coffee.

Joy finished hers, then clapped her hands and sat up. "Now, I hear you are in charge of food. Come in here and tell me what I can make for appetizers and such. I'm obviously going to contribute, so just tell me what is needed."

Aiden pried himself off the couch and followed Joy into the kitchen with his half-full mug of coffee. "Well, what do you think about a cheese platter?"

Joy nodded. "I'll make one for the guests and a separate one for Heath."

Aiden snorted. "And maybe another one for Jace, that man can eat, too."

Joy sighed, grabbed a grocery pad off the fridge and a pen and started to write things down. "All right, enough cheese to feed an army. What else?"

Chapter Twenty-Two

"Well, the motherfucking meteorologist gets to keep his job this time," Rayma said, the morning of the wedding as she scuffed out of her bedroom in her slippers and housecoat, looking not at all like a woman about to get married later that day.

Aiden had been up until midnight the night before cooking, and was up again at six that morning to continue prepping food. He'd put Jordan to work helping him wrap wontons and deep fry them, then he put his brother on dredging duty to take care of the broccoli and cheese stuffed breaded chicken breasts. But he still had a few more appetizers to take care of.

Rayma was up and dressed, as was Aiden. Just like they predicted, a few guests were unable to make it to the wedding due to weather. Either they couldn't get over to the island because the wind had canceled the ferries and flights or some people were located further north on the island and were facing even more snow than Victoria and couldn't drive.

Not that Aiden had been anywhere on Vancouver Island besides Victoria, apparently there was a big mountain called The Malahat that separated Victoria on the southern tip, from the rest of the island, and the road through the mountain passage was treacherous. And besides a ferry or a backwoods road, there was no other way to get to the city.

As of midnight, the night before, their head count was around forty, which Pasha said would be tight, but doable in their house. So Aiden needed to make sure they provided enough food for forty people.

He liked that he had a purpose and was able to help.

Rayma, despite everyone assuring her that the wedding would be beautiful, didn't really perk up at all. She was still devastated.

It didn't help that her mother had called her around dinner time and encouraged her to just cancel the wedding. That Rayma should have expected this and the fact that she didn't have a backup was so *like* her.

Rayma just turned into a hermit in her bedroom after that. Oona comforted her while Jordan helped Aiden with food.

Oona, for the most part, avoided Aiden.

Which he hated.

Because he'd done that.

He went and acted impatiently, rashly, and stupidly, and now their truce—sex and all—was gone.

While making food, he also put together breakfast for everyone. This time, it was eggs Benedict, but rather than an English muffin and ham, he used crab cakes.

"Coffee is here," he said to Rayma who pulled herself up to the kitchen island and took a seat. "And I can have eggs poached in a couple of minutes. Didn't want to do them ahead of time because, you know ..."

"Is that white shit still coming down?" she asked.

He frowned and nodded. "I'm afraid so."

"Maybe I should just go back to bed. Wake up in the spring like the bears."

"But then you'll miss your wedding. And I happen to know a lot of people who are working very hard to make this day happen and be special for you."

She glanced up at him, her eyes puffy from all the tears. "I know. And thank you. I haven't been in one of these pity pits in a long time. At least not one this deep."

"They can be pretty hard to climb out of. I know from personal experience." He poured her a coffee and added a splash of half-and-half to hers which was how she liked it, then slid it across the island to rest in front of her crossed arms. "I punched a drunk driver that I pulled over. He had his kid in the car. Someone else recorded me doing it and it went viral. I've been suspended for almost five months and mandated by the courts to attend anger management and counseling before I can return to work."

Rayma lifted her head and gaped at him, her eyes wide. "Shit, dude."

"As I'm sure you can guess, I have a bit of a zero-tolerance policy when it comes to driving impaired."

"Understandable, given Dallas and your dad and stuff."

Aiden's head bobbed. "Yeah, well, until I guess yesterday, I've been in this pity pit, as you called it. Feeling sorry for myself. Believing that I was justified in my behavior and that because Oona denied seeing me as a patient, she was holding my career hostage."

"You guys slept together. It would have been unethical."

"And I see that, now. But at the time, I was so deep in the pity pit I couldn't see daylight. Couldn't see reason. Couldn't see that Oona was trying to help me even when she couldn't treat me. That there are a lot of people who wanted to help me."

Her gaze turned coy. "I see what you're doing."

He shrugged. "Ready for breakfast?"

She nodded. "Oona's still sleeping, so is Jordan. But I'm hungry."

He put a pot of water on the stove to boil so he could poach a couple of eggs. "Having spent that day with your parents, I understand your reaction to them showing up early. And your mother's reaction to your dress and asking you to cancel the wedding is uncalled for. Hurt people hurt. It's what I'm realizing. I hurt Oona because I'm hurting."

"How the hell do you think Yanna Young is hurt?"

He shrugged. "All of her daughters moved as far away from her as they could? I don't know."

"Yanna Young isn't hurting. She just *does* the hurting."

"Maybe so, but I realized that it's up to us to decide *who* we let hurt us. People can try, but its up to us whether we allow them to penetrate the skin or if their barbs just bounce off. For too long, I've allowed every barb ever thrown at me to go down to the bone. And in turn, I've struck hard enough to hit bone, too."

"So you're saying that I'm choosing to let my mother hurt me? Are you victim blaming?"

"No. I'm saying, you have this rich and beautiful life that you've created. It *is* your armor. This family, this tribe that you've built, *is* your armor. Your mother's barbs should just bounce right off, because what you have here is so strong, what she thinks of it doesn't matter. It's weak and inconsequential." He held out his hands cupped together like a clamshell. "This is for you."

She bunched her brows at him in confusion.

"Open it," he encouraged.

She rolled her eyes, but with a smirk, pried his top hand away from his bottom one. "What is it?"

"It's a box of the fucks you have left to give about what your parents think of you."

Her mouth split into a grin and that golden sparkle to her warm brown eyes returned. "Thanks, Big Lassie."

A door creaked open and Oona emerged, yawning. She was in her black tank top and flannel pajama pants. "'Morning," he greeted her.

She smiled at him, her eyes taking him in, watching him with a keen interest that made his belly get warm. "Good morning."

"Eggs bennie on crab cakes. Two?" he asked.

Her stomach rumbled loud enough that even Rayma's brows shot up. "Yes, please." Then she sidled up to the barstool beside Rayma, wrapped her arm around her sister and leaned her head on Rayma's shoulder. "How're you doing this morning, kiddo?"

"Well," Rayma said with a sigh, reaching for her coffee and taking the first sip, "I'm getting married today. And thanks to Big Lassie here, I have an empty box of fucks left to give about Mom and Dad, so I think I'm good to go."

Aiden turned around from where he stood at the stove preparing the eggs for poaching. Rayma was beaming, and Oona was giving him some serious fuck-me eyes.

He turned back around to his boiling water, a stupidly big smile on his face.

Today was going to be a great day.

He could just feel it.

Oona's door had been open a crack when Aiden and Rayma started talking in the kitchen. And as much as she knew she shouldn't, it was impossible not to eavesdrop.

And holy fucking shit.

Aiden was incredible.

He said all the same things that Jordan and Oona had said the day before, but yet, coming from him they seemed to resonate with Rayma. Or maybe it was that Rayma had slept on things and was in better spirits. Regardless, his pep-talk worked.

He'd also confided in Rayma about his own trauma and that he was working on things.

He was growing. Evolving, and starting to do the work to get better.

During one of their many heart-to-hearts over the week, Rayma told Oona about the brothers' trauma from when they were younger. About their father hitting the kid and Jordan reporting it to the police. It made a lot more sense to Oona now, why Aiden didn't drink and why he was so black and white when it came to people driving impaired.

But given the fact that he misjudged that man the night before and assumed he was drinking when he'd had a stroke, most definitely added a few shades of gray to his way of thinking. Yes, driving while impaired is bad. But not all people who drive impaired are bad. Not all people who drive recklessly are impaired. Each and every circumstance needs to be addressed for its uniqueness and not painted with the same brush.

Aiden and Jordan were going to stay at the apartment and get ready there with Jace, while the bridal party and Oona and Rayma's parents all went to Pasha's.

Heath had come by earlier that day in his big truck with the studs on the tires and dualies on the back, to grab the food, and Oona and Rayma, and bring everything back to his house.

The way Heath fawned over Rayma like she was his baby sister was adorable. Oona knew the two of them had a special relationship, so it was fitting that he was the one she chose to walk her down the aisle.

They were all in Pasha and Heath's enormous loft-style bedroom on the top floor of the house with it's peaked ceiling, sitting area and gigantic bathroom with a tub that fit both of them—apparently it was custom made because Heath was a giant—and a huge walk-in shower.

The bridal party was dressed in their floor-length forest-green dresses and white faux-fur shawls, while they took turns doing each other's makeup and hair, since the hair and makeup people ended up canceling, too.

There was champagne and snacks and Joy fussed over everyone like a mother hen checking if they needed anything ironed, sewed, glued or taped.

Oona was in the vanity chair while Mieka did her makeup when the bedroom door opened and their mother walked in. She was dressed in a plain, dark gray shift dress with a matching bolero-style coat over-top. The dress fell to her knees and she had black stockings on underneath and plain black shoes. She looked like she could be heading to church, a funeral or the office, but not really a wedding.

Yanna Young also didn't believe in jewelry, besides her wedding band, so of course, she had nothing on her ears or around her neck.

Their mother cast her gaze around the room on everyone and as if drawn by magnets, she zeroed in on the tattoo on Pasha's shoulder. The grayscale one she'd had forever of her dearly departed pet rabbit Marigold. It was a beautiful tattoo and Marigold had been a lovely little companion for Pasha during her college years. The tattoo was a perfect tribute.

"Pasha Young!" their mother exclaimed, stalking over to Oona's oldest sister who was in the middle of curling Rayma's hair. "What on earth is this?" She jabbed a finger into the middle of Pasha's tattoo hard enough that Pasha winced.

"It's a tattoo, Mom," Rayma said, boredom in her voice.

"I'm not speaking to you," their mother snapped. "I'm speaking to Pasha."

Pasha continued to curl Rayma's hair. "It's a tattoo, Mom," she repeated.

"You know how your father and I feel about tattoos."

"Then don't get any," Mieka said.

"How could you disgrace your body like that? You know what your father says. It's like putting a bumper sticker on a Ferrari. You've just gone and cheapened yourself."

"Well now, hang on," Joy started. "That's a bit uncalled for."

"I'm having a conversation with my daughters," Yanna spat back.

"Yeah, loudly and in front of everyone," Mieka added. "You're unnecessarily making a scene."

Their mother rounded on her. "Mieka!"

Oona rolled her eyes, glanced up at her sister, and told her to back off with the eye makeup for a moment. Then she stood up, slipped the spaghetti straps of her sleeveless dress over her shoulders and let it pool to the ground at her feet so she was in nothing but her bra and underwear. "Mom, we all have tattoos. I have four."

Her mother's eyes doubled in size as they scanned Oona's body, taking in the hearts on her hip, the lily along her ribs, and when she lifted her arm, the compass on her tricep. Then she turned around so her mother could see the hummingbird on her back.

Oona faced her mother again. "And you know what, Mom. I'm also a doctor. I have my fucking PhD *and* tattoos. Pasha is a pediatrician *and* has tattoos, Triss is a speech path *and* has a tattoo, Rayma is a social worker *and* has tattoos and Mieka is a dancer *and* has tattoos. Having tattoos does not make you any less of a person. Any less of a success. Because I happen to think we're all pretty fucking successful. And hey, maybe I don't *want* to be a Ferrari. Or maybe I do and I want to cover myself in bumper stickers. Who gives a fuck? But the moment you kicked Rayma out of the house and turned your back on her, was the moment we all stopped giving a fuck about what you thought of us."

Their mother gasped. Her whole body trembled and for the briefest of moments, Oona thought perhaps she'd gone too far.

But, no, she hadn't. This was a long time coming.

"We did what we thought was best for her," their mother defended. "We raised her exactly the way we raised you four, and it just ... didn't work."

"Because I'm not a clone," Rayma said with exasperation. "None of us are. And it didn't *work* with all of us. We all have some seriously fucked up triggers from your parenting. From the constant shaming. The judgment. The comments about food, our bodies, our clothes, and our learning disabilities."

Every time one of them swore, their mother would blanch, flinch and suck in a rattled breath as if the words weren't just words, but a baseball bat and the person who swore was wielding the bat closer and closer to her face.

310

"Well, you turned out ... *fine*. I think we did the right thing."

"I turned out fucking spectacular, fuckyouverymuch," Rayma said. "And it's not because of *you*, its because of *this* woman." She pointed at Joy. "She took me in. She gave me the patience, structure, and freedom that I craved. That I begged for. That you were just too lazy to give me. I'm amazing in *spite* of you."

Yes!

Sing it, kiddo.

"You have five incredible daughters. Successful, amazing, brilliant and beautiful daughters who have so much going for them, and yet, all you ever do is focus on the negative. Chastise them for picking men with dangerous jobs, criticize them for getting tattoos, or showing skin. You pick us apart, when as our parents, as our mother, you should be building us up." Oona reached down and shimmied back into her dress. "All I have to say, Mom, is that my sisters and I have only grown closer over the years as we've bonded over our trauma of being raised by you. Commiserating has brought us closer. So, thank you, I guess." She shrugged and sat back down in her seat, lifting her chin at Mieka to finish her makeup. "You will be asked to leave if you make the bride cry," Oona warned before she closed her eyes so Mieka could apply the eye shadow. "I will escort you off the property myself."

Her eyes were closed, but she heard footsteps approach the door, the door open and that same gait head down the stairs. Then a kiss, followed by three more landed on her cheeks.

She smiled.

"You're fucking amazing, Oons," Rayma said.

"Brass balls, baby." Mieka swept the eyeshadow across Oona's lids.

Once her hair and makeup were finished, Oona left the "bridal suite" and headed downstairs to check on things. Jordan, Jace and Aiden had arrived and all three looked dapper in their serge blues.

She nearly swallowed her damn tongue when Aiden turned around, dressed in his uniform and with his beard freshly trimmed. Holy hell did he look good.

His eyes drank her in and darkened as his mouth split into a big smile and he walked toward her. Instantly, he took her hand. "You look amazing."

Heat filled her cheeks. "I was thinking the same thing about you."

"Come, see what we can accomplish when we put our differences aside and work together." Still holding her hand, he led her out the door from Heath and Pasha's kitchen to the deck. An awning had been set up, the wood patio cleared of snow and lined with small cedar trees in pots and bedazzled with white lights. The awning only spanned about eight feet, then they stepped down where a red velvet carpet was laid out on top of the stone patio and a cleared path of snow. The whole thing was tented by white tents that had panels all around it, protecting them. Heaters were in the corners and white lights strung across the support beams for the tents. Chairs formed rows on either side of the aisle, while more cedars decorated with red bows and more lights led the way to the alter. An actual arbor, covered in cedar boughs, lights, and holly stood waiting for the happy couple.

It was warm, it was inviting, it was magical.

She blinked up at him, tears burning the backs of her eyes. She knew Rayma would love it.

"Thank you," she whispered, her throat tight and the words coming out more like a scrape.

He nodded once. "Team work."

"We do work pretty well together."

His eyes darkened again. Nostrils flared.

That heat in her cheeks ramped up and her belly fluttered.

Her eyes darted around them. There were Harty boys and their wives milling around, kids everywhere, a few guests mingling. They were less than thirty minutes to the ceremony.

But she didn't care.

Grabbing Aiden's hand, she tugged him back into the house, made sure nobody was watching, and shoved him into the powder room directly off the laundry room. Locking the door, she shoved him up against the wall and kissed his face off. Kissed him like he held all the answers to every question she'd ever had, and every question she ever would have.

He kissed her back with the same intensity, spinning her around so it was her back to the door. Her dress had a high-slit, so it made jumping up onto his hips easy. He pressed her harder against the door, moaning into her mouth and devouring her whimpers as his tongue plundered and plunged.

She was riding a high.

Not only had they saved the day—with a whole lot of help from everyone else—but she'd finally told off her mother and holy hell did it feel fantastic. She hadn't seen her mother since she left the bridal suite upstairs, and frankly, she didn't care if she did again.

Yanna Young was toxic and there was no room for her on this joyous day.

There was no time for complete clothes removal, though. This had to be the quickest of quickies. A real true-blue, wham bam, thank you, ma'am kind of deal. Pull some fabric to the side, drop some pants just enough and go.

Aiden seemed to catch her drift, because he was already reaching beneath her dress. He found her center with his fingers by pushing her thong to the side, but she mustn't have been wet enough for him because he brought his fingers to his mouth sucked them but then put them back between her legs. Immediately, he pushed two inside her and his thumb found her clit. She was back on her feet and fumbling with the button and zipper on his pants.

"There's a belt, too," he said with a chuckle, taking pity on her, removing his fingers from her pussy and unfastening his belt and pants. She took that time to pull her thong all the way off, then his cock was out, in his palm and she was leaping back onto his hips, taking him inside of her with an ease that shocked both of them.

They made eye contact and both seemed surprised at how easily that worked.

"Nothing but net," he said, breaking into a big grin.

She tossed her head back against the door and laughed.

But then things turned serious again—and fast. She wrapped her arms around his neck and started to bounce up and down while Aiden bucked upward. She rode him hard and fast, letting the moment, the adrenaline, the triumph of the day fuel her orgasm and push her closer to the edge.

Aiden was beautiful in his serge. And the way he'd thrown himself into helping make this day special for Jordan and Rayma just made him all the more beautiful in Oona's eyes. His advice to Rayma had been spot-on, and was exactly what she needed.

He was growing. He was evolving. He was working to make things right and she had to give him props for it. But she also had to guard her heart.

This was a great start, but even plane crashes can have stellar take offs.

She'd worry about that later, though. That was for future Oona to worry about. For future Oona to figure out. Right now, present Oona was going to take the win and fill her brain with as much oxytocin as it could handle.

He wedged a hand between them, found her clit and gave it a pinch. She gasped and started to bounce up and down on him even harder. Squeezing her muscles on the way down. Grinding down harder onto his fingers as they ran circles around her throbbing clit, she raked her teeth along his jaw, then nipped at his neck. He growled, pinched her clit again, and she exploded.

Like a powder keg covered in rocket fuel, she went off. Her body shook like she'd been electrocuted as she settled down deep on his cock and pulsed around him. Her limbs tingling, center heated and full of crashing waves of pleasure. Pressing her head hard against his shoulder, she allowed every sensation to just ravage him.

A moment later, Aiden grunted and his hand cupping her ass tightened, his fingers digging into her cheek as his cock twitched and pulsed against her walls and he exhaled deeply through his mouth.

They stayed like that for a long minute. Arms around each other, connected, breathing ragged.

Eventually, though, noise beyond the door brought them both back to reality and she slid off him, then sat down to pee.

"Uh ..." He spun around to give her privacy.

"Sorry," she murmured.

"All good."

She finished what she needed to do, found her thong and put it on. Then they both washed their hands, and with Aiden sticking his head out the bathroom first, checked to see if the coast was clear.

It was, so he exited, then a moment later, she did.

She snagged his eye for half a second as she headed back to the bridal suite.

All they did was share a knowing, secretive smirk with each other, but it warmed her so thoroughly, she probably could have rolled around naked in the snow and melted all of it.

Chapter Twenty-Three

As predicted, the wedding went off without a hitch. Rayma loved the decorations, the food, and everything in between. Heath stoically cried as he walked her down the aisle and passed her off to Jordan. It was bizarre to see the big blond gorilla—who was also a killing machine when it was called for—cry, but also truly heartwarming.

Even though the florist had the bouquets ready to go so nobody was without, Rayma decided, last minute, to carry a pineapple down the aisle instead.

And when Jordan saw her carrying it, he cracked up laughing so hard tears were rolling down his cheeks. And when his vows promised to always have a pineapple on the counter, Rayma barked out a laugh that made the whole crowd start to chuckle.

It wasn't a serious ceremony, but it was one full of joy and love and beauty. Their vows had jokes, everyone laughed and Rayma even called him Lassie and told him that he could always come home.

Oona's parents sat at the back, and they had Heath drive them to their hotel within half an hour of the reception starting.

When they embraced Rayma and Jordan after the ceremony, neither of them made eye contact with Oona or any of her sisters. And they didn't even say goodbye when they left.

The party would be more fun without them anyway.

Rayma and Jordan decided that since their photographer also had to cancel, they would just get back into their wedding stuff another day and do pictures. Bella, one of the women who'd been at the bachelorette party, knew her way around a DSL-R pretty well, so she brought her camera and took photos of the wedding party, which were beautiful, but as far as the professional and stylized ones went, they weren't going to sweat them just now.

Oona was proud of her sister for rallying and rolling with the punches. It took a bit to get her out of her pity pit, but Aiden was the one with a long enough ladder and helped her climb out.

There were no designated spots to sit, everyone just mingled about, sat where they could and ate when they wanted. It was informal and casual and suited Jordan and Rayma—or Jordayma as Rayma told everyone to start calling them—to a T.

"So, no heartfelt apology and hug from Mom then, huh?" Mieka asked, as the sisters all sat with each other sipping wine—save for Triss—on the patio chairs around one of the heaters. Guests mingled and chatted, while children ran around giggling, probably hopped up on sugar from the cupcakes Joy made.

"I never expected one," Rayma said.

"Me either," Oona added.

"The woman has never apologized for anything in her life. We were just expected to adhere to their fascist regime without question. And unfortunately, I did," Pasha said, sipping her wine. "Took a big splash of cold water in the form of a seventeen-year-old rocking up on my doorstep to realize that they're not perfect."

Rayma snorted. "Far fucking from it."

"Heard Dad tell Heath that they're going to try to reschedule their flight and leave sooner," Triss said.

Rayma snorted again. "Good luck. Weather Network says this shit's coming down for at least another few days. And so far, the meteorologists have been right." She made a sarcastic expression. "Now they're fucking right. Mother-fuckers."

"It sucks that we couldn't have the reconciliation I think we all dream of with our parents. But we're better off," Pasha said, her face sad.

"It does suck," Rayma agreed. "But when I told Dad that Heath was walking me down the aisle, all he did was shrug and go, 'Okay.' Didn't seem disappointed or upset at all. And that tells me everything I need to know. This family, here, is the one that matters. Yanna and Royce have made their choice and that is to not be part of this family."

Oona and her sisters nodded.

Jordan appeared, his eyes a little glazed over from the open bar. "Wife," he said.

"Yes, husband dear, how can I be of service?" Rayma said in her best baby doll voice. "Would you like me to *service* you?"

Oona and her sisters all snorted and shook their heads.

"Later," Jordan said, holding out his hand. "But right now, we must dance."

Rayma giggled and took his hand, allowing him to pull her up and twirl her out onto the dance floor, which was outside under the tent on outdoor carpets that were usually used for camping.

Their chosen song came on and they twirled around the dance floor like two newlyweds with very little rhythm but a whole lot of love.

Oona sipped her wine and smiled as she watched her baby sister giggle and grin when Jordan dipped her.

Soon, the song changed and the dance floor filled up. Jace was dancing with Peyton, Mieka had Nate out on the floor, and Pasha and Heath were showing everyone that a married couple with kids could still grind like teenagers.

"Care to dance?" came a dark rasp that had Oona's nipples instantly pebbling.

Triss was off snuggling with Asher, his hand on her belly, rubbing it affectionately, so Oona had been by herself, until Aiden sidled up. She glanced up at him, then down at his outstretched hand.

Smiling, she took it and allowed him to pull her to standing and lead her out to the dance floor.

It was a song that shouldn't have been slow danced to, but they slow danced anyway.

She liked that.

"I want to take back what I said before," he said, his hand sliding further down her back.

Her brows knitted together and her heart rate picked up. "What do you mean?"

"I don't want to start things in Montreal."

Now her heart was threatening to shatter. What the hell? Her palm grew sweaty in his and heat sprinted up into her cheeks. Did someone just crank the heaters? Why was is so hot under the tents all of a sudden?

They'd just had sex in the bathroom, and now he was telling her to pound sand? Did she completely misread everything that happened in the last few days? The progress they'd made? The progress that *he'd* made. Was he going to tell her that the sex was terrible, too? Just drive that final stake into her heart for good measure.

She made to pull out of his embrace, but he held on tight. "Aiden, let me go."

"I don't want to start things in Montreal *until* I've done the work. You deserve me in a better way than I am right now. You deserve me *fixed*, for lack of a better term."

Oh!

Her heart softened. She reached up and cupped his cheek. "You're not broken."

"I know. But I'm pretty banged up. I need to heal, so that I can be worthy of being with you. You deserve me *after* I've done the work. And for myself. I'm not doing the work for you. And this isn't lip service. This is me, telling you that I want a second chance. Or maybe it's a third chance. But when I've done the work."

She smiled and blinked through threatening tears.

"I don't expect you to stay celibate or not date. So if you find the love of your life between now and when I'm *fixed*, that's okay. I want you to be happy." He squeezed her tighter. "I mean that with my whole heart, Oona, you deserve to be happy. But, if you're not with anybody, and still interested, I'd love to cook you dinner, tell you about my day and hear about yours."

Well, that had to be the most romantic proposal for a future date she'd ever received.

Her lashes fluttered and she blinked rapidly, trying to stave off the tears.

"I'm really sorry for everything I've put you through. For all the horrible things I've said. For all the horrible things I did. You are a remarkable, strong, brilliant, beautiful woman, and for the record, you're great at sex, too."

She huffed a laugh.

"And you didn't deserve a word of my anger. Every word I said to you, I was saying to a mirror. You were right. I was using you to hurt myself. And I'm sorry."

She smiled and closed the gap between them until their bodies were pressed tight against each other. "I'd love for you to cook me dinner."

He smiled and splayed his hand across the small of her back. "And you promise you won't try to pay for half the food and my utility bill?"

She snorted and rolled her eyes. "I promise."

Jordan and Rayma sashayed toward them, the newlyweds all smiles. "Hey," Jordan said.

Aiden lifted his brows. "Marriage suits you."

Rayma beamed. "Marriage to *me* certainly does."

"Just got a text from a contact at the hospital. Mr. Zhao survived his stroke. He's going to have a rough recovery, but they think he'll pull through."

"Thank God." As if imaginary weights had been stacked on his shoulders, Aiden exhaled and relaxed in her arms. His body loosened and his entire demeanor changed.

She hadn't realized it until now, but he'd been carrying around the worry and stress of the man who'd rolled his vehicle surviving since it happened.

"That's wonderful news," Oona said.

"The family has asked if they can reach out to you and say thank you. Thought I'd get your okay first, before I handed out your number."

A pink flush bloomed in Aiden's cheeks beneath his scruff.

Rayma swatted him on the shoulder. "Just do it."

Aiden rolled his eyes but nodded. "Yeah, okay."

Jordan and Rayma danced away, leaving Oona and Aiden on their own again.

"Wow," she said, "what amazing news. That family is going to have an okay Christmas after all. I mean, he's still in the hospital, but at least he's still with th—".

She didn't get a chance to finish her sentence before Aiden kissed her.

Smiling against his lips, she kissed him back.

It wasn't a long kiss, or with tongue or anything like that. There were kids around, and he did just say he wanted to wait to start anything until he'd done the work. But it was a kiss that said a million things, all of them wonderful. It was a kiss full of promise, full of healing, growth, and hope.

Pulling away just enough, he broke their kiss and they both opened their eyes. "Sorry," he said. "I know that we're not supposed to be starting anything, but—"

This time it was her turn. She cut him off and kissed him again.

The kiss didn't last more than a couple of seconds, and they both pulled away at the same time, smiling and opening their eyes. "I know," she said. "It's okay."

"Time to throw the bouquet," Rayma announced as the song ended.

"You're expecting us to catch a pineapple?" Peyton asked, fear on her face.

Rayma shrugged. "Yeah?"

Oona wasn't going to step forward into the mix of single women, but when she realized that it was just her and Peyton who would be standing there, she rolled her eyes and stepped forward. "Are we seriously the only two single women here?"

"I will fight you for the pineapple," Peyton said, bending her knees and hunching over, getting into a fighting stance and shifting back and forth on her heels.

Oona gaped at her, then waved her hand. "I concede. Peyton can have the pineapple. She wins. I'm not getting into a brawl over a piece of produce."

Peyton threw her hands up in the air. "Yay! Victory!" Rayma gently tossed the pineapple in an underhand throw and Peyton caught it easy peasy.

Then it was time for the garter toss.

Jace and Aiden were the only single men, and Aiden quickly conceded the garter-win to Jace.

Jace and Peyton hadn't been able to keep their eyes, hands, or lips off each other, so neither Oona or Aiden were chapped that they didn't win.

Aiden made his way back over to Oona as she stood inside the house picking at various things on the buffet table. All the food was amazing. "You outdid yourself, Big Lassie," she said, popping a fried wonton into her mouth and humming in delight as the Asian flavors did a happy dance across her tastebuds.

He handed her a glass of red wine. "When I like who I'm cooking for, I try to do my best."

The symbolism behind him bringing her wine was not lost on her at all. She could see it in his eyes and his whole demeanor, how dedicated he was to mending himself and getting better. To doing the work. Even though he was giving her most of his attention at the reception, he was a lot more social with the other guests than she remembered him being at the bachelor party. He was joking and smiling. Carefree and relaxed.

Everything about the Aiden Lassiter she met in her office a little over a week ago, and the Aiden Lassiter now, was different. And in all the best kinds of ways. Gone were the bags under his eyes, the angry scowl, the harsh lines between his brows. The angry energy that accompanied him like a rock in his shoe, were gone. His dimples were out and attacking everyone, and it was beautiful.

She swallowed the food in her mouth and sipped the wine. "You know, I'm not your therapist, but I am your friend?" She said that last bit with an upward inflection. "Right?"

He nodded and reached for a wonton, which forced his wrist to brush against her arm sending electric zaps coursing through her body. "I'd like to think that we're at the very least friends, now, yes."

She sobered herself by taking another sip of wine. "And friends talk about their problems. They help each other. They vent and commiserate. So, if you ever want to talk—as friends—I'm here."

He finished chewing his wonton, then wrapped his arms around her waist and tugged her until her thighs bumped his. Damn, he was a sexy sight in his serge. "Thank you, but I think I'll see how my therapist and anger management go, first. I don't want to burden my *friend* with my problems. Right now, I just want to get to know her because whether she's Oona *or* Luna, I happened to think she's pretty great."

Oona's heart wanted to leap out of her chest and wrap itself around Aiden. But she kept her cool and simply met his big dimply smile with a big one of her own as her arms floated up and rested on his shoulders. "I think Aiden *and* Caden are pretty great, too."

The next day was Christmas day and even though the snow didn't let up until the wee hours of the morning, the plows (eventually) went through.

But Aiden, Jordan, Rayma and Oona were still at Jordayma's apartment that morning, with plans to go to Joy and Grant's later for the enormous family dinner.

"Little Lassie, you shouldn't have," Rayma fake-crooned as she opened the jewelry box from her new husband to reveal a necklace with a pineapple pendant. "But it's perfect. I love it."

Aiden and Oona exchanged looks. Though Oona didn't seem to be nearly as confused as Aiden was. "I gotta ask," he finally said, "what is with the pineapples?"

Rayma snorted. "It makes your cum taste better."

Aiden nearly choked on his coffee. "Excuse me?"

"When Little Lassie and I first started dating and we were finally going to sleep together—after he strung me along *forever*—I told him to eat pineapple or drink pineapple juice as it made his cum taste sweeter. Then, when I showed up at his house that night, he had like forty pineapples on his counter."

"Not forty," Jordan said. "You make me sound like some weirdo."

"You had a lot of pineapples. And you still buy a lot of pineapples." She shrugged. "It's just become our *thing* now. An inside joke. Hence why I walked down the aisle with a pineapple."

Aiden, still bewildered, nodded. "Okay, then. Probably a bit too much information for me to have about my brother and his wife, and certainly this early in the morning, but educational nonetheless."

"I'm here to inform," Rayma said, removing the necklace from its velvet bed, undoing the clasp and fastening it around her neck. "I could make a pearl necklace joke here in some way, but I'm going to take the mature highroad and refrain."

"I think mentioning that you could make the joke eliminates the maturity of *not* saying it," Oona countered before sipping her tea.

Rayma stuck her tongue out at her sister. "Here, Oons, this one has your name on it."

Oona's brows bunched. "But I already opened the one from you."

Rayma lifted one shoulder and handed the gift to Oona. All it said was "Oona" on it.

"It's from me," Aiden said, softly.

"What?" Oona exclaimed. "We're exchanging gifts? I don't have anything for you. Up until, like, two days ago we didn't even like each other. I can't accept this." She held the brown box with the red ribbon toward him.

"You've forgiven me for being a total dick, Oona, that's worth more than what is in that box, trust me." He pushed the box toward her again. "Just open it."

With a weighted sigh and a confused glint in her eyes, she set the box on her lap and pulled at the red ribbon until it unraveled. Then she opened the box and pulled out the matching scarf and gloves. "They're beautiful," she said softly, gazing at him with glassy eyes and appreciation. "Thank you."

Nodding, but not wanting to get too mushy, he reached under the tree and grabbed the two small boxes he had for Rayma and Jordan. "Here. These are for you guys."

They opened them at the same time.

"Ooh, I love it. Matching toques for Jordayma! Little Lassie, put on yours, too," Rayma said, tugging the light gray toque over her caramel-colored hair. "And gloves, too. They're so soft." She fed her fingers into the gloves. "Bamboo?"

"Hemp," Aiden said. "From that place downtown."

Rayma's eyes widened. "I love that store. Thank you so much, Big Lassie."

Jordan had his toque on, too, and nodded. "Yeah, thanks, bro, I really like them."

Aiden shrugged, then stood up from where he'd been sitting on the floor beside the Christmas tree. "So, French toast sound good?"

"French toast sounds fucking fantastic," Rayma said, still in her toque and gloves. There was a knock at the door that had them all glancing at each other in confusion.

"Santa?" Rayma asked the room, heading to unlock the door. "Did he forget to leave my new Ferrari covered in bumper stickers or something?"

Jordan snorted a laugh from where he was tidying up the wrapping paper in the living room.

Rayma opened the door and even though her voice was low and Aiden was rummaging around in the fridge, he still heard her murmur, "Holy shit."

"Mom! Dad!" Oona exclaimed, getting up from her spot on the couch. "Uh, Merry Christmas."

"Merry Christmas," their father said, stepping into the apartment.

Their mother followed, carrying three small expertly wrapped gifts in her arms. "Good morning. Merry Christmas."

Oona approached her parents and embraced them both awkwardly. Rayma did the same.

"Coffee?" Aiden asked.

"Please," Mrs. Young said. Mr. Young nodded.

"Soooo, what brings you by?" Rayma asked. "You took off before the speeches, the bouquet toss, and everything last night. I wasn't sure we'd see you guys again."

"Yes, well, after Triss's wedding, we realized that everyone probably would have more fun when we're not there, anyway," Mr. Young said. "That we're cut from a different cloth than the people our daughters seem to like spending time with, and our idea of a good time is different from yours."

"You could have stayed for the speeches at least," Rayma said, her voice cracking a little. "Aren't parents normally supposed to say something when their kid gets married?"

"We weren't sure you would want us to," Mrs. Young added. "After," her gaze pivoted to Oona, "after everything that was said."

Rayma dropped her gaze to the floor. "Right. Well," she scuffed her slippers over to the tree and grabbed a small box from under it, then shoved it toward her parents. "This is for you."

"Thank you," Mrs. Young said, accepting the gift and in return handing the three boxes to Rayma, Oona and Jordan.

She unwrapped the box and squinted at the certificate that was inside. "What is this?"

"I bought and registered a star for you," Rayma said. "I wasn't sure what to get you, but I thought this might be cool. It's one you can see from your house all the time. I named it *Forever Young*."

Oona opened up the box from her mother. It was also a toque, only, Aiden could tell from where he stood making coffee in the kitchen that it would be itchy. It was also a terrible beige-color. "Oh cool. Thanks, Mom."

Rayma had the same toque, and Jordan's was just a slightly darker shade. He and Rayma pulled off the ones Aiden gave them and tugged on the ones from her parents, but their smiles were fake and Aiden's neck started to itch just thinking about the scratchy material against their skin.

"We came here to apologize," Mr. Young started, which caused Oona and Rayma to both go slack-jawed. "For sending you to Pasha without talking to her first. And for making you feel like we gave up on you. That wasn't the case. We just ... we didn't know *what* to do with you or how to help. We just knew we needed to get you out of Baltimore and away from that—"

"Gang," Mrs. Young said.

Rayma nodded.

Even Aiden could tell that their apology wasn't really an apology at all. They were simply justifying their behavior. What the fuck?

"You've all grown up to be successful young women and we're very proud of you," Mr. Young said. "We just ... don't really know you."

"No shit," Rayma murmured.

"Anyway, please know that we love you all. And even if we don't necessarily see eye-to-eye on everything, that doesn't change that we love you." He smiled. "Tattoos and all."

"Thanks, Dad," Rayma said, her voice stiff, posture even stiffer. Aiden focused on Oona. She was a little more relaxed than Rayma, but not much. She was also watching their mother. Yanna was quiet and her back was straight as a board.

"Mom?" Oona said. "You have anything you'd like to add?"

Yanna sucked in a deep breath through her nose, held it a moment, then released it. "I love my daughters. I just don't understand them. And I'm not sure I ever will. But I'm proud and ... I did the best I could." She smiled grimly, then turned to the door. "We should go, Pasha is expecting us."

Mr. Young nodded and they turned to go. "We will see you at Joy and Grant's later this afternoon."

"Oh, you're going?" Rayma asked.

"We were invited," their mother said. "And we were unable to reschedule our flights until the twenty-sixth, so, yes, we're going."

"All right, well, we'll see you there, then," Rayma said, following her parents to the door. She held it open for them. "Thanks for stopping by."

She closed the door and turned to face Oona, Aiden, and Jordan, inflating her cheeks with air, then blowing it out as her eyes went buggy.

"What the fuck was that?" she asked.

"An olive branch?" Oona asked.

"Shortest, weirdest fucking olive branch I've ever seen," Rayma said, shaking her head. "Big Lassie, make that coffee Irish, please."

"On it," Aiden said, pouring a healthy dollop of Bailey's into a mug before topping it up with coffee. He snagged Oona's eyes and hoisted his brows up. "Am I making your tea Irish, too?"

"I think you better," Rayma said before Oona could reply.

Oona grinned and nodded. "Thank you."

Rayma yanked off the toque from her parents and put on the one from Aiden again. "This one is so much nicer. The other one itches like crazy."

Aiden smirked. He fucking knew it.

Jordan had already removed his toque and his hair stuck out in every direction. Oona wasn't wearing her toque, but she had the scarf he gave her around her neck. She wandered into the kitchen and around the island, bumping her hip against Aiden's. "Thank you for my present. It was unnecessary."

"So was you forgiving me, so thank you."

She grinned up at him. He reached down and tucked a strand of hair behind her ear, but kept his hand there and cupped her cheek. "Merry Christmas, Oona. I'm really glad I'm spending it with you. With my brother and not alone in my apartment with nothing but my anger and bad attitude."

Placing her hand over his on her face, she leaned deeper into his touch and blinked up at him. "I'm really glad you're not alone on Christmas, either."

"You guys ..." Rayma sung behind Aiden. "Look up."

Not moving from where they were, they both glanced upward to see a sprig of mistletoe dangling from a piece of string which was attached to a broom handle. Rayma was holding the broom, exceptionally pleased with herself.

Oona rolled her eyes but smiled at Aiden. "We can wait and *start* things after you've done the work once we get back to Montreal. But for now," she wrapped her hand around his neck and pulled him down so his lips hovered over hers, "I think we've earned this."

Then she kissed him, on Christmas, under the mistletoe and it was the best fucking kiss of his life.

Epilogue

Four and a half LONG months later ...

Aiden pulled up to the red brick building just as the light from the setting sun started to fade in the sky. It was mid April, and finally the days were getting longer again. The air held less of a nip to it than it had a few weeks ago and there wasn't frost on his windshield every morning anymore.

The cherry blossoms were still a few weeks away from decorating the city with their lacy petals, but spring was definitely in the air.

He'd come straight here from work. It was his first official day back on the force, and even though it felt weird returning to the station, and having to ride with a partner, Aiden didn't let it get him down. His friends and co-workers welcomed him back with smiles and handshakes, and nobody seemed to look at him like the cop that lost his cool. Maybe that was also because during the last four months, he'd made a point of reaching out to everyone in his department and apologizing for his behavior and how it made the department look. He said he was doing the work to get better and looked forward to working with them all again.

That making amends stuff really was magical.

The cop he had to ride along with was a bit green around the gills, but he was also eager and very bright. Aiden felt less like he was being babysat and more like he was helping a new recruit *not* make the same stupid mistakes that he did. Paying it forward and all that jazz.

He changed out of his work clothes at work into jeans and a black, long-sleeve shirt, then jumped in his truck and drove across town to *All or Nothing Dance Studio.*

He and Oona talked on the phone regularly, and met for coffee usually once a week at least, but as far as dates went, there were none. No sex, handholding or even kissing.

And that was more on Aiden's insistence than Oona's. He wanted to prove to her that he was doing this for the right reasons and that he was going to see it through.

So they did what they said they were going to do, and got to know each other. They became friends. And she was a terrific friend. She introduced him to some of her friends, like Teal and Penelope, and he introduced her to a few of the cops that he hung out with off duty.

But now, he'd officially been given the green light by his therapist—who was fantastic—and the new anger management group he started going to in the new year was working wonders, too.

He was ready to show Oona that he was a changed man. A calmer, less judgmental, and more patient man. He would probably always hold a bit of a harder scrutiny toward drunk drivers, but at least now he knew to ask more questions, and get more answers before he jumped to conclusions.

Not all those driving reckless were drunk, and not all those who drink are going to drive.

The world is not black and white, but rather a million different shades of gray.

He pulled open the heavy glass door to the dance studio and was instantly greeted by a heart-pumping tune coming from one of the rooms down the hall.

Smiling at the front desk girl, he pointed down the hall. "Here to see Oona."

"I know," she grinned, batting thick fake lashes at him.

He nodded and headed toward the music.

Oona knew he was coming here, but that didn't mean he didn't want to watch her for a second while she was unaware. And thankfully, the door into the room she was in had a long glass panel running down the center of it, so he hung back in the shadows but close enough that he could see her on the pole.

She wasn't wearing her performance costume, just an emerald-green sports bra that did all kinds of crazy criss-cross things in the back, and a pair of very short booty shorts. In fact, they were so short that the bottoms of her butt cheeks stuck out a little.

It was a good look.

She leaped up onto the pole and wrapped her legs around it, spinning backward, counter-clockwise, then she let go with her hands and continued to spin, holding on with just her legs. She did two revolutions hands-free, then gripped the pole again with her hands and spun herself upside down, doing the splits with her legs in the air.

He hadn't watched her pole dance since that first night they met—besides her online videos—and he was realizing now just how much he missed it.

She'd taken on teaching another class once a week, so now she taught pole twice a week—two classes each on those days. A six o'clock and a seven o'clock, and one burlesque class a week. But today was her day off from teaching. She was here for herself. To work on her own routine and because, as she told him in a text—she missed freestyling on the pole. It was her happy place and where she could just let the outside world fade away.

So, to see her in her happy place, when she didn't know that he was watching, as she allowed the outside world beyond the four walls around her to fade away, was a privilege he wasn't going to take lightly. It was beautiful to witness her creativity and grace. As she did what just came to her mind in the moment. As she gave in to the spontaneity.

He watched her for another few moments, mesmerized by her strength and beauty. By Oona. Because even though he'd fallen for Luna and liked her very much, it was Oona who owned his heart. It was Oona who he was in love with, and wanted to be with.

The brilliant beauty with the heart of a warrior and a booty like two halves of a peach.

When she finally dropped to the floor and stepped off to the side to grab her water bottle, he opened the door. "Hello there."

She spun around to face him and her eyes lit up like two gold-flecked orbs. Then she set the water bottle down and skipped toward him. He didn't expect her to leap up into his arms, wrap her legs around his waist and kiss him.

But he wasn't complaining about it, either.

He held her tight, feeling the last four months of torture that they'd both endured pouring out of her into him. She squeezed him with her thighs and wrapped her arms around his neck.

He kissed her back just as hard, loving the moans that roamed up from the depths of her chest.

Finally, breathless, they broke the kiss. "Big Lassie! What took you so long?"

He grinned at her. "I came here as soon as I got off shift."

"How was your first day back?"

"Weird, but also great. Guy they've got babysitting me is pretty cool. Really smart and eager." He set her down on her feet and took her hand. "How was your day?"

Her sigh held an exhaustion that he could feel right down to his toes. "Long, but good."

"Ready to go?"

She nodded. "Yep, just let me grab my stuff." She stowed her water bottle and towel into her gym bag, then tugged on a pair of sweatpants over her booty shorts and a hoodie over her bra. "You're cooking for me tonight, right?"

He smiled at her ponytail as she led him out of the studio. "That depends ..."

She craned her head around. "On what?"

"On whether I'm cooking at your house or mine, because I have a fully stocked fridge, you usually have oat milk, salad mix and pre-cooked chicken in yours."

"Touché," she said, facing forward again and walking past the girl at the front desk. "See you tomorrow, Clara."

"Bye, Oona," Clara said.

Aiden gave Clara a wave and followed Oona through the parking lot to her car. "So, you'll follow me home?" He caged her in against the driver's side door of her car.

She bit her lip and looked up at him. "I will, yes."

And will you stay over?

That was the big question.

They hadn't talked much about what would happen once they decided to give a relationship a shot. Were they dating? Were they boyfriend and girlfriend? Were they going to take it slow and wait to sleep together?

He didn't want to push her, and he also didn't want to assume.

But judging by the way she flung herself into his arms when he arrived and kissed him like crazy, he really hoped she didn't want to take things *too* slow.

"I uh, I packed an overnight bag just in case," she said, her eyes shimmering with hope beneath the obtrusive LED street lamp directly overhead. "Hope I'm not being too forward or assuming things."

He shook his head and grinned down at her. "I was hoping you would."

Looping her arms back around his neck, she lifted up onto her tiptoes. "I'm glad you did the work, Aiden. These four and half months have been hard, but I've really enjoyed getting to know you and seeing your progress. You've done the work and it shows. You seem happier, more at peace."

"I am," he said honestly. "I don't think I've ever felt this good in my entire life. And I have you to thank."

She shook her head. "Nope. Not me. *You* did this all on your own."

"I know, but if I hadn't met a beautiful woman at a bar, spent an amazing night with her, and then fucked it all up beyond recognition, I don't know if I would be here now. With you, that is. You would have been my therapist and then we never could have been together. So, you refusing to treat me was the best thing that ever could have happened. Because not only did I get the help I needed, but I also get you."

Her smile held so much pride that Aiden's chest tightened almost to the point of pain his heart was so close to bursting.

"We're in this, right?" she said, her voice strained as tears welled up in her eyes. "You're my boyfriend. I'm your girlfriend. We've done enough of the preliminary stuff for months, that I think we can make it official."

Now Aiden's face hurt, too, because he was smiling so hard. "Oh, it's official. You, me and your dozens of houseplants that you've gendered and named. We're in this. All of us." Then he pressed her against her car and kissed her silly, because he could. Because he was her boyfriend and because he'd done the work and finally, after far too long, he liked himself and he knew he deserved happiness, too.

If you've enjoyed this book, please consider leaving a review wherever you purchased it. It really does make a difference and helps an independent author like me.

Thank you again.

Xoxo

Whitley Cox

Check out this book

It's all fun and
games until
somebody falls
in love

DOCTOR
Sexy

WHITLEY
COX

CHECKOUT DOCTOR SMUG

Grab Doctor Smug Here—> books2read.com/doctorsmug

CHAPTER ONE

RILEY

Tonight was NOT the night to be bringing in subs. The LA Kings didn't bring up players from the farm team during the playoffs, and we sure as hell didn't need to be bringing in noobs on a night like tonight.

I pulled the worn brass door handle of The Old Emerald Pub in downtown Seattle and stood aside so Greg could walk through ahead of me "So if you don't know what she looks like or what she does for work, can you at least tell me if she's any good at trivia? You *do* know this is like the World Series for me. Game seven, Kings vs Rangers. The eighteenth hole, two below par."

Greg snorted, lifted his chin in greeting to the hostess and headed toward an open four-top table in the dimly lit underground pub. "I don't think Emily would have invited her if she wasn't good at trivia. She knows how important this match is to us."

I took a seat, facing the stage. I needed to get into the zone.

Pub trivia night was no joke. I took this shit seriously.

Greg and I were undefeated all year with our teammates, two other doctors, Filip Renny and Will Colson, but they'd just accepted positions in Africa working for Doctors Without Borders, so now we were down two men.

I had a hard time giving them shit for abandoning us since they were off fixing cleft pallets and vaccinating children in remote villages so they wouldn't catch polio or some other horrible ailment.

Didn't mean I couldn't—and didn't—grumble their names in the privacy of my own mind. We'd been coming here since January, whenever we had Friday nights off (which we made sure was often) and in the last five and a half months had made a name for ourselves among the trivia crowd.

Normally, it wouldn't have been a disaster to be down two teammates—Greg and I could hold our own—but we were going up against some guys from a pub across town who'd heard about our success and wanted to make things a little more interesting. A friendly bet of five hundred dollars and paying the winners' booze tab hung in the balance. If Filip and Will had been here, it would have been like shooting fish in a barrel winning the trivia match, but down two men, I wasn't nearly as confident. And not being confident in something unnerved me almost as much as the thought of losing to a bunch of lawyers from across town did.

I wasn't sure if I wanted to rack up my tab tonight—because if we won, the other team would have to pay for it—or if I wanted to play it cool and hope that if, on the off chance, we did lose, karma would have my back and not rob me blind.

"Blonde, brunette, redhead?" I shelled a peanut from the bowl on the table. "I know Emily, and this is more than just someone to come help us win trivia.

This is a setup. She works with a shit-ton of guys. She could have invited any one of them, and yet she invited a chick."

Greg was the picture of innocence and simply smiled.

"Your sister is a meddler." I popped the peanut into my mouth and chewed. The last thing I needed was some doe-eyed, hopeful woman looking to land a doctor and distracting me from winning this trivia night. "Do I *look* like I need help with the ladies? I mean, come on."

Greg's eyes rolled hard.

"That's right, big sexy doctor man doesn't need any help with the ladies," a fake deep voice said behind us before the back of my head was swatted. "Damn, you're full of yourself, Pretty Boy." Emily took a seat between me and her twin brother.

I glanced up at her, ready with a witty comeback, when my tongue doubled in size and searched for a way out of my mouth rather than focusing on forming words.

Behind Emily, blue eyes blinked and a smile curled plump lips framed by freckles. Her face was covered in them. More than the beach had sand. Strawberry-blonde tendrils floated down around her heart-shaped face while the rest was pinned on the top of her head in some weird clip thing.

"Riley, this is my friend Daisy. Daisy, this is my brother's friend Riley. He's an egotistical jackass, surgical resident who knows he looks like a baby-faced underwear model. He also has a penchant for cheap beer, expensive scotch, and he's obnoxiously competitive when it comes to pub trivia." Emily's hand waved between Daisy and me. She caught the eye of a waitress and silently summoned her over before glancing back at me. "Does that about sum you up, Ry?"

"Don't forget playboy," Greg added with a cheesy smile.

My insides twisted.

Emily pointed at her brother and nodded. "Right. And *Pretty Boy*, hence the why you call him that at the hospital. Pretty boy playboy."

Yeah, I fucking hated the nickname *Pretty Boy*.

The twins needed to shut up and shut up now.

Daisy took a seat next to me, her expression amused but also wary. "Is everything Emily said true?"

I needed to find words. I needed to find good words. Smart words. I could do this. I was a surgeon at one of the best hospitals in the Pacific Northwest. I had good words in my head. Lots of them.

But the words weren't coming, and all I could come up with was a low, grunted, "Yeah."

Oh, for fuck's sake.

Color bloomed in her cheeks, which only made the freckles stand out even more. "None of those are very good selling points. For a friend, a teammate or otherwise."

Otherwise?

So this was a setup. I knew it. Emily was such a meddler. Greg was too, though, so I couldn't rule out his steady hand having a finger or two in this night.

I opened my mouth to respond, but like before, nothing came out. Her expectant gaze on me was so heavy, I thought I might crumple to the ground under the weight of it.

"What can I get you to drink?" the waitress asked, sidling up to our table in all black, her pen poised on a pad of paper at the ready. The pub was filling up. The crowd combined with the music made it difficult to hear people. When trivia started, things would quiet down.

"A pint of Pabst Blue Ribbon," I said before turning to Daisy, finally finding words again. "Only beer I drink. Keeps me humble."

Emily and Greg rolled their matching baby blues.

Daisy snorted, but the smile on her face was still there, along with the almost magical twinkle in her eyes, eyes a much darker blue than the twins'. "I'll have a vodka soda with a wedge of lime, please. In a tall glass with extra ice."

Emily ordered a rum and Coke, and Greg ordered a rye and tonic. We'd get food later, but for now we needed to talk strategy.

I turned to Daisy, adopting my game face. "How good are you at trivia?"

She and Emily exchanged amused glances, their eyes dancing in a way that meant they were having a full-on conversation without actually saying a damn thing.

Women were terrifyingly good at that.

Finally, she peeled her gaze from Emily to me, though rather noncommittal, and continued to take in the rest of the pub. She shrugged. "I'm pretty good."

I needed more than that. This game had a lot riding on it. "Yeah? Like *how* good?"

Her shoulder lifted again, and her head shook gently. "Like I loved *Jeopardy* growing up, still do. I'm pretty good at geography and pop culture. Know all the words to every Spice Girls song."

Emily made a noise in her throat that made Daisy slide her a sideways glance and a half-smile.

She was not giving me confidence that we would win this. In the three years I'd been doing trivia night, not once had a question been about a Spice Girls song.

Was she deliberately playing coy? "What do you do for work?" I asked, continuing with the interview.

Please say astrophysicist or professor of economics. I'd even settle for hoarder and reader of out-of-date American history textbooks.

I didn't get the hoarder vibe from her though. She seemed like she tossed her takeout containers in the recycling and didn't stack them on a shelf until they formed a leaning carboard tower just *in case* the craft bug bit her one day.

But then again, people had quirks and secrets about them that often came out of left field. Maybe she was a hoarder with pockets of rodents creating dens in her stacks of takeout containers.

I also wasn't trying to be an asshole here, even though Emily and Greg were both giving me looks that said I was being one. I just had a lot riding on this trivia match, and I needed to know we had winners at our table.

"I'm a matchmaker," she said, sitting up straight in her chair so her breasts strained against the sleeveless white button-up cotton blouse she wore. I hadn't paid much attention to what she was wearing when she walked in. Her face and smile knocked me off guard, and I'd been unable to focus on anything else, but now I could tell she had style and taste. Dark jeans, tight enough they could be painted on, black strappy sandals with a heel and that blouse that I was pretty sure harbored a red lacy bra underneath.

I needed to get my eyes off her chest.

Wait, did she just say she was a *matchmaker?*

I groaned.

Oh Christ.

"A matchmaker, you say?" Unable to keep the inflection or judgment from my tone. I'd never been the most tactful man.

I had the ego fit for a surgeon, but people said I needed to work on my poker face. Fair enough. Nobody was perfect.

"So what does that look like? You meet people, they pay you and you set them up on dates? Aren't there free apps out there for that?" I regretted the snort at the back of my throat the moment it happened because Daisy's eyes darkened and her brows narrowed.

"Something like that," she said, her tone harsh, reminding me of my mother when I'd pushed to stay up late one too many times as a kid, ultimately snapping the last of her nerves.

"So is this like a side gig, or is the matchmaking business a profitable one?"

The waitress returned with our drinks, and I immediately took a sip of my beer. Call me weird, but to me, there was nothing quite as refreshing or nostalgic as a good, cold pint of Pabst Blue Ribbon. It was what I drank all through college and med school. PBR got me through some tough times and helped me celebrate some epic ones. I couldn't turn my back on it now that I had money.

Glancing back at Daisy after setting my beer down on the table, I waited for her response. She hadn't said anything since I asked her if she made good coin in her job. Was she trying to come up with some clever way of saying it wasn't about the money; it was about helping people find true love?

When she set her glass back down, I heard the sound of ice cubes being chewed. I noticed a small birthmark on the back of her right hand just beneath her thumb. It was shaped like a perfect heart, about a nickel in size and so damn cute. "My latest algorithm is still in beta testing, but so far we're seeing very good results. We doubled our gross income since last year, and I've hired on three more full-time employees. Projections for next year are triple of this year. I also own my condo and have already paid off my student loans. I do okay. What say you, *doctor-man*, still neck-deep in those med-school loans?" Her confident smile and lifted brow of challenge only drew out a big, genuine grin from me.

I tossed my head back and laughed. "My apologies. I assumed there was no money in the matchmaking business, and I was wrong. How does a single guy like myself hire your company? Do you have a website? What's the name of it?"

"Daisy's Chain Attraction." She had a wall up around her now. She was on the defensive.

Shit.

Leaning forward, I planted my hands on the table. "So I just pay you money and then you start sending me women's numbers?"

To be honest, I'd never met a professional matchmaker before, and the fact that she made as much money as she said she did had me all the more curious to know how she found people their happily ever afters.

Perhaps this wasn't the setup I thought it was. Maybe meeting Daisy was a sign I needed to shut down my Huukup app profile and start looking for something real and with substance. Maybe I'd just found the person to help me do that. For a price, of course.

Unless ...

I dismissed that crazy thought before it had a chance to fully form in my mind.

I was not here to be set up; I was here to fleece a bunch of attorneys out of their money, and now that we were down two of our regular teammates, I needed to get my head in the game even more. But a second glance at Daisy's smile had me feeling a whole new kind of unease. I'd only had a sip of my beer, and already I felt lightheaded and like I'd just shotgunned a six-pack.

Her voice had me mentally slapping myself to clear my head. "You pay me money, fill out a very extensive, very personal, almost invasive survey, and then we match you with women in our system. The men do not get numbers or profiles or even pictures of the women until the woman gives the green light. If the woman is interested, we set up the first meeting in a safe, public location, and we have an escape plan in place in case she feels unsafe and needs a way to end the date safely. We do this for every first date for every client."

I let out a whistle. "That's hands-on customer service right there."

"It's why I charge what I do. I take the happiness and safety of my clients *very* seriously. This isn't a hookup app. It's people seriously interested in investing the time and money to find someone they're compatible with."

"So what got you into that?" I had her talking again, which was good. Her responses remained frosty though. Her arms had crossed in front of her chest, and she was leaning back in her chair, almost glaring at me.

"I have a master's in psychology with a minor in statistics and an MBA. I have a killer team of computer techs working on my algorithm, as well as trained marriage and couples counselors helping me match my clients. The algorithm does most of it, but before we let the women know of their matches, the counselors preview their profiles to make sure there are no weird outliers that could result in incompatibility between the couples. I *got into this* because I'm good at reading people and setting people up. We have an eighty-four percent success rate. But I believe that with our updated algorithm, we could bring that rate up to eighty-six by this time next year."

Jesus Christ. Now I felt like a real tool. She actually had her shit together.

"Could I take the survey?"

"That'll be five hundred bucks," she replied quickly.

My eyes widened.

"Fifteen hundred if you're a woman."

Holy crap. I blew out a breath that rattled my lips, kind of like a horse. "Surely you know just from meeting someone their level—even just superficially—of compatibility with someone else, no?"

Crystal-blue eyes narrowed, and her face darkened. "What are you getting at?"

I shrugged, giving her another one of my smiles that made the hospital nurses blush. She appeared immune. "You and me. How would we score on your very extensive, very personal, almost invasive survey?"

Daisy wasn't blushing. She also wasn't smiling. Her level gaze and bored expression had the hair on my arms prickling up. But my pulse was racing. "I can confirm right here, right now, *Doctor Smug,* that you and I are one hundred percent, irrefutably, undeniably incompatible."

Grab Doctor Smug Here—> books2read.com/doctorsmug

ACKNOWLEDGMENTS

There are so many people to thank who help along the way. Publishing a book is definitely not a solo mission, that's for sure.

To my editing team at Proofreeding by the Page, thank you.

Megan Macphail, Sharon Abrams and Author Brooke Burton for your beta-reads, thank you!

Author Kathleen Lawless and Danielle Young, thank you for helping me work through the plot holes and hangups I had with this book. Your insight was invaluable and I am eternally grateful.

Megan J. Parker-Squiers from EmCat Designs, your covers are awesome. I love these covers so much, you outdid yourself.

Author Ember Leigh, my author bestie, I love our bitch fests—they keep me sane.

My fabulous assistant, Megan Macphail of Kiss My Smut, what would I do without you? You are amazing and I SO appreciate all your hard work, beautiful graphics and organization. Thank you!!!

My parents, in-laws and brother, thank you for your unwavering support. The Small Human and the Tiny Human, you are the beats and beasts of my heart, the reason I breathe and the reason I drink. I love you both to infinity and beyond. And lastly, of course, the husband. You are my forever, my other half, the one who keeps me grounded and the only person I have honestly never grown sick of even when we did that six-month backpacking trip and spent every single day together. I never tired of you. Never needed a break. You are my person. I love you.

OTHER BOOKS BY WHITLEY COX

Love, Passion and Power: Part 1
The Dark and Damaged Hearts Series: Book 1
https://books2read.com/LPP1-DDH
Kendra and Justin

•

Love, Passion and Power: Part 2
The Dark and Damaged Hearts: Book 2
https://books2read.com/LPP2-DDH
Kendra and Justin

•

Sex, Heat and Hunger: Part 1
The Dark and Damaged Hearts Book 3
https://books2read.com/SHH1-DDH
Emma and James

•

Sex, Heat and Hunger: Part 2
The Dark and Damaged Hearts Book 4
https://books2read.com/SHH1-DDH
Emma and James

•

Hot & Filthy: The Honeymoon
The Dark and Damaged Hearts Book 4.5
https://books2read.com/HF-DDH
Emma and James

•

True, Deep and Forever: Part 1
The Dark and Damaged Hearts Book 5
https://books2read.com/TDF1-DDH
Amy and Garrett

•

True, Deep and Forever: Part 2
The Dark and Damaged Hearts Book 6
https://books2read.com/TDF2-DDH
Amy and Garrett

·

Hard, Fast and Madly: Part 1
The Dark and Damaged Hearts Series Book 7
https://books2read.com/HFM1-DDH
Freya and Jacob

·

Hard, Fast and Madly: Part 2
The Dark and Damaged Hearts Series Book 8
https://books2read.com/HFM1-DDH
Freya and Jacob

·

Quick & Dirty
Book 1, A Quick Billionaires Novel
https://books2read.com/QDirty-QBS
Parker and Tate

·

Quick & Easy
Book 2, A Quick Billionaires Novella
https://books2read.com/QEasy-QBS
Heather and Gavin

·

Quick & Reckless
Book 3, A Quick Billionaires Novel
https://books2read.com/QReckless-QBS
Silver and Warren

·

Quick & Dangerous
Book 4, A Quick Billionaires Novel
https://books2read.com/QDangerous-QBS
Skyler and Roberto

·

Quick & Snowy
The Quick Billionaires, Book 5
https://books2read.com/QSnowy-QBS
Brier and Barnes

·

Doctor Smug
https://books2read.com/DoctorSmug
Daisy and Riley

·

Hot Dad
https://books2read.com/Hot-Dad
Harper and Sam

•

Snowed In & Set Up
https://books2read.com/SISU
Amber, Will, Juniper, Hunter, Rowen, Austin

•

Love to Hate You
https://books2read.com/Love2HateYou
Alex and Eli

•

Lust Abroad
https://books2read.com/Lust-Abroad
Piper and Derrick

•

Hired by the Single Dad
https://books2read.com/HBTSD-SDS
The Single Dads of Seattle, Book 1
Tori and Mark

•

Dancing with the Single Dad
https://books2read.com/DWTSD-SDS
The Single Dads of Seattle, Book 2
Violet and Adam

•

Saved by the Single Dad
https://books2read.com/SBTSD-SDS
The Single Dads of Seattle, Book 3
Paige and Mitch

•

Living with the Single Dad
https://books2read.com/LWTSD-SDS
The Single Dads of Seattle, Book 4
Isobel and Aaron

•

Christmas with the Single Dad
https://books2read.com/CWTSD-SDS
The Single Dads of Seattle, Book 5
Aurora and Zak

Snowed in with the Rancher
A Young Sisters Novel
https://books2read.com/snowed-in-rancher
Triss and Asher
March 4, 2023

•

Second Chance with the Rancher
A Young Sisters Novel
https://books2read.com/second-chance-rancher
Mieka and Nate
May 13, 2023

•

Done with You
A Young Sisters Novel
https://books2read.com/done-with-you
Oona and Aiden
October 13, 2023

•

Rock the Shores
A Cinnamon Bay Romance
https://books2read.com/Rocktheshores
Juliet and Evan

•

The Bastard Heir
Winter Harbor Heroes, Book 1
Co-written with Ember Leigh
https://books2read.com/the-bastard-heir
Harlow and Callum

•

The Asshole Heir
Winter Harbor Heroes, Book 2
Co-written with Ember Leigh
https://books2read.com/the-asshole-heir
Amaya and Carson

The Rebel Heir
Winter Harbor Heroes, Book 3
Co-written with Ember Leigh
https://books2read.com/the-rebel-heir
Lily and Colton
March 18, 2023

NATALIE SLOAN TITLES

Light the Fire
Revolution Inferno, Book 1
https://mybook.to/light-the-fire
Haina, Zane, Alaric and Jorik

•

Stoke the Flames
Revolution Inferno, Book 2
https://mybook.to/stoke-the-flames
Olia, Maxxon, Cypher and Alaric

•

Burn it Down
Revolution Inferno, Book 3
https://mybook.to/burn-it-down
Zosha, Knox, Shade and Tozer
June 3, 2023

ABOUT THE AUTHOR

A Canadian West Coast baby born and raised, Whitley is married to her high school sweetheart, and together they have two beautiful daughters and a fluffy dog. She spends her days making food that gets thrown on the floor, vacuuming Cheerios out from under the couch and making sure that the dog food doesn't end up in the air conditioner. But when nap time comes, and it's not quite wine o'clock, Whitley sits down, avoids the pile of laundry on the couch, and writes. A lover of all things decadent; wine, cheese, chocolate and spicy erotic romance, Whitley brings the humorous side of sex, the ridiculous side of relationships and the suspense of everyday life into her stories. With single dads, firefighters, Navy SEALs, mommy wars, body issues, threesomes, bondage and role-playing, Whitley's books have all the funny and fabulously filthy words you could hope for.

FIND WHITLEY HERE

Website: WhitleyCox.com
Email: readers4wcox@gmail.com
Twitter: @WhitleyCoxBooks
Instagram: @CoxWhitley
TikTok: @AuthorWhitleyCox
Facebook : https://www.facebook.com/CoxWhitley/
Blog: https://whitleycox.com/fabulously-filthy-blog-page/

Exclusive Facebook Reader Group:
https://www.facebook.com/groups/234716323653592/
Booksprout: https://booksprout.co/author/994/whitley-cox
Bookbub: https://www.bookbub.com/authors/whitley-cox
Goodreads:
https://www.goodreads.com/author/show/16344419.Whitley_Cox
Subscribe to my newsletter here:
http://eepurl.com/ckh5yT